# HILLGATE HALL

## NICHOLAS BUNDOCK

ISBN 13: 9789493056220 (ebook)

ISBN 13: 9789493056213 (paperback)

Published by Amsterdam Publishers, the Netherlands

info@amsterdampublishers.com

Author's website: nicholasbundock.com

*My happiest hours, aye! all the time*
*I love to keep in memory,*
*Lapsed among moors,*
*ere life's first prime*
*Decayed to dark anxiety.*

**Charlotte Brontë**

# PART I

# 1

Hillgate Hall was jokingly called by pupils and staff alike Hellgate Hall. But for me, in the summer of 1995, hell it was. So much so, that it has taken me over twenty years to bring myself to write about what happened there. At the time, I thought Hillgate might give me some much-needed security and strengthen my then fragile mental health. I was wrong. My financial and health problems were as nothing compared to what lay ahead.

It is hard to return to that world of 1995 – modern but distant. No sophisticated internet, no social media, and before mobile phones were commonplace. It sometimes seems as remote as the Victorian England I love reading about. At other times it is as close as my fingers to this keyboard. To record is painful. To revisit my life before Hillgate is distressing enough, but to return to the weeks which followed is almost unbearable. But record I must.

\* \* \*

*Late April 1995*

'Leave me and my son alone.'

She didn't hear. She wasn't meant to. I was at the half-open kitchen window, seething the words. She was strutting my lawn, like a lady of the

3

manor visiting a poor tenant. My ex-husband Anthony and she, as usual on a Saturday, had arrived mid-morning to take James out for the day in Anthony's beloved old MG – roof down today. For her, collecting my ten-year-old son was never a weekly routine. It was a drama.

The chatelaine now became a model, using my lawn as a catwalk for her latest outfit – a navy and oat-flecked sweater above tight pink needle cords. Perhaps, I thought, I should get an excitable mongrel with razor-sharp claws. Not that I could afford dog food, let alone vet's bills.

Remaining at the window to delay meeting her again, I watched James hunt for his football in one of the wilder patches of a flowerbed. She floated towards him, ostensibly to help in the search, but paused by a clump of white flowers to allow an unseen photographer a couple of shots for *Vogue*.

Her satinwood blonde hair draped over the flowers as she bent down to read the plant label. More clicks and whirrs from the invisible Nikon.

Photoshoot over, she tossed back her head and called out, 'Oh, Pulmonaria Sissinghurst White.'

I winced at her shriek, her tone, her supercilious drawl.

'Ant,' she shouted,' staring towards me, 'we must go to Sissinghurst Castle one weekend with James. Did I tell you Granny knew Vita Sackville-West? Our place is only down the road, and it's about time we saw Mummy and Daddy again.'

I already knew about 'our place' – only last week I'd been told that my house reminded her of their gardener's cottage. I went out to say goodbye to James and to face any further insults she might have lined up for me. But by the time I reached the garden the football had been found, James was in the back of the MG, she was in the passenger seat, and Anthony was about to climb in. It looked like I was safe from any more of her venom. Feeling reprieved, I walked to the car. 'Have a good time,' I said to James. 'Enjoy yourselves, all of you,' I added, with more charity than I felt.

I shouldn't have bothered. Anthony turned to me and said, 'It's okay if B buys James a new pair of jeans, isn't it? His old pair are looking a bit past it.'

B (short for Beatrice – what else could it be?) looked up with a predatory smile.

'Buy him whatever you like,' I said to them.

Anthony, wimp that he now was, became defensive. 'There's this great kids' store in Southwold . . .'

'Enjoy your day,' I said.

I stepped away and waved to James.

'Bye, Mum,' he called.

Wimp got in and fired the engine. I walked to the house, but made the error of turning back to watch the car chug off through the gate and down the lane, allowing myself, before they disappeared, the sight of B's hand waving in my direction – more a victory salute than a farewell. Without talking, she had had the last word. Again. I felt abused.

Why did she do it? I wasn't a rival. I was far beyond the point of wanting Anthony back. I had nothing for her to be envious of. She was so much younger, prettier, had never known my money worries. Unlike most of her fellow-students, she even had her own house – late-Georgian, mortgage-free, in Wyatt Square in central Norwich. What did she want from me? Did she want me to crawl up to her, lick her Gucci sneakers, and apologise for my overdraft and my Yorkshire accent? James had told me she sometimes tried to make him lose his own accent, a cross between Norfolk and mine. She had made him repeat, 'I like to ride my bike at night,' and 'Monday's never fun for us, Mum,' the second more insulting than the first, since, when he repeated it to her, the implication was that she was his mother.

Or maybe she was envious of the fact that I had known Anthony – I had never called him Ant – before her, been to bed with him before her, had borne his child, although in my experience it was usually men who got more hung up about former partners than women. But then B was in her own category of twistedness, so who knows what phantoms haunted her mind?

Angry, I found a garden fork and stormed over to the clump of pulmonaria, intent on digging it up and consigning it to the compost heap. But as soon as the tines stabbed the soil I checked myself. The flowers had been a present from a friend, of which I had few – why should I let B influence what grew in my garden? I gently eased the fork from the dark earth, and, contenting myself with cutting off the plant label, threw that away instead. There was no chance I would forget the name printed on it. I collapsed on a bench. Looking at the 'gardener's cottage', I tried to forget about her.

We had bought Limepit House five years earlier at a poorly attended auction. At one end of the village, isolated at the bottom of a lane, it had been a wreck. To give Anthony his due, he did much of the work to make it habitable. But when it was almost completed, he gave up his job at an outdoor pursuits centre, and enrolled as a so-called mature student at the university in Norwich. At the time, I was teaching, and financially we could just about get by. All changed when Anthony met B, left me and moved in with her. Two months later Wingbourne Court, the private school where I taught, closed, and I failed to find another teaching post. My lack of any teaching qualification was always against me. I certainly couldn't get a job in the state system, which I would have preferred. Nor could I juggle the practicalities of teacher training. I needed money – fast. Looking back, I could have applied for all sorts of single parent benefits, but – perhaps it was my Yorkshire stubbornness – I was determined to be independent. I knew I'd get nothing from Anthony. He paid a pitiful monthly sum in child maintenance – 'ice-cream money' I called it. The divorce settlement gave me the house, but also the mortgage. My survival plan was my own business dealing in antiques. And at first it went well. But now, after fourteen months of trading on borrowed money, selling mainly at a seaside antiques centre, the scheme looked madness.

I looked up at the walls of my house and imagined them slipping away, brick by mellow Norfolk red brick, into the hands of the bank. I shivered, frozen to the wooden slats of my bench. During the last two years I had frequently experienced these debilitating bouts of terror. But I had also learned the painful lesson that I must wrench myself from my seat immediately and throw myself into activity, or the attack would worsen, hold me there a prisoner, chained, trembling. On waking each morning, before fear could set in, I recited my programme for the day, so I knew which activity to focus on at any time the terror struck – I suspected that counsellors and shrinks had a name for the technique, but I wasn't going to pay them to find out.

I repeated aloud the programme from now until James's return in the evening. 'Drive van to Cambridge. Take overmantel mirrors to dealer who is almost certain to buy them. Drive back with cheque. Gardening. Have drink before happy party in MG return.'

The mantra gave me enough strength to pull myself from the bench. Within ten minutes I was on the road.

## 2

These occasional visits to a dealer who was always happy to buy from me were the only profitable part of my failing business. I had learned that what he called 'furnishing overmantels' could often be bought cheaply at my local auctions. Mirrors wouldn't save my business, but they might help delay its demise long enough for me to find an alternative. I would have preferred to be dealing in pictures, about which I knew more, but the art I loved was totally beyond my pocket. I was always searching for the unrecognised masterpiece, begrimed, anonymous in a country sale. I had yet to find it.

At a roundabout before I hit the A11, a grating from the front of my Ford Transit reminded me that the wheel bearings should be replaced. The garage had told me they were worn, but it was another expense I had deferred. I was gambling they would make the round trip. The first hour passed without mishap.

Now the worst part of the journey – bypassing Thetford. Four more roundabouts to make me shudder at my growling bearings. Not enough traffic to distract my thoughts from money matters. Or from B. I imagined her with Anthony and James. Was my son between them holding their hands – like a happy family out for a Saturday afternoon by the sea? She wasn't old enough to be his mother, but at that moment, as I sat driving towards Elveden, that's how I pictured her. And what was I? The nanny who looked after him weekdays? Or a poor governess, releasing her charge when her ladyship could spare a few hours for her child?

Governess. I recoiled at the word, and thought back to the characters I loved reading about as a girl – Elizabeth Gaskell's ghastly Mrs Kirkpatrick, Anne Brontë's Agnes Grey, but most of all Charlotte Brontë's Jane Eyre, my childhood favourite. She might have known how to deal with B. She certainly knew what it was to feel, as I often did, vindictive. And she knew what it was to take insults in silence, having been forced to listen to the bitchy gold-digger, Blanche, vilify all governesses – comments addressed to someone else in the room, but intended for Jane's ears. I knew all about that sort of spite. It was B's stock-in-trade. But B, unlike Blanche, would never need to dig for gold or for anything else – certainly not scrape less than a living from old mirrors in the back of an ailing van.

That childhood hero was so distant now. Why hadn't she written about a single mother with a mortgage she couldn't pay? And I was so much older than Jane who, in her twenties at the end of the book, was happily married, with a son, and wealthy. I was thirty-nine – older than Charlotte Brontë when she died – divorced, with a son, and broke.

Beyond Elveden, passing heathland and roaming sheep, my mood changed. It was a fine morning, the road was free from thunderous lorries, and in a few hours I should be returning home with a cheque and a profit. There was reason to be optimistic. And I had so far managed the journey without a panic attack. Often, even on short journeys, I found it necessary to pull off the road, stop and recover equilibrium. Before any trip I reminded myself of the laybys and side roads I could escape to if necessary. I even knew all my escapes between home and Cambridge. But today I felt I might not need them. Perhaps at last I was regaining the confidence I had once enjoyed ... how long ago? Before Anthony left? Before marriage? Longer maybe. Again I thought back to my early years and to the books I had loved.

As a child I had felt so close to Charlotte Brontë, had read and reread her, knew some passages by heart – a friend remembering the voice of a distant loved one. Like her (and Jane Eyre) my father was a clergyman – books by daughters or sons of clergy (with some exceptions) have always attracted me. Like the Brontës, I was brought up in West Yorkshire. Our village, a few miles from Keighley, was not far from Haworth, and our Edwardian rectory, like Haworth Parsonage, adjoined the church graveyard – unlike theirs, not a cause of disease. And, like them, I'd been sent to an appalling school. I flinched at the memories, not helped by the fact that today I was driving south, and it was in the south where that school had been.

Now I was beyond the Newmarket bypass and into depressing rural Cambridgeshire. No wonder this was the setting for the saddest book I had ever read, Flora Mayor's *The Rector's Daughter*. Unremitting desolation, unlike Jane Eyre's fairy-tale ending. I would have settled for somewhere comfortably between the two extremes.

I left the A11 at Fourwentways and took the Babraham Road, driving up a hill, the best flat Cambridgeshire could manage. Nothing like my beloved Pennines. No moors, none of Charlotte Brontë's *moss-blackened* crags.

I parked in the yard behind Spenser and Greene Antiques, and entered the shop by the back door. Since the elderly Mr Greene was busy with a customer, I waited in the restoration workshop behind the main showroom, breathed in the comforting smells of wax and gesso, and looked at the furniture and mirrors in their various states of restoration.

Mr Greene, stooped and a little shabby in his creased grey suit, soon appeared, followed me to my van, and gave the three D-shaped mirrors a cursory glance.

'Ninety each, as usual?' he said.

'Fine,' I said.

Our dealings were always brief.

'I'll write you a cheque.' He was never one for cash.

I followed him to his desk in the showroom. At that moment his phone rang.

'If you could wait?' he said. 'I've been expecting this.' He began a conversation about purchasing a set of chairs from a college.

Through the shop's plate-glass windows I surveyed Cambridge's Saturday afternoon shoppers. It was good to be away from my tiny village of scattered houses, to be distracted from loneliness and introspection for a minute or two by this scurrying stream, none turning a head in the direction of the shop. At last, an elderly man in a well-cut suit – a wealthy retired academic perhaps – paused, attracted by an imposing Charles II mirror, set back from the window to be away from the sun. He eyed it with a connoisseur's gaze, glanced up at the shop sign and turned away.

The local shoppers may have been avoiding this place today, but for me it was a lifeline. A young couple with a small boy lingered by the window and stared at a Regency chest of drawers. For a moment I thought they would come in, but they walked past, making me recall shopping trips with Anthony and James a few years ago. They should have been happy memories, but B turned all memories sour. I felt she had always been nearby, offstage, waiting for her entrance – a dark presence about to work her malice. To suppress thoughts about her, I looked at the Sienna marble top of a console table beneath a towering gilt pier glass. But gazing at its veins and gradations of colour, I saw B's blonde hair. I touched its cold, polished surface, shivered and lifted the ticket. I gasped at the price – more than I had ever earned in a year. I thought of my overdraft.

'Be with you in a minute,' called Mr Greene.

When the phone call ended, there was a rare grin on his face. It remained as we unloaded the mirrors from my van and carried them to the workshop. I assumed the deal with the college had gone well for him. This impression was confirmed when he gave me the cheque – it was for £300.

'A little extra to cover time and fuel,' he said. 'And keep those mirrors coming in.'

I drove away with some elation, but at the Addenbrooke's Hospital roundabout the snarling from my front wheels returned, a beast at my ankles. I heard its ominous voice in my mind: 'That cheque in your bag is nothing – it may buy you food for a few weeks and pay an electricity bill, but it will contribute little to your monthly mortgage repayments and nothing to new wheel bearings, never mind about reinvesting in more stock.' I was glad when I hit the A11 and for many miles, cutting between fields green with growing wheat and barley, there were only straight, uninterrupted roads. But later, at each of the four roundabouts skirting Thetford, the jarring returned, and with it all the familiar anxiety. I thought of Anthony and B's easy life, and felt the emotion Jane Eyre knew all about. Envy.

# 3

'Pity about Norwich on Saturday,' said James.

'Yeah – gutted,' said Ben.

'Well, against Liverpool – could have been worse.'

I watched James and best mate Ben, mourn their local team as far as the gates of Ulford Primary School, where their own game of football took over.

'Bye, Mum,' he called.

The two boys threw down their yellow and green Norwich City scarves as makeshift goal posts at the edge of the playing field, more mud than grass, and littered with the faded confetti from an ornamental cherry tree whose mid-April gaudiness had now ended. Sliding on the damp surface, they took turns to be striker and keeper. Smiling that they had no more than football to worry about, I returned to my van and to thoughts about an unopened letter, waiting for me at home like a snake by a nest. I knew it was from the bank manager, telling me in the language of business plans and cash flows what I already knew. Yeah – gutted.

Back at Limepit House, I reversed the van close to the garage, so I could later load up the furniture I had restored and polished. Opening one of the garage doors, I remembered Anthony's obsession with orderliness: the clipped ranks of screwdrivers and pliers, their handles a red line of resistance against my natural untidiness. Further on, the heavy brigade of hammers and mallets. Next, the hi-tech weaponry –

power drills, electric saws, nail guns – all present and correct above the workbench. Plenty of room for his precious MG, the one possession he had taken with him, apart from his clothes, at least those which he had bought during the B era. The others I had with (in those days) mixed emotions taken to a charity shop.

I opened the other garage door and stared at the post-Anthony mayhem. The red line and other units had been dispersed, lost or fallen among the partly restored chests, tables and chairs – bandaged casualties in the battle with my bank. The workbench was a clutter of jars of wood stain and tins of furniture wax, from out of which wandered an orange cable towards the drill on a half-polished stool, where I had left it yesterday.

I inspected a foot I had fixed on a pine mule chest and decided that the glue had set. That could go to the antiques centre today; the stool too, if I could finish it on time.

It was not yet 9.00am, but I already felt drained. In that Georgian house in Norwich, Anthony and B, with no apparent worries about looming finals, were no doubt still in bed. What was more nauseating – the thought that they might be snug asleep, or the picture of them ecstatically awake?

Indoors, I scooped up the reptile from the doormat and skinned it. Everything predictable apart from the final bite: *Perhaps you would phone to make an appointment to discuss matters with me. May I suggest Friday.* No question mark. No chance of fobbing him off with another misleading letter. I had four days to find a way of charming the snake. The possibility seemed hopeless. Anyhow, even if I could evade the bank for a statement or two, I couldn't sidestep the truth: I and my home were saddled with a mortgage and loan I had no way of repaying. I foresaw a custody dispute in which Anthony and B could offer James the home and the security which I lacked. And they would win.

There was no point turning to my parents for help. Their old age pensions and my father's clergy pension didn't leave them with much to spare. Worse, since my father had dementia, their own futures were uncertain. At the moment, my mother could look after him, but eventually one or both of them would need professional care. As their only child, I should have been working out ways to help them.

Now was the vulnerable hour. Getting up, seeing to James, the school run had so far absorbed ninety minutes of Monday. If I could survive until 10.00am without wobbling to a chair, drawn into that black hole, passivity, which could reduce me to a soulless creature, powerless and sexless, then the day had a chance. Even now, when I have moved beyond that illness – to say 'recover' would be to invite a relapse – it is only with great effort that I can dare myself to recall it. At first, there had been the pills prescribed by my GP. Next, came the insistence of Ben's mother, Molly, a potter, that I spend some time with her each morning until, just before Christmas, I had risked my first danger hour alone. Even so, by noon, I had ended up shaking at her kitchen table, and over the next two months many times more.

It wasn't depression. The blackness which descended on me, the trembling isolation, didn't share its name with anyone else's illness; it wasn't the sharing sort. It knew me and gave me a tailor-made dark dress, measured, made and delivered while I was asleep. Bespoke, but not bespoken by me.

It was depression.

Through my daily mantras, with disciplined effort, through a business I wish I hadn't started – a toxic occupational therapy – I could now survive until magic midday. Beyond noon the risk of wobbling was minimal. I would turn on the radio: 'BBC Radio Four. The news at midday.' It was like an order of release. I never waited to learn what was happening in the world – the only news item I wanted to hear was that I was safe for another day. 2.00pm might find me asleep through the exhaustion of survival, but 12 noon was safety time.

On bad days – they were becoming less frequent – no amount of reasoning, no telling myself that every day was certain to have its midday, its high noon, would diminish by one shake or quiver the tremors of the morning – tremors which were skilled at finding for each day a different disguise under which they could unnerve me. If it wasn't money, it might be a blocked drain or a ringing phone – it could only bring bad news – or the phone call which cut off as soon I answered. Or the large stray dog which last week I had seen rooting about in the lane by my gate. Even on days I didn't shake, the memories of worse days persisted. And there had been that Wednesday last October when I had trembled at Molly's table until school came out.

I could sense the illness, a shapeshifting creature over my shoulder, waiting for its next opportunity. Last year it had hit me hardest in spring, its preferred season, and it was annoyed that this year it had been held at bay. I gave my head a quarter turn, half-expecting to see it, even challenge it. But it had become invisible. I knew better than to think it had left me.

To work. The routine. Radio on. Loud. Any programme. No,

something frivolous, please. No Third World Reports. No environmental scares – I can scare myself, thank you. Music or talking, but it must be light-hearted. Nothing religious – plenty of that in the past, sometimes too much. Talking's best. No, must talk myself. Phone Molly? Don't want to pester her. Who? Frank perhaps.

I phoned Farrier's Arms Antiques, a smart name for a former pub on a deserted crossroads between two villages. Frank didn't run a business – at whim he let it interrupt the love of his life, racing. He sometimes gave me tips, but I had seldom won any money from them. I had met him just after I had moved to Ulford, while on the hunt for an old sink.

'Frank? Phoebe.'

'How's my favourite clergyman's daughter?'

'How many do you know?'

'Not sure. Quite a few clergy widows though. Did I tell you that the other day . . .'

He drifted into one of his stories. Frank roamed freely in the North Norfolk retirement belt, where he would buy all manner of bric-a-brac and better, with the result that there would sometimes appear, in the back of his run-down shop, the odd Georgian chair or bedside cupboard which I could buy for stock. When I became aware that Anthony was increasingly staying away for the night, Frank was the first person I had allowed myself to talk to – even before Molly. Subsequently, through clouds of his chain-smoked Benson & Hedges, he had patiently listened to each episode of my divorce saga. Molly could sometimes make me laugh at my predicament; Frank could always manage it.

His latest story was at an end. 'Have you exorcised your husband from your life yet?' he said.

'I still have to see him when he collects James on Saturdays. And her.'

'At least you have the house.'

'And the unpaid mortgage.'

'Call in later – I've some rubbish you might like.'

'I need something.'

'Remind me to give you a group photo of the 1932 Ulford Pig Club. You can have it as a present.' He rung off. As ever, his voice had made me a nerve or two stronger.

Without thinking too hard, I phoned the bank, confirmed Friday's appointment – still hadn't trembled – and went out for the morning's inspection of the garden – another routine.

Walking along the edge of the still-wet lawn, I frowned at the ground elder in the beds by the lane. Trowel in hand, I teased it out, but it performed its usual trick: as I pulled out one leafy stem with white stringy root, even as I scanned the bed, hoping not to find more, others appeared to spring up, like Hydra's heads, in half a dozen other places. Every garden in the village, in Norfolk probably, had the weed, but I couldn't remember it at the rectory where my lifelong love of gardening was born. It was a love inherited from my parents. My mother tended the flowers; my father grew the vegetables. I cherished the old gardening book he had passed on to me two years earlier. He was well enough then to say, 'I shan't need it anymore.' I tried to protest, but a nod from my mother told me that to refuse it would hurt him. And so I accepted the saddest gift I have ever received, made sadder by a photo I found tucked in the back cover – a three-year-old girl standing next to him, her small homemade wheelbarrow brimming with rectory garden potatoes. I devoutly followed many of the book's instructions concerning soil types and sowing times. One sentence I particularly loved, will always love: *In districts north of the Trent plant two weeks later.* I was well south of the Trent now and even further from the Humber, beyond which my home county stretched towards the hills.

The sound of the phone dragged me indoors. I felt nervous until I heard Molly's voice.

'Are you going to the auction this morning?'

'When I've rooted out some more ground elder. Not that it's as bad as the unwanted blonde.'

'What's she done now?'

'When I think of the weeks Anthony and I spent viewing crumbling properties all over East Anglia before we found this place, then living in a caravan while we almost rebuilt it – was it all so he could bring her here every week to inspect my flowerbeds?'

I heard Molly's slow, patient exhalation. 'What did she say this time?'

'Nothing. It's her manner, her condescension. You'd think she was a duchess deigning to lower her eyes and pretend to admire a poor tenant's garden.'

'Well, it's your garden, not hers.'

'Right now it looks like the bank's. Why does she make me feel like some estate lackey?'

'You mustn't let her.'

'I can't very well forbid her to leave the car every time she turns up.'

'What time shall I meet you?'

'I'll be there half-ten.'

'Okay. Now I'll leave you to clear some more weeds and make space to bury your duchess.'

She was trying to make me laugh at myself. I couldn't do it.

Back in the garden, there was no more visible ground elder. I collected my hoe and walked over to the vegetables. The shallots needed weeding, but they would have to wait. *In on the shortest day, out on the longest*, were the book's instructions. A good size already, they promised an enormous crop by midsummer. It was a thought about the future. A twinge of panic. I gripped the hoe tightly and headed for the half-polished stool in the garage. Desperation forced me to finish it quickly. I carried it to the van. Next, I dragged the mule chest along on one of my indispensable pieces of old carpet and loaded that up too. Now I was ready to head for the Monday auction.

# 4

The local flint of houses and barns was almost shining under a massive sky, the sea-blue of classroom globes. I was driving into a heady spring morning, bright with a rare intensity and without the familiar wind. It was the sort of morning which could exhilarate me or shatter me. The creature over my shoulder knew it too. Again I sensed its annoyance at being outmanoeuvred. This gave me momentary confidence in my tactical skills. But I was on my guard, as I had been since the earliest signs of spring.

This year, determined to fight it, I had watched for the appearance of comfrey and red nettle by the back door, and had seen them as warnings. It was a hard lesson, learning not to love the plants in my garden too much – to see bulbs and blossom make their annual statements, and not to become too attached, since this season of hidden things breaking out, was also when depression could well up – my personal contribution to spring's loss account, as inevitable as the first sign of peach curl, or an abandoned nest of unfledged chicks. April may be the cruellest month, but now, on its last day, I knew I was not out of danger. Last year had taught me that May can be heartless too.

Tanner's weekly sale at Walborough – it eventually closed to make way for a housing estate – was one of Norfolk's last surviving general auctions where poultry, produce, secondhand cars, house clearances, antiques and miscellaneous outside lots came under the hammer at different points across an extensive saleroom. From all over the county it drew a motley following, rich and poor or disguised as either, so that a newcomer might have found it hard to distinguish the millionaire scrap metal man from the down-at-heal junk dealer, or the rabbit man from the dealer in period furniture. Some of the older faces, sizing up a pig or reminiscing by an old farm wagon, might have time-travelled from a George Morland painting of rustics; some of the younger clientele might have stepped from a page of *Country Living*. Before I started dealing I enjoyed attending sales here, and even now, if I failed to walk away with stock, I could console myself with a tray of young lettuces or some bedding plants. I knew that by now the car park would be crammed, chiefly with rusting pick-ups, all kinds of vans and 4x4s. I was lucky to find a parking space two streets away.

I found Molly by the table lots inside the main sale shed. She was pondering some 1950s Christmas decorations in their original boxes. Leaning over her shoulder, I said, 'Joining me in the junk trade, are you?'

'Certainly not. If I buy them, I'll use them.'

She unbent herself from the table, and with her miss-nothing grey eyes gave me the sort of look I had seen her use on pots fresh out of the kiln as she searched for firing faults. I felt that today I had passed the inspection. 'Anything here for you?' she said.

'I ought not to be looking. I've no money and I heard from the bank today.'

Molly scribbled down the lot number. 'Paul will probably murmur if I buy these.'

'An argument about paper chains – I'd settle for that.'

'That bad, is it?'

'The bank's on my back telling me I'm making a mess of what I know I shouldn't be doing. Meanwhile I can't help thinking of Anthony and her sipping their second leisurely coffee while they talk about Louis Zukovsky.'

'Who?'

'Part of their poetry project. They've even been talking to James about it. Why can't they just take him to football or fishing? But dragging him into their precious world . . .'

'Come and have supper tonight.'

She sounded like a therapist booking me in for another appointment. I was uneasy – there had been too many such suppers.

'Come to us for a change. I'll collect Ben from school and the boys can make mischief in the garden while I'm busy in the kitchen. How about seven-thirty?'

'Thanks, but can we say eight? I've been roped into the school fete committee meeting. It'll just be me and Ben – Paul's working late.'

I watched Molly leave the saleroom. Without her I would have ended up in hospital. She had been my one support in the face of two hopeless GPs, and a Relate counsellor in whom I could place no confidence, since she was also a lecturer at Anthony's university. Anthony never joined me for any of the three sessions; he was certain our marriage was over. 'Personal cul-de-sac' was his favourite expression. When I quoted this to the counsellor, she said, 'Is the blockage with you or Anthony?' I was annoyed that she accepted his description without question. 'Does it matter?' I countered. 'He's now hurtling down his personal highway with the twenty-year-old he found at your university.'

Half-heartedly, I viewed the furniture and noted two lots, an oak plank coffer, dirty and wormy but redeemable, and a walnut commode chair, complete with stained pewter chamber pot, which would convert into a saleable armchair. I knew I might have to bid against the local dealers' ring for both of them, but today, unlike during the Easter holidays, there appeared to be no holiday-homers, another group of determined competitors.

I moved to the outside lots. A few yards ahead of me I recognised the green tweed hat belonging to the mother of one of my former pupils at Wingbourne Court. She was talking to a man I knew to be Cosmo Butler, a dealer who ran a trade-only business on the edge of town. As I struggled to recall the woman's name, she looked up and recognised me.

'Mrs Burns,' she bellowed, 'how are antiques now that you've forsaken the classroom?'

I walked over and feigned some nonchalance. 'Tables and chairs are sometimes easier to deal with than children,' I said, but thought, they are also less profitable.

'I expect you know my neighbour Cosmo.'

'Across a crowded saleroom,' he said, beaming.

I recalled his reputation as a womaniser. Tall, with thick red hair, he had a hint of a Dublin accent which, I suspected, had all but disappeared at some expensive English school. He wasn't particularly handsome, but he possessed the deep confidence some women find irresistible. I'd heard various stories that his wealth originated from inheriting a fortune, drugs, or a series of questionable deals. The one clear fact about him was that he was very much king of the ring, and delighted in playing the mystery card, both in his private life and his dealings.

The tweed hat pointed to a heap of ironwork. 'Cosmo's going to bid for me on these railings, aren't you?' she bullied.

Cosmo made a guttural noise somewhere between 'Ahh' and 'Ooh,' then, 'I'll do my best, but don't tell the world. For all we know, our friend Mrs ... er ... Burns here might want them.'

'It's Phoebe,' I said. 'And no, the railings aren't on my list.'

'Thanks, Cos,' she said, moving away and giving me a token nod.

As he watched her disappear into the crowd, his eyes fixed on her tight jeans, I wondered whether the two of them were rather more than neighbours. Meeting her again made me recall my former, more lucrative job. I felt a surge of desperation. Cosmo was about to walk off.

'Ahh,' I said to him – I'd picked up his introductory grunt. 'Can I leave a couple of bids with you?'

He looked at me for a second as if he were viewing a lot of doubtful provenance. 'Yeah, alright. What have you got down?' He pulled an envelope and pencil from a back pocket.

'Lot 194, a commode chair. Ninety pounds.'

'Okay, Shouldn't think anyone much will want that.'

'266, a plank coffer ...'

'Er, I've got that down too. Do you want to sort it with me now?'

I hesitated. I wasn't sure how you could 'sort' a lot before it had been auctioned, but I didn't wish to appear ignorant. 'No, I'm happy to leave a bid. Two hundred and thirty pounds.'

Cosmo scribbled. 'Right. P. Burns, two thirty. Sounds like a jockey at Newmarket. That it?'

'Yes, thanks.'

With another grunt and a jowl-shaking grimace, which could have meant 'Goodbye' or 'Too much beer last night', he walked over to the used cars. I returned to my van, which probably wouldn't have got a bid had I put it into the auction. Now to the antiques centre in Sheringham.

Towards the coast, the hedgerows shouted late spring, and the verges had abandoned themselves to the tropical lushness of spreading alexanders. It was hard not to feel good about the day or the season – impossible to set myself, like the lonely church towers I passed, above, aloof from it all in riskless detachment. I was glad to see the Sheringham town sign with its absurd model dingy planted with wallflowers. Here spring was controlled among urban roads and gardens. I felt safer.

At the centre, in a former chapel built of harsh Midlands brick, Tara, a dealer in ephemera – it was one of her duty days – helped me unload the mule chest, talking as we struggled to carry it through two sets of double doors.

'So you didn't stay for the auction?'

'I left a couple of bids with someone.' I wasn't going to tell her it was Cosmo.

'That's better than leaving them with the auctioneer. You know what happens . . .'

'I pay exactly my limit, or I'm the under-bidder.'

'We've all been there. Can we put this down for a moment?'

Older than me, she needed to catch her breath. We looked at each other across the chest. Tara was of indeterminate age, somewhere between fifty-five and seventy-five. My guess fluctuated according to what she was wearing, since she had an extensive wardrobe of vintage clothing which, depending on the outfit chosen for the day, could flatter or age her. Today she had opted for a severe early-1960s navy dress which, with her short grey hair, reminded me of one of those secretaries in old films who went to work wearing hat and gloves – the head of the typing pool.

She stroked the top of the chest. 'Have you thought about moving away from furniture? It's a difficult area for women.'

I resented her tone. I felt like one of her junior typists. 'I've thought about moving away from antiques altogether.'

We lifted the chest again and wove our way along the central aisle, side-stepping the chairs and tables which always trespassed on what was intended to be a clutter-free zone.

'Women in furniture,' she said, 'always seem to have a husband in tow, or a lover, or henchman who can sometimes do their bidding, always do their carrying, and probably stand in the ring for them as well. You'll have to get a boyfriend.'

'No, thanks. I'm still recovering from a husband. And I prefer aching arms to a replacement partner.' As I said the last two words, a hazy image of a man's face formed in the polished surface I was staring at. It certainly wasn't Anthony, but there was something of Cosmo about the hair. As I frowned at the thought the face disappeared.

We found a space for the chest in my section between piles of leather suitcases.

Tara stretched her back. 'I'm glad I deal in pieces of paper, not lumps of oak and mahogany. I can't see the boys in the ring knocking out a box of old postcards and billheads in the back bar of the Dolphin on Monday afternoons. Coffee?'

'I must get home. Did I sell anything on Saturday?'

We walked to a broom cupboard of a room near the front door, with *OFFICE* pretentiously painted on it – probably Tara's idea. She thumbed through the day book.

'One pine washstand. Eighty quid.' She handed me a cheque.

'Ugh. Not even enough to cover a month's rent here.' I looked down the room at the various stands: the lamp man, the six furniture sections, the vintage clothes area, Tara's ephemera, a mini gallery of prints and pictures, a large section at the end under a gilded sign, *Interiors*, the book dealer's corner, my own jumble of country furniture and luggage. Not for the first time I felt a misfit here. Month in, month out, I seemed to do as well as anybody, but it wasn't a living. I suspected that I was the only dealer who looked to antiques as a primary source of income. The lamp man, a retired engineer, had his pensions, the gallery people owned flats in Cromer, the interiors woman had a husband in advertising, Tara had once mentioned 'a small legacy' from an aunt, one of the furniture people rented out a string of houses in Normandy, someone else had . . .

'Things will hot up in summer,' said the head secretary.

'I'm not sure the bank will wait that long.'

On the other side of the centre's leaded windows, the sun disappeared, allowing the building, despite numerous spotlights and table lamps, to revert to its natural Victorian Gothic drear. I turned to the front door.

'Good luck with the Walborough mafia,' Tara called as I left.

I didn't reply.

Outside, a sea fret had rolled up to the town, blurring the shapes of buildings and making an impressionistic haze of the rooftops. Back on the road, once I was a mile inland and higher up, although the sky was clearer, the morning had lost its earlier effusiveness. I felt more at ease. But going through woodland, I again thought about Friday's bank visit, and panic set in. I was nervous driving. I had to pull off somewhere. What could I say to them? My only defence was that I had advertised for a lodger, and had written to two local private schools for teaching work. Neither plan had so far produced anything. Back to regrets. I knew I should never have started in antiques. Did I also regret having met Anthony? I had asked the question a thousand times, often wanted to say yes. But to utter that one word was somehow to deny James his life, and that I couldn't do. Regret marrying him? Probably.

I stopped at a passing place in a narrow road close to one of the highest points in Norfolk, and counted the church towers dotted around a rural landscape spreading out in three directions with hardly a house in sight. A visitor to the area might have wanted to take a photograph. For me the scene was oppressive – nature tamed and ordered. It made me long for limestone ridges and outcrops, for my early childhood, for the years before I knew Anthony.

We had met at University College London, he in his last year reading geography, I in my first year of history. Armed with a good degree, the then Anthony, conservation-minded and waving every green banner, became assistant director of a field studies centre near Ongar. In London, bored with history in books and documents, I found myself missing lectures to spend more time with the tangible history found in art galleries, museums and auction rooms. I could have switched to a history of art course, but that also felt too academic. During the autumn of my second year I found a part-time job with a St James's gallery, and at the start of the following term I collected my grant cheque – no student loans in those days – and never went into college again. The gallery had given me a full-time job.

Within a year I was married to Anthony and commuting on the Central Line from the idyllic cottage which came with his job. We were happy, had our careers and even – unbelievable now – managed to save. The one shadow overhanging those days was the knowledge that Anthony wanted to move to more responsible, better-paid work, most likely further away from London, perhaps somewhere from which I couldn't commute. Luckily, his next job was near Ipswich, and I continued full-time at the gallery. By the time of his next move – to Breckland – I was pregnant with James and decided on a break from the art world. Four years later I returned to work, not at the gallery, but teaching history at a private school, Elveden College, near Thetford. The CV I had given to the headmaster stated that I had read history at London University. I hadn't added that I had dropped out degreeless before I was halfway through the course. The deception, if that's what it was, was never uncovered, and the head was sorry when I resigned, so that I could work with Anthony in restoring Limepit House.

I restarted the van and drove on, slowing at sharp bends, in the hope that the wheel bearings would remain silent. They continued to grind at every corner until I arrived at the Ulford village sign. Again I panicked. I needed to stop before returning home. On the main road, below the brow of the hill leading down to the village, I pulled into a layby near a group of ash trees. I had often stopped here, a place which afforded the perfect view of my house. A field of barley ran down to it – roof and upper floor visible above the swaying stalks. The lane between field and house was hidden, but its route was marked by a winding line of oaks which protected the property. How much longer would this place be my home?

In our search for a house, this was one of the more tumble-down remains we had encountered. But it was the most endearing, despite the nettles growing through the ground floor and the sycamore tree poking through the pantiles at the back. The village itself appeared unremarkable, but its overriding attraction was a flourishing primary school which had never been on the county education committee's hatchet list.

Whatever I think of Anthony now, I grant that his DIY fanaticism served us well for the two years it took to make the house habitable. He had given up his job in Breckland and worked long hours on the project. For my part, while I have always been happy to tackle the most daunting jungle of weeds, building work was an alien world. But I did my share, from clearing out the undergrowth inside the house to helping dig out the floor, spreading damp-proof membranes, even laying concrete.

There came a point – somewhere about the replastering stage – when it became clear that my skills, basic or newly acquired, were no longer needed. Added to that, since our money was running out, we were no longer able to employ Steve, a young brickie from the village, who helped at weekends. Hence my return to teaching. With the house almost completed, Anthony decided that he needed a career change and had visions of the world of broadcasting and journalism, for which a degree in media studies seemed to him essential. I had been the last person to discover why he, in his very first term, had switched to English and Drama studies – B's bloody course. I gazed down at the house, determined to hold on to it. Slowly, my panic subsided. Why hadn't those schools I'd written to replied? I would phone as soon as I was home.

'Yes, we're sorry not to have got back, but, as you may have heard, we are merging with Carrow College in Norwich, and it's no secret that there will have to be some staff reductions. We can't foresee vacancies, part-time or otherwise.'

So much for the first unanswered letter. I phoned the second school. Worse, it was closing at the end of term due to falling numbers. I slammed down the phone and wondered about Anthony and B. Where were they now? Not revising, I was certain. Their degree consisted of so much course work that finals appeared not to matter. I saw them drinking in a bar on campus where nobody bothered about the cost of the next pint. My stomach clenched. More regrets. Had I completed my own degree, adding a Postgraduate Certificate in Education, I would now be eligible for state school teaching, full-time or supply.

I carried a sandwich and coffee into the garden and sat down on an old kitchen chair by the iris bed. They had flowered early this year and now needed deadheading. I would do this later, if I had energy. But food and drink, rather than restoring me, only made me comatose. Exhausted, I clambered upstairs and threw myself on the bed. Experience had taught me to set the alarm, so I wouldn't be late collecting James from school. I reached for the clock, but it had been moved from its usual place on my bedside table to the window sill. Annoyed, I rolled off the bed and retrieved it. I couldn't remember touching it since last night, but was too drowsy to give it more thought. I slept deeply for an hour. Without the alarm it might have been many more.

Ulford Primary was a mile away at the other end of the village, along a road safe enough for me to have decided that, from the following September, I would allow James to cycle to school. The prospect of this gave me as much pleasure as it gave him. Playground parade with the Ulford parents was never my favourite part of the day. After my divorce, some of the married mothers kept their distance, as if marriage break-up was contagious. Nor did I like the daily nightmare of manipulating my Transit into impossible spaces outside the school among other vehicles, prams and children. The lollipop lady near the gate, fiercer than any sergeant-major, was also a self-appointed traffic warden, who delighted in singling me out for public reprimand and aggressive brandishing of her wand of office.

On Friday I had said to Molly, 'Why the hell does she always go for me? At least I don't double park every afternoon, like Mrs. High Heels in her Jeep Cherokee.'

'Ignore her,' said Molly. 'She's got it in for me too.'

'Need, got, need, got, got.' Ben and James swapped football stickers next to me as I drove home.

I heard the two words of their ritual say to me, 'Need money, need remunerative job, got house, got overdraft, need sanity, got friends – three or four – got ex-husband, don't need him, but need to get his girlfriend out of my brain.' I wished resolving it all was as simple as swapping stickers.

The boys played football in the garden, had their tea, returned to the garden. I watched them through the kitchen window. At this time of day, the desperation of the morning was as distant as some other woman's life in a radio play. I could imagine that the creature was asleep, or had never existed. The football rocketed over the greenhouse, followed by Ben hop-scotching over my vegetables to retrieve it. When this happened in the morning, as it often had during the Easter holidays, I would panic, imagine the sound of breaking glass, worry over a repair bill, regard a trampled row of chard as a threat to my home, overreact when I shouted at the boys. Now it was evening I could smile and not feel it was worth opening the window to call out to them to be careful.

Molly arrived with two bottles of village shop Spanish Soft Red and a cardboard box. She was still in her working clothes with their ever-present film of studio dust, which was also on her hair, normally fair but now a matt earth colour. She cleared a space on the dresser for the bottles, but placed the box by her usual chair. I brought out two glasses and the corkscrew. We sat at the kitchen table which, like Molly's, had been both the embalming table for my marriage, and the lab bench where my life had been dissected. Both processes had brought their peculiar mixture of angst and laughter, but had never threatened our friendship.

'Everything fine?' she said.

I wanted to say 'Yes, good,' but in the last two and a half years I had learned not to give way to the mood-swing glibness which is happy to forget that each day begins with a morning which, even if it could be negotiated tolerably well, could wear me down by early afternoon. 'After I left you at Walborough I got through till lunchtime. But I was totally out of it between two and three this afternoon.'

'But you're okay now?'

'I think so.'

'Sounds like you're winning.'

'Not the battle with the bank. I phoned the two schools I wrote to about a job. One's about to merge and make some staff redundant, the other's closing down.'

'Listen, I was talking to one of the school dinner ladies at the fete meeting . . .'

'Don't tell me – she needs a trainee washer-up?'

Molly smiled. 'No, her sister works in the kitchens at Hillgate Hall, and apparently a recently appointed French teacher failed to appear at the start of term.'

Hillgate Hall was the one private school I hadn't written to. I had ruled it out, because its reputation for attracting problem children suggested that my teaching skills would be inadequate.

'Why not give it a try?' said Molly.

I downed half my glass, looked at Molly, thought of the bank. 'French, was it?'

'So I was told.'

I had never taught French, but I had taken it at A-level, and since leaving school had improved my fluency. Looking down at the scrubbed pine table top with its open grain, wine stains turned blue, and indelible marks from James's felt-tips, I searched for some excuse not to approach Hillgate.

'I suppose it's a possibility,' I said.

'Phone the school first thing tomorrow.'

'Shouldn't I write?'

'No, move in quick before anyone else.' Molly reached down to the box by her chair and produced a parcel wrapped in red tissue paper. She pushed it towards me. 'A little nonsense from the studio.'

I unwrapped the layers of paper, beneath which I could feel the hard forms of two pieces of pottery. The first to appear was a stoneware beaker with Molly's characteristic laurel-green glaze. Its companion was a saucer, the well of which was surrounded by a collar. The foot of the beaker fitted so exactly into this collar, that, when I tapped the saucer, there was no movement between the two pieces.

'This is amazing. Precision potting.'

'I based it on an eighteenth-century design. *Trembleuse* it's called.' She pointed to the saucer. 'You didn't notice the inscription'

'Let me guess. "To my trembling friend".'

'Not quite.'

I lifted the beaker, turned the saucer over and read out the words scratched on the base, 'Bugger pills.'

'I was going to write the names of the drugs you were on, but I couldn't remember what they were.'

'Prothiaden and Ativan.'

They had been prescribed by the senior of the two GPs in our local practice. I had first seen his arrogant young partner, whose promises of a Prozac heaven I had rejected when he had begun writing my prescription before I had finished telling him how I felt. His older colleague was more of a listener, and I walked away with different drugs. But when I had been on them a month, I felt worse, felt my nerves change from hot wires to damp cotton wool, and thought I was going (or had gone) mad. Years later I was told I might have been suffering from a combination of diurnal depression and seasonal adjustment disorder, added to a pre-existing bipolar disorder. Drinking alcohol in the evenings might have made it worse. At the time, I wasn't aware of any of this, and had never heard of bipolar. My mother had often said to me, 'You're up like a rocket, down like a stick.' Perhaps she understood. Anyway, it was Molly who helped me exchange chemicals for her kitchen table therapy. Finally, I had thrown the two plastic bottles into her woodburning stove, where they had melted with an angry blue flame, like an updated rite of some ancient ceremony.

Molly seized the wine bottle. 'Shall we christen your present?'

She filled my beaker and her own glass. We lifted them in a toast. 'Bugger pills,' we said together.

I stood the beaker on its saucer again. '*Trembleuse* sounds better than *depression*,' I said. '*Depression* is too much like a weather forecast.'

'And makes you feel there's nothing you can do to change it.'

James and Ben came crashing through the kitchen door. Running with sweat, they made straight for the sink, gulped some water from the tap, and charged back to the garden.

'You're lucky James has come through everything unscathed,' said Molly.

'He shows less than he feels. Unlike me, night-times are worst for him. Anthony always used to read to him; now, when I read to him, I can see memories in his face.'

'Does he talk to you about it?'

'Not much. I wish he would. He's seen me upset and shaking a few times, so I suspect that he feels he has to be brave for both of us, which is hardly fair on him. But it's impossible for him not to pick up what's happening in my head.'

'Does he open up to Anthony?'

'Sometimes. I always know when, because Anthony makes capital out of it. On Sunday night, after he had dropped off James, he leaned his head through the car window and said, "James tells me you've been upset about things. He seems very distressed. Is it sensible for you to unload all your stuff on him?" And, needless to say, *she* was next to him wearing a suitably concerned expression.'

'Bastards.'

'I can take what he says, but saying it in her presence – it's as if she's written the script for him.'

'Fight them. Phone Hillgate first thing tomorrow.'

# 5

I was not misled by the euphoria I felt at 5.30am the following day. The village shop Soft Red was a hardened deceiver. I knew that, although more sleep was impossible, I should resist the urge to tidy the house, finish the ironing, and polish furniture in the garage. The energy felt there, perhaps it was, but it would be needed to fight the masked hangover which would drop its disguise well before mid-morning.

After a mug of tea, followed by two glasses of foul-tasting mineral water, I unearthed my box file marked *Teaching*. For a minute it stared up to me from the kitchen table as I searched for the courage to open it. To do so was a physical admission that my business was failing, just as my marriage had done. I shut my eyes, lifted the lid and pulled out my most recent CV. I looked at my surname. Now was a chance to return to my unmarried name. The opportunity was tempting, but I had always preferred the name Burns to my maiden name, Wilson. Jane Eyre's best friend had been Helen Burns, and I was glad to share her surname. It was one of the better results of my marriage. So Phoebe Burns I remained.

Under *Education*, I had listed St Michael's College Bramshead and University College London (History), not mentioning my lack of a degree. Since the deception had slipped past Wingbourne Court as easily as Elveden College, I wasn't going to alter it for Hillgate Hall. I retyped it all on my old portable typewriter – no PC in those days. My one alteration was under *Present Employment*. Here I wrote *See attached*. I then typed a covering letter, explaining that my business allowed me time to do another job, a lofty lie, but as much as I was prepared to put in writing. Before I had signed it, I noticed the two empty wine bottles by the kitchen bin and remembered how Molly had suggested I phone the school. Such a direct approach worried me, but it would at least, I supposed, bring a quick response, and I had endured more than enough waiting for never-to-appear letters from headteachers. Later, I would phone them. If there was the slimmest chance of a job, I would drop in my CV by hand.

8.30am. Another drive to school, another tilt at the lollipop dragon, another watching James, unburdened by my worries, dash through the school gates. He was very much at one with village life, as I had been as a child. Recently, he and Ben had taken up coarse fishing, with the ambition to catch a pike. We were lucky in living near several large lakes where their ambition might be fulfilled. Although never an angler myself, I knew that my childhood river, the Aire – the inspiration for Jane Eyre's surname – was even better for coarse fishing, including pike; perhaps one weekend I would take him and Ben there, if I could afford it.

8.50am. Back home, still no tremors. But I knew I must not relax as I waited to make my phone call. In the garden I weeded, pushing the boundary of the vegetable plot into the wild area near the south hedge, where, among yard-high nettles, a dark home for caterpillars, stood the old caravan in which we had lived while the house was restored. A briar from the hedge was creeping over the roof, and moss was shrinking the windows – nature intent on countering this metallic intrusion, like new tissue around shrapnel. It had been the first home we owned after we left the Breckland tied cottage, just as this garden was the first to be truly ours. Those two cramped rooms had been a cosy refuge on the many nights when it seemed that the house would never be ready. Somehow, we had become adjusted to its confines, had taken on the gypsy spirit, and even felt some sadness when we forsook it for bricks and mortar. James had cried, insisting that he leave his drawings behind on the cupboard doors, and for weeks returned to it, making it his playroom. Maybe he had some premonition that life in the house boded an unhappiness the caravan had never known. From the undisturbed ivy around the door, I guessed he hadn't been here lately – no bad thing. Perhaps it was time to have the thing removed, before further leafy encroachments made me forget it was still here. The ever-helpful Steve would know how to dispose of it. But I would first consult James. 9.30am. Time for the phone call.

Three attempts found the headmaster's office engaged. To remain calm I scribbled lattice designs on the phone pad. On the fourth attempt, against a background of children's voices, a woman answered. I heard a deep, drawn-out 'Hello.' The one word reminded me of a stalwart spinster in my father's church choir, who was happy to move from contralto to tenor if one of the men was absent. Another 'Hello' pulled me into the present.

I stammered, 'My name is Mrs Phoebe Burns . . . I'm a teacher . . . I'm phoning . . . I gathered you are short-staffed because . . . anyhow, since this is my subject, I wonder if you have a part-time vacancy. Up until recently I taught at Wingbourne Court. Could I send you my CV?'

'Yes, do send it to us, please. No, even better, come and see us.'

I imagined a blue stocking behind an ancient black Remington typewriter.

'The headmaster is away at a conference today. How about tomorrow morning?'

'Er . . . yes.' I couldn't believe my incoherence had gained me an interview.

'Eleven, shall we say?'

'Thank you.'

'No, thank *you* for calling. Tomorrow then.'

She rang off. In disbelief I looked at my scribble, an untidy mesh, as confused as my telephone voice. I wish I hadn't said 'Mrs' – it had slipped out in my nervousness. But I had an interview. I phoned Molly.

'It was too easy,' I told her. 'Like buying a piece of furniture for nothing at an auction, because you're the one idiot who hasn't seen it's riddled with woodworm.'

'Don't be so harsh on yourself. You've got an interview for the good reason that they're hard-pressed and you heard about it first.'

'Don't think I'm ungrateful, but I can't help wondering . . .'

'Forget gratitude. Just get yourself that job.'

With cautious optimism about my future, I set off to see the 'rubbish' Frank had for me. The prospect of this animated me more than thoughts about tomorrow's potentially more lucrative interview.

It was a hazy morning, giving to my cross-country route an added isolation, which made my van an intruder in a Gainsborough landscape. Two miles from Frank's, the road fell into a gentle valley where, between high hedges, then a wood, it almost became a cart track. A favourite stretch, it often made me think, at this moment no one knows where I am; here nothing can get to me. It was a feeling which reminded me of a day in my teens on Nidderdale Moors. A girlfriend and I were on a summer hike. At some point, we had thrown ourselves down on the bracken and watched a buzzard ride the thermals. We felt completely alone and happy. Nothing since that day had recaptured the experience, but this remote Norfolk road went some way to recalling it. On the other side of the valley, the feeling disappeared – the wood ended and the road became a straight line between vast fields of young beet and barley, different greens giving way to each other without dividing hedges, apart from a few leafless stag oaks, standing like grey saguaro cacti.

Farrier's Arms Antiques is an austere Victorian building. Since no other house is in sight, it is hard to imagine how anyone would have wished to build a pub here. Frank had told me that he had bought it in the 1970s because it was cheap, and had moved in with a view to improving it and selling. But it was clear that he had never got around to doing anything, apart from painting *ANTIQUES* on the former pub sign. I parked in the front yard by a grimy window which retained some of the white letters of *Private Bar*. Opening the door, I was hit by the ever-present smell of stale tobacco, and the sight of Frank's stock, seemingly unchanged since my last visit. The shop bell rattled for a few moments while I double-checked that there was nothing new to interest me. Frank, who, I supposed, was at the back of the house in the kitchen, poring over the *Racing Post*, had heard the bell and guessed it was me.

'Tea, Phoebe?' he shouted.

'Yes, please,' I shouted back.

I heard the sound of newspapers and china, then he shuffled in, wearing green cord slippers, grandad flannels and a shapeless brown hand-knitted sweater. His fat Jack Russell followed him. Today had obviously been one of his occasional shaving mornings, so that even with his jowly face and half-bald head he looked in his mid-fifties, not his usual late sixties. He slopped two mugs of tea on the glass display cabinet which served as a shop counter, and dropped into a chair behind it. I found myself a stool, removed the tea bag from my mug, and nestled it in the saucer of dog-ends on the counter.

'Your bits are in the back of the car,' he said. 'I'll show you in a minute.' Never in a hurry, he lit up a Benson, leaned back on his chair and stared up at the boarded pub ceiling. It was nicotine brown and cobwebbed. 'Wonderful the power of a dirty joke,' he said.

I sensed this was the preamble to some story, so settled down to hear it – he'd listened to me enough in the past. Behind him was a wall of shelves crammed with miscellanea. Within a lazy arm's reach of the kitchen door, it was his favourite dumping ground for recent acquisitions. I scanned the familiar cracked china, dented Sheffield plate, unsaleable trinkets, stoneware jars, and boxes of castor wheels. Since Frank was in the habit of forgetting what he had placed here, there was no point in asking if he had anything new. I had to search it out for myself.

'Same old rubbish up there, I'm afraid,' he said.

I nodded, but the clutter had somehow changed since my last visit.

'The Brigadier,' Frank continued. 'The old boy came in here out of boredom. We swapped jokes, watched the Cheltenham Gold Cup on TV, and then he suggested I sell a few things for him.'

I noticed an odd-shaped box on the bottom shelf. It hadn't been there before.

'Of course, he'd tried the smart auction houses first. One of them sent a couple of besuited twerps. Knocked on the front door. Asked the man in the boiler suit and woolly hat who answered to tell the Brigadier that the valuers had arrived. From then on, the suits were on a hiding to nothing. And he refused to pay for the leather-bound valuation they sent him.' He gulped his tea.

The box was about four inches long and sarcophagus-shaped. It had no lid. What was it?

'Next, that flash dealer from the TV. He bought a pair of library chairs for a pittance. A week later the old boy's cousin spotted them in a shop in the Fulham Road. The price had gained a couple of noughts. Exit the smart end of the trade.'

I guessed it might be a miniature tea caddy.

'So I end up with the job. I tell him I wouldn't buy the better things, but I'd place them for him in suitable auctions, or smuggle them into country house sales. Providing he gave me first refusals on the also rans.'

'Is that box one of them?'

'Where's that?'

I pointed. He tipped his chair back and grabbed it, spilling sawdust from it as he placed it on the counter.

'I was going to mention this. I found it in his kitchen cupboard.' He handed it to me. 'One pin cushion holder minus pin cushion, which must have been stuffed with sawdust. Not on the twerps' inventory. Yours for twenty quid.'

'I'll have it.' I wanted it for myself, couldn't justify the expense, but knew I would enjoy making a cushion for it. I'm good with a needle, even if I'm not up to governess standard. I pulled out the cash from my bag before thoughts of my bank balance could prevail.

Frank wrapped it in newspaper. 'When you've made a wax model of the blonde, you can use this to store your pins.'

'No, it's much too nice to be associated with her. It's a present to myself for getting an interview for a teaching job.'

'Not giving up antiques?'

'Augmenting my income.'

'And the lucky school?'

'Hillgate Hall.'

'You're brave. The kids call it Hellgate.'

'Frank!' The shout came from the back of the house. It was Connie, his wife, a mobile hairdresser, who was seldom at the house when I called. 'Frank, if you're going out today, we need some more dog food.'

Frank groaned his way out of his chair and led me to where his Vauxhall Cavalier was parked. He lifted up the tailgate.

I looked at some leather cases, still with old clothes inside. There was also an empty Gladstone bag, a hat box complete with top hat, and a pair of riding boots with their trees.

'Hundred and thirty pounds the lot. Cash. My profit's the thirty. If you find a diamond ring hidden in a pocket, good luck. You needn't pay me now. Hat box is worth that.'

It was. I told him I'd pay as soon as possible. While we loaded the things on my van, from the back garden Connie shouted out more of her shopping list.

As I drove away, I knew the visit had been a tonic. Never able to take himself seriously, Frank was able to make me do the same. I had never questioned him about his past, but I suspected a deep sadness was hidden there. When I worked in London, the gallery next door had once displayed in the window two of Georges Rouault's paintings of sad clowns. Frank was like them – able to see the comedy, the absurdity of life, despite or because of an inner grief. Perhaps this was my world too.

I spent the rest of the day coaxing myself into interview mode. Clothes first. At my earlier teaching posts, I had discovered that a woman, once on the staff, can dress almost as casually as she likes – even more so than male teachers – but an interview was different. I pulled out the dowdy tweed skirt and jacket I had bought for my Wingbourne Court interview, but had hardly worn since. It was slightly too big – I had lost over a stone in the last two and half years. My hair was a mess, but I couldn't bring myself to make an emergency appointment with Ulford's equivalent of Connie. I found some green tights, and dusted down my sensible brown interview shoes and the bag which almost matched. Opening the tea caddy I used as a jewellery box, to see if my favourite amethyst ring was there, I sighed as I saw my wedding ring beside it. I could understand why some women threw away their wedding ring after a divorce, but I couldn't quite do this myself. 'When I'm ready,' I muttered, 'when I'm ready.'

It wasn't until midday that I remembered I might have bought furniture at yesterday's auction. I looked up Cosmo's number and phoned him. There was no answer.

The next morning Molly, whom I hadn't seen at the school gates, phoned to wish me luck. 'Paul suggested you borrow our VW, if you think the van might give the wrong first impression.'

'A kind thought,' I said, 'but experience has taught me that to own a van is considered an asset at a private school. Moving equipment, stage scenery – that sort of thing. Tell Paul I shall be parking where I hope it will be seen.'

Dressed and ready by 10.00am, I spent a few minutes looking at my CV again, persuading myself that I was qualified to teach French. In the van, my apprehensiveness about the wheel bearings was allayed when, on the first sharp bend, they made no protest. I considered this a good omen.

Hillgate Hall is about thirty minutes away from Ulford, on heathland two miles from the coast. I had driven past once or twice, but had never ventured beyond its tall iron gates. From the road at the top of the drive, I had assumed it was built of local grey bricks. Now, as I drove through the gates and down an avenue of oaks bordering playing fields, to my surprise I realised that the early nineteenth-century house in front of me was built of stone. It was in Gothic style. The only brickwork was a later addition to one side – for classrooms, I guessed. Using whitish bricks and a few token mullioned windows, some attempt had been made to match its design with the older part. The greyness, the mix of old and new, I found unnerving; it was how Jane Eyre had described Lowood Institution.

Nearing the hall, I saw that there were touches of Regency about it, especially the fanlight above the front door. It was an in-between style which reflected the way I felt, suspended between dealing and teaching, uncertain of both. Newly dug flower beds lined the end of the drive, and, in front of the hall, was a large circular lawn with a central bed of amber-coloured roses. Here the drive forked, one way leading to the classrooms.

I took the other way, between box hedges, following signs pointing to the car park, a shingled area between the main hall and tennis courts. Beyond the courts was a tall yew hedge, behind which, according to another sign, was the headmaster's house. Half a dozen other cars were parked here, two looking so clapped-out that my van didn't seem out of place. Walking towards a side door, I could see clearly into a room which, from its armchairs, pigeon holes, notice-boards and coffee cups, could only be the staffroom. I suspected morning break had just finished. This was a relief. When I arrived to be interviewed at Wingbourne Court, afternoon break was in full swing, and I ran a gauntlet of eyes and whispers, 'Is she the new teacher?' Then I had to wait in a secretary's office while a succession of staff passed through, each glancing my way with the same unspoken question, a leering male teacher adding others.

The back door was flanked by campagna-shaped stone vases filled with compost, awaiting their summer plants. This side of the building was covered with Virginia creeper which in autumn, I imagined, would provide a striking contrast to the elephant-grey stonework. My arrival must have been noticed, since the iron-studded door in front of me opened before I could reach the handle, and the blue stocking appeared, only her stockings were beige fifty denier, and the office into which she ushered me had two computers instead of the imagined black Remington. The rest of my down-the-phone picture of her – large-boned, late sixties, short grey hair and all-seeing efficiency – was accurate.

'Dora Prideaux,' she introduced herself, giving me a heavy handshake. 'Do sit down, Mrs Burns. Dr Lennox won't be a minute.' She pointed to a hard-seated chair by a door with *Headmaster* painted in black lettering on one of its panels. The chair forced me to sit straight-backed, like a pupil in trouble waiting to see the head.

Miss Prideaux settled herself into a leather revolving chair opposite. She wore a lovat tweed skirt, of a different generation and weight from my own, but with superficial similarity. Establishing affinity, this was reassuring. Tonight, I thought, Molly and I may laugh about my clothes, but right now, in front of Miss Prideaux, I am pleased with my choice and certain that those tawny owl eyes have noticed my cream silk shirt. Hers was white and cotton, billowing about her chest like my father's surplice. Beaming at me, she tried to put me at ease – perhaps my desperation was showing itself.

'It's a real godsend, your contacting us, Mrs Burns. Mr Osborne was meant to start at the beginning of term, but his mother's illness has obliged him to stay with her in Nottingham, and he won't be with us until at least half-term. And at short notice it's so hard to find a Latin teacher.'

Latin. I nodded and smiled, but felt a hammer blow. Again I looked at the owl eyes. They shrunk me to a mouse of a creature, who had a minute to apologise for a misunderstanding, or to become proficient in a language I had happily forgotten at O-level. I might have taken the honest course, but the shock had rendered me speechless, while inner desperation urged me to bluff my way through. A disturbing vision came to me of my dark blue school Latin grammar book, the first page with *mensa*, a table, set out in all its cases. Uncomfortable on my penitential chair, glancing at the remorseless electric clock on my right, I couldn't get beyond the vocative, *table, O table*.

Miss Prideaux was saying something about Dr Lennox covering a few classes himself, but his Latin was rather rusty. What was mine? Corroded beyond use. But I needed the money. *Table, O table*. What was Latin for chair? Had I ever known? Was it the same as those stone seats in my father's medieval church, *sedilia*? I had no idea.

Miss Prideaux was now talking about her own school's Latin motto. I didn't catch what it was – my brain repeated table, *O table, table, O table*, but as the minute hand on the wall clock moved to eleven, the chant inexplicably changed to *Vive la, vive la, vive l'amour*, and I wondered if my sanity had left me. When, later, I told this to Molly, she said that it was my subconscious mind failing to accept I was being asked to teach Latin, not French.

'Sorry to have kept you waiting.' David Lennox, tall, mid-fifties, greying, stepped from the adjoining room. 'Do come in.'

In his office, the voice in my head receded enough for me to absorb my surroundings: two walls fitted with oak bookcases in the same gentle Gothic style as the building, and a library table of the same period. He pointed me to the only modern chair in the room, and settled himself behind his desk – 1830s I guessed. On the wall behind him was an inscribed oar from a Durham college. Miss Prideaux, who had followed us, seated herself in a button-back armchair. I had enough mental and physical agility to produce my CV from my bag and lay it among a collection of snuff boxes in the only space on the desk. David Lennox glanced at it.

'Ah, you read history at UCL. My wife was at London University –

psychology.' He said this with a derisive smile. This slowly changed to a tight, unsettling grin, which lingered until Miss Prideaux spoke.

'When I was in London thirty years ago, I used to visit a friend near UCL.'

'Where was that, Dora?' he asked.

'The Hotel Russell – she had a suite there.'

I began to wonder who was being interviewed, her or me, although she probably knew more Latin.

'Now, Mrs Burns,' he said, 'to be frank, Hillgate Hall is not Elveden College. We have only a hundred and forty on the roll, and you would find them somewhat different.'

'More challenging perhaps,' said Miss Prideaux.

'We couldn't offer quite the rates you're used to, but we could pay you at the level we had agreed with Neil Osborne, which is, as head of department, a graduate with, say, ten years' experience, approximately eighteen thousand per annum.'

Miss Prideaux added, 'Which we can pay you on a weekly basis until we know when he can take up his appointment.'

This was way, way beyond what I was earning week by week with antiques, but I think they regarded my silence as surprise that the pay was less than I expected.

'Does this sound reasonable?' he asked.

'If you have any queries . . .' she said.

I was stunned that, without being asked questions, I was being offered the job. From politeness I asked about the hours, weekend commitments and out-of-lesson demands, which at Elveden College were more onerous than anything in the classroom. He or she gave me answers, but I was so much in shock that it required more concentration than I could summon to remember what I was being told, apart from registering the fact that Latin was not taught beyond GCSE level. I was in a haze of bewilderment: *the words they uttered seemed indistinct and blurred.*

Frenetically, I tried to estimate how far out of my financial troubles a few weeks' teaching would lift me, hoping old Mrs Osborne's illness would detain her son in Nottingham until the end of term. Now Miss Prideaux was speaking. I regained my concentration as she explained the school's policy of admitting a proportion of disadvantaged children and those, for various reasons, expelled from other schools. All the while Dr Lennox examined his snuff boxes: first, a tortoiseshell example, then, an enamel box in the shape of a swan. Seemingly relieved that his Latin problem was solved, he slouched back in his chair, so that his bright green paisley tie lopped over the waistcoat of his ridiculously old-fashioned brown herringbone three-piece suit. His polished brogues pointed towards me from under the desk. His socks, I noticed, were a yellow almost too garish to blend with the rest of his clothes; perhaps part of him was resisting the outward formality.

Miss Prideaux stressed that staff were expected to attend assembly, conducted most mornings by the head. Here he looked up, grinned, pulled out a pipe from a pocket and placed it between his teeth, clearly longing to light it. Now that the exposure of my bogus teaching credentials seemed less likely, I was more relaxed. I looked at his longish face, furrowed, I guessed, with frustration that a doctorate and thirty years' teaching had propelled him no further than a small school, which was probably surviving because it welcomed children other schools had rejected. Our eyes met and he grinned again.

'The school is a nineteenth-century foundation,' he said.

I tensed.

'Lady Widwell, our founder, was by all accounts a very devout woman, although she seldom attended any church and believed education should be secular. For the early 1800s, very much ahead of her time. However, she did stipulate that mornings and evenings there should be, not prayers or readings, but three minutes' silence. It has been said she had Quaker ancestry. We do include RE in the curriculum, but there is no school chaplain or any of the usual religious trappings of a private school. You'll see her portrait in the dining hall when Dora gives you a guided tour.'

This information dispelled some of my preconceptions. None of the compulsory daily chapel of my own school – certainly none of Lowood's hour of prayer and Bible readings every morning.

He stood and, picking up my CV and letter, gave them back to me; perhaps they were spoiling his arrangement of snuff boxes. At any rate, he seemed glad to hand me over to his secretary.

'We look forward to seeing you on Monday,' he said, grinning and extending a hand.

I shook it. It felt cold, robotic. His eyes were focused elsewhere.

Our first stop was the dining hall, originally a ballroom. It was set out for lunch with small tables. Miss Prideaux explained the self-service arrangements. I had half expected more formality than this, even the sort of High Table which had dominated the hall at my old school, but here the one traditional dining hall feature was the portrait of the founder, life-size, over the chimney piece. Had it hung in the gallery where I'd worked, the label would have said *Follower of Sir Thomas Lawrence*. She was seated in a garden, wearing a long red dress, a book in her lap. In the background was Hillgate Hall which, without its later additions, was both elegant and severe, as was Lady Widwell's face.

Miss Prideaux led me along a green-painted corridor, past some dank-smelling changing rooms, towards the classroom block, joined to the old building by a short cloister. I shivered: the stone columns of the arches reminded me of the school where I had endured four unbearable years, St Michael's College Bramshead – a Victorian school, founded to educate, according to its charter, *the sons of poor gentlefolk*. It had decided to go co-ed in the late 1960s, and I had been one of its unenviable first intake of girls.

'Would you like to see the Latin room first?' asked Miss Prideaux as we entered the 1930s classroom block.

My room was at one end of the building. Its windows looked towards the circular lawn and rosebed. The interior was bare, apart from chairs and desks, waiting for the head of Latin to give it some character. For a moment I tried to forget my scant knowledge of the language, and to imagine ways of livening up this anonymous space. Posters? Pictures of Roman life, villas, soldiers? Younger classes could do some of this. My guide opened a cupboard and showed me a selection of current text books. I gasped – none bore the remotest resemblance to the Latin grammar book I remembered. This was both a comfort and a worry. I would not have to return to hated but familiar ground, but I had no longer than four days to familiarise myself with new books. Casually, I pulled one from a shelf and flicked through its pages. I shuddered. This was not the Latin I had once learned. Was it possible for a dead language to have changed so much in the twenty-three years since I had last studied it? I glanced at the line drawings and cartoons of a Roman market place, and a chapter titled *Shopping for Clothes*. All this was new to me. I turned to the vocabulary at the end of the next chapter, *The Dining Room*. Here were words – *triclinium*, *ancilla* and many others – I never remembered learning. My weekend was going to be spent as if I were cramming for exams.

'I'm afraid your predecessor, Henry Chilvers, didn't leave any notes about his teaching,' said Miss Prideaux, 'but since you're only filling in for a week or two, I don't suppose it matters.'

I told her I would borrow a few books for lesson plans, thinking, for my education as much as theirs.

My first glimpse of children came when we arrived at a nearby class. A maths lesson was in progress. Twelve pupils, girls and boys, all in green blazers, had their heads in exercise books. Their teacher was circulating and looking at their work. He paused by the desk of a dark-haired girl.

'Alan Carter, Year Tens,' whispered Miss Prideaux, anxious not to disturb them. 'He's also assistant head.'

I was impressed by the atmosphere of concentration, until the teacher shouted at the girl with a vehemence which no possible mistake in her work could justify. The others didn't raise their eyes, but bent their heads closer to their books. I shuddered again. This was a class controlled, not by good discipline, but by anger: *the obedience of fear*.

Miss Prideaux hurried me into the next classroom, devoid of children but with every table and shelf laden with cardboard models and miniature plastic figures. Paintings and diagrams covered every inch of the walls, while, hanging in corners, there were costumes and wooden swords. I guessed it was an art room shared with a drama teacher.

'Renwick Percival's room. History and RE,' she said.

I examined the models and realised that they represented various events in world history. The American Civil War was clearly one of his favourites, with the Battle of Gettysburg taking up two tables. If Latin was all domestic life, history at this school was still fixed in the world of warfare. On the teacher's desk, a battle from classical times was being fought. I made the mistake of pausing to examine it.

'Ah, as a historian and classicist, you must enlighten me,' she said.

I was lucky. Along a river which divided the two armies, someone had pencilled *Issus*. Unearthing some of my meagre ancient history, I said confidently, 'Battle of Issus – Greeks versus Persians.'

She seemed impressed with my knowledge. If this was the extent of the examination in Classics, I had got off lightly. My growing confidence lasted only as far as the school computer room. There was no class in progress here, but she proudly unlocked the door and led me in.

'Henry Chilvers had always planned to do some Latin work here,' she said. 'So if you wish to use this room a few times each week, I'm sure it can be made available.'

I gave an interested look towards the machines and nodded, wondering how long it would take Molly or James to make me computer-literate.

'If you need any technical support,' she continued, 'then I suggest you . . .' Shouting from the other side of the classroom block distracted her. She frowned. 'We'd better investigate.'

I followed her, the noise increasing, to a classroom overlooking a small clump of birch trees. Through the glass-panelled door I saw a minor riot. Two boys of about fourteen were waving chairs in the centre of the room where the desks had been pushed to one side. Two other boys were on the floor fighting. Three more were at the back, urging on the others. One alone was at his desk. He was wiry, with close-cut dark hair and malevolent pleasure on his face, like a boxing fan given a free ringside seat at a prize fight, out to enjoy the violence, never mind the winner. I thought their teacher must be absent, but then I saw a white-faced young man in a badly fitting suit and creased floral tie, standing in a corner, holding a book and trying to make himself heard above the din.

Before Miss Prideaux could place her hand on the door, the boy at the ringside shouted, 'Watch out – the old bag!'

Instant silence.

As we entered, the teacher said with unconvincing composure, 'Now we'll try that section again, with a little more acting and rather less fighting.' The comment was directed more to us than to the class.

'Good morning, Mr Devlin,' she said, looking at the boys, not at him. 'Let me introduce you to Mrs Burns who will be joining us to teach Latin for a few weeks.' Then to me, 'Brian Devlin teaches English.'

He shuffled forward and gave me an awkward, muttering handshake. 'We were just acting out a scene from *Of Mice and Men*.'

The sniggering from the two boys, covered in grime from their fight on the floor, confirmed that the class had been completely out of control. Miss Prideaux looked at them. The sniggers stopped. The boys turned their eyes to me. Even as I stood there under the wing of Dora Prideaux, I felt that they were plotting to make sure my first lesson with them would be hell. Their looks made me long for the familiar discomfort of an auction room, where the disdain of the local ring of dealers was far preferable to the fermenting hostility in front of me, the fiercest of which emanated from the boy at the back, out for revenge because his entertainment had been cut short. His steel-blue eyes fixed me with hate.

'That was Year Nine, lower set,' Miss Prideaux said, as we walked towards the science block, a newer building, joined to the main block by a covered walkway, happily without cloisters.

We looked in at a chemistry and a technology lesson, both of which appeared cheerful and well-conducted. In the physics lab, however, after we had knocked and entered, we found an obese and scarlet-faced teacher blasting away at a boy for some trivial act of stupidity. He continued to do so as we stood in the doorway, working himself up to a rage, partly, I thought, for our benefit.

'You pathetic imbecile,' he concluded.

He turned and introduced himself with an unrelenting handshake and loud bonhomie. 'Douglas Morris. Physics. CO, Naval Section, Cadet Force.' Then in a whisper, 'Everyone calls me Duggy.'

A cursory look around his room showed that his naval interests had invaded the physics department. He was clearly a Nelson aficionado, since pictures of the admiral, his battles and contemporary men-of-war hung on every wall. There was even a display cabinet of Nelsonia – commemorative plates and mugs, lengths of rope and an inscribed cannonball.

'Visual aids,' he explained. 'Nearly all the basics of physics can be illustrated by reference to ships.'

When we were outside, Miss Prideaux said, 'Dear Duggy has his own individual style.'

It was unclear if she was defending or criticising him.

'Is he an ex-naval officer?' I asked.

'Heavens, no. Teaching's all he's ever done, apart from running a seafood restaurant for a year. I don't believe it was a great success.'

We were walking back to her office through a lavender garden behind the main school when, from out of a shrubbery ahead of us, charged a line of children holding long poles. Behind them, encouraging the slowest, was a short grey-haired man who looked far from fit.

'You must meet Mr Percival,' said my guide, stopping as the tiny army advanced.

The children halted, their poles inches from our faces, and encircled us. Their teacher, sweaty in shirt sleeves and dirty brown trousers, panted up to us.

'Civil War. Skirmish in Virginia,' he spluttered. 'Reduced to pitchforks.'

We were introduced. He shook my hand furiously.

'Mrs Burns is going to be teaching Latin,' she said. 'But you'll be interested to learn her degree was in history.'

'And probably better than my poor second from Bristol.'

'I'm sure it's not,' I said, smiling to hide the uneasy truth.

'Troops to the billet,' he bawled, and led his band of eleven-year-olds towards their classroom.

'Games hall and squash courts over there,' she said, pointing to a new building in some woods beyond the classroom block. 'No need for me to take you there. Library next.'

We entered the old hall by its front door. The library was through the first door on the left, an enormous room whose walls were fitted with mahogany shelving. The lower shelves housed the school library books. The upper shelves, accessible only with a ladder, were filled with leather-bound volumes.

'This is where we hold assemblies,' she said. 'A lovely room – it is also home to some of the founder's own books and furniture.'

I noticed a grey-painted Regency sideboard, an interior decorator's dream. I imagined it standing at a smart London fair with a five-figure price on the ticket.

'I don't think there's much about Latin or the ancient world here,' she said, 'apart, of course, from the *Asterix* books. Now, biology. Ruth Stebbing.'

The biology room was housed in an old stable block beyond the headmaster's house. Before we arrived I heard a no-nonsense voice, which reminded me of a friend of Molly's, a local Pony Club organiser. But when we entered, I didn't find the imagined martinet in jodhpurs, but a petite, urbane woman, a few years older than me – the first professional-looking teacher I had so far encountered. Her chestnut hair was immaculately shaped and tinted, and from her designer summer dress, fashion cardigan and the expensive handbag by her desk, I guessed she either spent all her salary on clothes and accessories, or, more likely, had another source of income. The quantity and variety of plants in her room suggested that the biology she taught had a bias towards botany. Unlike any of the teachers I had so far met, she was pleased to introduce me to her class of Year Eights, and asked one of them to tell me about the seedling they were studying. After my experiences with English, history and physics, it was comforting that there would at least be one person in the staffroom with whom I might hope to enjoy a normal conversation.

When the tour was over and Miss Prideaux had thanked me for 'saving the Latin department', I returned to my van, and, watching a gardener mow the circular lawn, wondered what sort of school I had joined – fraudulently joined. I hoped I would drop into my work here as easily as I had at my other teaching posts, but I had worrying reservations: my false pretences, the school's overriding oddness, most of the other staff and, worst, the perturbing echoes of St Michael's Bramshead. Returning to a timetable would also be strange after working for so long on my own. But when I considered the pittance my freedom earned me, all misgivings evaporated. As for my lack of qualifications, a little deception – almost a misunderstanding – in this school, where the academic standards did not seem very high and where the teaching skills were very mixed in quality, seemed no great crime.

Driving home, I was torn between my urge to carry my good news along with a celebratory bottle of wine to Molly, and my conscience, ordering me to drive straight to Norwich and buy a large Latin dictionary and grammar to add to the books beside me. I had a few miles to go before I needed to make the decision. As I deliberated, the face of B appeared on the windscreen. She was wearing the smile she wore when I saw her with Anthony at the County Court on the day of our divorce hearing. She had said nothing to me then. Now she was saying, 'So you've returned to the blackboard, I gather.' She had appeared like this before. As on previous occasions, I accelerated and switched on the wiper blades in a mad attempt to throw her off. Why had she come to scoff when I had good news to celebrate?

I rejected the dictionary-buying trip and drove to the village shop, where I bought a bottle much better than my usual choice, then headed for Molly's. Our celebrations extended until we collected the boys from school.

*Ancilla*, a serving maid. Of course. How had I forgotten? *Triclinium*, a dining table. Once I may have known that too. An hour or two over my text books that night drove away most of my fears; the weekend would not be one of sleepless revision after all. Anyhow, I told myself, my pupils were probably as worried about their new teacher as I was of them. Apart from Year Nine, lower set.

I told James about the new job.

'Does this mean we'll have more money?' he said.

'My work's only for a few weeks.'

'Any chance of a holiday? I'd love to go fishing somewhere new.'

I thought about the river Aire. 'We'll have to see.'

'I'd rather go away with you than with Dad and B.'

'Let's hope we can.'

'Ben's going to Brittany in the summer.'

The mention of Brittany unintentionally hurt me. For several years before we moved to Ulford, Anthony and I had rented a cottage near Concarneau – James's first seaside holidays. Living in his workplace, Anthony was never truly relaxed unless he was away from home – my father was in a similar position with his rectory. Did the new Anthony, I wondered, ever think back to those weeks in France? James's first tentative steps into the sea. The *moules marinières* in the restaurant up the road. The church festival we attended – I could still remember the hymn, sung to a melody from the *New World Symphony*. And the bonfire and fireworks late into the night. I had never guessed what sort of new world Anthony would find a few years later.

I felt a wave of anger, but with it an assertiveness which lasted until the next day. I phoned the bank, insisted on talking to the manager, and told him that I was about to start a well-paid job. I mentioned the salary, omitting to tell him it was only for a few weeks. I enjoyed saying, 'Head of the Latin Department at Hillgate Hall.' It impressed him enough to agree to cancel Friday's meeting. For the first time in months I felt in control of my life, and it was only 10.00am.

On a high, I phoned Cosmo again. Once more I had no reply, but a phone call to Tanner's informed me that I had bought the commode chair for £60, and that the plank coffer had made £210. Since it was not in my name, I knew it must have been bought by the ring, one of whom, I supposed, would now owe me money. With the volume of the van radio turned up, Elton John's *Made in England* accompanied me as I set off for Walborough.

The creature over my shoulder hit me late that day. Driving back home with my chair, I was filled with misgivings about my ability to stand in front of a class. For no reason, the earlier self-confidence was gone. In my driveway, I could not even bring myself to leave the van. For a few minutes I sat looking at the house, listening to the birds and the murmurous insects in the garden. Above me, the candelabra branches of the horse chestnut tree by the gate, the conker supply for James and Ben, brushed the top of my van. It was a restful sound.

I had retained as many as possible of the trees and shrubs we had inherited, the best of which were four apple trees, still in flower. These, like the old-fashioned roses, now in bud and rambling over them, were a variety I had not yet been able to identify. Beneath them was a rough lawn made from the orchard grass I had found there. My eyes lifted to the largest tree, perhaps an ancient James Grieve, one of whose branches was supported by a mossy oak post. I looked at the grass below it, to the exact spot where I had first set eyes on B.

It was one Sunday afternoon in the third week of Anthony's first term. He had invited some fellow students to Ulford. Most I never saw again, but I can remember the faces of all eleven of them: the four boys who played football with James; the head-girly type who insisted on washing up the tea things; the girl who amused us all with her impersonation of Margaret Thatcher; the boy from New England who wanted to know details of Ulford's history I couldn't supply; the serious couple in black I saw rolling joints in the greenhouse, like witches performing some arcane ritual; the simpering girl, a tenant of B's who never left her side; B herself.

Wearing a blue and white floral-printed dress with cross-over straps against her long spine – a cold choice for a Norfolk October – she held court under that apple tree, seated on a wooden bench. I was walking among the windfalls, carrying a tray of tea and cake, while Anthony was showing someone round the house. He was a good host although, I remembered, B was the one person he ignored all afternoon, the significance of which I was too naive to recognise at the time. As I stood, tray in hand, she stretched out a bare freckled arm towards me, took a cup in her long fingers, smiled a thank you and stroked her hair with her left hand, a prelude to an extravagant gesture.

'This would be a lovely space to play *A Midsummer's Night Dream,*' she said.

None of the courtiers around her, nor I, had any doubt who would be cast as Titania. It was at that moment, standing close to her, that I was surprised by her perfume, the sweet, heavy smell of lily of the valley. It drew me back to a great aunt who used to stay with us at the rectory. When she was out of the house, playing whist in the village hall, I would creep into her bedroom and sniff my way along the row of tiny bottles on her dressing table, a far more exciting selection than my mother's. Floris' Lily of the Valley was always there, never my first choice, but still winning my secret award for pungency. Had this favourite of great aunt Hilda's, I wondered, now become campus chic?

November had been a month of wormy suspicions. Anthony's first night away followed a 9.00pm phone call, telling me he wanted to attend a late-night seminar with some visiting professor who had given an evening lecture: 'It makes sense if I stay over in halls.' Next came the department drinks party: 'You could come too, but it's really just a faculty do. I think it would be best if I spent the night here.' Perfectly plausible, apart from a curious tone. Then the nights away in London on theatre visits. Why not? It made good sense. His new course included drama. But I had to wait until Christmas to discover what changing courses really meant.

The wind had dropped, and the branches no longer brushed the top of the van. I turned my eyes to the house and watched the sun catch the metal plant labels nailed on the south wall. There were four, spaced at different heights, names stamped on them: *Walburton's Admirable Peach, Beurre Bachelier, Doyenne du Comice* and *Josephine De Malines*. All four fruit trees had disappeared before we bought the house, but I had plans, with soil improvement, to plant replacements beneath each label. In the sunlight they were taking turns to glint, like an unseen hypnotist dangling his watch in front of me. I recalled my nights of sleepless suspicion during Anthony's second term.

Over Christmas there had been a hollow joviality about him, alerting my doubts more than his feebly explained absences in term-time. We made love twice, but Anthony was more dutiful than loving. After the second time I almost shouted at him, 'What the hell's going on? Don't you know you're in the same bed as me?' But I said nothing. At this stage a part of me wanted to rationalise, to argue that his emotional absence was due to a preoccupation with academic work. But a week into New Year, when he began going into Norwich for 'vacation reading in the library', I sided with my intuition – there was another woman. I admitted the fact quite calmly, while on a walk round the frozen Blickling lake. Once the truth was accepted, I knew exactly who she was, and felt I had known from the first.

To begin with, I felt no anger, merely the wish quietly to say to him, 'It's B, isn't it? Tell me.' But as the start of term approached, and I watched him move about the house performing everyday tasks as if life were normal, my feelings changed and I wanted to challenge him, to disturb whatever he was doing with a sudden punch, or kick him, his books or his car, and shout at him to admit it was her. But I held back. Nor could I talk to Molly about it.

The breeze had returned and the sun, flickering through the swaying branches above me, was now playing on the *Doyenne du Comice* label, like a signaller flashing a message. I recalled Anthony's second term, with the increasing excuses for his staying nights in Norwich. Even now, I don't remember what reasons he gave, only that I didn't believe him, and that the nights away were easier than the occasions he said he 'might be staying over', a euphemism which made me feel sick. Awake, often until the early hours, waiting for phone calls he never made, I felt my marriage drain away. And making it more painful was the intuition that Anthony and B were getting high on the deceit. Late one Saturday morning he had appeared with flowers and some excuse about not being able to find a phone. I threw his daffodils on the floor.

'Give them to that prima donna you're screwing.'

He did his best to look shocked, ignoring the accusation. 'Don't be silly, darling. You've no idea how demanding this course is. Returning to academic work is bloody difficult.'

'Is it *academic* work?'

'I said I'm sorry I didn't phone. He began to pick up the flowers.'

'Take them to B. Unless you give her orchids.'

'Why don't we go out for lunch?'

We did, and I felt like a child being taken out for a treat. In the pub, over something horrible in a basket, I said, 'I suppose you feel this is doing your duty to your family.' Since James was with us, I suppressed the urge to send my food the same way as the daffodils. That evening, I sneaked a look at his diary and discovered B's address. It had already been arranged that the following Wednesday James would be spending the night at Ben's. Since Wednesday was also, amid all the variable days, Anthony's regular 'staying over' night, I decided to use the opportunity to investigate Wyatt Square.

The messages from the plant labels were becoming spasmodic – clouds were disrupting their signals. I recalled that night. I didn't go to bed, but sat watching TV until after midnight, followed by a video Molly had lent me before Christmas – a strangely suitable film about the triangular relationship between a painter and two women. Most of its two hours, much in silence, was shot from behind the artist's shoulder, as he turned for inspiration from the older to the younger woman.

At 2.30am, my planned departure time, I set off to Norwich in the old Renault I then owned. I felt like a burglar driving to work. A half moon lit up the road. My ineffectual car heater did little to counter a bitterly cold night. I drove slowly along the icy lane and joined the empty Norwich Road. In the darkness, I was in an unfamiliar country where I was a spy. A rush of guilt made me formulate an excuse in the event of being stopped by the police: 'No, I haven't been to a party or drinking. I couldn't sleep, so I'm driving to get rid of insomnia.' The guilt was short-lived. As I approached the outskirts of the city, I found a strange pleasure in what was becoming an adventure. For once I was ahead of Anthony and B. In control. And it felt good.

I saw no traffic until I stopped at traffic lights on the ring-road, where a convoy of lorries roared across in front of me. Their noise was reassuring, a feeling which lasted until I turned off into the residential streets of west Norwich, whose stillness insisted I was a criminal. Again I told myself I was breaking no law, but I was aware that I was breaking faith with myself, with my marriage and maybe with James too. At this

49

point I could have turned back, were it not for the recurring picture of that girl on the garden bench the previous autumn. That expression on her face goaded me to continue. But I was becoming tense and nervous.

Somewhere I took a wrong turning and was forced to weave in and out of unfamiliar streets. They were car-lined and asleep. I was an intruder, scared, but I needed a final confirmation of my suspicions. Now, at last, I found my bearings. I turned into Wyatt Square. I didn't have to check the door numbers – Anthony's MG was parked outside one of the almost identical double-fronted houses. Quietly, I said, 'You rat, you cornered rat.' I gazed into the night, barely able to breathe.

My first emotion was, not anger, but a tide of relief at this decisive end to sapping suspicion. It released in me an energy and palpitating rage. I lowered the window. Outside, the city was cold and lifeless. To calm myself I tried breathing deeply, a futile act which told me I had been calm for too long. After perhaps ten minutes my mind was clear enough to let me say, 'I can go home now. I can't be deceived anymore. I can look to the future.' But another feeling, maybe the desire to savour this victory after months of deception, detained me. I needed a closer look at the house.

I got out of the car as quietly as possible, but the metallic click of the closing door sounded loud enough to wake the whole terrace. I looked around, half expecting sash windows to open and heads to appear. But nothing. I walked a step or two and shivered. I have never liked urban cold. Sharp frosts on my lawn and hedges, in lanes and fields, I love, but not the city frost which steals in unnoticed under the glare of sodium lights.

I told myself I would walk to the front door, stroll round Wyatt Square and return to my car – a desolate lap of honour after my triumph over uncertainty. But when I arrived at the front door and had checked that the number was the same as in Anthony's diary, I looked up and saw a dull yellow light. I pictured a scented candle on a bedside table between empty wine glasses. The thought made me long for a stone to hurl through that sallow window with its thin chintzes. I looked down at the small lawn either side of the path, but saw no stones. I felt helpless. I stared at the door. There was enough light for me to see that it had been recently painted dark blue and given a repro brass knocker. I reached towards it. I wanted to bang it and wake the whole neighbourhood. But I restrained myself. This gave me a momentary feeling of power over the house and its occupants.

Lowering my arm, my knuckles inadvertently touched the door. It opened an inch. I looked at the gap between door and jamb. Had Anthony, in his haste to be with her, forgotten to close it? Or had one of her tenants dared to be negligent? Again I reached forward, this time wanting to pull the door shut by its knocker, but against my will I pushed it further open.

In front of me was a narrow hallway. To the right there was a staircase, at the top of which the yellow glow was stronger. I stepped in and half closed the door behind me. I had to go on. I stole up the stairs, pausing at each step. Near the top, a board made a creak like an axe splitting kindling. Heart pounding, I froze, certain the whole house had been disturbed. On the landing, I saw that the light was coming from a front bedroom whose door was ajar. I was certain this was their room.

Silence was no longer important. I walked along the landing and into the bedroom. The light was to my right – from a small table lamp by a double bed where two sleeping forms lay under the covers. My foot knocked a shoe. Automatically, I picked it up. It was one of Anthony's. Holding it by the toe, I slammed it into his head. Then again and again, but the blows slid off and hit the pillow. Why didn't he stir? At last he moved, turning, so that a blow came down on his cheek. I heard a shriek. I realised I was hitting B. Amid shouts, I found Anthony at my side, restraining me.

B screamed, 'Get off, get off! Ant!'

The shoe was wrenched from my hand. Someone else, another girl, was now in the room, shouting, and in the cacophony a brighter light was switched on. I looked at B's face bleeding on the pillows, until I was pulled away by Anthony and bundled downstairs, he all the while talking to me in an uneasy blend of reprimand and apology, punctuated by voices upstairs and shouts of, 'Get that mad woman out of here. Get her out of my house.' I resented Anthony touching me, but was trembling too much to shake him off. Several times he said, 'Phoebe, we really must talk.' I found myself in a kitchen, pushed down on a chair. Again, 'Phoebe, we must talk.'

'Talk to you is the last bloody thing I'll do.'

A green nightdress appeared at the door – the simpering tenant. 'Anthony, she's really quite bad,' she whispered.

I shouted to him, 'Run to the bitch. I'm leaving.'

I forced myself onto shaking legs and made it to the door. He tried to restrain me. I glared at him, and his hands fell away. I staggered down the hallway to the front door, but some neighbour must have phoned the police. A uniform was in the doorway. I knocked into it. A zip or button scratched my face. I recoiled, stepped backwards, dazed. Nobody in the house was shouting anymore. I wanted to run past the policeman, but was frozen where I stood, the newel post of the staircase pressing into my back. I blinked towards the door and the motionless policeman. Some other lights came on.

I was breathless and cold and there was cramp in one of my legs. The sun had gone in, and the plant labels were no longer giving their signals. I had often had the dream, but never in daytime. And each time, as now, was a new experience. Afterwards, on reflection, each version contained fresh minor details and one or two nagging differences, suggesting I would have to return again and again to the house to establish the true facts. Once, I had hit only Anthony; once, B had hit me back; another time, I had ended up in an excrement-smeared police cell and had crouched in terror on a hard, rexine-covered bed. This time, the blue nightdress was an addition. Always, I had woken cold and trembling, needing to remind myself that the assault had never happened. True, I had driven to her house and had seen Anthony's car outside. But after that I had simply returned home in tears. A week later he moved in with her.

It was just after 2.00pm – I had been asleep for almost three hours. I was thirsty and my legs were stiff as I hobbled towards the back door, trying to restore my circulation. The dream had destroyed my confidence about next week. Self-doubts had returned in force. I wasn't sure if I was an antique dealer turned teacher or a teacher turned dealer. Or something else pretending to be both. What jobs would Anthony and B end up with? I wondered. I was certain she would talk her way into a successful career, and, if he were at a loss, find something for him – if they were still together.

# 6

Awake and alert at 5.00am on Monday, I listened to a persistent wood pigeon, whose call seemed to tell me that all good things were possible and no problem insurmountable. Over the weekend I had revised what Latin I knew and pored over much that was new, until I felt equal to Hillgate's likely requirements. Even so, I opened some text books to reassure myself that nothing had been forgotten overnight. Next, in a rare fit of domestic fervour, I tidied most of the house. Then, after a leisurely bath, I returned to my bedroom, and, letting my dressing gown fall from my shoulders, looked into the mirror. For the first time in years I felt good about myself. In two months' time, I thought, I shall be forty, almost twice B's age, but there is not a whisper of grey in my dark hair, and if my face has changed since I was twenty – I recalled my wedding photos, unseen for years until divorce sent me thumbing through them – then I am pleased to have thrown off the bony naivety which stared out from that ridiculous white veil. I didn't care that pregnancy and breast-feeding had reshaped my breasts – so different from the waiflike protrusions which were almost imperceptible beneath B's floating dresses. And why was I making these absurd comparisons? From now on she would be of no account – nothing but a minor annoyance. And last night, when Anthony had brought James back from a fishing trip, she had stayed in the car. Perhaps this was a precedent. I would forget her.

Optimistic about my new job, I saw how easily I had allowed the most trivial of upsets to unnerve me when depressed. How asinine to imagine, as I had done too often, that she was laughing at me, as if by some Titanian magic it were she who had brought about each tiny setback affecting my home, my son or my business. B probably didn't give a toss about my life – she was much too busy with . . . why should I care what she was doing? I had Latin to teach, money to earn, antiques to sell.

Molly had offered to have James on Sunday night and take him to school in the morning, making my return to teaching as pressure-free as possible, but I had refused, wanting him with me as I prepared for my new work. He had already quizzed me about Hillgate: 'What sort of computers have they got?' I couldn't tell him. 'Do they have a swimming pool?' I didn't think so. Up early too, he persuaded me to join him on a computer game. In Streetfighter I did well, before capitulating to the strangely metamorphic woman warrior. Sensing I was a poor opponent, he asked, 'How about a game of Grand Prix?'

'Find your school bag,' I said. Mine had been packed and double-checked two hours earlier.

At 8.00am Molly was effusive with her 'Good luck' and assurances. 'You won't have any marking on your first day,' she said, 'so I demand every detail when you get back. The bottle will be open and waiting.'

'Wouldn't mind some now.'

'You can't enter assembly with booze on your breath.'

When I arrived at Hillgate, groups of children were heading for the main door and the library. As I climbed from the van, I felt their eyes on me. At the other end of the car park, Volvo estates and 4x4s predominated, as parents of day pupils dropped off their children. Before I was in the door Miss Prideaux was at my side. She led me to a staffroom already fogged with early-morning cigarettes. Our entry silenced an animated conversation.

She introduced me. 'For those of you who have not already met Mrs Burns – she will be taking over Latin until half-term.'

'Or maybe longer,' added Duggy.

'Or for ever and ever,' intoned Renwick.

'Renwick,' said Miss Prideaux, 'only you will be here that long.' She left the room.

Someone pointed out my pigeon hole and indicated my lessons on the timetable. With that I was ignored, while Renwick and Duggy, clearly the staffroom double act, tried to outdo each other with stories about a boy named Jarritt – 'impossible to teach' and 'seriously deranged'. The rest of the staff were a smiling audience. My isolation lasted only a minute. Ruth Stebbing entered the room and welcomed me. The comedians meanwhile directed their wit to Brian Devlin.

'No wonder his classes are a shambles,' said Duggy. 'Look at his suit.' Duggy now glanced towards us. I suspected we were his next target.

'Ignore them,' said Ruth. 'Their mockery is not always as light-hearted as it seems. Have you found out where everything is?'

'Apart from the loo.'

'I'll show you on the way to assembly.'

In the library, now filled with lines of chattering pupils, there were already two other women teachers. One wore a black and pink track suit and white trainers. 'Joan Tatham,' Ruth told me. 'She takes all the games, rugby included.'

The other woman, frail and in a cardigan of almost the same length as her dress, was standing in front by a piano.

'Don't be deceived by Linda Baird,' said Ruth. 'When she starts playing, she'll deafen you. She teaches music and special needs.'

When the other staff were lined up with us on one side, by the towering bookshelves, Dr Lennox entered wearing a grey three-piece suit and academic gown. From the rostrum, he surveyed the school with his hallmark grin. He appeared to be dreaming he were the head of some major public school, about to address an assembly of seven hundred. The chattering died away.

'Good morning. The Founder's Silence,' he announced.

The three minutes seemed interminable, but the school was obviously accustomed to the tradition. So different, I thought, from the ghastly morning hymn we had been obliged to sing at St Michael's, followed by seventeenth-century prayers with their beseechings and vouchsafings. And yet there was an atmosphere here disturbingly similar.

When the Silence was over, Dr Lennox told a short moralising story about Baden-Powell and 'stickability'. No one, as far as I could see, was listening, and I realised that I hadn't been at the school for more than half an hour and I was already longing for a table of junk at Tanner's Monday auction. Dr Lennox made a couple of announcements about punctuality and litter, but to my amazement made no mention of the school's new Latin teacher. There followed more announcements by other members of staff – mainly by Joan, who threatened all manner of sanctions against members of the senior cricket team who failed to attend nets practice after last lessons. Renwick and Duggy were whispering – probably about her. She noticed their inattention and glared at them

'And we still need two more players to make up the Headmaster's Eleven for Speech Day,' she said.

Dr Lennox now gave Linda Baird a nod. She promptly broke into a Sousa military march with all the *fortissimo* Ruth had warned me about. It felt like a protest against the founder's quietist spirit, negating any hoped-for spiritual benefits of wordlessness.

Ruth accompanied me to my room and stayed until the start of my first class, a group of thirteen Year Six pupils. 'If I were you, I'd spend the next hour just getting to know them,' she said.

I followed her advice, forgot about lesson plans, and mentioned Latin only in relation to the ancient names of their home towns when I knew what these were – *Norvicum*, *Lindum* and *Londinium*. I told them a little about myself, including my dealing in antiques. By breaktime I considered myself part of the school. My confidence lasted as far as the staffroom. Even before I stepped in the door the stale air and smoke engulfed me, carrying me back to St Michael's where I was knocking on the door of the staff common room, handing in a late essay.

I pushed open the door to dispel the memory, and to assert the fact that I was a teacher a generation later at a school 200 miles away. Through the thick atmosphere beyond the door I could see Ruth wasn't there. I found a cup of coffee, and from a safe corner watched Renwick pacing the floor, perspiring and spilling his own coffee over his shirt, as he worked himself up into paroxysms of disgust about a boy in his last class.

'He tried to tell me that if he didn't wear his blazer back-to-front, to protect his shirt from paint smudges, his mother would do him bodily harm.'

'If only she would,' said Duggy.

'I wouldn't mind if his history was improving, but this year he's dropped from a predicted GCSE C grade down to the abyss of Unclassified. I mean – a back-to-front blazer. It looked more like a bloody straitjacket. More appropriate for the mad Jarritt.'

'If his spelling improved,' said Brian Devlin, 'I wouldn't mind if he came to my lessons in fancy dress.'

'Following the example of his English teacher,' said Duggy.

I was about to introduce myself to Linda Baird, who was marking a pile of books at the table, when Renwick dragged me into the conversation. 'Mrs Burns, you must forgive our little banter about certain unspeakables you're yet to meet in this cesspit of no-hopers which passes for a school.'

'Not to mention the unspeakable Devlin whom you have met,' said Duggy.

Renwick continued, 'It's just that when you have encountered some of these poor specimens . . .'

'As you will have done by lunch,' said Duggy.

'. . . then you will appreciate what all of us are up against. Hellgatitis we call it. They all seem to catch it.' Renwick dropped into an armchair, exhausted.

'I've only met Year Six so far,' I said.

'Most of that lot haven't caught the disease. Yet.'

I disliked this conversation, now that it had moved from what they called banter to cynicism, but, as a newcomer, I asked, 'What characterises this illness?'

'Wait until you've been here a few more days,' said Joan, without removing the cigarette from her mouth.

Linda Baird looked up from her marking. 'Or wait until you've attended the half-term staff meeting.'

'Tee tiddly tum-tee tum-tee tum tum,' sung Renwick with Sousa gusto.

Linda ignored him. I was glad to see Ruth enter the room.

'Late for break, Biology,' said Duggy. 'Did you lose your way on a nature walk?'

Ruth looked around the room, fanning away smoke with a hand. 'I could lose myself in here,' she said. She smiled at me.

I walked over to her and whispered, 'Tell me about Year Nine, lower set. I see them after break.'

'Not easy. One or two in particular certainly have problems. But if you accept that you are not going to get them through GCSE, and don't try to bully them through it, as some of our colleagues try to, they're fine.'

With this in mind, I decided to conduct my next lesson with the same approach I had used for my first. But from the outset I found they had no wish to talk about themselves or their homes. I might have been a prison visitor, discovering that personal questions are sometimes best left unasked, unless raised by the inmates. The boy at the back who had enjoyed last Wednesday's fight proved to be Mark Jarritt. I felt him eye me, assessing me for any weakness. Looking at one or two of their books, I saw that Dr Lennox had been struggling to teach them Latin grammar. I looked at Jarritt's aggressive face and made a sudden decision.

'You seem to have done nothing about the Roman army and their weapons,' I said grimly, and watched his eyes change. 'We will begin with the use of the sword, *gladius*.'

So warfare became the theme for the lesson and several others later in the week. I felt it was a cop-out, a deleterious step towards Renwick's mock battles and Duggy's warships, but it worked. And my old vocabulary with its militaristic emphasis was put to good or bad use: *valete*, goodbye, shopping and kitchens.

The next class was, in comparison, a pleasure. Motivated by looming exams, they asked me to cover areas where they felt uncertain. Here my weekend's cramming saw me through, and my dread that a precocious child would ask me to translate a passage from some obscure Latin author never materialised. When the lunch bell sounded, I was certain my Latin teacher persona had been accepted.

Hungry, but with mixed thoughts about school food, I made my way to the dining hall. I met Ruth in the corridor.

'School lunch is not obligatory,' she said, 'and my packed lunch is enough for two. After that, since today we're free until four, why not join me on my usual shopping trip to Walborough, while everyone else is wearing themselves out on the playing fields?'

I said I'd love to, and walked with her towards her car, a metallic-red Mercedes. 'My husband's,' she said. 'Mine's being serviced.'

The car was blocked in by a dark blue ex-Coastguard Land Rover.

'Damn that Duggy,' she said, giving one of his tyres a kick with a patent leather shoe. 'He'll make such a fuss about moving it.'

'We can use my van,' I said.

Amused by the idea of travelling in an old Transit, she climbed in and produced some gravlax rolls which we shared on the way to Walborough. I explained how the antiques side of my life had forced me to return to teaching.

'After one morning do you feel you'll settle in?' she asked.

'I don't know, but I'll only be here a few weeks before Neil Osborne takes up his appointment.'

'That's what you've been told, is it?'

'Isn't it true?'

'Well, I started off filling in for someone for a week or two, and I'm now in my ninth term.'

I parked in the supermarket car park. 'I still ought to keep an eye on antiques,' I told her. 'Can I catch you up at the cheese counter?'

I jogged the hundred yards to the sale ground, where the familiar world of the auction was a salutary change after Hillgate, but I felt guilty about slipping away from school at the first opportunity. And if Ruth's suggestion were true, that my job might be for much longer than I envisaged, then it made sense to be seen around the place as an enthusiastic new member of staff.

Since I had never arrived at Tanner's so late on a Monday, the sight of furniture being moved from the morning auction made me uneasy. I felt like one of my pupils late for a lesson. But the quick calculation that I had already earned over £30 at Hillgate for half a day's work softened my anxiety.

In the 2.00pm sale there was only one lot which demanded my inspection. It was a winged armchair whose stained loose cover could not quite conceal what was below. Someone else had been at the chair before me, since a corner of the hessian underneath had been pulled away to reveal the beechwood seat rails. They looked as genuine as the mahogany underframe. I replaced the loose cover.

'Yeah, hide the evidence,' said a familiar voice from behind me.

I turned round, but before I had the chance of speaking to Cosmo he nodded to the saleroom door and started walking towards it. I followed until he halted by the sale ground café.

'I think I owe you some money from last week,' he said. 'Can it wait until later? I haven't a penny on me at the moment.'

For a moment I thought he was going to walk off again, but I said quickly, 'I won't be around later, but can I leave a price with you on the wing chair?'

'Ah, chair, yes,' he said, as if he'd forgotten about it in the space of twenty yards. 'How do you want to do it?'

'Can I just leave my price with you again? Five hundred.' This was more than I had in my account, but I was fired up with new job confidence, added to which I was certain that the chair was completely genuine and worth over £1000 to him.

The notebook from the back pocket. The pencil. The grunt. He was gone.

On the way back to the supermarket, I felt caught in limbo between teaching and antiques, avoiding both in a double truancy. I found Ruth behind a trolley laden with what for me were luxury foods – artisan salamis and cheeses, expensive hams and the sort of seductively boxed desserts which James would sometimes try to sneak into my own trolley. At the checkout, my basket of special offers and cheap wine was through in a minute. I helped Ruth pack her shopping into boxes. There was no wine. 'Hugh's department,' she said. 'You must meet him. We're having a party in a couple of weeks.'

On our way back to Hillgate we exchanged family details. She had no children. Hugh, her husband, considerably older than her, was senior partner with a firm of Norwich solicitors, and the reasons for her teaching did not include the need for money.

Turning into the school entrance, I could see that Joan Tatham's world of sport had taken over the playing fields. She, assisted by a floppy-hatted Brian Devlin, was supervising a group in the cricket nets, Dr Lennox was umpiring a junior game, while we could see, in the distance, some figures swinging golf clubs. When we arrived at the car park, I saw mixed doubles were being played on the tennis courts.

'Watch out!' Ruth shouted.

I braked hard. The tyres bit into the gravel as I allowed a group of runners, shepherded by a sweat-soaked Duggy, to pass in front of me. Two boys at the rear laughed at the near miss. Duggy scowled at me. He wanted to swear, but any words were choked by his panting and gasping.

'Not a way to endear myself to the school,' I said.

'Might be best to avoid the staffroom this afternoon,' Ruth advised, 'although running across the main drive without looking was pretty crass of them. Now, this is always a good time to clear one's pigeon hole.'

When her shopping was placed in her car, she led me into the empty staffroom, littered with coffee cups and fugged with after-lunch cigarettes. Since my last visit, a label with my name had appeared above my pigeon hole – an encouraging sign. Inside were two notes. The first was a general information sheet headed *Half-Term Arrangements*. As I stared at it I felt protective towards my job. I wanted my name to stay above this pigeon hole in this grimy room and not be replaced by that of the shadowy Osborne.

I turned to Ruth. 'If I teach up until half-term, do you think I'll be paid for the week of the holiday?'

She sensed my money panic. 'I really don't believe you have much to worry about. I've seen all this before at Hillgate. My betting is that you'll be here until at least the end of term.'

The second note was handwritten: *Will you be able to do evening duty on Fridays? It's time-consuming rather than onerous. Perhaps you would let me know. D.P.*

60

Ruth looked over my shoulder. 'Tough luck,' she said.

'How late's evening duty?'

'Till ten-thirty. Not much to it apparently. No extra pay, but they give you a bottle of wine.'

'You don't do an evening?'

'I managed to avoid it,'

'I suppose I'd better say yes.'

'It might help your case. You may be able to get out of it later.'

'If new-girl keenness is called for, I think I'll make a tour of the games fields.'

'Don't get bullied into any more duties. I'm off to my room with a book – not a school one.'

On my walkabout I made first for Joan's cricket nets. This was a mistake. Brian had disappeared, and, as soon as I was within earshot, she shouted to me, 'Hold the fort here for five minutes – I've got to organise catching practice.'

I took up her position near the bowlers, who were happy to ignore me. Despite my Yorkshire upbringing, I had no great love of cricket, but it was very much Anthony's game, at least in the pre-B era – now I suspected he had dropped it entirely. Never before having paid much attention to cricket nets, I was intrigued how so much power – the bowler's, the batsman's, the ball's – could be dissipated within such fragile netting. To listen to the zip-zipping of ball on net was to hear what happened in my mind when trembling attacked: a sound of slowing down, of momentum lost against some barrier or wall, in itself almost without substance – no more than an outline – but able to drag all things down, absorbing their energy. The pattern was too familiar. I wanted to walk away. I would have done so, had Joan not returned at a sprint to take over.

'Do you play cricket?' she asked.

'I'm afraid not.'

'Tennis?'

'Not since school.'

'Go and look at the tennis courts.' It was an order.

At the courts, I looked through the wire and saw a woman I'd not seen before. She was showing a boy the ideal position for serving, which he immediately changed as soon as the ball was in his hand. The girls in this mixed-doubles game suppressed giggles; the other boy was torn between amusement and the fear of being the next to be coached. The teacher was about my age, slim, with long raven hair contrasting with the brilliant white of her tracksuit. I supposed she was a part-time games assistant, until the boy on the baseline spoke to her.

'But Mrs Lennox, I really can't stand like this and keep my balance.'

'You could if you tried.'

'But I can hit the ball hard enough at the moment.'

'Yes, but you could be so much better.'

Noticing my approach, she told her class to continue playing.

She walked up to the fence. 'All enthusiasm and no discipline,' she smiled. 'Now you must be Mrs Burns.'

'Phoebe, please.'

'Kate Lennox – head's wife, part-time hockey teacher and unpaid tennis coach. I do hope you're settling in.'

'Thanks. I'm sure I'll enjoy my week or two here.'

'Might be longer than that – if you can tolerate us. You must come to dinner sometime.' She looked over her shoulder and shouted, 'Run for it, Sarah. Don't be a wimp.' She turned to me. 'Excuse me. Good meeting you. Better get back. The girls are as bad as the boys.'

I watched her return to her coaching. With her long legs, clearly defined by tight track suit bottoms, she wouldn't have been out of place on the pages of a sportswear catalogue. An unlikely wife for such a husband, I thought – at least ten years younger, but different by a whole generation. I couldn't imagine Dr Lennox exchanging his brogues for her Nike Air Soles. Then I imagined Dora Prideaux's voice saying, 'My dear, they complement each other wonderfully.' Perhaps they did. I was still too close to my divorce to have an opinion of someone else's marriage.

Confident that my visits to cricket and tennis constituted a sufficient display of keenness, I passed the remaining time of the games period in my classroom. I found in the book cupboard a map of the Roman Empire, along with two posters about Roman Britain. I pinned the map on the wall, stared at it and decided it was not an improvement. Dog-eared and alone in the bareness, it created the atmosphere of a World War Two Air Force briefing room, awaiting the arrival of the men in flying jackets. I added the posters. They too were old and damaged, but at least moved the room forward a generation, so it became a classroom of the 1970s. I would replace them with young people's work as soon as possible. It was 4.00pm. There were tea and biscuits in the staffroom, but I stayed away. I considered searching out Ruth, but felt too tired for conversation; my little remaining energy would be needed for my last two lessons.

The double period with Year Eleven called on resources I didn't have, and more than expended my remaining energy. The class began with a burst of enthusiasm, asking for 'the date of next month's GCSE' – I hadn't yet discovered; 'this year's most likely questions' – I had no idea; 'Roman art. There's always a question about that, Miss' – I said we'd look at it next week. Next, the question I wanted answering as much as they did: 'Can you stay to the end of term – we've had so many Latin teachers?'

For the first half hour I borrowed an exercise book and recapped earlier work. Their enthusiasm flagged. This was probably my fault. I felt bad, but told myself that even the most experienced teacher would have little chance of making more than a marginal impact on their eventual exam results. On the other hand, I remembered, it was often the marginal differences which determine a pass or a fail. This made me feel worse. At the end of the first period I sensed that they were as tired as me. We had a two-minute break, as much for me as for them, after which I opted for a vocabulary test. A boy at the back, who had lost his books, tried to write his name on the sheet of A4 I had given him, but the surface of his desk was gouged with years of graffiti.

'Haven't you anything to lean on?' I asked.

He slouched back. 'Yeah, the wall.'

I failed to hold back a smile. The Percivals and Morrises of the school might have worked themselves up into a tirade, but I felt too sympathetic towards this weary comedian to remonstrate. To relaunch the children of this school into academic work at 4.30pm, after games, was absurd. When the final bell rang, I could have joined in the general cry of 'Yessss'. But any sense of achievement that I had survived my first day was wiped out by a glance at Tuesday's timetable. Last lessons were double Year Nine, lower set. I also noticed that I took them for last lesson on Friday.

Having no need to visit the staffroom, I made straight for my van. The closing of the door marked my entry into a different world, like the slam of a prison gate behind a released inmate. I pitied the Hillgate boarders. Halfway home, in exhaustion, I parked in a lane and cut the engine. With a window open, listening to the wind rustle the tops of hedgerows, I closed my eyes and let the day blow over me. So this was survival. I recalled my two previous teaching jobs. Then, as now, I had desperately needed the money, had felt half-dead after my first day's work at each school, but Hillgate . . .

Listening to the drone of a faraway plane, I opened my eyes to see a small flock of finches. Further up the lane was an overgrown entrance to a track which led to some disused farm buildings. I wondered how long it would be before they were converted into dwellings, and whether they would ever look as lovely as they were now in dereliction. They made me think of our first sight of Limepit House and brought back memories of Anthony. Then thoughts of B. Did she ever feel tired after a day's work? I doubted it. And had B ever considered teaching drama after university? I doubted that too. A classroom was way beneath her aspirations. Again I felt her powering ahead of me, hot in pursuit of her career – stage, TV, the media – while I was stranded at Hillgate. I restarted the engine. I needed Molly's kitchen.

'Phoebe,' she said, 'unless you're seeing things through terminally jaundiced eyes, the school is a complete madhouse.'

I had described my day to her. She had listened for about half an hour, a bottle was almost empty, and James and Ben were in front of the TV, eating village shop burgers.

'I wish you could see the place. Especially the staffroom.'

'Ruth sounds reasonably normal.'

'Largely because she avoids the others.'

'So would you take up a full-time job if it were offered?'

'Eighteen thousand a year. Can I turn it down?'

'What's your sanity worth?'

'That's the worry. I'd have to avoid the staffroom as much as possible.'

'To think there are parents out there who pay to keep a school like that going.'

'It makes me sorry for the kids. I feel I'm on their side – in league with them against their parents and teachers.'

'But can you do the job?'

'Tell you on Friday.'

I gulped my glass and warmed to the safe familiarity of the kitchen. The paraphernalia of gardening, cookery and pottery vied for space on every surface. On the dresser opposite me, letters and newspapers were piled between trays of seedlings, trial ceramics and kitchen utensils. When Anthony and I had come for supper here, he had found it all too chaotic to relax. On what proved to be our final visit together, arriving early, we watched Molly roll out pastry on the table top, where, five minutes before, their muddy-pawed cat, Bullace, had walked across holding a small, furry, squeaking creature in her mouth. Two hours later Anthony left most of his plate of chicken pie untouched. Then, I had smiled at his fastidiousness. Now, I never entered this room without looking out for Bullace, normally visible by the profile of her head, staring down like a one-eyed gargoyle from the cornice of the dresser. I would wink at her knowing eye to confirm our complicity in emotional matters, and to acknowledge the cat's higher wisdom.

In the kitchen and throughout the house Paul's drawings and paintings were spread haphazardly over the walls. The subjects were mainly landscapes and local buildings. I particularly liked a series of studies of Salle water tower, and a group of oils of the mausoleum at Blickling Hall. Between the dresser and the window was a watercolour of the tumble-down cricket pavilion at Sennowe. It was one of a pair; the other he had given to me and hung in my own kitchen. Near the staircase were a number of drawings of Molly. There were others upstairs – very good, I thought, but she sometimes moaned that four nude studies on the landing reminded her too much of 'how I looked before childbirth'. Her only decorative contribution to the walls were four terracotta tiles, hanging in their bedroom, depicting the seasons as women: Winter, lean and shivering by a fire; Spring, small-breasted with a basket of flowers; Summer, a mother, standing, sheaves of corn in her arms, like Ceres; Autumn, older and carrying bunches of grapes.

The sound of Paul's car at the side of the house sent Molly off in search of another bottle. I eased myself back into the Windsor chair which in the last two years had almost become my own, and stared into their long back garden – its size more than compensated for the absence of one at the front, where the pavement of the main village street ran along the wall of the house. Outside the kitchen was a brick terrace, where herbs and miniature lavenders filled stoneware containers made by Molly. A ragged lawn sloped down to a well-tended vegetable plot. It made me wonder how I would now find time for my own garden.

Paul appeared at the kitchen door. His curly, dark brown hair, neat in the mornings, was in its usual late-in-the-day state. It matched his creased navy linen suit. He was a friend almost as much as Molly but in different ways. We shared a love of fine art, but he always approached a painting from an artist's standpoint.

'So the antique dealer has turned teacher again,' he said.

'Yes, but after a day in the classroom I don't think I'm cut out for it.'

'I'm still not sure I'm cut out for teaching drawing, and I've been doing it twenty years.' He sat at the end of the table.

Molly appeared with two bottles of white Burgundy, discovered at the back of the shoe cupboard. She handed one to him. He dusted it down with a sleeve, and, failing to find the corkscrew among the table's clutter, set about the bottle with the corkscrew on his penknife, while I described my afternoon at Hillgate.

'Normal new-job syndrome,' he said, without looking up – he was struggling with the cork. 'You'll just have to take it day by day.'

'And pay-cheque by pay-cheque,' said Molly.

The cork broke under Paul's exertions. He frowned at the bunged-up bottle neck. Automatically, Molly, who was opposite me, leaned back on her chair towards the dresser, reached for a wooden spoon and tea strainer and passed them to him. With the spoon handle he pushed the stubborn cork into the bottle and poured himself a glass of wine through the strainer. It was a ritual of partners. Anthony and I had had them once.

When he had filled the other two glasses, he raised his own. 'To the end of the week and to a full-time job,' he said.

'If I haven't died of exhaustion.'

'First-day fatigue,' said Molly, and brushed a speck of filter-passing cork from her mouth.

'The trouble is I feel guilty about it all.'

They looked at me, Molly, with her kitchen-counselling look; Paul, as if he were pondering which way to draw my expression.

'Not only do I feel sick about teaching Latin on false pretences, but I feel really bad at missing the early furniture auction at Tanner's. Right now, I'm caught between the one school mad enough to employ me, and antiques, where part of me says I can still make a go of it.'

'Maybe in time you can do both,' said Molly. 'But I guess adjusting to teaching will take a week or two.'

'Two weeks may be as long as they want me – perhaps as long as I can manage. On the way back I stopped near a derelict barn. You know what I thought?' They stared at me. I looked away, catching Bullace's eye above Molly's head. 'I thought, I hope this pile of bricks will be allowed to disappear into nettles, not put on some architect's life-support machine, then reconstructed and filled with my furniture and other nostalgia I sell to people who send their kids to Hillgate to learn a dead language from an impostor. There's something dependable about a ruined barn.' I looked at Paul. 'It reminded me of one of your cricket pavilion watercolours.'

'A weakness for Romanticism,' he said glibly, tossing his head back.

I wasn't sure if he was referring to me or his paintings. Either way he annoyed me. I knocked back my wine and brought the glass down heavily on the table. Molly topped it up.

66

'I haven't seen you so spirited for months,' she said. 'Hating your job and the world after the first day has got to be a good sign. What would be disconcerting for us is if you came back whizzy and ebullient with your plans to change the English education system.'

Over supper with them my new-job anxieties subsided.

James and I arrived home late that evening. As we entered the back door he stood still and asked, 'Why did you move the doorstop?'

'I didn't,' I told him, but I could see that the iron Mr Punch stop had been shifted from its usual place to a few feet further along the wall. I remembered my alarm clock and shivered. Had we had an intruder? I also remembered an old man in the village saying that the house had a reputation for being haunted. In desperation, I tried to recall on which day I had noticed the clock had been moved, and when I had last touched the doorstop. I couldn't remember. I decided not to share my suspicions with James.

'I must have been tidying up this morning,' I told him. 'Shows how rarely I do it, if you notice.'

Since nothing else in the house had been disturbed, I believed what I had told him. After all, my uncharacteristic bout of early-morning tidying was so long ago in the pre-Hillgate past, that I could hardly remember which parts of the house had received my attention and which had been overlooked. I considered phoning Molly, but the idea of an intruder who did no more than move clocks and doorstops seemed ridiculous. As for a haunting – this would have to be the least troublesome of ghosts. Nevertheless, when James was in bed, I began to phone her number, but changed my mind, then, in the wish to speak to someone, anyone, phoned Cosmo instead.

'Yeah,' he answered.

'Phoebe. Er, wing chair?' Again I was echoing his perfunctory grunts.

'Amazingly, just you and me. We should have bought it for forty quid, but some private punter had a bit of a notion about it. At any rate I owe you one eighty.'

I lay in bed, reflecting on the irony of having had a good day's dealing for doing almost nothing, when I had tried only to be a teacher. Then my thoughts returned to the moving alarm clock and doorstop. Had Anthony, I wondered, come to the house in my absence? Did he still have a key?

That night I dreamed I was ordered to be at Hillgate at 5.00am. Scared I would be late, I set out before dawn. But a mile from school, my van broke down, and I continued the journey on foot, my anxiety increasing to panic. I arrived at the gates with minutes to spare, but as I stared down the drive through the early morning mist, Hillgate became Jane Eyre's Thornfield Hall. Somehow I was transported to her bedroom. In the dim light I was disturbed, as she had been, by screams from a remote part of the building. I woke, wondering if James had been crying. I went to his room. He was quietly asleep.

# PART II

# 7

'Good morning, Jehu,' was my Tuesday morning staffroom welcome from Duggy.

'*And Jehu drove furiously*,' said Renwick. 'First Book of Kings, if you don't know your Bible. We've heard of your attempts to run over the athletics team, Mrs Burns.'

'And we'd have settled just for the flattening of their coach,' mumbled Brian.

Duggy pretended to spit. He looked at Renwick. 'You're the religion man – what's the feminine of Jehu?'

'Why don't you ask our Latin lady?'

'Do your Classics skills stretch to Hebrew?' said Duggy.

'No,' I snapped, 'though I believe Jehu drove a chariot, not a Ford Transit.'

'Perhaps we should call you Boadicea,' said Renwick. 'There's that marvellous statue of her driving a horned chariot.' His eyes became salacious. 'We could even get you a whip.'

At this point Ruth entered, glanced around and guessed the conversation. She fixed Duggy and Renwick with disdain. They looked at each other, like children caught misbehaving. Alan Carter stepped forward and pushed a packet of Marlboros towards them. They each made a show of pulling out a cigarette – their way of asserting adulthood.

During assembly I stared at the line of Year Nines and wondered how I would occupy them at the end of the day and what was passing through their minds during the Founder's Silence. When Dr Lennox banged on about less shouting between lessons and better manners in the dining hall, I found his voice strange and impersonal. How did it differ, I thought, from the way he talked to his wife over breakfast? Or in bed?

In the post-assembly scramble I lost Ruth, but my Year Nine worries were eased as I walked off to first lessons. Linda Baird ran up to me and caught my arm. Since leaving her piano stool – it had been Scott Joplin's *The Entertainer* this morning – she had put on a dark grey light-weight mac and a sombre headscarf. She reminded me of an elderly nun with a message for a young novice. She pressed a video tape into my hand.

'It's none of my business, Phoebe, but Jarritt and company can be very trying during last lessons. I recommend bribery. Twenty minutes' light work with the promise of fifty minutes of film. Educational, of course. That's *Spartacus*. Kirk Douglas should keep you going for a week or two. You can borrow my TV and video from the special needs room. I'll get them dropped off to your classroom. Must fly.'

The Sister of Mercy rushed away, only to be replaced by the Mother Superior.

'I assume you're happy about evening duty,' said Dora Prideaux, ruling out discussion. 'I've asked Duggy Morris to show you the ropes this Friday. Then there's only one Friday before half-term. Duggy can be almost pleasant when he's out of the staffroom.' She beamed and walked off.

By lunch on my second day I felt I had taught at Hillgate for several years. This was both heartening and alarming. In contrast to the day before, I was now worried that I was finding it too easy to fit into a school which Molly had called 'a complete madhouse'. I was eating a packed lunch Ruth-style in my own classroom. The school and grounds were eerily silent. As I looked out over the circular lawn, I was back again at St Michael's Bramshead. I was ill in the sanatorium, an eccentric Arts and Crafts house at the edge of the school grounds. Recovering from a severe bout of flu, I was looking through the diamond-shaped panes of glass across a playing field and towards the older buildings of the main school, where I could make out a small group of figures in maroon blazers. Feeling better, I wanted to be out of my isolation room, a bleak cell without carpets or curtains – even the fever room at Lowood had its curtains. There was some pleasure in being away from the day-to-day school life I hated, but my illness and loneliness in that stark sanatorium, with its heavy oak doors and highly polished floors, made me long to be back with the others. As I unearthed those memories the maroon blazers turned to Hillgate green, worn by children walking around the circular lawn.

Following my first afternoon lesson, in a spare period I relaxed in an empty staffroom. I opened all the windows. Just before 4.00pm, when a tea tray was brought in by one of the kitchen staff, I poured myself a cup and carried it to my classroom, where I set up the TV and video.

The last-lesson bribery worked. The film's connection with the ancient world, however tenuous, was sufficient to satisfy my pliable conscience, while its violence held even Jarritt's attention. So in the evening Molly encountered a very different teacher from the stressed probationer of the previous day, and she was happy to send me on my way much earlier.

Back home, James, to my surprise, did not rush to a computer game, but suggested we go for a walk. I readily agreed, since an overcast day had given way to a true summer evening. I hoped that this was a good sign; the previous two summers had been uncertain seasons between a late spring and a seemingly five-month autumn, beginning in July, when the first fields were returned to plough, and lasting until late November.

In the field opposite the house, a low sun was burnishing the heads of verdigris barley, while, further down the lane, sugar beet the size of my newly planted lettuces was wilting for lack of rain. James, more interested in wildlife, rushed ahead to the first of two ponds where, standing at the edge, still as a heron, he surveyed the surface. I watched him stoop down to examine a damsel fly hovering on the surface, his light brown hair falling in front of him. Like this, he reminded me of Anthony in his field studies work, teaching a group of children the joys of pond dipping.

We looked at the coots on the next pond before walking on for half an hour. We were halted by the sight of a yellow hot-air balloon hanging, like a second moon, on the horizon. As we watched it drift over some woods, then out of sight, I told myself that I would allow B to float away from my life with similar unencumbered ease. A successful day had given me a confidence which I would set between myself and any of her machinations.

James had enough energy for another mile, but my thoughts were on tomorrow at Hillgate. I steered him home where I marked books, while he sorted through some old computer games.

'Some of these are almost antiques,' he said.

He pulled out an old Nintendo console and I watched him reach level nine of Saloon Gang. Then I took the gun and, to his amazement, shot my way to level three, where the gaunt bandit in the top right window finally outdrew me. There was a hint of B in his face.

# 8

An envelope containing a cheque for my first week's teaching appeared in my pigeon hole during last lessons on Friday. Half an hour later I began my evening duty which, according to Duggy, demanded my presence in the staffroom. I felt I was an officer at a police station, hoping for peace but expecting trouble.

'Of course,' he told me, 'we could go on patrol. But what's going on out there is so inevitable that we might as well leave them to it. The smokers will be among the rhododendron bushes, and the fornicators will be in the music rooms. The premises and grounds are so vast that our meagre interventions would only transfer their misdemeanours from one place to another.'

Accepting his counsel of despair, at least for the present, I attacked a pile of marking, while he thumbed through a wad of estate agents' brochures. He had found a cash buyer for his house in Dereham and was hoping to move nearer to Blakeney, where his boat had its mooring. By the way he scowled at every glossy page, I guessed that nothing on the market appealed to him, or was within his price range.

He looked up. 'I'll happily bet you your evening duty plonk that you'll be here at the end of term. In fact, I don't think there was ever a chance in hell of that Osborne guy coming here.'

I put my marking aside. 'Did you meet him when he was interviewed?'

'We all did. Nice bloke. But no fool. Had this place sussed. Renwick reckons he had some other job lined up, which he's probably accepting about now, and this was just the reserve. All this illness nonsense was just buying time. Are we going to open that wine?'

I didn't like the 'we', having planned to take the bottle home with me. But I was desperate to hear more of these rumours. 'Have you a corkscrew?'

'Of course.' Duggy leapt towards the bottle, whipped out from a pocket a folding corkscrew and removed the cork faster than a harassed wine waiter. Paul could have learned a thing or two from him.

'If he's not coming here, shouldn't he .. ?'

'Oh, don't worry. The cunning sod will give Hellgate a buzz the day before half-term, refusing the appointment, and then Lennox will offer it to you – your virtue meeting his necessity, so to speak.' He sniffed the cork and smiled. 'That's how things work round here – hellgatitis in every plank from stem to stern. But what else can you expect with the mad doctor in control?' He handed me the bottle.

'I got the impression Miss Prideaux was more in control.'

'Dora? Let's call her the figurehead. Can't you just see her as one of those bare-breasted maidens on the prow of a tea clipper, the salt spray tickling her nipples?'

I found a smile. Duggy was repulsive, but the apparent good news about my job made me humour him. It was a mistake.

'Welcome aboard,' he said, going to a cupboard labelled *Combined Cadet Force*, where he found two wine glasses. 'God, what a floating disaster. Lennox at the helm, mad as Captain Ahab. And some of the crew are almost as bad. Renwick, for a start, should have been pensioned off years ago.' He poured two glasses, downed half of his quickly and paced the parquet floor, as he did with his breaktime audience. 'What a lousy ship, and what a cargo we struggle to keep in order.'

'You make the school sound like a slave ship.'

'Not far off. Ferrying the unfortunate from the tribal warfare of their homes to a pretence of civilisation.' He sank the rest of the glass and drifted his eyes towards the bottle. The prep bell intervened. 'Topsails and gallants, Mrs Burns. I'll show you what passes for junior prep.'

I followed him to the classroom block.

'Idiot! Stop swinging on that door or it will soon be as unhinged as you are,' he shouted at a boy as we entered the maths room, which housed prep for Years Six, Seven and Eight.

Duggy marched past the waiting line of juniors and into the room where, with an exaggerated waving of arms, he threw back the dividing doors which separated the room from the adjoining classroom.

'The littluns are meant to have a separate room from the rest,' he whispered, 'but my system makes life easier for us.' Then, loudly, 'You've all met Mrs Burns. In future, she will be on duty Friday nights. Enter.'

As the boys filed in, I was ashamed to be standing next to him. Had caning not been banned, I was certain he would happily have carried it out – Hillgate's equivalent to Lowood's Miss Scatcherd.

'So I stay here for ninety minutes?' I said.

'Heavens, no. Get them settled, then go over to the seniors and pick a prefect to take charge. I recommend Lee. I sometimes let him have the last two inches of the bottle in payment. After that you're free to read, mark, learn or inwardly digest whatever in peace. Being Friday, you could even watch the Pipistrelles.'

'Pipistrelles?' I couldn't imagine that Duggy was interested in bats.

'Not the flapping variety. They're a local cricket team who borrow a pitch on Friday evenings for a limited over thrash. Better viewing than watching juniors deface exercise books.' He glared at the boys. 'Quiet, all of you,' he shouted. 'A prefect will be here in a minute. Mrs Burns and I will not be far away.'

As we walked out, he said, 'You should be untroubled until nine. Have a prowl around in forty-five minutes, if you're feeling keen. See you for Founder's Silence and bedtime – I've an appointment at the Gryphon.' He winked and marched off to his Land Rover, leaving me in charge of a school, most of which I was yet to explore. I knew that somewhere inside the main building was the matron's flat, and she was supposed to supervise the girls, who boarded in one wing and had their own prep and bedtime arrangements. Apart from that slim assurance, I was alone.

I found Lee in one of the senior studies – tiny rooms, partitioned only by eight-feet-high walls in the main building's former drawing room, whose elegant ceiling looked down on them. He was an ox of a sixteen-year-old, an obvious choice as Duggy's henchman, being a younger version of his master. To Lee's surprise, I accompanied him to the prep room, where I made sure that everyone had enough work to occupy them. Alone again, I wondered what I could do for ninety minutes. The school, a different place at this time of day, made me feel like a visitor to a deserted foreign village. I decided to follow Duggy's advice and watch the cricket. On my way there, near some maintenance sheds, I saw two Year Eleven girls smoking. When they saw me, they dropped their cigarettes.

'Sorry, Miss, we're just on our way to prep,' one mumbled.

I looked down at the cigarette protruding from under her foot.

'Please don't report us,' pleaded the other. 'I'll be suspended – I'm on my last warning.'

I knew I should issue some sort of reprimand, but couldn't. They had pulled me back to St Michael's, where they were girls with whom I was sharing Silk Cuts by the rubbish bins. 'Make sure you finish tonight's Latin,' I told them.

As I watched them hurry to the main building, I justified my leniency with the knowledge that there seemed little point complaining about cigarettes, when, a few miles down the road, in Walborough, a whole menu of Class A drugs was available in the recreation ground. Duggy would have understood my logic.

The sound of a struck leather ball, followed by gentle clapping, reached me a hundred yards from the cricket field, stirring more rankling memories of my old school. I resented these nagging tugs into the past. I began to suspect that the creature over my shoulder had found a new way to undermine me. I longed for the safety of my garden or Molly's kitchen. But then I noticed that the fielder near the boundary in front of me had the unmistakable hair of Cosmo. In his cricket whites and part of a team, he looked out of place. I watched him as the bowler started his run-up. Cosmo walked forward a few paces with token concentration, and coughed in disgust as the batsman blocked a slow ball. He then turned and jogged back to his position, as if this were his only way of staying awake. I walked towards him.

I suspected he had seen me well before I arrived at the white boundary line, but he still performed an exaggerated double take when I reached him.

'Hm, we don't usually get spectators.'

'I'm not really here for the cricket.'

He pulled a face in the direction of the wicket. 'Not sure if I am either.'

'So who exactly are the Pipistrelles?'

'Wooh. Excuse me.' He walked a few paces towards the wicket, watched another ball prodded back to the bowler and returned. 'As you can see, we're odds and sods who like to pretend we're twenty years younger for two or three hours between work and pub. You with the other lot?'

'No, I teach here.'

'What? Oh, here we go again.'

This time the batsman hit the ball with a vengeance to make amends for his earlier caution. Cosmo rushed over to a fielder who looked well into his sixties. The older man stopped the ball cleanly, but was happy to flick it to Cosmo, who threw it hard into the wicket-keeper's gloves. He ran back panting.

'Fielding for two sort of keeps you fit. What do you teach?'

'I try to teach Latin.'

'Benedictine monks tried to do that to me.' He held out his hands. 'I have the scars on my knuckles to prove it. So you have two strings to your . . . I used to know the Latin for bow.'

'*Arcus.*' I had learned or relearned the word yesterday.

'Very good.' He looked towards the pitch. 'Oh dear, hold up. Batsman's got shoelace problems.' He put a hand into a back pocket, pulled out a wallet, counted out £210 and gave me the notes. 'Chair and the other thing.' He turned back to the game. 'Here we go again.'

He walked two or three steps forward, groaned at another blocked ball, and turned round. 'This batsman's not what you'd call a risk taker.'

Next ball he was clean bowled. Cosmo rubbed his hands in sham excitement. 'Ah, we should be back in the pavilion in twenty minutes. Will I see you there?'

'I'm supposed to be on evening duty.'

'Does this teaching thing pay better than antiques?'

'It pays.'

'More than some of my customers are doing at the moment. Hm. Change of bowler apparently.' He gave me a goodbye bow and moved closer to the wicket.

Walking over to check the studies, I made a detour past the headmaster's house, a white brick, characterless 1950s building, surrounded by a tall yew which obscured it from almost any line of vision. It reminded me of the vicarage in the parish next door to ours in Yorkshire. Near the rear of the house I paused. I could hear shouting. My first impression was that it was from some seniors who had abandoned their studies before time, but then I realised that the commotion was coming from the other direction. I retraced my steps a few yards towards a small gap in the dense hedge, from where I heard the intermittent crescendos of a domestic argument. I couldn't make out individual words or phrases, but sudden bursts of anger shot out like sparks from a fire.

For half a minute there was silence. I almost walked on, but then came an echoing, 'No I shall not.' It was Dr Lennox's voice.

I turned round towards the cricket field, expecting to see all faces looking in my direction. But since the white figures were plodding on with their game, I assumed that the trees around the ground had absorbed the shouts. A moment later an upstairs window was slammed shut, closing the Lennox's married life behind it.

I imagined situations which might have led to that four-word outburst. I tried to picture Anthony shouting those words at me, but, for all our arguments, I couldn't remember his using that exact phrase. It was too emphatic for him. Several times before he admitted his affair, I had said to him, 'Why don't you go away for a few days and decide whether or not you want to continue being married?' His answer was always the evasive, 'Why should I?' Was Dr Lennox having an affair? I wondered. The heavy beat of a sound system from the direction of the studies blasted towards me, dispelling the thought. Going to investigate, I told myself that there was no reason the argument should have been about their marriage. Perhaps Kate Lennox saw her husband as head of a more prestigious, more academic school than Hillgate. I could picture her in that boring box of a house throwing a *Times Education Supplement* at him and shouting, 'For God's sake – for my sake – apply for another headship. We're stagnating here.' I could hear him thunder back, 'No I shall not.' If this were a bad guess, no doubt Duggy, on his return, would have his own explanation. The episode made me feel so sick about the school that I began not to care whether it might or might not have a full-time job for me.

In the studies, work seemed to be in progress despite the deafening heavy metal. There was a rule about silence in prep, but I allowed myself to be persuaded by the boys that the other teachers didn't mind, providing the volume was turned down. I thought, why should I care? At that moment I couldn't see myself teaching at Hillgate much longer – why disturb the school's warped approach to work and discipline?

Twenty yards from the junior prep room, I heard Lee barking insults to one of his charges. In his voice I detected the tone of Duggy. Next week I would find a replacement. I should have sat with them myself for the last half hour, but feeling too tired to be of any use, I wandered back to the staffroom and collapsed into a chair.

How did I come to be here? The question welled up repeatedly as I tried to relax in that dingy room among the detritus of the day's teaching – overflowing ashtrays, sports equipment, a duffle coat, a corner piled high with boxes labelled *PTA FETE*, another area littered with lost or confiscated property. The room was a home for the misplaced, and it was trying to make me part of itself. I looked up at my pigeon hole, but felt none of the morning's pleasure at seeing my name written above it. Then I noticed that where the label with my predecessor's name had been ripped off, a scrap of paper had remained stuck on. I could read the final two letters. I felt that this depressing room begrudged its occupants leaving. I suspected that however much Duggy and company moaned about the school, complained of hellgatitis and probably dreamed of teaching elsewhere, nevertheless, the place had a way of attracting misfits, then clinging to them until they had nowhere else to go. Was I its latest victim? Yet again the figure, £18,000, lit up in front of me. But it was unreal, like the score rattling up on an old pin-ball machine which rewards you, not with money, but only another game. It would take more than my first pay cheque to dispel the illusion.

The bell for the end of prep sounded, followed by the roar down the drive of Duggy's returning Land Rover. From the staffroom window I watched him skid to a dusty halt. Half a minute later he staggered in, all sweat and smelling of beer.

'Conversation about catamarans. Argument about origins of. Couldn't get away. Apologies. Any of that wine left?' He helped himself, poured a mean splash into my own glass and leaned against the mantelpiece. 'All quiet on deck?'

'Apart from the headmaster's house.'

'One of his dinner parties? Strangely, they can be quite good fun. He's a different man after a glass or two.'

'No, it's just that I heard raised voices from the house. He and Kate were having some sort of argument.'

'Probably some nonsense about his wardrobe. She's been trying for years to give him a sartorial makeover. So far, she's won the battle of the ties and socks, but he won't let her near those silly suits he wears.'

'It sounded rather more than an argument about clothes.'

'He's got a lot to get worked up about. For a start, eighteen kids are leaving in July, and to date there are only five firm bookings for September. We're hardly viable as it is. I'd be tearing my hair out if I were him.'

'It was more like he was pulling his wife's hair out.'

'Sounds fun.' He leered, and I knew I would get no more sense out of him.

I picked up a crumpled *Daily Mail* and tried to complete Renwick's attempt at the crossword. Duggy was restless – perhaps he needed more of an audience. He fidgeted his way to the door. 'Got some kit to sort out in my classroom. We're free until nine, when we meet again for Founder's bloody Silence.' I was glad to be rid of him.

Tired and dispirited, I needed a dose of Molly. I rang her from the staffroom phone.

'I'm not sure if I can stand this every Friday night.'

'What happened?'

'It's like one of those dreams where everything is askew, but no one can see anything abnormal.'

'But you've had no disasters?'

'None I've noticed,'

'Would you prefer the school to catch fire?'

An image of Jane Eyre's fire-gutted Thornfield Hall appeared in front of me. I gasped at the *grim blackness*.

'Phoebe?'

'Sorry. Right now Ulford feels a thousand miles away.'

'You only do this one evening a week.'

'Still a fourteen-hour day. I wouldn't mind, but I'm so numbed mentally. And stuck in this staffroom.' I looked around the room where, in the evening gloom, the oak-panelled walls, the carpet, furniture – everything – had become one depressing brown.

'You there?' Molly's voice was like a paramedic's trying to keep a badly injured road victim awake.

'Yes. It's just that the room's so funereal.'

'That all? Take a tin of paint with you next week. Do you want to speak to James?'

'Hi, Mum. See you tomorrow morning. Must go. Ben's got *Jurassic Park*.' He rang off.

I was alone in the room again. I opened a book labelled *Use of Phone* to enter my call. Since the last entry was over a year ago, I closed it and headed for the library.

A few stragglers were shuffling in as I entered. Duggy was already on the rostrum, red-nosed, more subdued than normal, perhaps trying to hide his drunkenness. After a roll-call he announced the Founder's Silence. To no one's surprise but mine, this lasted less than a minute, being broken by, 'Don't forget to read the bath list and don't stew in the bath beyond your time, or Mrs Burns or I will put you on mopping duty until half-term. Dismiss.' He walked over to me. 'Locking up time.'

During the next half hour I became a trainee prison officer, marching behind a senior colleague as he rattled a heavy bunch of keys and secured all doors. I was an unenthusiastic deputy, more than ever feeling forced to relive my own deprivations at a boarding school. Up in the dormitories, converted from the bedrooms of the old hall, divans and duvets had replaced the iron beds and grey blankets I remembered, but this did little to divert my focus from a past I had hated. I looked at Hillgate, but saw another school. And I began to realise how much of my loathing I had forgotten over the years. My head contained innumerable records of simple dislike, but all pictures of pain had been tucked away, like badly exposed negatives at the back of an old photo album. My evening duties were prising them out. I was upset. I slipped away and let Duggy look after the remaining bedtime rounds.

'Where did you get to?' he asked later.

'I needed a drink,' I told him.

He looked at the empty bottle. 'Don't blame you,' he said.

At lights out, I followed him round from dormitory to dormitory. Towards the end of a passageway were two very small rooms. 'These are the one-bed dorms for miscreants,' he explained. 'Like solitary confinement, though Jarritt, who permanently has one, says he prefers it.'

Duggy indicated a door at the opposite end. 'Sanatorium,' he said. 'Empty at the moment.'

I winced, remembering the two weeks when I had been ill at St Michael's.

Back in the brown room at 10.15pm, we waited for the sound of Brian Devlin's Lada returning from quiz night at the Gryphon. When he arrived, Duggy shot off in his Land Rover without saying goodbye to either of us.

Brian wasn't surprised. 'Still ten minutes before last orders,' he said.

Driving home, my window open, as I put miles between myself and Hillgate, the weight of the evening fell from my shoulders. No longer a prison officer, I was now a released prisoner throwing off my shackles into the back of the van, or into the hedges and cow parsley which lined the road to Ulford.

* * *

I woke in a panic at the sound of a vehicle outside the house. It was Saturday morning and I had overslept. Anthony and B had come to collect James. He was still at Molly's. Anthony would revel in this point-

83

scoring opportunity. B too. I crept to the window, wondering which outfit would be gracing my lawn while Anthony waited at the front door. But the drive was empty. Up the lane, the tractor and sprayer which had woken me were turning into a field. I looked at the alarm clock. 8.30am. Time for everything to be done, apart from expelling the ridiculous fear of an ex-husband and his irksome girlfriend.

An hour later my tractor alarm had Molly choking over her coffee. 'I wish you had overslept,' she said. 'Then you could have sent them round here for James. I've only seen her twice.'

I laughed with Molly and Paul, but when the MG arrived at my house, as ever it changed the atmosphere.

'Mum's teaching again,' announced James.

'Back to the history books again, is it?' said Anthony.

I disliked his patronising tone. 'Latin, in fact. Hillgate Hall.'

'You sadist.' A half smile. 'I didn't know you knew any Latin.'

'Enough,' I said.

B was making a point of being ever so helpful in arranging James's fishing gear in the car boot. She was in a navy T-shirt, braless, and fawn linen trousers.

'I quite liked Latin,' she chirped. Then a giggle. 'We were forced to learn Catullus's *Hymn to Diana*. All very dull. But the previous poem in the anthology was much more fun – all about buggery and thieving in the public baths.' With a flourish she closed the boot.

'Sounds like a poem which would appeal to my Year Nines,' I said to Anthony.

'Don't get yourself sacked,' he said. 'Money good, is it?'

'Not particularly.' It was safer to appear poor.

When they were about to drive away, he called out to me through the driver's window. 'Oh, by the way, there may be some technical problem in the divorce settlement. B's father's lawyer is looking into it. You'll be getting a letter in due course.'

James waved as they drove away, while B again raised a Queen-in-coach hand and shot me a steely glance – the goddess of the hunt seeing her arrow strike home.

I limped back to the house. At first, I suspected that Anthony was bluffing, and that his intention had been to diminish my low reserves of self-esteem now that I had a new job. But the malice had worked. He, they, had hit the target again, so I soon began to wonder if there might be some truth in his wish to have the divorce settlement reconsidered – another battle, another legal bill. And it might also have indicated that

Anthony had been snooping around the house in my absence, looking through my papers, examining my financial affairs, searching for information to give B's father's solicitor. Perhaps it was time to change the locks.

During a morning's weeding I recuperated. At lunchtime I phoned the antiques centre to see if I had sold anything. I hadn't. Mowing the grass, I managed to avoid thoughts about Anthony or B, but later, as I set about the task of pruning the camellias, I felt like a witch as I snipped off each unwanted shoot, wishing B out of my life with my secateurs and sympathetic magic.

# 9

---

'Risking a second week?' said Duggy

'You've crossed your Rubicon' said Renwick.

Re-entering the staffroom on Monday morning was like intruding backstage at a pantomime, as the actors preened themselves for another performance. Only there was more sarcasm than humour in their tired scripts. I pitied their young audience. I wouldn't have wanted James to have been taught by either of these two, or most of the others, whose classes carried the risk of infectious cynicism. I too felt in danger. It was tempting to join in the banter, to become a member of the cast, but I refused to do it. I had no wish to be in their sickening play. Had I been stronger, I might have taken them on, as Ruth could, but not at the moment. And I was wary of the art of the smart riposte – that was too near B's territory. I needed an aloofness while bruises healed. I ignored them and turned to Ruth.

'Are you on for another lunchtime escape?' she asked.

'I'll go now if you like.'

'Ah, but escape's all the sweeter after a morning's teaching.'

In assembly, after the Founder's Silence, Dr Lennox, somewhat in breach of Lady Widwell's secular wishes, recounted a story about an uncle saved from certain death in 1943 in Italy, when a sniper's bullet lodged itself in the thick cover of the Bible he always carried in the top of his pack.

Ruth whispered, 'If uncle was like nephew, I find myself on the side of the sniper.'

Dr Lennox, in booming voice, then read out a prayer the lucky uncle had written on the flyleaf of his Bible. Meanwhile, I wondered what he and Kate had been shouting about on Friday night.

Halfway along the path to my Year Sixes, I decided to change my lesson plan. Following last week's introductory lessons, I had intended to tackle some formal grammar. But assembly had put me off formalities. I opted instead for some role-play about masters, mistresses and servants in a Roman villa. Perhaps the pantomime dames of the staffroom had given me the idea of drama as a teaching aid. At any rate, the result was successful, if noisy.

Walking back to the staffroom, I met Duggy. 'For a dead language, your Latin this morning was very lively,' he said.

'That was just the Roman household. Wait till we get to the market place.'

He frowned. 'Just watch out for the good doctor. Renwick's mock battles are frowned upon, and Brian keeps getting little notes in his pigeon hole about the riots he calls English lessons.'

'If the headmaster's worried about someone's teaching, why doesn't he have a quiet word with the individual?'

'Lennox doesn't have a quiet word with anybody, from God downwards. At the last staff meeting, he gave us all a bollocking about classroom discipline and warned us that there might be sackings.'

Renwick, who had been following us, caught up with the conversation. 'There will be sackings,' he mimicked. 'There will be sackings,' as if by repeating the phrase he would somehow safeguard his own job.

Unable to face the staffroom and its undrinkable coffee, I headed for the seclusion of my van. Managing my classes, I decided, was within my capabilities, coping with the staff was not. Once again, the reassuring click of the Transit door isolated me from their world. I stared towards the empty cricket field surrounded by its mature oaks, and the green weatherboard cricket pavilion – it almost persuaded me that it had grown there with the trees. Along the drive a gardener was planting out geraniums. It was a sight which might have made a favourable impression on those much-courted prospective parents.

Now I was back to the day when, aged twelve, I was taken to see my future school. Hands clenched, I was standing between my parents as we stared across the vast playing fields of St Michael's, watching giants of boys play rugby. We were being shown around by the headmaster and his wife, whose combined efforts to make me feel that these expanses of maleness and Victorian Gothic masonry would welcome the arrival of a dozen girls, left me in disbelieving terror. I could only think of the friends I would be leaving behind, many of whom I had known since primary school – I was then in my second year at grammar school and loving it.

On the way back home, we called in to see great aunt Hilda, now in a nursing home in Epsom. It was through her benevolence that the possibility of my going to a public school had been presented to my parents. Weeks earlier, my young arguments against the plan had been rejected with a salvo of counter-arguments. 'It's a wonderful opportunity.' 'It's very kind of your aunt.' 'You'll love it once you're there.' 'You'll see your old friends in the holidays.' I hated it. My old friends were never quite the same. They didn't say, 'You're right posh now,' but I knew they thought it. Worst of all, my parents had played the guilt card: 'You should be grateful.' I wasn't. I never fully forgave them.

That day, when I saw Hilda, bed-bound and incontinent, it was difficult to be angry with her. The old stalwart of the baize tables and perfume bottles believed she would be helping me, and I couldn't bring myself to look at her withered face and argue my case.

Returning by train, I cried my way past all those stations whose names still stiffen me with fear: Raynes Park, Worcester Park, Motspur Park, parkless places, I thought, with little green in evidence – nothing like Cliffe Castle Park near my home. Before we arrived at Waterloo Station I made a final effort to change my parents' minds. Dismissing my objections, they promised some treat in London. Having none of the skills of protest, I was finally reasoned round to their thinking, from which escape was impossible. I had already read *Jane Eyre* three times. Forced, like her, to a school many miles away, I read the book again.

I never enjoyed St Michael's – the most I did was learn to endure it. So strange a world I found it, that in my first term I gave secret names to all the members of the staff to match their seeming unreality. Most of these names came from *Alice's Adventures in Wonderland* or *Through the Looking Glass*, childhood favourites. In my thirteen-year-old eyes, the characters in the books resembled the mad people around me. The headmaster was the Frog Footman, his wife the Red Queen, my housemaster the Mock Turtle, his wife the White Queen, the chaplain Father William, his assistant the Young Man. Another teacher was the Walrus, someone else the Lizard. I told no one these names. Placing them in a different world was a way of distancing them. Sometimes I even felt I was controlling these would-be figures of authority – an unseen puppeteer holding invisible strings. It was one of my techniques of surviving the place. Survival was the greatest achievement of those four years.

I was ecstatic the day I left. Great Aunt Hilda, still clinging to life, had the last word by paying for me, without my knowledge, to be a life member of the Old Pupils' Society, whose magazine, *The Archangel*, had somehow (with no help from me) found my every change of address. For years I thought it was she who was informing the school of my current whereabouts. But even after she died, the magazine continued to make its annual appearance on my doormat, no matter where I moved. Can the dead, I asked, send change of address cards on behalf of the living? I had intended to cancel my membership, but that meant contacting the school. There was also a compensatory pleasure each year in throwing away the magazine unread in its unopened envelope, identified by the school crest (archangel slaying serpent) printed on the back. Two years ago, in a hurry to go through my mail, I had opened it by mistake. I gave its pages a token look. Several of my former teachers were still at the place, including the Mock Turtle. I wondered if they and the school had changed much over the years, but to read further would be to dignify its existence. Into the bin it went.

Blinking back to the present, I saw, in my wing mirror, the girls I had caught smoking disappear into a bushy corner of the car park. I hoped that today they would be undisturbed.

There remained ten minutes of break. I looked round to the back of the van. The suitcases I had collected from Frank over a week ago remained untouched. I had planned to sort through them and price them over the weekend, but the garden had fully occupied Saturday, while on Sunday, a walk on Stiffkey marshes, followed by Molly and Paul coming for lunch, had taken up the day. I climbed over the front seats and began to rummage.

The top hat retained the label, *Gamps of Picadilly*. I found myself valuing it in terms of my teaching pay – two or three days at Hillgate. I looked through one of the cases. There were a few back copies of a textile magazine – they might provide interesting reading in my spare lessons. Next, I found some torn curtains fit only for rags, a couple of '30s dresses – with luck worth a day's teaching – and an unsaleable mink stole with two handbags – not worth a lesson. The second case was packed with meticulously laundered white cotton nightdresses – not quite Brontë vintage, but definitely late Victorian and worth about two days' teaching. Beneath them were bundles of Methodist temperance leaflets. Perhaps Tara would want to buy them. If not, when the staffroom was empty, I would secrete them into Duggy's pigeon hole. Smiling at the idea, I noticed a pink corner of silk, which I thought was a camisole or a pair of bloomers hiding under the case's demure upper strata. But on removing the leaflets, I discovered, wrapped in a piece of old rug and protected by tissue paper, a pair of squares made from coloured strips of silk sewn together – pinks, blues, mauves and black, embroidered all over with tiny stars. They were clearly part of some costume, Middle Eastern I guessed, but I had no idea what they were called. With the end-of-break bell calling me to my classroom, I left my van. What were the silk squares worth? Half a day's teaching on my Hillgate index? I looked at the old textile magazines, hoping there might be an article about them, but found nothing relevant.

On the other side of the car park, the two girls were emerging from cover. Their looks suggested their temporary escape from school had been as stimulating as my own. I returned to my classroom with my magazines.

The vision of my eastern textiles, illustrated in a London auction catalogue, gave my pre-lunch teaching extra confidence. I even took to heart Molly's advice that in time I could both teach and deal. In the lunch hour, on our way to Walborough, I mentioned this to Ruth.

'If a couple of silk squares give you and your teaching a shot in the arm,' she said, 'it's got to be better than the nicotine and cynicism of the staffroom.'

'I don't find it easy avoiding them every break.'

'Don't worry about it. It's what I do. The staffroom's a contentious little club.'

'There was a staffroom club at Elveden College. Only they called it the Common Room Club and had their own president, committee, opera trips and dinner.'

'Sort of thing David Lennox would love.'

Ruth, joining me for a quick look at the afternoon auction, was pleased to find some edging bricks which matched those along her garden path. She left a bid with a porter. I was looking at a pile of potato baskets when Cosmo appeared.

'Anything here?' he said. 'I missed the morning show.'

'Only these,' I said.

'I've more than enough baskets to deal with as it is. Nothing else?'

'What do you call those Middle-Eastern silk stripy things?' I indicated their size. 'Some sort of clothing.'

'Er, got some here, have they?' He sounded excited.

'No, I recently picked up a pair. I can't remember what they're called.'

'Oh, mm, *khatraaz* or something. Not really my thing, but can I have a look at them?'

'If you like.'

'Friday night? Mid-wicket boundary?'

I nodded. Cosmo made a half bow and disappeared into the saleroom.

As we walked back to Ruth's car, she put on a schoolmarm voice. 'And perhaps you can tell me precisely what you two are up to?'

'Nothing, Miss. Only business.'

'Really? Under the trees on the cricket field?'

'No, honestly.'

'Actually, he has a certain charm about him.'

'He also has a certain reputation.'

'I quite liked the way his red hair fell forward when he made the little bow. Not sure about the gutturals though. Hardly the gift of the Blarney.'

She was starting to annoy me. 'He's another dealer, that's all.'

When we were in her car, I said, 'I'm not ready for a new relationship, Cosmo or anyone else.' I gave her the history of my divorce. As I talked and she listened, we both stared ahead through the windscreen to the car park fence, our eyes not meeting, like patient and analyst. I told her about Anthony and B, and my inability to handle our confrontations.

'Have you considered a counter attack,' she said.

'What can I do?'

'Perhaps you need a game plan.'

'Game playing's their thing, not mine.'

'Depends how you do it.'

After a few moments' silence she slowly turned her head to me and smiled. 'You could borrow Cosmo for a day. Get him to open the door when they arrive one Saturday morning to collect James.'

We laughed. The therapy session was over.

At 4.30pm I settled down with my Year Nines for the next instalment of *Spartacus*. All the class were happy with this arrangement, apart from Mark Jarritt. He spent the first part of the double lesson gazing out of the window, ignoring and ignored by his classmates. My attempts to engage his concentration failed so hopelessly that I succumbed to his peers' view that, like this, he was beyond communication. I hoped the film might distract him, but after five minutes he folded his arms on his desk, let his head sink down and went to sleep. No one took any notice of him. I wondered what Dora Prideaux might have thought had she passed by, or Dr Lennox with one of his sought-after parents. But I didn't disturb him; his problems were beyond my expertise.

After lessons, catching Ruth before she left for home, I asked her where I was failing with him.

'You're not necessarily failing anywhere,' she assured me. 'It's really an issue for his house tutor.'

'Who's that?'

'Brian Devlin, I think.'

'Is that where his pastoral welfare ends?'

'Probably, but it's not for us to change the system. The school has its tutors, residential staff, a matron – leave them to it is my advice. You still okay for our party Sunday week? Should be fun. Fancy dress, I'm afraid – Hugh's idea. "A *Charley's Aunt* Gaudy" he's called it.'

'I'll look forward to it,' I said, more through friendship than enthusiasm.

Driving home, I wondered why on earth Hugh had picked on a late-Victorian farce for his party theme. If he wanted fancy dress with a theatrical theme, why not choose *Les Misérables* or *Cats*? Perhaps one of the old dresses in the back of my van would do for the party. No, they would be too dowdy for a summer's day in 1890s Oxford. I was struggling to remember if I had anything else suitable, when the juddering from my wheels returned. I should get the van fixed as soon as possible.

# 10

Over the next three days, waiting for news of the ghostly Neil Osborne, I checked my pigeon hole between every lesson, hoping for the invitation to stay on beyond half-term. So my visits to the staffroom were more frequent, a fact noticed by Duggy.

Towards the end of the week he said, 'Good to be seeing more of you, Mrs Burns. For a while we thought you and Biology had opened up a secret women's room.'

'The nearest we get to it is Sainsbury's in Walborough.'

'So all you do is go shopping together. And there we were, thinking you were avoiding us.'

'I'm sorry, but sometimes we do have to drag ourselves away from this stimulating environment.'

He eyed me suspiciously, like an old man in a country pub, offended by the comment of a newcomer. 'A hint of sarcasm, I think,' he growled. 'The first symptom of hellgatitis.' He went off with most of the others to change into uniform for the Cadet Force afternoon.

I turned to my pigeon hole. Again it was empty. In fact, it was the only empty pigeon hole on the wall. Other members of staff were receiving letters and circulars by the pile, but I was being overlooked as a stand-in teacher who needed only the barest information. Alan Carter's pigeon hole, which was next to mine, was crammed with brown envelopes addressed *Head of Maths Department*, from the educational press and other interested bodies. Either heads of Latin didn't attract such letters, or Dora Prideaux was holding them all back for my successor.

With only eight days before half-term, I needed my uncertainty dispelled. Had I been brave, I would have knocked on Dr Lennox's door and asked him outright if I might be required until the end of term. But that perfectly reasonable question felt out of keeping with the school's decision-making process. I also had a superstition that any direct approach would somehow work against me: *to prolong doubt was to prolong hope.* Opting for an oblique approach, I carried a Latin text book to Dora Prideaux's office, ostensibly to do some photocopying. In the corridor outside her sanctum, a khaki huddle was by the Army Section notice-board, reading their orders. Inside, Dora was seated at her desk. We nodded hellos, and I switched on the copier, filling in the record book while the machine warmed up. Since it was impossible to use the machine without her seeing and no doubt counting every sheet of paper, the record book, unlike the staff phone book, was up-to-date. Opening my text book at random, I ran off a dozen copies. I collected them together and started to leave the room, but paused by her desk.

'Any word from Neil Osborne?' I tried to sound offhand, suggesting I'd rather be back dealing in antiques, but might just be persuaded to teach until the end of term.

'Nothing as yet, but I phoned last week, and he said he would be writing shortly.'

I mumbled, 'Oh, right,' and left feeling the familiar pang of uncertainty.

I wanted to trust Ruth's intuition that my work was secure until the end of term, and there were even moments when I believed with Renwick and Duggy that my full-time appointment was a certainty. But my rational self insisted that Dora Prideaux, who was the one person at Hillgate who knew the true facts, right now had no idea. I must face another eight days of waiting.

Not being involved with playing soldiers and sailors, under a threatening sky I wandered over to my classroom with the idea of half an hour's quiet doze, with the cupboard door open to screen me from outside. I nodded off, but was disturbed from sleep by a deafening woman's voice.

'Platoon, shun! Platoon, right turn! Stand at ease!'

I stretched my neck beyond the cupboard door to see that Joan Tatham had exchanged her tracksuit for a uniform. She was drilling a dozen teenagers carrying rifles. I watched her reprimand them about keeping in time, before marching them off again in front of the classroom block. She shouted again. They did a gravel-crunching about-turn at the end of the path. Back they came towards me. It was a mixed platoon in which, to my surprise, the boys and girls equally were enjoying themselves. At St Michael's, the Combined Cadet Force, obligatory for boys, was hated by all but a few who were labelled 'corps swots', a term of ultimate abuse. As Joan Tatham's happy soldiers marched past, I thought back to the voluntary service I had carried out on school corps afternoons. My task was gardening for an elderly woman, altruism which turned out to be light weeding on the professional gardener's day off, followed by an hour's tea and gossip in an elegant drawing room – a weekly escape I had looked forward to.

The platoon reappeared, this time running and without rifles.

Joan, shouting again, initiated an army cadence: 'Left right, left right, keep in time.'

'Left right, left right, keep in time,' echoed the platoon.

'Eyes to the front and stay in line.'

'Eyes to the front and stay in line.'

They passed my window, sounding more like US Marines than English schoolchildren. A minute later they returned.

'If I die, they'll send me back.'

'If I die, they'll send me back.'

'Boxed up with the Union Jack.'

'Boxed up with the Union Jack.'

I wondered what a school inspector would make of these lyrics.

As their voices faded in the distance, I thought I had seen the last of them, but they promptly returned, again with their rifles. They halted in front of my classroom.

'Now I will demonstrate rifle drill,' shouted Joan from under her officer's hat. She borrowed one of the rifles and threw it around her body with the same enthusiasm I had seen her teaching batting strokes in the cricket nets.

I edged back to the cupboard door, escaping again. Why had I done so much of this in my life? At school, quitting university early, and now, not only avoiding disagreeable parts of school life, but also feeling that antiques and teaching were escapes from each other. I envied Joan's uncomplicated world, where there was a right or a wrong way to bat, bowl, march, hold a rifle. I doubted whether she had ever needed to escape from anything. I leaned forward again to watch.

'Present arms,' Joan shouted to a girl who had difficulty in lifting the rifle and holding it vertical. She almost dropped it, but recovered her grip. I admired her tenacity.

Out on the circular lawn, Linda Baird, ridiculous in baggy fatigues, was demonstrating the use of an ancient stretcher to a civil defence squad. The absurdity of the sight reinforced my own sense of unease. I was glad to watch them driven indoors by a cloudburst.

The rain continued all that day and most of the night. On Friday, North Norfolk, with blasts of cold and sleet, had slipped back to winter, reminding me of the day Anthony and I moved from Thetford to Ulford, driving through a freak snow shower. It had been the first day of June. Perhaps I should have seen this as an omen. Just after 8.00am I dropped James off as usual at Molly's, then rumbled off in my van to Hillgate.

The thought that today was pay-day, and that later a cheque for another week's teaching would appear in my empty pigeon hole, cheered my drive along flooded roads. It also occurred to me that, unless the weather cleared by midday, the Pipistrelles' cricket, and hence my meeting with Cosmo, would be cancelled.

The weather had affected the whole school. Assembly, taken by Renwick today, was given a watery theme. After the Founder's Silence, punctuated by receding thunder, he gave a nauseating sermonette about the Dutch boy who plugged a leaking dyke with his hand. I imagined he had come up with the idea in the early hours as the rain beat on the roof of his house, an old gamekeeper's cottage at one corner of the school grounds. Linda picked up the theme with a deafening rendition of *A Life on the Ocean Wave*. Duggy whistled the tune all the way from library to staffroom.

'Reminds me of Mel,' he said, throwing himself into a chair and grabbing *The Telegraph*.

I looked to Ruth for enlightenment.

'Mel is Melford College, where Duggy taught for a time,' she whispered, 'although, from what I gather, he wasn't there quite as long as he would have us believe. Mel' – she enunciated the word with sarcasm – 'has a strong naval tradition.'

We looked over to him. His head was in the sports pages. The occasional drop of rain from his hair was dampening the paper. His eyes were wet; clearly, he had been moved by the music.

'Why did I leave the state system?' Ruth muttered.

I looked around at my other colleagues in an unusually subdued staffroom, where silent faces stared up from the armchairs. No one was in a hurry to get to first lessons. Only Joan Tatham showed any animation. She was standing by the window, hands on hips, glaring at the rain and throwing her head from one side to the other, as she looked for a break in the clouds. Once or twice she murmured, 'Wind chill factor.'

Again I looked to Ruth.

'It's the sudden change of weather,' she said. 'Affects them all. You get the same thing with the inmates of a mental hospital.' She winked. I wasn't entirely certain that she was joking.

The suspension of summer had made the children restless. My normally conscientious GCSE class banged and shouted their way through the door, knocked desks and chairs, and sat down like drunks from an all-night party taking over a café. I succeeded in quietening them, but since even the brightest were distracted by the overflowing gutters and flooded paths, I decided that for my later classes I would change the lesson plans. In one of my textile magazines, I remembered, there was an article about a tapestry depicting Luna as goddess of water. Year Seven could draw Luna in her chariot, sprinkling water on the earth, and giggle at her bare right breast, while Year Eight could look at her attendants, the naiads, dryads and satyrs with their fascinating behaviour.

The strategy worked until mid-afternoon. I was with a class of Year Tens.

A usually reticent girl said, 'Miss, why does Luna's long hair hang loose round her shoulders, but her helpers have a kind of French plait?'

I tried to explain the symbolism of unbraided hair, but, as the rain drummed down on the flat roof of the classroom block, my voice, tired from a week's teaching, struggled to compete. Under this pressure, I lost touch with my class and with myself. From a distance, I heard myself describing Luna's wilder aspect. I was scared. I wanted to end the discussion. The teacher continued to talk. I couldn't stop her. I felt convinced that Luna, the giver of water, had made me a beneficiary of her other gift, madness. From behind and slightly to the left of myself, I watched a half-familiar woman talk to her class and tell them to continue with their drawings. Then I saw her sink into her chair behind the desk. Very slowly I drifted back to her. When I had recovered enough of my senses to move, I looked at my watch and discovered there were only a few minutes of the lesson remaining; I thought there was much longer. A boy in the front, who had been looking at me on and off for some time, asked, 'Are you alright, Miss?'

'Yes, thank you,' I said and tried to smile. 'For a moment I felt a little faint. It must be this wretched weather.'

He nodded in sympathy.

During the five-minute respite between lessons, I opened the classroom windows as far as I dared without letting in the rain, and breathed in deep lungfuls of damp air. I considered going to the school office and declaring myself sick, but stubbornness, coupled with a fear of going from a room where I might leave part of myself behind, restrained me. I walked over to my desk, closed the magazine and placed it in a drawer. There would be no more Luna today, certainly not during my last lesson, the Year Nines. I had no idea what to teach them, but a friendlier deity must have been smiling on me, since, when they entered the room, there were fewer than usual – three boys were in a squash team playing an away match. In addition, one of the remaining children handed me a note in Alan Carter's handwriting: *Would you teach these morons Roman numerals. Subject came up in my class. More your department.*

So for the last thirty-five minutes of the day the sober world of numbers occupied us, apart from Jarritt, distant as ever in his own thoughts. His only contribution, five minutes before the end of the lesson, was to give an example of a modern use of Roman numerals: the Mirage IV fighter plane. This rare positive input gave him some pleasure. After the bell he approached my desk.

'How's antique dealing, Miss?'

'I don't get much time for it now.'

He nodded, understanding that education and dealing were an uneasy mix.

At the final bell I was first out of the classroom. The rain had stopped. I felt stronger now, in need of any adult company, and for once the prospect of entering the staffroom was almost a pleasure. But my colleagues were in no mood for talking. Silent in armchairs, without end-of-week cheerfulness, they were even more subdued than they had been after morning assembly. In my pigeon hole I found a brown envelope with my pay cheque. I felt the need for some sort of celebration, but this was not the place for it.

When Ruth entered, I whispered, 'What's wrong with them all?'

She nodded towards the headmaster's notice-board. I walked over to what had been since I arrived at the school an empty square of green baize. Now, in the centre, was a notice headed *Half-Term Staff Meeting.* The third item on the agenda was *Autumn Term – Staff Rationalisation.*

This euphemism for redundancies was clearly the cause of the ambient gloom.

Renwick looked up. 'Don't worry, Latin, your subject's safe. It's even written into the Founding Charter. History they can always merge with some general studies monster.'

'But you teach RE too,' I said. 'That must be safe here.'

'Not on your life. They're thinking of bringing in part-time a retired clergyman.' He looked at Duggy. 'Almost as bad as the plan to merge physics with chemistry.'

'If that bloody man sacks me,' Duggy snarled, 'then who the hell will run the Cadet Force Naval Section? I've put thousands of pounds of my own money into this dump of a school. Kick me out and I'll damn well sue them for compensation.'

Joan Tatham must have felt more secure about her own job. She began to whistle the *Hornpipe*.

Duggy exploded. 'Pissy little school.' He barged his way past Ruth and slammed the door behind him.

'They didn't have sackings at Mel,' said Ruth.

I smiled, but no one else had the stomach for mockery.

Before tea I changed into jeans and T-shirt. This earned me a wolf whistle as I entered the dining room. After enduring a Hillgate macaroni cheese, I returned to an empty staffroom, while the residential staff were claimed by the Gryphon or Dolphin, and the children disappeared, spirited away by an invisible Pied Piper. By a similar magic, during tea, the bottle of duty claret appeared on the staffroom table. I phoned Molly to tell her about my earlier disorientation. She made light of it.

'Only one attack in two weeks' teaching. Not bad going,'

'Once was more than enough.'

'But none of your class saw you levitating to the ceiling?'

'That was the worst of it – being an observer of myself while trying to teach children who noticed nothing unusual.'

'Any attacks since?'

'No.'

'So everything's normal.'

'Apart from getting a wolf whistle from a fifteen-year-old at teatime.'

'Is that so bad?'

'I think he was being ironic.'

'In that case, I'll get Paul to give you a heart-felt whistle when you get back here.'

'I'll settle for a glass of wine.'

In the free time before prep, too tired even to read a paper, I remained in a chair by the window and looked down towards the cricket ground. Puddles glowed amber in the evening sun, while one marshy corner was dotted with seagulls like miniature players. I knew that tonight even the most fanatical amateurs would be unable to play here. The prospect of three more hours of duty within the confines of Hillgate was dispiriting. I longed for sleep, but somehow, the heavy bunch of keys in my hand, I dragged myself over to the senior studies, where I found a replacement for Duggy's henchman to supervise junior prep.

When the boys were settled into their work and I was about to return to the staffroom, I heard voices from the tennis courts on the far side of the classroom block. The disturbance annoyed me. I was planning to relax with my wine, not chase after stray children. Rather than walking all the way round to investigate, I went upstairs, with the idea of looking across the courts from the large window outside the special needs room. From there I would be able to see them before they could slip away. But from the first floor I was relieved to see, not children, but the Lennoxes on a hard court, talking to each other across the net, he in a blue track suit, she all in white. I couldn't hear their conversation, but from their body language it appeared a less vituperative exchange than last week's slanging match.

I watched the game. He served with some power. She returned the ball without effort. There followed a fiercely fought rally. I stepped back from my vantage point. This was a private contest, and it would be embarrassing if one of them looked up and saw me. But standing a safe six feet from the window, I had a restricted view and failed to see who won the point. Was there somewhere outside, I wondered, from where I could be an unseen spectator? I was about to go down the stairs, when I turned to the locked door of the special needs room and realised that its key was on my duty bunch. Within a minute I was watching the game from behind the net curtains of Linda Baird's room, the window a few inches open.

Kate Lennox was the better player. Quicker on her feet, she placed the ball with a precision which infuriated her husband. He was struggling to keep his head, relying on a strong but not always accurate serve. When he struck the ball well, he hinted at a past talent. But such shots were rare, and he was forced to run around the court, looking for a fitness he no longer enjoyed. At last he found some form, summoning a hat-trick of aces, each point cutting years off his age.

He took delight in calling the score. 'Forty – love,' roared up to my window. But next came a double fault, followed by some long rallies which saw him racing in every direction, while she hardly moved.

'Forty – all,' he called from the baseline. He was doubled-up, panting.

At the other end she waited, swaying in composed concentration, her eyes fixed ahead.

When he had unbent himself, he tore off his tracksuit with a roughness which said, 'Now we'll see the serious tennis.'

For the next point he recovered some of his earlier authority. For once she did the running, and he won with a lethal passing shot. But she was unruffled, and after his next serve taunted him with lobs which sent him gasping back in pursuit. Again his stamina failed him. He looked done in.

This time she called – a sharp, 'Deuce.'

During the next point he slipped on a wet patch near the net.

'Bad luck. Play the point again,' she shouted. It was no sporting gesture. Now in control, she was happy to delay her victory.

With an awkward jump, he pulled himself from the ground. He reminded me of one of James's perch, hooked and near the landing net, but still with enough flick in its tail to fight on. The next point he was do or die.

'Out, darling,' she called to one of his crashing volleys, overstruck by a clear foot.

'Nonsense,' he shouted. The whole school must have heard him.

'Out,' she insisted.

'We'll play it again.'

'We just did. The ball was out. My advantage.'

He gave way, lost the next point and the game, and marched out of the court towards his house. No word to her. Very slowly, she walked towards his tracksuit, picked it up and folded it over her arm.

I locked Linda Baird's room, wondering about the game beneath the game. Anthony had been good at those.

After a tour of the studies I returned to the staffroom to open my wine. But although there were glasses in the CCF cupboard, there was no corkscrew. I tried the kitchens, but they had been locked by the catering staff, and none of my keys fitted either the inner or outer door. My last hope was that a boy might have a Swiss Army knife with a corkscrew attachment. I made my way round the outside of the school towards the studies. It was now the brightest part of the day, but the flower beds at the end of the drive were a dismal sight: the geraniums had been beaten almost leafless, and the wet soil was spread with a carnage of broken stems and red buds. If the gardener had planned colour here for Speech Day, he would have to replant. I wondered if I would be here to see it.

Comforted by the smell of drying earth, I delayed my penknife hunt and wandered down to the cricket field. The gulls had gone, and mist was hovering over puddles. I stood under the oaks on the boundary and let intermittent drops of water fall on me from their black branches. Beyond the cricket field the occasional car passed by. The sound, approaching, then dying in the distance, made the school a desolate place. I began to circle the boundary, again asking myself if I really wanted a full-time job here, even if one were offered. Yet again I told myself I needed the money.

As I neared the flooded corner of the field, the grass was becoming unwalkable. I turned towards the central square, weighing up my pay cheque against the demands and privations of Hillgate. Then I heard, in the distance, a car turn off the road and come up the drive – Brian Devlin, I guessed, was returning early from the Gryphon to catch up with his marking. I wondered how Anthony and B were passing the evening. The thought made me feel penned up in this melancholy place. I wanted to blame them for it. From the edge of the cricket square, where the close-mown grass was much drier, I surveyed the boundary, trying to pinpoint the place where I had met Cosmo last week.

I saw the classic car first. It was parked at an odd angle in the staff car park, its brash chrome mocking the late sun. Next, I saw Cosmo, under the oaks, in pink shirt, hands in jeans' pockets, standing still and looking towards me. His appearing like this, while I was alone in the centre of the field, unnerved me. I felt a thousand eyes were watching from among the trees on the boundary. At the same time his presence and the sight of that sleek '60s convertible lifted the evening's dreariness.

It felt a long way to the boundary. For a minute, I became a defeated batsman walking with slow regret from the wicket. Ten yards from Cosmo I received the signature bow.

'Er – a bit late for a pitch inspection,' he said.

'I was idling away prep time.'

'And if the kids are like I was at school, they'll be idling too. Been waiting long?'

'I wasn't expecting you at all. I was just walking. With the cricket cancelled I thought we'd meet up another week.' It sounded a poor excuse for being where I was.

'Oh, right,' he said, but I heard him think, why the hell were you scanning the boundary from the middle?

'The textiles are in my van,' I said.

Walking over the car park's wet gravel, we were silent, but my head was abuzz with thoughts about the price I should ask for the embroideries. We came up to the car, a black Ford Galaxy. To look at it without comment was impossible.

'I'll swap you my Ford for yours,' I said.

'At fifteen to the gallon I might take you up.'

I looked at the blood-red leather seats. 'I like the pleated upholstery.'

'Yeah, tuck 'n' roll. Ugh, the old junk we surround ourselves with.'

'Come and see the rubbish I've got in my van.'

Then I realised the keys were in my bag in the staffroom. I dashed back for them. Before leaving the staffroom I looked at myself in the mirror above the fireplace, brushed my hair with my fingers, and immediately frowned at myself for doing so.

We both climbed into the back of my van. I unwrapped the embroideries and spread them on the floor. Cosmo bent down, flipped them over, shut his eyes, turned down the corners of his mouth and swayed his head from side to side, like a child rolling a boiled sweet from one cheek to another.

'Mm, not really me,' he said. 'What do you want for them?'

'Three fifty,' I said firmly. I had no basis for my asking price, apart from paying for my new wheel bearings.

He looked at them again, while I wondered if I had asked too much or too little, and if he knew any more about them than I did.

Cosmo stood up as far as he could in the low-top. 'No, I don't think they're for me,' he said. 'Probably about the right money though. If I were you, I'd bung them into auction.'

I folded them and covered them with the piece of carpet.

Cosmo turned round as if he'd forgotten something. 'How much is the bit of rug?'

He had said the words a fraction too quickly.

Now it was my turn to make noises. 'Er, well, I was thinking of keeping it. I've got this stupid thing about fragments.'

'Can I tempt you with an amazing four hundred?'

I was tempted, but he'd wised me up.

'No, I'm sorry.'

'Sure?'

'Yes.'

He looked annoyed. We walked back to his car without speaking. I wanted to start some sort of conversation.

'Where would you date the embroideries?' I asked.

'Mid-nineteenth, I suppose.'

'Turkish?'

'I'd say Persian.' He opened the car door. The discussion had ended. For all his reputation as a charmer, he was now somewhere between terse and rude. The slam of the Galaxy's glossy black door felt like a goodbye.

Through the open window I said, 'You don't by any chance have a corkscrew I could borrow?'

He sat back on his tuck 'n' roll and dropped the dealer look. 'Oddly enough...' He opened the glove compartment and pulled out a woman's legs corkscrew. The flesh tones above her striped stockings matched his shirt. It was an object which suited the car. 'Have this. It came with the motor, but I never seem to use it.'

For a moment I thought he was expecting to be invited to share my wine, but he started the engine.

I held up the corkscrew. 'I'll let you have it back on Monday.'

'Keep it, but let me have first refusal if you want to sell that scrap of rug.'

The Galaxy cut a wide sweep of the car park and sped down the drive under the oak trees. I thought of one of James's elusive pike darting out of sight among reeds. I looked at the corkscrew. The toe from one of her boots was missing, but it still had a value.

As I walked back to the van for another look at my remnant, a black and white springer spaniel bounded up to me.

'Tabloid,' shouted Kate Lennox from the path by the yew hedge. Still in tennis kit, she was carrying a lead.

The dog threw itself around, kicked back gravel at me and charged back to its owner.

'Heel,' she ordered. Again it obeyed, following its mistress towards me.

She looked at my mud-spattered jeans. 'Sorry about the beast, but he missed his early walk because of the rain, so he's rather more lively than usual.'

'Don't worry. It's only mud.'

'Tabloid!'

The dog had made a bolt for a patch of scrub between the Lennox's house and the cricket field.

'Oh, God, no. The filthy animal was playing with a dead rabbit there yesterday.'

I followed her to the place where Tabloid was all nose in his flat, damp carrion.

'You bugger, come away.' She clipped the lead to his collar. For a couple of yards, she was forced to drag him skidding over the earth, until he anchored himself to the ground and drew his four legs together in a defecatory squat. 'Not here, you rat-bag.' She tugged at him, but he had already haunched out his coil. She looked on in disgusted resignation as the dog kicked up deep scoops of earth behind him. 'Tabloid, you're the pits.'

'How did he get his name?'

'The answer we give enquiring parents is that the first thing he tore up was a copy of the *Daily Mail*. The truth is, from a puppy, he's always been diligent in covering up his own shit, but revels in rolling in everyone else's. How's everything going?'

'Fine, thanks,' I said. This wasn't the time to mention my out-of-body experience in the classroom.

'Hillgate is probably very different from what you're used to.'

'Quite a few children do seem to have special difficulties – Mark Jarritt, for example.'

'Ah, yes, he's one of our statemented children. There are some home difficulties there, I believe. Tabloid!'

The dog was trying to pull her towards some laurel bushes, but she was in control, using his acts of disobedience as opportunities to display her authority. It was similar to the way she had treated her husband on the tennis court.

'You must come to dinner,' she said. 'I'll find a date and let you know.'

I thanked her as the bell called me away to post-prep duties. I was pleased at the invitation. Dinner would provide an opportunity to clear away the uncertainties surrounding my job. If I failed to get an answer from David Lennox, perhaps Kate, who seemed a rare natural ally in the school, might be more forthcoming. It also occurred to me that it would be interesting to gain a first-hand view of Lennox domesticity.

After more key turning I returned to my van, collected my fragment and carried it to the staffroom. There I uncorked my bottle with the leggy corkscrew, poured myself a glass and sat down with the piece of rug on my lap like a thick woollen apron. I now regarded it with new respect. Apart from one corner, it was extremely worn. I counted over a dozen holes, some of which must have been caused by moths or other insects. It was predominantly blue, but when I compared it with the colour of my jeans, it had a greenish tinge. Over this blue ground was a lacework of dull yellow and rust meandering lines, sprouting shoots, like the unearthed roots of some strange shrub. The whole piece needed cleaning, but where it was least dirty I could discern floral sprays like pressed flowers. As I agonised over what Cosmo knew and I didn't, the design mesmerised me, and I was looking at a Victorian stained glass window decorated with childish sprigs, and which a sinuous creeper in the churchyard was doing its best to obscure. When I turned the piece over, the flowers were less faded and grew in harmony with their surrounds, while the roots became branches which no longer choked the sprays, but encircled them with flowing arabesques. It had the tattered remains of a border – more winding branches, but now dark blue and ivory – which was separated from the main design by a strip of what looked like one of the folded-paper row of clowns' heads James had made in kindergarten. Each clown had a mouth but no eyes, as if the child, in a hurry to unfold the handiwork, had failed to complete it.

Slowly, I appreciated the exquisite beauty of the fragment and formed a picture of the complete carpet. I assumed that, like the embroideries, it was Persian, but as to its age and rarity I was at a loss. I tried to recall the exact tone of Cosmo's voice when he had wanted to buy it, and his annoyance at failing. This encouraged me about its value. Perhaps he was now thinking, as I was, that had he offered me £40, instead of £400, I would have remained in ignorance and sold it, and that the gift of the corkscrew which, even damaged, could be worth £15, was a payment to secure his right of first refusal. Alternatively, I thought, perhaps Cosmo the gambler might have been lucky in the past with rare carpet fragments, and was now doing no more than trying to take a chance with a speculative investment about which he knew no more than me. Arguing both cases in my head, I set off for another round of locking up.

When all doors were secure, I went to the library and searched among the shelves labelled *Art*, in the unlikely chance that there might be a book on antique textiles. There was nothing, but when I passed the children's section and saw a row of stories by Noel Streatfield – *Ballet Shoes*, *A Vicarage Family* and many others – memories were stirred of the books of my early childhood. Written by a clergyman's daughter, they had particularly appealed to me. I still had them all. One or two I had read to James, but unsurprisingly they weren't his favourites; he preferred books about rivers and fishing, which meant that the only modern classic we both liked was *The Little Grey Men* by Denys Watkins-Pitchford – a clergyman's son.

Before leaving I looked around for some other book with which I could fill the remaining spare time in evening duty. This again was fruitless, until, in the history section, I found two volumes on Roman and Celtic religion. These, I thought, might fill some of the gaps in my GCSE pupils' (and my own) knowledge. In the staffroom I tried to read, but my concentration was interrupted by occasional glances at my piece of carpet. Finally, I became absorbed with an account of Gallic priestesses, their rituals and rivalry, and might have finished the chapter, had not a prefect informed me that the boarders were assembling in the library. So, leaving the old religion for Lady Widwell's idea of the new, I stood by the Regency painted sideboard for the obligatory three minutes' silence, gave the customary warning about bathroom and bedtime punctuality, and felt that I had been teaching at Hillgate all my working life. The ease with which I had slipped into the system disturbed me.

In different ways my duties on the dormitory corridor were also unsettling, since I again felt hauled back to my own school. The door marked *Sanatorium* was particularly distressing. There were no sick pupils in the room, but it transported me back to that summer term at St Michael's when I had spent a week in a solitary room. For two days I had been delirious and beset by thoughts of the epidemic at Lowood Institution and the deaths of girls, including Jane's best friend Helen. Could the school doctor be trusted? I had asked. Was his diagnosis correct? The sanatorium blanket was red. My fevered mind recalled that it was in *the red-room* where Jane Eyre had once been locked. Total recovery had taken a further week.

I was glad when it was time to switch off the lights in the last dormitory and I could return to the staffroom for a final twenty minutes with my book and fragment. The arrival of Brian Devlin's Lada at 10.30pm signalled my escape until Monday.

I shared the remaining half of my duty wine with Molly and Paul, who pumped me for an account of my day. Fatigue made me give them the briefest description of my bilocation in the classroom. I was relieved they didn't press me for details. Molly was more interested in Cosmo and my piece of carpet.

'So you were forlornly pacing the cricket pitch,' she said, 'when he appears under the trees and you tell him you weren't expecting him.'

'I wasn't.'

Paul took up her tone. 'And then you said, "Come to my van and look at my textiles." '

So, helped by another bottle, the late evening drifted into its familiar winy absurdities, while my week receded into a past so unreal that it was like a restless dream, with only the pay cheque in my bag to confirm its reality.

At around midnight I bundled James into his bed, glad that he wasn't a boarder at Hillgate. Before going to my own bedroom I looked through a pile of old auction catalogues, pulled out two specialist carpet sales, took them upstairs and threw them on my bed for some late-night research. But here I hesitated, staring at the bed covers. I tried to remember if I had been in a hurry when I had made the bed that morning, since I had failed to follow my usual practice of placing the pillows so that the mouths of the pillowcases point away from the door. It's a silly domestic fad – I don't have many – but one I devoutly follow. I remembered the alarm clock and the doorstop and thought again about possible prowlers, of whom Anthony remained chief suspect. But exhaustion prevented my dwelling on the matter, and after looking through my catalogues with their totally unhelpful illustrations, I fell into a restless sleep.

I was woken by a 4.00am blackbird. Twenty minutes later it moved to a different part of the garden, and I slept deeply. I had one of my driving-to-B's-house dreams, but it never progressed beyond the lorries on the ring-road. Then I was at Molly's house, but around the kitchen table there was different company: Dora Prideaux, Great Aunt Helen, and a woman I had never seen before, who was wearing one of the drab old dresses I had bought from Frank – perhaps she was its original owner. We were passing around Cosmo's corkscrew, like a panel of experts on a TV programme. When it was placed in my hand, I saw that there was some writing on the handle, but the letters were indistinct, and I was unable to read them. The three women looked at me, demanding I decipher the word – a factory name perhaps – and were irate when I failed. As I tried again to make out the inscription, I became desperate with my lack of success. The three women were becoming impatient, tapping agitated fingers on the table. I was sweating, then crying. I couldn't see the object in front of me. Their faces glared at me and became drawn and haggard. Terrified, I wanted to get out of my chair but couldn't. Vestiges of common sense told me that Great Aunt Hilda had died eighteen years ago, the woman in the drab dress was probably dead too, and I had nothing to fear from Dora Prideaux. All three responded by becoming gaunt, then skeletal and closing in around me.

With no other defence, I threw down the corkscrew on the table. Shocked by my action, they shrank away. This gave me confidence. I wrenched myself from my chair and rushed to the back door and into the garden. I looked down on the familiar brick-weave path, but when I looked up, I was in the classroom in front of my Year Nines. They were laughing at me. Their mocking guffaws refused to fade as I woke. Slowly, I realised that James was downstairs watching Saturday morning TV with the volume turned up.

Rationalising, I staggered to the bathroom. My dream could be explained away by the events of yesterday blended in a foul brew after too much wine with Molly and Paul. Its taste, I told myself, would be washed away with two cups of coffee. But I wasn't convinced.

When Anthony arrived, his first words were, 'How's the blackboard?'

'Forgotten until Monday.'

James appeared carrying his fishing kit.

'You won't need that,' said Anthony. 'B's brother is staying with us, and he's going to take you fly-fishing.'

'Great,' said James.

'Will you go with them?' I asked.

'I'll see how time goes. B's rehearsing for her play this weekend, and I'm helping with the scenery.'

'What play's this?'

'*Major Barbara*,' called out B from the car. 'You'll welcome to see it. I'll get you a ticket.'

'Thanks,' I called back, thinking, over my dead body. I didn't have to ask who was playing the title role.

B was now getting out of the car. 'James will be quite safe with big bro,' she said. 'In the summer holidays he can take James salmon fishing. Norfolk's no good for that, but Hector's got a beat on the Esk.'

I recoiled under the multi-pronged attack. B's family were now, not only taking my son from me and promising him the sort of fishing which was far beyond my pocket, but also, since the River Esk was in Yorkshire, they were claiming lordship over my home county – already they had fishing rights there. At a stroke, my plan to take James to the River Aire had been belittled, shattered, and me with it.

'When Hec and James get back,' said Anthony, 'I'll take him swimming in the university pool.' He turned to James. 'Alright, matey?'

I went into the house to find James's swimming things. The 'matey' was a new form of address, but James seemed to accept it. His ability to adjust to the A and B world was disquieting. As I pulled out James's swim shorts from his chest of drawers, I was the old *hausfrau* left behind to do the ironing and gardening while the youngsters went off to have fun. But a few minutes later, as the MG pulled away under the horse chestnuts, I thought of Cosmo's Galaxy, and Anthony became an old fogey, caught up in a ridiculous image of himself and as pitiful as Duggy. Cosmo could laugh at his car, and would no doubt sell it for the right price; Anthony had an earnestness about his which made parting with it unthinkable. It was all so precious – like his relationship with B. 'Alright, matey?' I said to myself and went out to sow some runner beans.

As I gardened, I thought ahead to my third week at Hillgate and determined to be mistress of my timetable, not its harassed servant. This would be my last opportunity to advertise myself as the best choice for the Latin department if Neil Osborne was still faltering. On my vegetable plot, I worked myself into a blissful optimism. It remained with me during the afternoon, which I spent on duty at the antiques centre. In the long gaps between customers, I tried to research my fragment with an encyclopedia of carpets borrowed from the book dealer's shelves. It contained copious colour plates, but none resembling my piece. At the same time the author advised against looking at pictures when making attributions and comparisons, recommending instead technical analysis of the weaving. Here I knew I was a floundering amateur and soon gave up. Back with the colour plates, I saw there was some possibility that my remnant was from a vase carpet, but would only have value if it were sufficiently early. I had been here before. In recent months several finds I had considered 'early' had been buried under the epitaph 'nineteenth-century copy'. I imagined an auction house specialist looking at my fragment and using those same words. Over half-term week, I decided, I would take my fragment to London for an expert opinion.

At 5.00pm, when I left the centre, my optimism had seeped away, perhaps because I had sold nothing from my own section. So on Sunday, hoping for a change of mood to divert my thoughts from Hillgate and antiques, I took James and Ben to Salthouse, and walked along the beach to Cley, matching their punishing pace all the way and skimming stones with them on a millpond sea.

Sitting on a shingle bank, watching seabirds dive, James asked, 'You don't mind, do you, if I go to the dress rehearsal for *Major Barbara* in a few weeks' time?'

'Of course not,' I told him. There, in the solitude, we might have been on a desert island, where B and her antics were in a different hemisphere.

## 11

On Monday morning, as I drove to Hillgate, I encouraged myself that by the end of the week I would know if my job was to continue. I felt confident – perhaps yesterday's walk had released a good dose of endorphins – and I told myself that even if I couldn't stay at this school, I would be sure to find another post elsewhere.

The staffroom too had a fizz about it, but with my colleagues this was caused by the anticipation of half-term. Gone were Renwick's moans about miscreants, Duggy's tantrums and the barbed asides of the others. All conversation was about holiday plans, making the atmosphere in the room almost civilised. In break, three or four heads were buried in maps of planned destinations, while Joan Tatham and Linda Baird sat staring with idiot grins at the ceiling, as if there were joints, not Marlboro Lights, in their fingers. Duggy, who had dismissed his class five minutes early, had been seen running out of the classroom block while pulling on a blue mechanic's overall, like a quick-change artist late for the next act. For once, the staffroom wasn't his stage – he spent the whole of break (and several others during the week) with his head under the bonnet of his Land Rover. Ruth and I watched him through the window. She did one of her impressions of him, 'I'm bloody well going to service my engine in Lennox's time, not my own.'

The atmosphere had changed in the classrooms too, where, by Wednesday, games and magazines prevailed after a token ten minutes' teaching. Discipline was easy, work a doddle, my fear of aberrations forgotten. But with it all I felt a sense of finality. While the other staff eased themselves out of teaching mode, and the children became members of a summer camp, I found myself isolated in anxiety about my job. The morning's positivity had evaporated. I was tempted to call in again to see Dora Prideaux, but superstition restrained me. I decided to suffer in uncertainty until Friday. In several classes I was asked, 'Will you be here after half-term, Miss?' I was upset I had no definite answer.

One advantage of the phoney week's teaching was that the general slackening meant less marking, leaving my free periods truly free. This enabled me to view several auctions during school time. On these trips I hoped I would avoid Cosmo, since it was vital to know about my carpet fragment before I saw him again. At the same time, I made the picture of him driving away in his Galaxy a defence, an antidote against any debilitating thoughts about Anthony and B. In my mind, Cosmo had the power to diminish those who for so long had diminished me. As it happened, at Walborough on Monday and at the viewing of two other sales during the week, he was not to be seen. However, viewing a sale in Norwich during a Wednesday lunchtime, a dealer I knew only by sight, but whom I'd heard called Wesley by his friends, approached me.

'You're not the mystery lady, are you?'

'I shouldn't think so,' I said. 'Why do you ask?'

'Oh, it's just that we were knocking something out a week or two ago, and Cosmo said some woman dealer had left a price with him.'

'It may have been me.'

'And there we were thinking he was lying.'

'Why should he?'

'You know – putting an absent person in the ring to get an extra share.'

I didn't understand this explanation, but said, 'No, he wasn't lying.' I felt embarrassed at defending him.

A grin appeared, framed by his greasy hair. 'There's nothing much in this sale. I'm going to the café. Feel like a coffee?'

'No, I must get back.' I foresaw a chat-up which would have all the charm and finesse of one of my Year Nines.

As I drove to Hillgate for afternoon lessons, I was surprised to find myself feeling an affection for the school. And sad that Friday morning might be the last time I would drive through its gates. There was no logic to this. To be sad at the loss of income, yes, but affection for a school which was unsuitable for any child's education or any teacher's career, an emphatic no. I had heard that long-term prisoners, on release, sometimes experienced an inexplicable sense of loss. Was this happening to me? But how could it – I had been teaching here for only three weeks?

Friday drifted through a pretence of lessons until 4.00pm. An hour later, the last of the Discoveries and Volvos had left the car park with their jubilant passengers, leaving behind a smoke-filled staffroom waiting for Dr Lennox to appear and begin the half-term meeting. I felt scared.

Ruth did her best to reassure me. 'You'll hear something within the next hour – everything's last minute here. He'll announce that Neil Osborne has turned down his appointment, and you'll find yourself offered work until at least the end of term.'

Dr Lennox, wearing a heavy tweed suit, arrived and chose for himself a hard-backed chair at one end of the staffroom table. This gave him a physical superiority of at least a foot, since the rest of us were scattered about the room on low armchairs. It also dispelled any illusion that we were fellow teachers. At best, we were junior management in for a rant from a dictatorial director. His entry had silenced us, but he nevertheless banged the bowl of his pipe on the table with such force that he might have been calling to order a querulous public meeting. He then placed the stem between his teeth, and, keeping his lips apart, scanned the room with a frown, so the upper part of his face scowled and the lower smiled; perhaps, unsure of his mood, he was accommodating both extremes. His eyes failed to settle on anyone in particular, but, had they done so, it would have been difficult to decide if his look showed disgust or approval. In the end, I decided it was manic, and he had become – I reverted to my schooldays – the Mad Hatter.

'Pupil numbers,' he announced through his teeth. 'That's the issue which decides whether we all continue here or not.'

He had ignored the agenda on the notice-board beside him.

'In September,' he said, 'we shall have lost twenty-three and at the most recent count gained five. This makes the next month or two the most critical we've been through.'

He paused to allow the silence to stress the point. His eyes were becoming wild. I watched them dart about the room. He was a predator selecting prey from a herd where I was the weakest. I looked away and listened to what sounded like a call to arms, with talk of 'a campaign' and 'a recruitment drive'. The 'losses over the summer' could have been casualties at the front. In two minutes a bullying company director had become a wild animal, then a belligerent Field Marshal for whom the interests of children were not worth a mention.

He removed his pipe and held it by the bowl so the stem pointed to us, an extended finger of reproof. He now raved about falling standards – 'due to staff slackness'; staff scruffiness – 'a bad impression on parents'; the misuse of the school equipment – 'a waste of money which impacted the wages bill'; the private use by the staff of the school minibus – 'the equivalent of stealing'; not entering phone calls – 'downright dishonesty'.

He ended by waving his pipe above our heads. 'And unless things change, come September, there won't be the money to pay you all.'

I looked towards Renwick and waited for, 'And there will be sackings.' I was disappointed.

'Right now,' he said, banging down his pipe, 'I'm looking at redundancies.'

He then called on each head of department to make a report – another on the hoof item to his agenda, which had me dreading my turn and frantically composing a suitable response. I had plenty of time, since, as the first reports were given, he butted in with questions reflecting his overriding worry about numbers. As Brian Devlin stumbled through the position of the English department, he interrupted, 'Why aren't parents getting a school play this term?' Then, as Joan told us we had two cricketers in county youth teams, he demanded, 'Why aren't there more matches on the fixture list? Parents love coming to watch.'

Frenetically, I searched for something to say about Latin which would be appealing to his precious parents. I could think of nothing. The obvious answer, 'Get a permanent teacher,' was unlikely to impress him. But I was in luck: Latin was last on his list, by which time his appetite for staff abuse must have been satisfied.

'And . . . er . . . Latin next,' he said. 'Well, on account of unavoidable difficulties, there have been problems here. Now, the Speech Day programme. Linda Baird's been organising this.' He pointed his pipe in her direction. He might have been offering her a chew.

I was too angry to hear which General was giving away prizes, what displays were being put on for visitors, or who was allowed in which marquee for tea. I felt ignored and lumped in with the problems of the Latin department. I thought, as soon as your insulting tirade is over I shall insist you give me an answer about my future.

His one deference to the original agenda was *Any Other Business*.

Here Duggy used the opportunity to outline plans for a naval section yachting holiday in Devon, the subtext of which was, I'm doing more to impress parents than the lot of you put together. To outdo him, Renwick described a planned summer expedition to American Civil War battlefields. He added pointedly, 'I desperately need three more helpers, from yourselves or parents.' His subtext was, my history department needs more staff, not redundancies.

When Renwick had finished his pleading, David Lennox stood up. If there was more *Any Other Business*, he didn't want to hear it. Ignoring the women present with, 'Thank you gentlemen,' he left the room. When he closed the door, we looked at one another, for a few moments speechless.

'I'm looking at redundancies,' said Renwick.

No one even smiled.

'Pompous prat,' said Ruth.

'Good of him to mention me,' I said to her.

'He's not worried about us. What's on is mind is the next Governors' Meeting. If numbers look like plummeting in September, they'll give him a dose of what he's given us. And he'll need more than his pipe to find answers.'

'I need an answer from him myself.'

As I stormed down the corridor, I wondered how I could get past Dora Prideaux, who often was as much his watchdog as his secretary. But when I opened the office door, I found an empty room with the computers covered for the night. I knocked on the headmaster's door and entered without waiting for an answer. David Lennox was at his desk, pouring pale sherry from a decanter into a rummer.

'Ah, Mrs Burns.' He looked down at his drink. I guessed he might have hidden it, had I given him the vital few seconds between knocking and entering. 'Will you have one too?'

Unprepared for this, I said, 'Thanks,' and let him pour me a glass as full as his own.

'Good health,' he said. He downed a third of his rummer and pointed to a chair.

He sat behind his desk, settled his glass among the snuff boxes, and gave me a tight smile. 'At half-term one needs to wash down the chalk dust. And the May staff meeting is always rather fraught.' He looked up to his bookcases, frowning, as if trying to locate a lost volume. 'And in a small school like this keeping up the numbers is always going to be a challenge. Never had the problem at Dean Notley. In fact, we chose who we took. We wouldn't look at a boy unless he averaged sixty-five per cent in Common Entrance. And now what have I sunk to? Advertising in Spanish magazines, saying that Hillgate caters for children with rudimentary English. Meanwhile I'm looking for a part-time TEFL teacher for September.' He drank another third of his sherry and topped up the glass. 'And as for our predicted GCSE grades this year . . .'

I listened to him make further comparisons with his former school. At first, I waited for a pause when I could put my case, but, as he continued, I saw he was so pleased to have found a new ear for his problems that I thought it best to let him moan on, hoping that, when eventually he stopped, he might be more ready give me a sympathetic hearing.

He moved from the number and quality of Hillgate children to the condition of the school buildings and the inadequacies of the headmaster's house, not neglecting mid-sentence sips of his sherry. After a protracted gulp he lost his drift.

'Dr Lennox, regarding Latin . . .'

'We may well find that some of the children we get from Spain have a greater aptitude for it than our present lot.'

'But that's after September.'

'One or two may be spending a few days with us towards the end of term. Makes for a more gentle baptism.'

'Will I be needed after half-term?'

'What?'

His look reminded me of James when I woke him for school. I wanted to tap David Lennox on the shoulder, and pull him out of his dreams of Dean Notley and his fantasies about Hillgate's future.

'Is Neil Osborne arriving after half-term?'

'Osborne?'

He reached for his sherry again. The gesture infuriated me – made me feel like a reluctant counsellor. I waited while he drunk his way into the present.

'Of course,' he said, 'you'll want to know something.'

He pulled his pipe from his pocket and slotted it between his teeth. 'I suppose we ought to wait until Monday before we do anything. Can I get Dora to give you a ring during the week?' He gave me another taut-faced grin. It slowly registered my look of annoyance. 'Naturally, we'll pay you for the half-term week. Shall we call it a retention fee?'

After his last word his lips remained drawn back in a superior smile, like one of B's acolytes uttering the sacred name. I knew there would now be no arguing with him and felt lucky to have secured a week's pay for doing nothing. I found a smile and a thank you and placed my half-empty glass on a coffee table. He noticed.

'Driving,' I said.

He rose from his chair, looking as if he wanted me to stay and listen to more of his problems. I guessed that by the end of the third glass I would even have learned about the real game on the tennis court.

'Good of you to step in like this,' he said.

I didn't know whether he was referring to my teaching or walking into his office and listening to him. As I left the room, I thought, a different man would have asked, 'How have your three weeks with us been?'

Pausing on the other side of the door, and wondering what Dora thought of this man, I heard footsteps, followed by the chinking of glass on glass. No doubt he was pouring my undrunk sherry into the decanter, or into his rummer.

Ruth had waited in the staffroom amid the litter of educational jetsam. The room, like the staff, needed a holiday. As I recounted my sherry-fuelled meeting, she became more angry than me.

'The bugger. Why the hell didn't he appoint you to the end of term and have done with it?'

'I think he switched off decision-making when he pulled out the decanter stopper. How serious is the booze problem?'

'Lennox's? Or Duggy's, or Renwick', or Brian's? Let's get out of here. Found a costume yet for Sunday night?'

'Of course,' I said, but I hadn't thought about the party all week.

# 12
---

One of Hillgate's few similarities to the state system was its choice of dates for half-term. I envisaged a quiet week, since Molly, Paul and Ben were taking James to the Loire Valley where they had rented a *gite*. I had agreed to keep an eye on the house, feed Bullace and water the garden. On Saturday morning, with a promise not to forget the tomatoes in the greenhouse, I waved them away and, with mixed emotions about James's absence for all of the holiday, drove to the antiques centre for my first full day's duty in three weeks.

Opening the doors of the old chapel and switching on its lights was like evening duty at Hillgate in reverse. As I moved among the sections of each dealer, turning on their spotlights and table lamps, each selling space became a distinctive room displaying the character of its tenant, unless one looked to the beams and rafters; then the building took on a makeshift feel, like the Hillgate drawing room with its partitioned senior studies. Since many of the centre's customers lived in conversions – barns, farmhouses, maltings, pubs and other redundant chapels – perhaps the building suited its clientele.

Before turning the sign on the door from *Closed* to *Open*, I looked at my own section and wondered what it said of my character through its hotchpotch of furniture, luggage and hat boxes. It all needed rearranging – like my life. And whatever else it said, it told me that I would be better off teaching.

Half-term had brought visitors to the town, giving me a brisk morning in which I sold something from most sections, including my own – the riding boots I had bought from Frank. To be occupied like this was far preferable to the many wearisome winter days when I had shivered by a sputtering gas heater, selling almost nothing. But the morning's activity did little to convince me that I belonged here. If Hillgate had not yet fully succeeded in making me part of its world, then it had certainly distanced me from this one.

In those days, before eBay and online auction catalogues, Saturdays were when collectors were on the prowl – the postcard hunters, the china enthusiasts, the lamp men, the treen lovers. Two railway buffs almost came to blows when they made the simultaneous discovery, in the unlikely place of the *Interiors* room, of a *Ladies Waiting Room* sign which had been salvaged from the long-closed Overstrand station. Enamel signs were their holy grail.

'Excuse me, I was about to buy this.'

'I'm sorry, but I was here first.'

'I don't think so.'

'Have you seen the price?'

It was £150.

'Yes, but they're rare in this condition.'

A mutual glare.

'A pity the other one's not here.'

'You mean the *Public Waiting Room*?'

'It would have been *General Waiting Room*.'

'Oh, of course.'

'An unusual red for the Norfolk and Suffolk Railway.'

'Some fading, that's all.'

In even louder voices they entered into a debate about railway sign paints, relishing their common interest. There seemed no end to the minutiae they needed to share with each other. By another throw of the dice they might have been art historians poring over an old master and talking pigments. Their conversation enforced my sense of unbelonging. Half an hour later I was delighted to see them leave, almost arm in arm, on their way to the Sheringham terminus of the North Norfolk Railway. Neither had bought the sign.

At 1.00pm Tara appeared. Impressed by the morning's sales, she insisted I take a lunch break. Beyond the centre's Presbyterian brickwork the town was in holiday mood. The Bed and Breakfasts on the main road sported *Sorry, No Vacancies* signs, the outdoor market surged with coloured shirts and dresses, while beyond, on the old station platform, steam enthusiasts waited with their cameras. I walked to the bridge at the top of Church Street. Below, an engine whistled, and belched nostalgia towards me. I jogged forward before the smoke billowed over the parapet. I escaped, but behind me a railway fanatic allowed himself to become engulfed, emerging with a smile, like a pilgrim through incense.

I walked past the putting green, the theatre and the town clock, towards the seafront. Halfway down the street, before gift shops, ice-cream stands and arcades took over, I bought some prawns and a couple of rolls and drifted with the crowds to the point where the road ends, not with any architectural flourish or civic statue, but with a concrete wall, greyish brown like the sea beyond it. I peered over to the beach a hundred feet below, where groups of irrepressible holidaymakers were making the most of the damp strip between the incoming tide and the imported car-size rocks which serve as coastal defences at the foot of the sea wall. It was odd that more people were sitting on these escapees from a cubist landscape than on the local sand. Fifty yards away, at the water's edge, a few boys in swimming shorts dared each other to go in. The sea, while not rough, was unfriendly enough to persuade them to play football instead. I strolled towards the zig-zag path to the beach.

Ahead of me, a child was pestering her father to let her look through a coin-in-the-slot telescope. 'I want to see the boats, the boats,' she screamed. There wasn't so much as a distant tanker on the horizon, but, giving way to her innocent optimism, he relented. She might have been six-year-old me, with my parents on a day out to Scarborough. I sighed for my childhood beaches and cliffs and remembered walks over the rocky headland to the castle. And the excitement of going home via Pately Bridge to visit the world's oldest sweet shop. I would take James there one day.

On the sand, I sat on a washed-up log, and with my back to a breakwater ate my lunch. It was much cooler here than in the town above which, when I looked up, was now shrunk by the coastline on either side. For a few minutes it seemed far away, as did the antiques centre, Hillgate, Anthony and B.

The boys' orange football rolled towards me. 'Ball, Missus!' one of them shouted. I threw it towards them, wondering if James and the others were by now on the ferry from Portsmouth. The thought made me remember those holidays in Brittany, and, in another attempt to make some sense of my life, I began to recall all that had happened since, in the hope that systematic recollection of the past would gain me some new, life-enhancing insight. The process failed. I was left low and brooding in a world where everyone but me was having fun. I wondered how Anthony and B were spending a rare Saturday without James.

The orange ball again arrived at my feet. I hurled it towards the middle of the beach, surprised I could throw so far. It made me think of my meeting with Cosmo on the cricket field eight days ago, and Molly's barely concealed encouragement of me, later that evening, to think about a new relationship. Not yet, I thought, not yet. Any new commitment at the moment would be too much under B's shadow. For the last time I retrieved the boys' ball before climbing back to the town. At the top of the steps, the sight of a group of women in straw hats told me I needed to find a costume for tomorrow's party.

At the centre, Tara helped me try on a few dresses from the vintage clothes area. The most promising candidate was a lime-green beaded flapper dress. It suited my short hair. Tara rummaged around for a suitable headband, while I looked in a cheval mirror, trying to envisage Ruth's party. But the dress felt too formal and urbane, and when Tara crowned me with a ridiculous plumed diamante head-dress, which turned me into Daisy from *The Great Gatsby*, I rejected it. It was all too 1920s.

Next, I tried on a white rowing blazer piped in purple, with crossed oars embroidered on the top pocket. Below were some club initials and an illegible date. Again, this was early-twentieth century, but more or less passed for the 1890s – rowing blazers must be the most timeless of garments. An inside pocket carried the label of a Reading tailor. Near enough to Charley's Oxford, I thought. Tara found me some old cricket whites and a blue-striped tie for a belt. The legs were far too long, but when we rolled them above my ankles, I felt ready for a punt with my chums on the river. To complete the outfit, I pulled on a boater from my own section, looked into the mirror and knew I had solved the problem. But my dresser, less easily satisfied, whipped out an eye-liner and with a couple of strokes gave me a moustache. I thought this was a mistake until she made me use a hot pink lipstick. This underlined the burlesque and made me wonder who was staring back at me from the mirror. Turning, I saw a couple standing in the doorway and gaping. While the wife elbowed her husband for looking too intently, I grabbed my jeans and sweater and retreated to the storeroom.

# PART III

# 13

An itinerant clown, I thought. Party-bound on Sunday evening, I was looking into the rear-view mirror. I picked up the boater from the passenger seat, tapped it on my head, and the clown became another person. This was true escape – I would keep the hat on for the night. I hadn't quite succeeded in copying Tara's well-drawn moustache, several attempts at which had made me look like a camp Hercule Poirot. In the end I had settled for an understated tash, which gave more force to my lips and added some naughty to the 1890s.

A real evening drive to Norwich was a rarity – much less common than the dream of driving to Wyatt Square, with its alternative endings. Earlier I had phoned Molly and company at their *gite* near Blois. James was ecstatic.

'There's an *étang communal* outside our cottage, and last night there were loads of fish rising, and Ben and I will be having a go at them this evening.'

'And I'm going to a fancy-dress party.'

'Mum's going to a fancy-dress party,' he shouted.

Some voices shouted back.

'Molly says you must get a photo taken.'

'Tell her she wouldn't recognise me.'

More shouting, then 'She says, "Who are you going as?"'

'An idiot in a rowing blazer.'

He relayed the message. More shouting.

'Paul says you're to wear a life jacket.'

'And don't you fall into your pond.'

I felt I was sharing at a distance their holiday spirit.

At a roadworks, I waited behind an estate car for an interminable red light to change. A sevenish-year-old boy in the back of the car pointed wide-mouthed towards me, nudged two older brothers and all three waved and laughed. I waved back. This made them disappear behind the seat, only to re-emerge wearing party hats. I waved my boater at them. They tried waving their hats back at me, but ended up hitting each other. Their mother turned round from the passenger seat to prevent a full-scale fight. Through my half-open window I heard Vivaldi strike up. I guessed that the music had been put on in a futile attempt to pacify them. The boys now pretended to dance. In party solidarity, I reached for my tape compartment, but discovered there was only one there – James must have taken the others with him to France. I pulled out the one tape he'd rejected, *Romanian Folk Music*, which the previous owner of the van had left behind. I had once played part of it, but hadn't let it run beyond a mournful bagpipe which sounded like an old 45 vinyl record played at 78. I put it on.

When the lights turned green and I moved forward, an instrumental piece at breakneck tempo filled the van, its wild rhythms evoking all the colours and carousing of a gypsy wedding. Like the kids in front of me, I wanted to dance. I settled for increasing the volume, so it echoed round the metallic void behind me. Pan flute, whistles and strings urged each other on in speed and virtuosity. For a mile or so it was this whirling abandon, not the vehicle, which carried me to the outskirts of the city.

In the suburbs, memories of my November night drive resurrected themselves, but another touch of the volume knob expunged them from my head. I wished now I'd played the whole of this tape earlier. At the next lights, the estate car was again in view. I pulled into the left-hand lane and moved alongside. Waiting for the lights to change, I drummed my hands on the steering wheel in time with the music. The party-hat heads stared in amusement. We exchanged waves. Their parents were embarrassed. I opened my window as far as it would go and gave them a full blast of Romania. Linda Baird would have been proud of me. The boys rolled about laughing on the back seat, while their parents looked at each other with frowns of disgust. When the lights changed, the car shot off in a racing start – driver dad had had enough.

As I pulled away, the next track on my tape began – a woman singing a love song, all hot blood and passion, a dagger tucked under her dress. It gave another boost to my party spirit. But at the next roundabout, I felt a ripple of sickness. At first, I put it down to nervous excitement – when had I last had that feeling of going to a party where I would know hardly anyone? The optimism lasted only a minute, when sharp pains in my stomach had me thinking back to an early-evening snack – the remains of yesterday's prawns. In annoyance I banged the top of the dashboard, steeling myself to ignore what my guts were telling me. As a distraction, I concentrated on my newly discovered music. The ploy worked, since by the time I left the ring-road the upset had receded.

Ruth and Hugh lived on Addington Hill, a quiet road lined with plane trees. Beyond generous front gardens stood sedate early-Victorian villas of local white brick. I didn't need to look at the house numbers to find the party. Towards the top of the hill, a path leading to a large double-fronted house was flanked with bunting, hung in an upward sweep from gatepost to front door. Below a bay window, an enormous bunch of Oxford-blue balloons hovered above a myrtle bush, like mutant berries. In my search for a parking space, a concentration of cars in this part of the road forced me much further down the hill. At last I found a space, but on a steep slope – I hoped my handbrake was in better condition than my wheel bearings. As I climbed out, it occurred to me that that this was the sort of residential area where the presence of a dirty white van would be enough to send the Neighbourhood Watch rushing to their telephones.

On my way to Ruth's house, the old gym shoes I was wearing protested at every step, but at least the sickness had gone. I prepared myself for the 1890s. Walking down the gravel path, I could see through the balloon window two women in Victorian-style dresses, smoking incongruous cigarettes and talking intently. I hoped the party would be more frivolous. I didn't ring the bell, but, pushing the half-open front door, entered a wide hallway lined with Spy prints of judges and politicians. Cigar smoke hung in the air. At the far end was a melee of striped blazers and ankle-length summer dresses, from out of which Ruth appeared, wearing a long-skirted tennis outfit. She dashed up to me, the ends of a navy silk hair band flowing behind her.

'Phoebe, wonderful,' she said, looking me up and down. 'Our first cross-dresser. All the men have been too chicken to drag up as Charley.'

'I feel like a clown.'

'We're all meant to be clowns tonight, though you might find some of Hugh's colleagues a little staid.'

'So what's with the tennis? I didn't know you were sporty. I shall have to inform Joan Tatham.'

'Don't you dare. And tonight all mention of Hillgate's forbidden.'

As Ruth ushered me towards the blazers and dresses, I felt I was stepping into a Victorian painting of Henley Regatta. She introduced me to Hugh, very tall with an apologetic stoop which made his vermilion-striped blazer hang awkwardly about his lean body. Most of the other men's outfits were let down by their footwear, but Hugh wore an impressive pair of correspondence shoes which would have looked well among my luggage at the antiques centre.

Ruth disappeared with, 'Talk later.'

'Ah, Reading.' Hugh addressed my blazer, not me, and I took this to mean Reading University. 'Now you're piped in purple because . . .' A tedious monologue followed about university colours. He had small, darting eyes, but it was difficult to look at his face for long, since he had the habit of standing sideways, so that I had to rely on occasional turns of his head to register the fact that it was me he was talking to. I wondered whether this might be some habit of the courtroom, where it was necessary to keep an eye on witness and judge at the same time. When he had finished his lecture, he sidled off to find me a Pimms.

A small woman in a bulbous black dress, which made her look like Queen Victoria in mourning, fussed her way up to me 'You must be Hugh's new PA,' she said. 'Now aren't you somebody's sister?' As I sifted through some possible replies, she looked me up and down, then yapped, 'Sorry, wrong person,' and bustled off. I began to realise why Ruth enjoyed teaching at Hillgate.

Hugh handed me a drink. 'I've been instructed not to mention the school,' he said, one-eyed again, 'but I gather you're also an antique dealer. Did you see my Spy prints as you came in?'

I nodded.

'They cost me twenty-five shillings each from a shop in Charing Cross Road in the 1970s. A good investment?'

'Oh, I'm sure they were.' I wasn't sure. Thinking back to my London days, I suspected he'd overpaid.

'Very brave of a lady to come as one of Charley's pals. Your father's rowing blazer, is it?'

'No, just an item of stock borrowed from another dealer. Were you an oarsman?'

'Number eight. Never heavy enough for anywhere else.' His eye darted away again, but this time over my head. 'Ah, it's Adam, come to mystify us.'

I turned round and saw a younger man threading through the stripes and paisleys towards us. Half Hugh's age, he was wearing a mauve shirt and jeans. On his chest hung a gourd-like object, suspended from his neck by a leather bootlace, a baffling concession to the party's dress code. He eyed me from boater to gym shoes, as I stared at what looked like a witchdoctor's ju-ju.

'Our new partner,' said Hugh. 'Clearly a fancy-dress minimalist.'

'Brazil nuts,' said Adam. 'It's how they grow – in this capsule thing.' He gave it a rattle.

Hugh lifted his eyes to the ceiling and quoted, *I'm Charley's aunt from Brazil. Where the nuts come from.*

'I've never seen the play,' I said.

'I saw a bit of it on TV once,' said Adam. 'All this late-Victorian stuff is very much your thing, isn't it, Hughie?'

'Everyone has their pet periods,' he said defensively. 'Now, this lady here is an antique dealer – she'll tell you.' Host's duties performed, he slipped away.

Adam and I looked at the retreating blazer, then at each other. He was good-looking in a laid-back way, with untidy brown hair almost the same colour as the object on his chest. I was struck by his pale blue, slightly glazed eyes – perhaps he had needed a couple of drinks before he could face the party. For a moment, he reminded me of a boy home from university, attending an adults' party out of duty, not choice.

'Does everyone really have *their pet periods*?' he asked, mimicking Hugh.

'Old collectors and dealers used to hanker after the eighteenth century.'

'And young antique dealers?'

'I don't seem to meet many.'

'What's this thing worth?' He again rattled his curious pendant. 'Is someone out there collecting them?'

'There's a collector for almost everything. Can we find some fresh air?'

He led me through the kitchen to a morning room, then through a conservatory and out into a textbook town garden. He was as glad of the escape as I was. Outside, on the lawn, by some well-mulched roses, I felt less sick. We walked to the far end, where a York stone path led to a weathered bench. Together we sat down and looked back at the house.

'I thought I was going to throw up,' I said.

'Hugh's parties are like that.'

'No, I mean physically sick.'

'It was very claustrophobic.'

'I suspect it was some prawns I ate before coming here.'

'Can I get you anything?'

I shook my head. For a minute we were silent, watching some guests flow into the conservatory, like tropical fish tipped into an aquarium. By turns hot and cold the upset was spreading through my body. To calm myself I tried long, deep breaths. I was glad to have Adam beside me, far preferable to the alternative I imagined indoors – a fluster of long dresses competing to help me to a bathroom. My guts surged.

I stood up. 'I think I felt better when we were walking.'

We left our glasses on the bench, his empty, mine untasted, and walked around the perimeter of the garden. Inside the house someone had put on *The Pirates of Penzance*. A path of mossy pamments led us along an ivied wall towards a side gate. Some of the fish were flapping out of their tank and moving to the lawn, but a wisteria gave us enough cover to make our exit unnoticed.

Adam opened the gate for me. 'As Hugh might say, shall we take a turn or two down the street?'

I hesitated, but a fanfare of laughter from the house made up my mind. I felt bad about leaving Ruth's party, but my stomach felt worse. At the front gate, an ice-pick stab bent me double. My hat fell off. Motionless, I stared down at it, afraid any movement would turn the blade in my body. When I felt safe, I raised my head and looked at Adam. He said nothing, but his face spoke deep concern and sympathy. He retrieved my boater and took my arm. I risked a few wary steps.

Waking was a palliative. The thought that, without embarrassment, I could be sick in the gutter drove away the need to do so. After twenty cautious yards I attempted a normal pace, feeling well enough to imagine that Ruth was staring down the street from an upstairs window, smiling as I disappeared under the plane trees with a man at least fifteen years younger. I stopped for a moment, shoulders back, hands on stomach, daring the pain to return. I felt nothing.

'Back to the knees-up or go on?' he said.

I thought about the faux-Victorian jollity, the crowded kitchen, the cigar smoke, the blazers on the lawn. 'Can we walk round the block?'

At the top of Addington Hill, we turned into a street of small terraced houses.

'I'm sorry you're unwell,' he said, 'but any excuse to leave that party.'

'Not my kind of do either.'

'Are you a friend of Ruth's?'

'We teach at the same school, or at least . . .' I couldn't bring myself to explain the precarious nature of my job. Adam didn't pursue it. We walked down the street to a pub at the bottom of the road. The heavy beat of a live rock band pulsated towards us. There was a banner on the pub wall: *Stanhope Arms – '50s Night*. We looked at each other.

'Another bloody theme party,' said Adam.

It was my turn to mimic. '*Everyone has their pet periods.*'

He pulled off his pendant seed capsule and dropped it over the low wall of a front garden. We walked past the pub and into Stanhope Road, but the din from the band and the smell of beer pulled me up. This time it wasn't a sharp pain but a rising tide.

I said quietly, 'I'm about to be sick.'

'Gutter, or can you make it to the pub loo?'

'Pub, I think.'

We edged our way through a group of bikers in the doorway and into a bar full of girls in A-line dresses and boys in drainpipes. If anyone looked twice at what I was wearing, I was too ill to notice. The music was deafening. The colours and smoke blurred my vision. I felt unsteady. I doubted I would make it as far as the *Toilets* sign. The vocalist was screaming out the Elvis version of *Hound Dog*. My stomach heaved. I thought I was falling. I felt Adam's hand under my elbow.

'Straight ahead, then left,' he shouted.

With his hands on my shoulders he steered me forwards.

Inside a cubicle – no time to bolt the door – I had the briefest glimpse of water and vomited a torrent. I stared down at it, relieved this hadn't happened over some lawyer's polished shoes. It was hard to believe that I had eaten enough to produce the soup I saw in front of me, and yet I felt I could still bring up more. I wiped my mouth, flushed the loo, locked the door, waited. A finger down my throat made me retch, but brought up nothing. The background beat and pub loo stink made me feel I should be drunk. I hadn't felt so sick since I had been a student. I remembered an evening when a gang of us had tried to drink half a pint at every pub between the college union bar and Trafalgar Square. Somehow, I had made it to the Salisbury in St Martin's Lane, where the mirrors and gilding of its Victorian interior started spinning in front of me, forcing me into an alley round the corner where I was sick. I remembered little else of that night, apart from being bundled into a taxi.

I stared at the factory name on the ceramic pedestal, but the letters jumped about and I couldn't read them. I felt spasmodic churnings. Still nothing happened. It was like waiting between contractions before James was born, only no gas and air or Pethedine. The band was now playing softer music. Some girls came in. The door let in the words of the song, *It's All in the Game*. Then it banged shut.

One of the girls sung a few lines.

'Quite true, of course,' said another voice.

No cubicle door closed. I guessed they were preening themselves in front of the mirror.

'You really mean that, don't you?' said one of them.

'Of course, darling. It's only a game.'

I froze. I knew that voice.

'But what about people getting hurt?'

'People can get hurt in any game. There's a whole bloody industry in sports injuries . . . I think fifties lips were redder than this.'

'So you and Anthony – it's all a game?'

'If you like.'

'For him too?'

'I expect so. Lippy when you've finished.'

'So if he buggered off one morning for an away match, you wouldn't mind? All part of the game.'

'Oh, academic question. Anthony wouldn't.'

'Sounds like it's not a game after all.'

'Yes, it is. Give me that bloody lipstick.'

Another voice slurred out, 'B's right. Anyhow, the fun and uncertainty of a game has far more chance of surviving than some formalised fucking marriage.'

'And who makes the rules of this game?' said the dissenting courtier.

'I do of course,' said B.

They all laughed. One went for a pee. As she sat she called out, 'So you pick them up and play with them like puppy dogs?'

'Something like that,' B shouted. 'Big trusting eyes, slobbery tongues, wagging tails.'

'And what if someone plays games with you?'

'Just let them. All part of the fun.'

'So you wouldn't mind losing?'

'Well, I wouldn't go sulking about like some pathetic housewife.'

A cistern flushed. There was a tap on my door.

A voice – not B's – said, 'You alright in there?'

I managed a muffled, 'Yeah.'

As they left I heard the song *That's Alright, Mama*. I wasn't alright. I unfroze and was violently sick. This time there was nothing left behind. In seconds I felt better. Before I returned to the bar I glanced in the mirror. Someone had written on it in lipstick *It's a game*. The middle stroke of the final Greek *e* continued to form a smiley face which grinned out at me. I tried to rub it out with a tissue, but only smudged it.

'I can play games too,' I told the mirror.

Adam was outside the door, downing a half pint. I took my hat from him and rammed it on my head. He spoke to me, but the music and bar hubbub drowned it.

He bent his head to my ear. I heard the final words, '. . . feeling better?' I nodded. Already I had forgotten the sickness. Now my head was ablaze with anger. From under my hat, a safe disguise, I scanned the pub, but B and court were not in sight – probably in the back room, where I could see flashing lights and a tangle of jiving bodies.

'Let's get out,' I shouted.

It was much easier leaving than entering.

On the pavement Adam said, 'You're looking more lively. Before, you were the colour of your blazer.'

I glanced towards the pub-door loiterers. Adam noticed.

'Someone you know?'

'Not really.'

He raised his eyebrows as if a client had given him an unsatisfactory answer, but didn't pursue it.

'Look, I'm starving. Is there a chippy round here?'

'Are you sure that's wise?'

'And a large bottle of lemonade.'

'Along here.' He led me down the centre of a street of small terraced houses, with the confidence that there would be no traffic.

As the noise of the Stanhope Arms faded behind us, I felt the first tremors of real rage spreading through me. It scared me. I clenched my fists to hold back its flood. But it changed from a liquid within me, in my blood, and became a force shooting out from me like laser lights. Yellow, red and green shafts were striking walls and rooftops where every brick and tile was B. With it, there was a ringing in my head which drowned our footsteps and the sounds of the city, but not the words repeated again and again in my mind, 'I can play games too.'

133

When at last I looked at Adam, I was amazed he showed no sign of seeing what I saw. For a minute I became an urban terrorist testing a new weapon, finding its power and range. Its capabilities seemed infinite. I remembered a story of a woman who, on seeing her son get run over and trapped under a car, found the superhuman strength to lift the car and release him. I had doubted the truth of the report; now I knew it was true. This new strength at first scared me. Until I pictured B with James. Then it was pleasing.

I glanced at Adam, a man in a different world. If the lasers were lost on him, he had noticed my distracted eyes and white-knuckle fists.

'You must stop for a moment,' he insisted.

'No, really.' I slipped with ease between worlds. 'Just get me to those chips and the bottle of fizz.'

I tried to uncoil my hands, but, like a poor swimmer daring to release her fingers from the wall at the deep end of the pool, my hands refused to respond. An uneasy minute later we turned into a wider road, where the rush of traffic switched off the laser show, but for another minute it flashed chevrons in my eyes, like a receding migraine. At last I unclenched my fists and put an arm through Adam's. He snugged it to his side. This was a comfort, but at De Rico's fish bar I felt awkward and was pleased to be left sitting on a low bollard outside while he joined the queue.

Staring down at the sloping concrete forecourt, I became aware of my ridiculous clothes. I looked up at the chippy queue. Only Adam was looking my way. He raised a hand and pulled a face. I nodded back. The wait became a pleasure. If it is possible not to think of anything for a short while, this is what I enjoyed. Inside myself I was aware of a new power, but for the moment I did not need not consider how I would use it. In due course its time would come.

The chips and lemonade were effective medicine. On a circuitous amble back to Addington Hill, we talked trivia – favourite music, pubs, best chip shops – mine was in Whitby, his in Covent Garden. He jokingly suggested we visit both one weekend and make a comparison. I couldn't remember when I had last enjoyed this sort of conversation with a man. Anthony and I must have done so once.

At the foot of the hill we stopped.

He smiled ironically. 'Back to the party?'

'I can't face pirate kings and modern major generals. I'll give Ruth a ring tomorrow and make my apologies. What will you tell Hugh?'

'Shan't see him for a day or two. I'm in Leicester tomorrow, London Tuesday.'

'I've got to go to London one day this week,'

'Come with me. I'm driving down. I have to see a fierce old widow in Hampstead about her will. I'd love some company.'

I accepted, suggesting I meet him somewhere in Norwich, but he insisted it would be as easy for him to meet me in Ulford. Back at my van, I scribbled him some directions.

'You're sure you're okay to drive?' he said.

'A couple more swigs of fizz and I'll be fine.'

In my van rear-view window I watched him disappear, then drove off in the direction of the pub. I pulled up at the house where Adam had thrown away his ridiculous necklace, walked into the garden and retrieved it as a memento of the evening. When I drove past the Stanhope Arms, I didn't even glance towards the door.

# 14

The next morning, I woke heartened with a sense of purpose. The mundane tasks of the morning – the inspection of the garden, the drive down to Molly's house, the watering in her greenhouse, giving Bullace her food, were no longer a routine but a delight. I allowed myself a lengthy coffee break in Molly's kitchen, and watched Bullace devour her food, then glide up to her lair on the dresser, from which she fixed me with her usual hexing stare.

At the Ulford garage, I left my van to have its wheel bearings replaced. It would be ready, I was assured, by 5.00pm, and they lent me an old Fiesta van for the day. Sitting on its oily-smelling seat, cushioned by newspaper, listening to Radio Broadland, on which the radio was permanently fixed, I roared and bumped my way to Walborough in discomfort, but enjoying the anonymity of a strange vehicle. It was a form of disguise. I thought of the fancy-dress party, and of Adam.

A sense of euphoria told me that I would have no difficulty in parking, even at this time. I wasn't disappointed – despite the warm weather and the usual half-term crowds, I soon found a space. But the goods on offer were a let-down. Outside, there was a huge consignment of plant containers from a bankrupt garden centre. This had left no room for the bygones and old flower pots I always hoped for. Inside the main saleroom, things were equally bleak, with row upon row of modern dining suites but little else. The afternoon sale was no better, being crammed with the contents of a Yarmouth private school which had closed the previous year. Desks, chairs and battered, leather-covered vaulting horses filled the front room. I wondered if one day I might see Hillgate's contents in an auction. I was about to return to the van when I noticed a pair of library steps, which were wedged between tea chests full of old text books. They were heavily varnished but undoubtedly Georgian. I tried to look at them without being noticed.

'Only lot here, darling.'

It was the ubiquitous Wesley.

'Want to leave a bid with me?' he said. 'Cosmo's away this week.'

'No, I'll be here for the sale. If it's bought cheap, we can sort it out, can't we?' As I said the words, I was shocked at the assertive tone in which I was inviting myself to join the ring. Wesley didn't argue – perhaps he was too surprised to object.

'Want an ice-cream?' he said.

'No, thanks. See you later.'

I spent the remainder of the morning pacing the town, agonising over the workings of an auction ring, a subject about which I knew nothing. Bluffing my way into teaching Latin was easy in comparison. I phoned Frank for advice, but he was out.

Later, in a stifling saleroom, my chest tightened as the lot number of the steps drew closer. The auctioneer, who normally sped through the selling, today seemed unbearably slow. I stood near the huddle of dealers around Wesley. My heart pounded. I watched one of them buy the steps for £22. One by one they followed him out. I tailed behind. Away from the saleroom, we headed for a corner of the car park. I caught up with the slowest, a shabby old man with half a week's stubble.

'Doesn't this normally take pace in the Dolphin?' I asked.

'Not since we were barred.'

The others were climbing into the back of Wesley's Renault high roof van. I was last in. They sat on the dirty floor. Under the bulkhead, Wesley's mongrel was sleeping on a pile of brown blankets. I perched myself on the left wheel arch. A man in front of me ogled. I was glad I was wearing jeans.

There was other business before the library steps.

'Anyone want the table?' Wesley said.

Everyone but me raised a finger. I didn't remember seeing a table worth buying.

There followed a clockwise mumbling of numbers which I found impossible to follow. I had not the first idea how this secondary auction was being conducted. Looking at the grimy machismo around me, I knew that there was no chance I could join in when it came to the library steps. It was like observing a form of cardless poker with unfathomable rules. I glanced at the dog. It was awake now, alert. Even this animal appeared to have more idea of what was going on than me.

When the mumbling came to an end, the new purchaser of the table paid out the others from a roll of notes. Two other pieces of furniture were similarly reauctioned.

'Steps next,' someone said.

I had had enough. Being near the door, I could easily make some excuse and leave. But as I got to my feet, the dog hunched its back, retched and threw up at Wesley's feet. I froze between wheel arch and door. The others stared at the steaming mess on the van floor, and the shreds of plastic wrapping brought up with it. As the dog returned to its blanket, they all, apart from Wesley, broke into raucous laughter.

'What have you been feeding it?'

'Were you too pissed last night to unwrap its dinner?'

But the stink cut short their amusement. Instantly, I was reminded of my experiences at the Stanhope Arms.

Someone said, 'I'm not staying here any longer,' and bolted.

Wesley held him back. 'There's only the steps left.'

The old man said, 'Give us some bits of paper, and let's get it over and done with.'

A few moments later a scrap of paper was pushed into my hand.

'Write your prices and be quick about it,' said the old man.

This at least I could understand. I scribbled £450. The stench was overwhelming. I thought I might join the dog and throw up.

Wesley collected the papers. 'Wilf holds it at six and a quarter,' he said.

There followed a quick discussion about the size of each share of the payout.

Wilf said, 'Ladies first,' and handed me £50.

I couldn't open the door quick enough. I leaned against the side of the van, breathing fresh air.

I heard someone inside say, 'Do you think that was her first time?'

More laughter.

Infuriated, I considered shouting back a suitable reply. But my new-found inner strength told me to ignore them. As I walked off, the others jumped out coughing from the back of the van. I was glad to get away. At the same time, it occurred to me that for all its picaresque grubbiness, the previous half hour had been more democratic than last week's Hillgate staff meeting.

Driving away from Walborough, I was surprised at the surge of elation of a kind I hadn't felt for years. I was a child going on holiday. Memories surfaced again of Scarborough – Runswick Bay too. This was a familiar road, and I was in a dirty borrowed van, but I might have been in the back of my father's Morris Minor Traveller on the way to the seaside. I wanted to ask, 'When will we see the sea?' My dream segued fifteen years and I was now a young woman, designer-clad, in a TV advert, racing along roads lined with plane trees in the south of France, unlimited cash in my handbag. In the background a woman was singing *Un homme et une fille.*

The fantasy soon faded, but for another mile I felt I was driving high above the ground, free as a swallow, the mid-afternoon fields stretching before me. At Ulford garage, my repaired van was waiting, and I was brought down to workaday reality, but my sense of elation returned when I was told with apologies that my bill wasn't ready – they would send it at the end of the month, and no, they didn't need £50 cash on account. The swallow again spread its wings.

As soon as I was home, I phoned the textile departments of two London auction houses to make appointments for the next day. Neither, however, had a specialist available until Friday. I asked myself if I should cancel the trip. Perhaps I should phone Adam and call it off. Or should I go anyway, and, if so, did I need a new reason, a pretext for spending time with him? Undecided, I phoned the Victoria and Albert Museum, but while I was waiting to be transferred to the appropriate department, an inner voice told me to ring off and try the Textile Institute in Gordon Square instead. Here I was in luck – someone would be happy to see me at 11.30am. I felt relieved that tomorrow was back on track, without any need to vex myself looking for excuses to join Adam.

Next, the uncomfortable task of phoning Ruth with apologies for leaving the party so early. She was out or not picking up. I heard her recorded message and left my own, omitting any mention of Adam. Buoyed with the prospect of a rare day in London, I walked down to Molly's for the watering and hoeing.

An hour later, while Bullace silently attacked some scraps, I sank into Paul's chair at the end of the table and breathed in an almost eerie stillness. This room was normally a place of chatter, banged doors and a ringing phone, but not today. The smell was more intense than usual, the iron-on-damp-linen smell of a lived-in room at rest. Molly must have given the place a five-minute tidy before they left, enforcing a semi-neatness everywhere. Heaped together on a worktop were opened and unopened letters, copies of the *Eastern Daily Press* and school books. In the rack on the draining board stood a few plates with signs of having been washed up in a hurry. A pile of rough-folded school shirts was on the chair next to me. Odd, these tidy-up dashes, I thought. Ten minutes before they left, the room would have been its normal comfortable muddle, and would revert to that state within minutes of their return. And I was certain that Molly hadn't tidied for my benefit. For whom then? The cat? Back on her watchtower, Bullace read my mind and asked the old philosophical question, 'Who sees the object when no eye is in the room. Unobserved, does it still exist?' Back again to Alice, I thought, caught up in highbrow debates with animals.

I looked down at the table top, as scarred and scribbled on as my own. Here, my mind had been spread out and the Anthony-B maze explored a hundred times. These things, like the room, were tidier now, but whether temporary or permanent I couldn't be sure. I ran my fingers over the pine boards and the crumb-catching shrinkage between them. This table and this room were secure, like one of those zones in the games James and Ben played, where you couldn't be caught or shot. Or like the low limestone wall at my old primary school, which we used to leap on when we played off-ground touch, and which was the safe area when we played witches and fairies. I wanted to stay here longer, but Bullace looked down with a disdainful eye, reminding me that this was her home, not mine, and disapproving that I had borrowed, without asking, Molly's large leather shoulder bag for tomorrow's trip. She was telling me that, if all duties had been done, I should be on my way.

# 15

Next day, at 7.20am, I was again at Molly's house, putting out food for an absent Bullace. Five minutes later I was at the village shop, buying a paper and expecting to be the first customer of the day. But a retired gardener who often talked vegetables with me was already at the check-out.

'Lovely morning,' I said.

With no hint of contradiction, he replied, 'Every morning's a lovely morning,' putting me in my place as the city girl I had morphed into, with my creaseless summer dress and light raincoat, one hand on the shoulder bag containing my fragment.

For a few minutes I waited at the edge of the green, a lonely commuter watching cars pass by in twos and threes on their way to Norwich – Ulford's token rush hour. The air was damp from the dew on the rough-cut grass so hated by one or two newcomers to the village, who had recently petitioned, without success, for a manicured green complete with flower beds. I shivered and was pleased to see a red VW Passat slow down and stop alongside me. Adam was at the wheel. The jacket of his grey suit was untidily thrown on the back seat. Wearing a blue gingham shirt and striped silk tie, he was a very different sight from the Sunday night youth with the pectoral gourd. He must have thought something similar of me.

'I prefer you without the moustache,' he said, as he climbed out and opened the door for me.

'And that tie might just have the edge on Brazil nuts.'

'By now they're probably sprouting shoots in someone's garden.'

'They looked far too ancient for cultivation.'

'I've heard that poppy seeds can lie dormant for a century.'

'You'll have to make regular inspections,' I said, thinking of the memento I'd hung on my garage wall.

The speed of his driving at first unnerved me. I wondered if he was out to impress. But after a few miles I realised that it was months since I had travelled in any vehicle, apart from vans with a top speed at a shaking 60mph.

'I guess you haven't seen Hugh or Ruth since Sunday.' I said.

'No. I sent a card – that's all. You?'

'I phoned Ruth and left a message.'

'And blamed me, no doubt, for your deserting the fun.'

'I blamed only the offending prawns.'

He turned on the radio and I read my paper. When I looked up, we were on the A11 beyond Thetford. I watched the flower-heavy elder trees on the roadside dash past us like clouds, and felt that yesterday's new confidence had in no way diminished. I looked at Adam. He smiled back. His mobile was between the seats – I didn't own one myself – and I fantasised about phoning Molly to tell her I was being driven to London by a good-looking man I had known for less than forty-eight hours.

He glanced at my paper. 'How about the quick crossword?' he said.

I read out the clues and together we completed it before Baldock. Meanwhile Cambridgeshire had come and gone unnoticed. The crossword might have been finished much sooner, but the exercise became a source of fun, and I had the unfamiliar experience of laughing in the morning. It was the first time I had shared a crossword since Anthony and I used to do the *Observer Everyman* together, never a cause of humour, since he always had a competitive edge. Games of Scrabble with him had been unbearable.

For the next hour we exchanged our pasts, although I held back the more distressing episodes of the Anthony and B story. He apologised for his conventional upbringing.

'It hasn't made you like Hugh,' I said.

He spoke little about his work. He seemed to regard it as an adjunct to life rather than a career to which he was dedicated. The impression he gave was that, good though he might be at his job, he would prefer to be pursuing other interests which he hadn't yet discovered – an unspoken sentiment I shared.

He dropped me off at Highgate tube station – we were to meet there again at 4.00pm. I breathed in the smells of London with its memories. These were reinforced on the train, where I was surrounded by a gang of students on their way to an exam, several grim-faced and flicking through packs of revision cards, the others all nerves and forced laughter as they made plans for a party after finals. Theirs was an experience from which I had excluded myself, but today I felt no regret. This surprised me and I was unable to find any reason for it. I wondered if the events of Sunday night contributed to this new-found acceptance, but the movement and rumble of the tube rocked my reasoning to inertia. At Goodge Street, I shared a silent lift with the examinees up to the daylight, where they disappeared into the crowds, leaving me open-mouthed and hesitant, like a tourist taking bearings.

Early for my appointment I walked past my old college, then on to Gordon Square and the Textile Institute, part of a terrace of Georgian houses. Here I was admitted into a grave-quiet building by a taciturn secretary who pointed me to an airless waiting room. On a table were a pile of magazines. I selected a copy of *Hali*, the specialist textile magazine, but through nervousness was unable to settle into any one article. I discarded it but found, at the bottom of the pile, a stray auction catalogue – a surprise in an academic environment. I wedged it into my coat pocket to read on the way home.

A moment later a small, sharp-eyed woman with close-cut hair and wearing a shimmering ethnic dress slipped through the door, and introduced herself as the Research Director. Her handshake tailed off in the direction of my bag, indicating that she wanted to get this appointment over as quickly as possible, so she could return to the more important work which I had interrupted. I let her unwrap my fragment with her spindly fingers. She laid it out on the floor in front of us and stepped back in frowning thought.

After half a minute's silent reflection, she dropped to it like a starling attacking a morsel. Crouching, she picked it up, examined its knots and fibres, smelt it, and at last looked at me, finding a condescending smile.

'It's not quite my field – I'm primarily a tapestry specialist. I'll see if Dr Urgup is available.' She flew away, leaving me staring at my fragment on the waiting room's industrial cord carpet.

Several minutes later she returned with Dr Urgup, a heavily built man with the look more of a carpet dealer in an Istanbul souk than a London-based academic. He possessed more than enough charm to compensate for his colleague's brusqueness. He picked up the remnant and nestled himself in a chair by the window, holding it up in front of himself as if reading a newspaper. The Director stood at his side, impatient as he asked me where I lived, how I had come across the piece, and whether I had any other fragments. There followed some mutterings and whispers between the two of them which I was unable to follow. At one point her eyes darted to me to see if I had overheard some confidential information.

Finally, she turned to me with another difficult smile. 'Your fragment seems to have come from an old Kirman carpet, known to us by several other similar pieces. But we can't say much more until we've carried out further research.'

'An interesting find though,' said Dr Urgup. 'Seventeenth-century fragments like this . . .'

The Director interrupted. 'If we could borrow the piece for a week or two, we would be happy to carry out further research for you.'

'Thank you,' I said, 'but I would like to hang on to it for a while.' I was pleased that she looked disappointed. Dr Urgup beamed and graciously handed it back to me.

'Is it a collectable item?' I asked.

Dr Urgup was about to reply, but she interrupted again. 'We are solely an academic body. We're unable to give opinions about value and collectability. Your fragment really requires a little more study before it can be placed in its true context.'

'So I was right not to throw it away?'

Before she could restrain him Dr Urgup burst out, 'Oh, most certainly. That would have been a very great pity.'

'The study of small pieces like this is very much Dr Urgup's area of expertise,' she said, in an attempt to lift the conversation back to the world of scholarship. But they had told me all I needed to know.

With a reluctant handshake from her and an effusive one from him, his card furtively pressed into my palm, I left. Outside, I was glad to inhale London air fresher than the stale atmosphere of that waiting room, and to see real starlings pecking at crumbs on the pavement.

I looked into my bag and patted its contents. How much are you worth, I thought, how much? I tossed figures around in my head as I walked to Oxford Street. I knew that it didn't take much of a seventeenth-century scrap of carpet to be worth a thousand or two. Before I had reached the bottom of Tottenham Court Road, I had decided to have some good photos taken of it, send them to a few auction houses, choose the most promising autumn sale, sell it and unload the proceeds on my mortgage. The weight of the fragment in Molly's shoulder bag felt lighter. Life too.

In Oxford Street I bought James some summer clothes. Next, I walked to South Moulton Street to indulge a few fantasies and search for a summer sale. Before facing the shops, I sat in the café at the top of the street from where, over coffee and a sandwich, I watched lunchtime London pass by with all its self-assurance. I tried to catch some of its sparkle. Wandering down, I discovered that none of the shops had a sale, and things I liked in Labels for Less were still more than I could afford. Over the road to Colefax and Fowler for more fantasies, and on to a few galleries, which reminded me that my stock in the antiques centre was, in comparison, so much rubbish. I couldn't bring myself to walk down to the gallery in St James's where I had worked, so I returned to South Moulton Street, where I succumbed to some shoes, persuading myself that they would be ideal for teaching. As I paid, an inner voice assured me that my job had every chance of continuing, then becoming permanent. With this encouragement, at the top of the street, I treated myself to iced coffee and another quick peep at my fragment. To see it wrapped, snug in my bag, was almost to have the deeds of my house back in my hand.

When I met up again with Adam, he was exhausted and there was dust on his trousers. In the back of his car were some old tin trunks.

'I go to help her rewrite her will and end up clearing her attic,' he said. 'I hope your day was more successful.'

I told him about my fragment.

'So you have something to celebrate.'

'Possibly, but it's too early for champagne,'

During a ten-minute wait at Apex Corner we were hemmed in by coachloads of foreign students. Later, on the A1, when all looked clear, we joined another frustrating tail-back. Even with the air con the car was hot. Tired, I leaned back and slept.

I dreamed I was back at my old school in the sanatorium. John Copeford, the Mock Turtle, was visiting me. I was almost too feverish to know he was there, let alone speak. Through drowsy, half-closed eyes I saw the red blanket in front of me and the blurred outline of the iron bed-end. For a moment, I smelt his tobacco breath on my face, but he moved away. And then I felt his hand under the covers between my legs. He was hurting me. I was too terrified or too comatose to move or shout.

In the car, I woke shaking, perspiring. We were driving in darkness. I thought Adam must have touched me.

The car moved out of the underpass into daylight. I stole a glance towards him.

'Hatfield,' he said gently. 'You've been asleep half an hour.'

I lowered my eyes. I felt no physical pain. Slowly, I accepted that Adam had not assaulted me. Even so, against reason, I did not immediately dismiss it as a dream. I stared ahead and waited for the terror to disappear. But it did no more than distance itself, where it remained fixed, looking at me.

'We should have bought an evening paper,' he said.

'What?'

'For the crossword.'

'Sorry. I wasn't with you.'

The journey sped by. I saw signs to Knebworth and Stevenage, but the blanket, the iron bed and the face remained as pale silhouettes in front of me, like the shadows of a colour plate in an old book which have leached through the paper and the protective tissue to the next page.

To distract myself from the dream I pulled out the auction catalogue I had taken from the waiting room. I tried to read. I was unable. John Copeford remained too close. Nor was I ready for conversation with Adam. It wasn't until we were beyond Baldock that a part of me, deeper than reason, accepted what my head knew to be true: I was now fully safe. Again I looked at my catalogue.

'Anything interesting?' asked Adam.

I read out one of the cataloguer's more fanciful descriptions: '*Even the Bactrian camel which voided on this rug could not obscure its essential beauty.*'

'Pissed on but okay,' translated Adam.

I wanted to smile, but couldn't. I read out some more descriptions. Slowly, the terror shrank from sight. I talked to Adam about Anthony and B. He listened and said little. I looked out of the window at the fields. The barley had changed since the morning to a tarnished copper which, at times, in the evening light became a hazy mauve.

Near Norwich, he suggested we stop at a pub for supper. Knowing I wouldn't be the best company, I said I would prefer to get home. It felt ungracious, but I was unable to put aside the pain of the dream and a picture in my mind of the unseen face in the room.

When we arrived in Ulford, I directed him to Molly's so I could check over the house. To make up for my earlier unsociability I invited him in. I told him to find himself a beer while I watered the tomatoes, but he insisted on helping. His clumsiness with the watering can made me suspect that this was his first ever stint of gardening.

Afterwards, in the kitchen, unable to find any beer, I opened a bottle of wine. We sat opposite each other – the first time we had done so.

'Do you always help yourself to other people's drink?' he said.

'Only here. They do the same in my house when I'm away.'

I told him about Molly, Paul and the village. I thought it would sound very parochial to him, but he listened attentively, and when I apologised for the mundanity of it all, he pressed me to continue.

'What's social life like in the village?' he asked.

'Whatever we make it. For clubs and organisations, people go to Cantisham.'

I thought he was about to make some comment, but he remained silent. Our eyes locked for a few seconds. I saw the faintest smile on his face. It felt that this was the first time we had met. In that silence, I thought he might rest his hand on mine, but I turned my head away, and the moment passed. When I turned back, he was looking up at Bullace; he had only just noticed her. She was, as usual, surveying the kitchen from the top of the dresser. The stillness in the room was both exhilarating and disquieting.

Perhaps to break the silence, he asked, 'So how do you keep yourself sane in the country?'

'One or two friends, James, my garden. I scribble the occasional poem.'

I hadn't intended to add this last – it was a private pastime. I may once have mentioned it to Molly, but to no one else.

'I write a little myself,' he said. 'We should exchange efforts.'

'Yes, perhaps,' I said, quickly standing to leave. I felt uneasy with this sort of conversation, in this room, across this table which was special for Molly and me. I wish I'd gone along with the pub suggestion.

As the Passat turned into my drive, Adam made some comment about the house, and I wanted to invite him in, but a deep-seated caution overcame the wish. I merely thanked him for the lift, adding, 'You must come for supper sometime.' It was a comment which satisfied neither of us.

When I was alone indoors, the dream resurfaced. There was a good hour of daylight remaining. To clear my mind I set about my vegetable plot with the hoe. But for once my gardening failed me – the more I exerted myself, the more the nightmare persisted, to the point where I was no longer staring at the earth in front of me, but at that solitary room where I lay in lifeless terror. Then – and I can remember the exact place at the end of a row of dwarf beans two yards from the greenhouse, and can even now see the blade of the hoe turn and freeze where it happened – I saw the first glimmer that this was not dream but memory. I screamed and threw down the hoe. I rushed to the house, trampling on plants. By the time I was pulling off my boots in the bathroom I was streaming with tears. I turned on the bath taps and wept above the noise of running water.

Later, unable to face my own bedroom, I fell into James's bed. But the possibility of sleep was absurd. I went downstairs and made myself hot chocolate. For several hours I remained in a chair, recalling every detail I could bring to mind of my life at the school, searching for the slightest recollection at the time of what had been done to me. And throughout this searching I held, suspended in front of myself above the table, the two faces of John Copeford – the respected public face of the young schoolmaster and the face in the room at the sanatorium. But nowhere could I find any trace of knowledge of this second person who, until now, I knew, had been successful in concealing himself. The shadowy silhouette remained, but the engraving on another page had been carefully cut from the book.

Outside, the darkness was turning grey. I was cold and wrapped a scarf around myself. I wished that Molly were here. I imagined a conversation with her.

'You know about false memory,' she warned.

'*This* is true – I know it.'

'But you could never prove it,' she said gently.

'I don't have to. I know. That's enough. Every day of my life since then has been neutral, living out my time in a half-existence, somewhere between drift and avoidance.'

'Were you considering taking your case further? If your memory is correct, there may be other victims.'

'I don't yet know what I'll do.'

She frowned at me, then quietly said, 'Are you certain that one unverifiable event, so long ago, could have had such consequences?'

'It happened,' I shouted. 'And the proof is in everything I have felt, or rather haven't felt, since.' I broke into tears. 'No wonder my marriage collapsed. If Anthony's life had some flaw, God knows what mine was like.'

Molly tried to calm me. 'Even if what you say did happen, terrible though it was, can you be certain of its impact?'

I lost patience with her. She seemed to be accusing me of making a fuss over some minor upset in my distant past. Now Paul appeared and talked about the butterfly effect – one small, faraway, unnoticed beating of wings which can trigger a tornado.

Alone at my table, I sat sobbing, again and again asking myself whether one act of abuse of a few minutes duration could affect a lifetime. Each time I asked the question I saw John Copeford's face, felt his hand, felt helpless. I reviewed my history.

Slowly, I began to own a sexual reticence, a long-lost trust in myself and an inability to be spontaneous. I sank into self-pity – pity that for so many years I had suffered life without ever finding deep pleasure, and had expected nothing more. No wonder Jane Eyre had been a kindred spirit, with her harsh precept: *we were born to strive and endure.* I had endured long enough. I felt a rising anger. I knew that as soon as possible – today – I must drive to Bramshead and confront the bastard. This, at least, was neither drift nor avoidance.

# 16

I t was 4.30am, but sleep now was impossible. Hadn't I had too much
sleep over the years? My life owed me a heavy debt of wakefulness. I
would phone St Michael's first thing to see if John Copeford was in
residence. I had no idea of their half-term dates. Perhaps he was away, or
in the last two years had moved schools. This made me think of Hillgate,
and I realised that, such had been my state the previous evening, I had
failed to check my answer machine. There was one message: *Dora
Prideaux. Tuesday morning. Phoebe, I do hope you can be with us after half-
term until at least the end of the summer term. Please phone me.*

A few days ago this news might have been a cause of celebration.
This morning it was unimportant. Even so, I replayed the imperious
voice to hear again the critical words 'at least', hinting of further work in
the autumn. Tonight I would phone and tell Adam. Ruth too. And
Molly? I was too angry to want to speak to her. I checked myself. My
conversation last night with her had been imagined – how ridiculous
that my confidante of the kitchen table should be relegated to third on
my list, with three-day Adam first.

At 9.00am I made the phone call and gave a false name to a St
Michael's secretary. 'Yes,' she told me, 'Mr Copeford is in residence, but I
must tell you . . .'

I rang off. I didn't want to receive some officious advice about making
appointments to see members of staff.

Less angry, I set off for Surrey, enjoying the summer morning and a strange aura of calm. The first hour and a half was on the roads we had used yesterday, but they felt new to me, like travel in a foreign country. I had no clear plan for the day. I certainly didn't trouble myself with an imagined conversation with my former housemaster – there had been enough imagined conversations last night. Paramount was my urge to look him in the face with my new-found knowledge. Now, twenty years later, I realise the stupidity, the danger of what I was doing. But on that Wednesday morning, heading for the M25, I was beyond reason. I had a single blinkered aim – face-to-face confrontation. Much later Paul said this was brave of me. He was wrong. I was on the edge, acting on an impulse which had little to do with what the rational world calls bravery.

At the first motorway services beyond the Dartford Crossing, I stopped to eat. I felt at peace, took my time, satisfied a voracious appetite and read the papers. It might have been the first day of a holiday. I had had no sleep last night, but wasn't tired. Not until I turned off the motorway did the Surrey landscape remind me that I was close to where I had spent four years of my life. And it struck me as it had when I had first seen it – a London dormitory pretending to be countryside, and lacking the clear boundaries provided in my native county by the Pennines, the Dales, the North Yorkshire Moors and the sea. And as before, the Surrey light was filtered – dimmed compared to the light I remembered from early childhood, and certainly not that of my adopted county. Beyond Guildford, even the apparent wildness of the Devil's Punchbowl felt artificial, as if designed on a massive scale by some nineteenth-century landscape architect.

Turning off the A3 into Bramshead, I felt I knew every building and tree. Over the years the leafy roads, the tall beeches, the driveways with their azaleas, and the shrub-filled gardens had hardly changed – they might have been waiting for my return. I was now half a mile from the school. In the main street, only one shop remained of the row I remembered, and I was sad that the antiquarian bookshop I had once loved was now a private house. I slowed as I passed it. Here, in my second term, I had discovered Langdale's *Topographical Dictionary of Yorkshire*. Since it was published in the county in 1809, there might have been a copy in Haworth parsonage. The bookseller had apologised that, among other damage, its map of the turnpike roads was torn. I didn't mind and happily paid £5.00 for it: *a piece of extravagance I could ill afford*. It absorbed some of the many hours when I was bored at school; reading it was to be back home. I could remember some of its entries: *Keighley, Fairs, May 8 for Horned Cattle and Horses*. I had imagined them selling unicorns. I was now close to St Michael's.

My first sight of the school was the stone spire of the chapel. To see it again was to hear the sound of four hundred voices, predominantly boys, haranguing God with a hymn at the daily assembly. I have never lost the faith of my childhood, but over four years that chapel did its best to extinguish it. Even now, if I attend a church service, I prefer one without hymns. I was glad when the spire disappeared behind pine trees.

Avoiding the front entrance of the school, I approached St Michael's via the playing fields, the sight of which revived the terror I had felt on seeing them with my parents that first time. I shot one glance to the sanatorium before quickly turning away; I had no interest in the place of abuse, only the perpetrator. I parked in the car park near the dining hall, a stone-built Victorian Gothic building with a central tower. From here, the sight of groups of pupils in their maroon blazers told me that this week was not St Michael's half-term.

Driving down, I had considered confronting John Copeford outside the staffroom, but now this felt unwise. First, there was a possibility the staffroom had relocated – I was annoyed I had not read the old pupils' magazines which might have contained details of such trivial but now crucial information. Secondly, he would have safety in numbers. My experience of staffrooms was that, while teachers might fight among themselves, when a colleague was threatened, the others, like a pack of animals protecting one of their own kind, would rush to defend him. No, I needed a better strategy.

I thought about the school timetable and where he might be that afternoon. After all these years I was in no hurry – why not look for him at the end of the school day, perhaps at his home? I didn't know for sure where this was, but could soon find out. As I listened to the clatter of pans from the kitchen's open windows – a sound which had not altered during the generation since I was last here – I noticed in my wing mirror a workman repairing a net in the tennis courts behind me. I climbed from my van and walked towards him.

'Excuse me,' I called through the wire. I tried to sound like a visiting parent. I certainly looked the part, with my floral-print dress and the shoes I had bought yesterday. 'I'm looking for Mr Copeford's house.'

He looked up from his work. 'Number four, The Aspens.'

I remembered The Aspens, a row of 1920s school houses at the edge of the grounds. I then recognised the man as the same young assistant groundsman who had started working here when I was at the school. He made me wonder how the years would have changed John Copeford. Back in my van, I considered ways of filling the hours before 6.00pm, by which time he was likely to have returned home. But my impulse reasserted itself, and I drove straight to The Aspens.

I parked at the end of the row of near-identical black and white mock-Tudor houses. They hadn't altered since I had last seen them, apart from tarmac drives where I remembered badly drained shingle. Each building expressed its individuality through the smallest of spot-the-difference details – the height of the chimneys, the shape of a small upstairs window, the turnings of the oak posts which supported the porch; perhaps, at St Michael's, near-identity but not exact uniformity was deemed the appropriate style for schoolteachers' houses. It was disturbing how well I remembered these architectural niceties. I left my van and walked to number four. The low walls, the privet hedges behind with their sour smell, and the varnished double gates of each house had not changed with the years. And the flagstones on the pavement were still uneven; my feet remembered every contour.

With no idea what I would say to whoever answered the door, I rang the bell. There was no answer. Perhaps he was, after all, in the staffroom, or elsewhere in the main school. I was about to ring a second time when the door was opened by a grey-haired woman in a faded green linen dress. It was only when she smiled that I recognised her as the White Queen, Bridget Copeford, who for a time had taught me English.

'Phoebe, how lovely,' she said.

I struggled to adjust to the fact that this was the same person who had carried out the day-to-day running of the girls' house, the attractive woman who had been fantasised over by so many of the boys, and who had made heads turn in Sunday chapel, where her stylish clothes and auburn hair stood out among the dowdiness of the other masters' wives.

She gave me a hug from which I shrank.

'So many old pupils have come to visit John,' she said. 'I've been quite overwhelmed.' She showed me into the hallway and whispered, 'He's very weak. Come through to the kitchen and tell me all about yourself over a cup of tea, then we'll see if he's awake.'

I followed her into a tidy kitchen where every work surface was spotless, uncluttered. We sat on wicker chairs by French windows overlooking an equally well-ordered garden dominated by two large beds of deep pink peonies.

'It must be very hard for you,' I said, hoping this would elicit more information about her husband's apparent illness.

'Motor neurone disease is a long haul, but I hope he can stay here at home for as long as possible.'

'I am so sorry,' I said. It was a lie.

As she made the tea, she told me that over the last three months a succession of pupils had come to visit him, and it was unlikely that he would survive the year. I felt cheated. I had come here to confront him, not make a sick visit.

Trapped, angry, I fought to make some conversation, giving an abridged and rosy account of my life. I then listened to a description of the illness, which made me understand why a woman I guessed to be in her early fifties looked ten years older. She looked away from me when she told me how devastating it had been when the illness was diagnosed. I felt sorry for her. I doubted she had ever known about her husband's secret life.

She turned back to me and smiled. 'I shall always remember studying *Emma* with you,' she said. 'I can still hear you protesting that we should choose another set book. "Charlotte Brontë didn't care much for Jane Austen. Nor do I," you said. Did you ever change your mind?'

'I'm afraid not. Did you know I used to like sneaking phrases from the Brontës into my essays on *Emma*?'

'I never spotted that,' she said.

I returned her smile. We both looked out on the peonies and sipped our tea. She had been one of the better teachers. In an attempt to make our set book come alive, she had taken us all for a picnic on Box Hill, where she had read to us Jane Austen's account of Emma's picnic in the same place. I had been impressed by her kindness, but had not been won over to Jane Austen.

She moved to the present, describing the horrors of John's gradual loss of movement in the limbs, his wasting away, his loss of speech, his struggle each day against inexorable deterioration, his frustration and anger – both increasingly hard to express. I listened and saw the tears in her eyes, but had not a drop of sympathy for him. It was no more than belated justice. It gave me some pleasure.

A downstairs room, his study, had been transformed into a bedroom. Outside the door, she whispered, 'He's unable to speak anymore, but his hearing is perfect. Sometimes I manage to lip-read what he says.'

When she led me into his room, no description could have prepared me for the creature I saw on the bed. At first, nothing about him bore any resemblance to the energetic man in his late-twenties I remembered. Could this papery-skinned wreck of humanity, with hands as pale and creased as the white sheet on which they lay motionless, have any connection with the housemaster I remembered? Or the history teacher whose dynamism in the classroom was so infectious, whose drama productions were, for this school, so revolutionary? Or the squash player who could beat anyone in the school, staff member or pupil? Or the visitor to the sanatorium?

Bridget sat on a chair to his right and held his hand. I sat on the other side. He looked towards neither of us, but stared towards shelves of historical biographies, not noticing our presence. I was sure his head had shrunk, but around the eyes, which seemed too large for his face, I saw hints of the person I remembered. My slow recognition of him made me draw back.

'Someone has come to see us, John,' Bridget said.

He moved his head to me a fraction, but no more than was necessary for those oversize eyes to meet mine. It was also as much as his withered neck could manage. His face carried no glimmer of emotion.

'It's Phoebe Wilson,' she said. At the mention of my maiden name I was a pupil again. I shivered.

There followed some spasmodic blinking, and I felt those sea-creature eyes pierce through me. He knew who I was. I looked back with an equal lack of emotion. As I did so, his face muscles tensed and his mouth began to open and close. I was reminded of a stranded fish, not quite dead. He clearly wanted to speak. This was too great an effort for him since, after a few seconds of contortion, the muscles relaxed and his eyes resumed their vacancy. I thought this was the end to our communication. Again I felt cheated.

In another part of the house a phone rang. Bridget left the room to answer it. While she was absent, I leaned over his bed and again looked into those eyes.

Slowly, I said, 'I've come to say I know what you did all those years ago, when I was fourteen.' More firmly, restraining myself from shouting, I said, 'I know. Yes, I know all about your past – what you did to me when I was ill. You thought I would never know, but I do.'

His face muscles tightened again, but his head was motionless. I felt the power of his will. I was terrified that, despite his condition, he would find the strength to sit up and glare at me, once again move a hand. Finally, I assured myself he was incapable. Struggling to overcome my anger, in a low voice, I said in his ear, 'It has taken me twenty-six years to discover – all my adult life, you bastard. How many other victims do you have?'

His features tightened once more, his mouth opened a little, and he let out an almost inaudible groan, the effort of which sapped his strength. It sounded like the cry of a wounded animal heard from a great distance. It made me shudder. Frail though this remnant was, he could still make me afraid. Once again he stared ahead. I wanted to hit him, but had no wish to make physical contact. I stood upright and looked down on him. For the first time, I realised that I was the stronger person. And it was from this vestige of life, spent though he was, that I was drawing strength. I smiled at his weakness.

Bridget returned to the room. She laid her hand on his again. He turned his eyes to her. His lips made slight movements.

'He has something to say to you,' she said. She concentrated on the small tremors on his mouth. 'He says, "I . . . am . . . sorry." ' She paused. The tremors continued. 'He says that he's sorry you find him like this.'

His face now became contorted. He was clearly distressed by the misunderstanding of what he had tried to say. Again she looked at him.

'He says, "I am sorry. I am sorry." '

His face sank back to the stare.

She released his hand and turned to me. 'He gets very upset that he can no longer communicate with his friends.'

His eyes were now shut, but his mouth remained open. I thought he was waiting for the strength to say more. For a minute there was no further sound. She pointed to the door. If she had any notion of her husband's secrets, she had become as adept as him at hiding them.

In the hallway she said, 'It is so good of you to come.' There were tears in her eyes. Whether she knew about his past or not, I again felt sorry for her.

Halfway back to my van, the shock hit me. I felt it as a slight stumble, as if my confidence in knowing every paving stone had been upset by recent subsidence. I grasped hold of the wall for support. I looked down at my feet, waiting for my balance to return. The swaying continued in my head, but, by concentrating on the leaves in the hedge and by breathing in their smell, I restored my balance. Down the road, a boy and girl in school uniform were holding hands. They reminded me of the notices John Copeford used to pin up, forbidding what the school called PDA, public displays of affection. And for all these years, I thought, he has been concealing what was infinitely worse. I feared for the drive home and tried not to think of him.

For the first mile, I drove with excessive caution, expecting the swaying to resume, and making impossible efforts to empty my head of him. But those enormous eyes, like the eyes of a great fish seen through the glass walls of a walk-through aquarium, fixed themselves in my mind. And his groan remained in my ears. Driving now became increasingly difficult. It would be unsafe to continue the journey. I stopped and looked at the map. I had forgotten how close I was to the RHS gardens at Wisley. Here, I knew, there was a chance I could expunge him. The decision held him at a distance, so that on my way I was able to recall my one previous visit. This had been a girls-only outing, organised by the headmaster's wife, during my first term at St Michael's. It was her idea of a welcoming gesture. None of us had really enjoyed it, and if the gardens appealed to me more than to most of my companions, I felt it safest to keep the pleasure to myself. This wasn't difficult. I found it hard to enthuse over the most spectacular September flowers, since they all shared the unforgivable fault of being in the same county as the school, and so far from home. I was more willing to criticise than to enjoy, and it was these negatives which now provided my strongest images of the place: clumps of fierce orange callas, in my mind more suited to the Mediterranean, and neat lines of colchiums which cried out for disorder.

The car park and entrance buildings had changed since my first visit – a pleasing discovery. I bought my ticket and walked in, looking for the first quiet seat I could find. On another occasion, I might have ambled about, notebook in hand, Surrey forgiven, pausing at every bed to read plant labels. Today I dropped onto an empty bench and looked ahead. In front of me, beyond a billiard table grass border, was the rectangular pond Wisley calls The Canal, a name which annoyed me, as it had years before, being nothing like the Leeds and Liverpool Canal near the old rectory. Beyond, I could see raised beds with the Conifer Lawn behind them. In themselves they held no interest for me. I was hoping the atmosphere here would offer some peace. But there was none. I was too angry. The water lilies in front of me transformed themselves into John Copeford's fish eyes. I turned away. Looking to my left, I saw the building called the Laboratory, built to look like a Tudor manor house – more sham. Done with deception, I got up from the bench. The rose behind me was labelled *Caritas*. I felt charitable to no one.

On next to the Formal Garden with its summer bedding plants. Again, all too organised and disciplined. Now the Walled Garden with its fountain, intimate, romantic – not what I was looking for. What I needed was very different. I found it down the steps as I entered the Wild Garden, losing myself under the trees among the hostas and trilliums.

I blamed all three of them: my great aunt and my parents for listening to her. As soon as I had left home, I had become vulnerable. How right my own judgement had been at the time. I blamed myself too, for not fighting harder to stop them getting their way. And I blamed the school. And that wasting, bedridden body. Why had he done it? Had his wife been so admired, such a social success, that even he, something of an educational star himself, felt eclipsed by her, perhaps envied her, before turning elsewhere to gain whatever sort of gratification or power he craved. I hoped that my visit had shaken every remaining cell in his body, and that he had sufficient time left to agonise over it. He once must have been delighted to find me barely conscious. I was delighted to have found him alive enough to hear me accuse him.

Walking by a stream banked by ferns, I seemed to have the garden to myself. So I sat on the ground and examined my life from that time in the sanatorium to the present. I had done so last night, but anger had clouded my thoughts. Now, listening to the gentle sound of rippling water, I reviewed the years with clarity. It wasn't many minutes before the dominant threads of detachment and indecision appeared on the surface. I had spent my life pretending to live, limping in a twilight world where the shadows couldn't tempt me to believe that there was some reality beyond them. It wasn't a world of an arrested childhood, but a world whose reality deserved so little credit that to commit myself to it was utterly pointless. Hardly surprising that my history course at university seemed futile compared with my interest in art, so much of which was closer to my way of thinking. No surprise the three unsatisfactory, short-lived relationships before Anthony appeared. And God knows how he and I got together, or stayed together for so long. If only this had been simply about physical sex. It wasn't. That diseased creature had not simply touched me, but my whole world. No wonder Anthony and I had split up. How long can anyone live with a ghost?

I got up and walked in the direction of a towering sequoia by the lake. Now the paths were more open. No wonder I had been depressed. When had I not been? Not since about the last time I was in these gardens, pretending I liked them better than I did – a more innocent deception than many since. What chance the counsellor? What chance the pills? At least Molly was right there. I found myself walking among pines and maples in a far limb of the garden. I tried to think of the future. It felt a hopeless task. I was only beginning to emerge from an illusory existence – what did I know about (or could hope from) a world of substance? Allowing the colours to distract me, I wandered around a field of heathers near the river, then back through the pines, peopled now with groups of visitors.

I looked ahead and was surprised by the new restaurant staring at me across the lawn. At least the building looked what it was – no pretence here. I walked in through the chattering tea-drinkers, bought a drink, found the one remaining table, and looked down towards the lake.

'Can we join you, love?'

Before there was time for me to be fully aware of their presence, two elderly women were settling themselves at my table.

'We're not disturbing you, are we?' said one.

'I was just about to leave.'

'Don't let us rush you away.'

I wanted to go, but their voices struck warm memories, and I made room for them, resuming my gaze through the window, while they argued whether one of them 'could manage all those steps to the top of Battleston Hill.'

I looked at the old biddies with their northern accents – Leeds, I guessed – and whose clothes and mannerisms were like those of Aunt Hilda's whist-playing cronies. Odd, I thought, how each generation produces identikit geriatrics.

'I'll never make it t' mixed borders, let alone trial field,' said the heavier one. Then she turned to me. 'Do you have a garden yourself, love?'

I nodded. They returned to their bickering about which part to visit next, about the Wisley facilities, the coach trip, the driver, their arthritis. I resented the intrusion.

To put a stop to the argument, I said, 'I'm on my way out soon. I'll help you up the steps to the borders.'

Their gratitude was almost as tiresome as their squabbling. So they finished their tea, and with the occasional, 'Come on, you can do it,' I manoeuvred the large Irene, weighty and sweaty under her white cardigan and polyester dress, up towards the borders, where her friend, Margaret, produced a camera and took photos of the more showy flowers, then one of Irene and me in front of some hideous, flame-coloured lilies.

Irene turned round and admired the beds. 'Ooh, they're a proper show, aren't they?'

'Wonderful,' I said.

We slipped into a conversation about our favourite flowers and our gardens at home.

'Which part of Yorkshire are you from, love?'

'Near Keighley.'

This set them going on whether someone they knew still lived there, an argument which took them down to the gift shop, where they insisted on buying me a tea towel and a cookery book. I was glad to see them onto their coach with thirty other pensioners. But as they waved from a window, I realised that for an hour I hadn't thought of John Copeford, and wondered who had done whom the favour in the gardens. At my van, I collapsed in my seat and slept for an hour.

Back in Ulford at around eight, I drove straight to Molly's for the daily chores. From there I phoned Adam's flat. I wanted to tell him about my day, but was unable. Instead, I shared with him my job news.

'Wonderful. Now, for God's sake get yourself a contract,' he said.

'I'm sure they'll advertise the vacancy and have interviews.'

'Nonsense. Be insistent. They know you're brilliant at your work. Make out that you've had other schools approaching you.'

'I'm not sure about the "brilliant".'

'Of course you are. I enjoyed yesterday. Do you want two empty tin trunks?'

'Any bearer bonds left inside?'

'Sadly, no. Shall I drop them round sometime?'

'That would be kind.'

'I'm being sent to New York for four weeks. Can I call you when I get back?'

When he rang off, I felt I had been unnecessarily cold. I wished we had made a more definite time to meet. I blamed the weight of the day for dulling my conversation. I should have postponed phoning him until morning.

Bullace looked indignant: yesterday's food had been early, today's was late, and what was I doing using their phone? Even so, I phoned France. There was no reply. I dragged myself down to the vegetables and greenhouse. Our local efforts aren't quite Wisley standard, I thought. But when I had finished the watering, I realised that the gardens of afternoon and evening had done their work, and had returned those saucer eyes to the shrunken man staring at books he would never again read.

After garden duties I decided that Bullace must have forgiven my behaviour, since, waiting on the back step, was a present of a pair of yellow feet, the remains of a young moorhen. I had intended to make myself a cup of tea, but since the last of the milk was in the cat's dish, I settled for a large gin and tonic which I drank in Paul's chair. This time there was no animal to frown at me – perhaps she was out searching for more macabre offerings.

The following day I phoned Hillgate Hall. I told Dora I could teach until the end of term, and pressed her about work in September. It was wasted effort.

'I will certainly pass on what you say to Dr Lennox,' she said.

I was left with the same feeling I had had during the divorce process, when each solicitor's letter, with its reported steps of progress, only opened up a few more twisting byways I was forced to explore.

Next, I again tried the party in France. Molly answered, said all was well with them, and asked me about Sunday night. I told her about Adam, omitted everything about the Stanhope Arms, mentioned the trip to London, but said nothing of yesterday; some news deserves better than a phone call.

'It sounds like you've been making the most of our absence,' she said.

'Oh, and I've got teaching until the end of term.'

'They should give you a full-time contract.'

'That's what Adam said.'

'So it's "what Adam said" already, is it?'

'No, it's not.'

Commotion in the background was summoning her to some holiday emergency.

'Tell me more about Saturday night,' she shouted.

'When you get home,' I said.

She passed the phone to James, who shared with me some discoveries about sinking lines and lures.

Lastly, I phoned Ruth who was delighted with my news and not in the least offended by Sunday night's abrupt departure. It was a relief too that she said nothing about Adam.

The remainder of the day and most of the week was absorbed by lesson planning or gardening. I was determined never again to be stranded, scared and devoid of ideas in front of a class of hardened teenagers. So I devised reserve strategies to meet the frequent occasions at Hillgate when my initial teaching plan floundered. I found myself calling these my 'safety nets'. Educationalists, I was certain, would have pulled my system to pieces, but I consoled myself with the thought that my methods had to be better than Duggy's or Brian's for all their degrees, Certificates in Education and greater experience. For three days, apart from a wet Saturday morning in the centre at Sheringham, when rain rattled the old chapel roof, as if divine vengeance were being wrought on the building's secular use, I did little about my antique business. Once Frank phoned.

'What's all this I hear about you becoming queen of the ring?' he said.

'I was enthroned on the wheel arch of Wesley's van.'

'And what did they drop you with?'

'Fifty pounds.'

'More than I've made in a fortnight. Look in sometime.'

I said I would, but it wasn't to be that week. These were a few days when I needed peace. It was a time of convalescence. But my equanimity was shaken on Saturday morning when a letter arrived from Adam, posted from the airport.


*Heathrow*


*Dear Phoebe, Here's some doggerel I've just written during my flight delay:*

> *Which word in our peripheral chat*
> *Materialised the sleeping cat*
> *Above us on the dresser shelf?*
> *Or when our conversation failed,*
> *Was their some hesitation, pause*
> *Or glance which conjured up a tail?*
> *No stopping now, we added claws,*
> *Head and body – kitchen-dust fur*
> *Made up the feline integer*
> *Whose full, then evanescent grin*
> *Spoke wonderlandish origins:*
> *A cellared must, but whose the yeast,*
> *Tell me, whose summons stirred the beast*
> *To show its effervescent self?*


*Good luck with the teaching. I'll phone from New York. Love, Adam.*

* * *

I was intrigued, perhaps a little flattered – I had never before been given a poem. I was also disturbed. I was uneasy about the weight he had placed on the pause in our conversation. Yes, the moment had been there, but, whatever it was, I preferred it to remain wordless, not shaped into this irregular sonnet. And my spine shivered at the word 'wonderlandish'. Adam had no knowledge of my childhood fondness for the Alice stories, or of my reuse of the names of the characters. His making Bullace into the Cheshire Cat felt not so much a coincidence as a psychic intrusion into my past. Nor was I happy with the implicit comparison of the Cheshire Cat with myself, not least because the Cheshire Cat was male. And in the story, it disappeared whisker by whisker, not, as in Adam's poem, appearing in that way. And I resented Adam's use of the word 'beast'. The beast in my life had been depression caused, so I now knew, by the creature I had confronted yesterday. Adam had no right to apply the word to me. As for 'effervescent', he was way off the mark – 'incandescent' better suited my mood. Jane Eyre's pious cousin had given her a poem – albeit not one he'd written himself – and that relationship had gone nowhere, to her cousin's annoyance, but much to Jane's relief. Maybe this was the destiny of Adam and me.

Despite all this, a little later, as I placed the letter in a drawer, I felt sad. Four weeks was a long time. Perhaps the fact he'd taken the care to write the letter was more important than its irritating content.

Around 8.00pm on Saturday Molly phoned to say they were home. I drove round to hug James, hear the news, watch the kitchen return to its familiar mess, and help them empty two of the many bottles of wine which had filled every spare space in the car.

'So let's hear all about him,' Molly said.

'There is nothing. Really.'

'Oh, come on.'

'He gave me a lift to London and he helped me water your garden. That's all.'

'But you'll be seeing him again.'

'He has some old tin trunks for me.'

'Trunks? He's not moving in?'

'Of course not.'

'Phoebe, you're not telling us everything. She's not, is she, Paul?'

Paul frowned at me.

'Almost the only news is about my job,' I said.

'Almost?' said Paul.

'Well, I've had some luck with a piece of carpet.'

I told them about the fragment, and invited them to lunch the following day. It felt the worst of betrayals of friendship to say nothing of my visit to Bramshead. But that Saturday evening, with its unpacking and homecoming clamour, was not the time. I needed a childless house, when Paul was absent, to tell Molly everything. Since I was stronger now, in no need of her hand as each new emotional wave struck me, I could wait for the right moment. And I was beginning to bask in the self-assurance that what I had discovered since they had been away had been my own achievement. There was no requirement for it to be laid out in front of Molly – I would feel I was exchanging my latest package of problems for the box of French supermarket goodies she had brought back for me.

I was glad when the time came to return home and cajole a weary James upstairs. I thought he would be in bed and asleep within minutes.

I had hardly left his room when he shouted, 'Why have you muddled up my football programmes?'

I returned to see his perturbed face. 'I promise I haven't.'

He began to rearrange them on the shelf.

'Why don't you leave it till the morning?'

'But they're all out of order.'

'I must have tidied up your room when you were away.' I hadn't. I had entered it only once, and then briefly – on the sleepless night when I had ended up in anguish in the kitchen.

'It looks like you've shuffled them. It'll take me ages to sort them out.'

'I'm sorry. Can you leave them for tomorrow?'

Tired, he agreed. I said goodnight and again wondered if Anthony had been prowling. But why would he move football programmes? I thought back to Tuesday night and decided that I had been in such mental turmoil I must have knocked them off the shelf, and haphazardly put them back without remembering having done so; my mind had been focused elsewhere. And I wanted to dismiss my worries about a possible intruder as a phobia which belonged to a former life, out of which I was building a new, confident self. In consequence, the inspection of the other rooms of the house which followed was brief, and yet again nothing else was out of place, nothing missing. All the same, after that, every time I left the house, I made sure that the bedroom windows, which I normally left open, were now securely closed.

On Sunday morning, as soon as he was awake, James re-organised his football programmes and much else in his room He called me in to inspect. I congratulated him on his tidiness – almost certainly inherited from Anthony. Pinned to a shelf was a handbill for *Major Barbara*. I remembered that in two weeks' time he was seeing the dress rehearsal. Not long ago I would have found the presence of that handbill upsetting, but not now. Yes, I knew I had to protect James from her influence, but to be annoyed that he was going to see a rehearsal for the play was not the way. She and her machinations would no longer irk me. My life had decisively moved on.

Any unease I had felt on Saturday evening with Molly and Paul had melted before they arrived for a barbecue lunch. Paul set to work on the charcoal, and there might have been the chance of a good chat with Molly, but the sun was blazing and the boys were soon in their swimming shorts and engaged in a water fight with garden hoses and water pistols. The adults were bullied or soaked until we joined in, and the opportunity for conversation passed. I wasn't disappointed. Sometimes I felt too close to her – we might have been sisters. But, as with many sisters, there were places not shared. James and Ben, on the other hand, behaved as blood brothers and were probably more ready to share anxieties with each other than with their parents. Paul too had some part in this extended family, where he was often more relaxed with James than Anthony could ever be. If Anthony took James fishing, it was not a shared pleasure but a duty to be done. Paul, however, relished such outings. The fishing in France had kindled a desire in him and the boys to do more trout fishing. This pleased me. James didn't need largesse from B's brother when Paul was always at hand. He had plans to take the boys to Graffham Water the Sunday after next, and was looking forward to the trip with all their reel-sorting, fly-tying fervour.

# 17

My memories of the two weeks after half-term are fragmented. Perhaps, in my struggle to recall the distant past, my powers of recording the present were temporarily impaired. Or perhaps, in the light of what was to follow, I allowed those early June days to slip into insignificance.

\* \* \*

I remember the hours spent with Ruth in her classroom during breaks and afternoon games. I can see the two of us marking exams and making notes for reports, she meticulous and professional, I trying to emulate her. I have convinced myself that my future is in teaching. Antiques have become, at best, the secondary source of income which they are for the other dealers at the centre.

It is an enjoyable time, when I feel in control, focused, and when my hours in the classroom have been less tiring, partly because invigilating exams is easier than normal lessons. There have been school exams as well as GCSEs. I am particularly proud of the exam paper I set for Year Seven. This included questions based on paintings with mythological subjects. The artwork has been carried out, under Linda Baird's guidance, on a school computer and scanner. I have shown James my efforts and he has been both surprised and impressed. They have become part of my Speech Day display, a task I have completed a day before Ruth has finished hers.

At times I glance up from the exam papers to look at Ruth's small, deft fingers with their quick-as-thought writing – an exact, legible hand I wish were my own. On one such moment she looks up, tilting her head so that her impeccably shaped hair falls to one side, and raises her eyebrows with a quizzical smile. 'Have you heard from Adam?' she asks. 'I gather he's in New York for most of this month.' It is the first time she has mentioned him.

I pretend not to be caught off-guard. 'We spoke on the phone before he left,' I tell her. 'And I've had a couple of postcards.' I said nothing of the poem.

'If I weren't so disciplined, I could become a teeny bit envious,' she says, and returns to her pile of exam papers.

'There's not much to be envious of,' I tell her, and gaze out of the window towards the cedars and Norwegian pines on this side of the grounds, the last survivors of a Victorian arboretum. A little later, Ruth and I go for one of our occasional walks in this direction, then onto some heathland near Renwick's cottage, testing each other's knowledge of wild flowers as we go, sometimes disagreeing about the names – gentle arguments which continue until we are back in her classroom, where one of her reference books gives its verdict. Adam hasn't been mentioned again, but I think of the second postcard he sent me – it showed a corner of a Persian carpet in the Metropolitan Museum. We return to our marking, I as conscientious as my companion. I remember Jane Eyre's feelings for her friend and fellow teacher Miss Temple: *her friendship and society had been my continual solace.* I feel the same way about Ruth. Of course, I have no more told her about my trip to Bramshead than I have told Molly. It is so much my own exploration into my past, so much a journey from which recovery must be made alone, that I am not yet ready to speak of it. I am glad of the structured framework given by my exam timetable, and of the demands of my work. Within myself I am becoming stronger than I can remember.

I recall also that in those two weeks I have learned from Ruth not to be affected by the mood of my colleagues. Led by David Lennox, who is stalking the corridors, pipe between his teeth, like a rabid lurcher with a stick, they are working themselves into a lather about GCSEs, the CCF inspection and looming Speech Day. One incident remains in my mind of the atmosphere – the echo of Duggy screaming 'Bloody Army Section' in Joan Tatham's face when he learned that his Naval Section was to be inspected a full hour after the army cadets. There followed the crash of the staffroom door as she stormed out, for once offended by his aggression, leaving Brian Devlin eyeing the ashtray, where her unlit cigarette, bent tick-shaped, lay discarded in anger between packet and lips. Since that incident, on the first day after half-term, my avoidance of the staffroom during breaks has been total.

This time of self-assurance reaches its peak on the Friday after the holiday. It is my duty evening and I am convinced that most, perhaps all, of those feelings of incarceration at Hillgate Hall I had experienced in the weeks before half-term stemmed from my own schooldays. But now, because I have revisited the source of my fear, faced and overcome it, such feelings have disappeared. I am pleased at this discovery, achieved, like so much in the last few weeks, entirely without the help of my unofficial therapists, Molly, Ruth and Frank.

Through the staffroom window I watch the tiny figures of cricketers drift like pieces of paper over a green vastness, beyond which a mass of poppies at the margin of a wheat field are aflame in the late sun. Cosmo may be there somewhere. I don't care. My foray into his territory is over. My future is in teaching, not in a grey world of intrigue, poker-playing and notes exchanging hands in the backs of vans. I even suspect that the mystery he affects is mostly a cloak to conceal a void below. I have an evening stroll, but it leads me in the direction of the stream in another part of the grounds, where there has been a sighting of otters. I fail to find any, my search not helped by a dog I see splashing in the water. It is Kate Lennox's Tabloid. She joins me, and together we walk back to the main building.

'Now, that dinner date,' she says. 'There's a tradition that the headmaster invites the head boy and his two deputies to dinner on the evening before Speech Day. I would be delighted if you could join us. I'm sorry there's no head girl to help even up the numbers.'

'It will be a pleasure,' I tell her, knowing that my continuing work here is as good as guaranteed.

That evening I sip my duty wine, toast my own success and feel exuberant in the knowledge that, now I have unmasked my past, I can defy any odds, conquer anything. I feel the lightness of release. My life cannot return to limping heaviness and uncertainty. Elated, I go over to my classroom to admire again my Speech Day display. I look at my work with pride: Jason and the Argonauts, with the help of Orpheus, sailing safely past the Sirens; Echo, watching Narcissus fall in love with his own reflection; Icarus, plunging to earth, overconfident in his homemade wings. I would not dream of applying any of these stories to myself.

# 18

The MG, roof down again, appeared early on Saturday to take James to Norwich and the dress rehearsal. Since I was busy in the greenhouse, James and I shouted our goodbyes across the garden, and I returned to my tomatoes. But then I heard the car engine stop. I looked back to see Anthony, annoyed, impatient, striding over the lawn towards me. Standing by the side of the car, talking to James, was B. Her hair was shorter than I had ever seen it – I guessed she had had it cut for the play.

Anthony thrust his head into the greenhouse. 'What's all this nonsense about Graffham Water tomorrow?'

'Paul's taking James and Ben there,' I said quietly. 'Do you and B want to stop for a coffee – I'm just about to make some?'

'But James is meant to be seeing the play tomorrow evening.'

'No, the plan we arranged was for him to see the dress rehearsal today, and for you to bring him back as usual this evening.'

'But we told him he could stay and see the opening night.'

'That's the first I've heard of it.'

I put down the watering can and moved to the door.

He blocked my way.

'Well, it's all been arranged. James must have told you.'

'I assure you he didn't. He would have said something about it when we were arranging the fishing trip, which he's really looking forward to. Do you honestly think he wants two doses of Bernard Shaw over one weekend?'

'I think he's mature enough.'

'And I think he'd prefer fishing.'

'Have you asked him?'

'I don't need to. But let's put the question to him. Excuse me.' I tried to squeeze through the half-blocked doorway.

He shoved himself in my way again. 'Phoebe, be cooperative – this weekend's been arranged for ages.'

'By you, perhaps. Not by James and me.'

He clenched his fists and banged them on his thighs. I thought he would have preferred to punch me. 'What the hell's got into you?' he shouted.

I saw B look in our direction.

'Let's ask James what he would like to do,' I said.

'Very well,' he snapped and stepped ahead of me. Then he turned, beckoning me with his knuckles as if he were signalling to a disobedient dog.

I followed him towards the car, where B's bobbed head was in deep conversation with James.

Before we were off the lawn she announced, 'All settled, people. James says that just this once' – a smile here to James – 'he would prefer drama this weekend to fishing. I'll make sure he has that day on the Esk to compensate. So no prob.' She threw her arms wide, expecting applause.

I looked at James. I could see from his face that he had been bullied into this decision.

'Paul and Ben were looking forward to taking you,' I said.

'I'd better go to the play, Mum. Say sorry to Ben.'

B opened the car door for James.

'Very well,' I managed to say. 'Your decision.' I knew it was not.

B closed the door with an extravagant sweep.

I couldn't have argued with James in front of them. Not only would it have placed unfair pressure on him, but, whatever the outcome, B would somehow have managed to turn it to her advantage.

'Everybody happy then?' she called as she got into the passenger seat.

I turned to Anthony. 'In future you must phone first about changes of arrangements.'

He said nothing.

'By the way,' I said, 'have you been snooping while I've been out?'

'Don't be mad,' he said, as he dropped into the driver's seat, from where he looked at me and groaned, treating me like a child coaxed out of a spat.

Up until this point, my strength had held, and I might have sighed and waved them goodbye, had B not said, in a stage whisper, 'I hate all these fits of pique.' Her eyes now met mine with the same smile she had given me in the County Court car park.

Anthony started the car.

I looked at the pair of them, smug in the front seats. Through my teeth I said, 'Everybody happy then?'

As the car shot out into the lane throwing up gravel, from the back seat James lifted an arm towards me. Not a wave, it was more a sign of capture, or an apology for allowing himself to be browbeaten by her. But I waved back.

'No, not happy,' I said. 'Not happy at all.'

A month earlier, I might have thrown myself into an hour's cathartic weeding, in order to quell my anger. Not anymore. I walked slowly to the front door, where I stood and listened for the sound of the MG turning out of the lane and onto the main road. Looking beyond the trees to where the noise was fading up the hill, I made a decision.

'Since it's a game,' I said, 'this is where I start to play my hand.'

# 19

The farmhouse looked deserted. The window shutters were closed, and on the flaking black paint of the front door a cobweb stretched from the keyhole, over the jamb, to the brickwork of the wall. I lifted the heavy iron ring of the lion-mask knocker and struck it twice. There was a beating of wings as a pigeon lifted itself from the roof, then silence. I gave it another hard knock. The echo from inside the house suggested the place was empty. I waited and stared down at a rusty boot scraper set in a massive block of stone and almost totally concealed by ivy. It must have been years since it had last seen a muddy boot. I wondered whether I had come to the right address.

While I was considering going to the rear of the building, I thought I heard from inside, perhaps upstairs, the sound of a closing door. I continued to wait and looked up at the facade, a typically eighteenth-century arrangement of five identical sash windows on the first floor, and four on the ground floor, two each side of the front door – like Haworth parsonage. All were in need of repainting. The garden too needed serious attention. The lawns either side of the path behind me had been recently cut, but the roses and lavenders in the beds beside them were in losing competition with an army of weeds.

Since there were no further sounds from within, I decided to try the rear of the house, walking along a narrow path encroached upon by catmint, pungent in the mid-morning air. The farmyard buildings which came into sight were equally deserted, although here all woodwork had recently been painted moss green. I was about to round a corner of the house when I heard noises above me. Looking up, I saw the shutters of an upstairs window thrown back, followed by the scrape and rattle of an opening sash window.

Cosmo, his hair dishevelled, leaned out. His shoulders were bare. Clearly, he had just got out of bed.

'Is it urgent?' he growled.

'Yes,' I shouted.

He snarled, then shouted, 'Back door.'

The window closed with a crash.

The back of the house had none of the symmetry of the front, making it hard to discern where the Georgian original ended and the chaos of Victorian additions began. Over a door was an elegant iron lamp, far too ornate for the rear of a farmhouse. I heard several bolts pulled before the door opened to reveal Cosmo in an acid yellow dressing gown. He wasn't pleased to see me.

'Coffee,' he said. 'Can't think this time on a Saturday morning without it. Through there.' He pointed down a dingy passage, but went off in another direction, barefoot on the flag floors.

The walls of the passage were hung with empty gilt frames, while various side tables under them allowed minimal passing space. At the end was a hallway dominated by a marble-top centre table covered in letters and auction catalogues. I hesitated, looking up a staircase, the walls of which were hung with fragments of carpets and tapestry. Not lingering, I made for an open door ahead of me. The room I entered, lit only by two table lamps, had that random mixture found in an antique dealer's house of what was probably permanent furniture – two sofas, a coffee table and an Edwardian leather armchair piled high with newspapers – and items of stock – mainly chests of drawers and console tables, some of which still had auction lot numbers stuck to them. A few items, like the ebonised clock and the bronzes on the mantelpiece, looked semi-permanent – part of the furnishings, unless an irresistible offer were to be made. I was uneasy, surrounded by half a dozen pieces, each of which was worth more than my entire stock. An English impressionist painting on the wall – by Stanhope Forbes perhaps – reminded me of my gallery days. I never envisaged myself dealing in works of this quality. I felt a fool in coming here.

'Milk? Sugar?' he shouted from the depths of the house.

'Please,' I shouted back. I wondered if he had heard me.

Grunting and shuffling, Cosmo appeared with two mugs which he placed on the coffee table, moaning as he bent down. He then went to a window and opened the shutters to their widest, blinked at the sun and half closed them. As he walked away a diagonal shaft of light cut through the room, revealing the dust on the furniture.

He looked up at the clock. It had stopped. 'What time is it?'

'Ten-thirty,' I said.

'God, I'm meant to be playing cricket this afternoon. You haven't got a cigarette, have you?'

I shook my head.

He yawned and pushed the pile of newspapers off the leather chair. He found a lady's silk headscarf among them and held it up, pretending he had never before seen it. Frowning, he smelt it, then look repelled. He was enjoying his role as the half-awake roué. He picked up his mug and looked at me.

'I suppose it's about yesterday's sale,' he said.

'No.' I felt my heart pound. 'I've come to offer you a deal.'

His eyes ignited, then too soon dulled. 'What? You'll play in the cricket team instead of me?'

'My rug fragment in exchange for you sorting out a certain young woman.'

'Sorting out?' He laughed. 'Sorry, I don't do hit jobs.'

'I mean inviting her out a few times, entertaining her, then dumping her at a suitably distressing moment.'

'Bloody hell.' He got up and moved to the door. 'While I go and get my smokes, I'll think of a polite way of telling you to eff off.'

He left the room. I felt like a three-year-old caught being spiteful to another child. I contemplated leaving before he could reappear, but somehow the room, which was like the storage basement of a stately home, held me captive among its discarded furnishings – a punishment for vindictiveness. I thought of Jane Eyre, accused of spitefulness and locked in a room with dark furniture and dusty mirrors.

From upstairs came a banging of doors. A minute later he returned, a cigarette in his mouth, the packet in his hand. He was wearing a pair of monogrammed slippers. He sat down, blowing the smoke of his Gauloise towards me. Leaning back, he took another drag and this time exhaled towards the ceiling. I felt diminished by each second of silence. I drained my coffee and was about to get up. He raised a finger towards me. I saw some sort of rebuke coming.

'Okay, you're on,' he said.

'What?'

'Since I couldn't think of a polite way of refusing your offer – and one doesn't like bad manners – I'll try my luck with your *deal*, or whatever you call it.'

Speechless, I stared at him.

There was no sign of emotion in his eyes.

He looked towards the clock. 'Who is she? Boyfriend's new floozie?'

'Ex-husband's.'

'This won't get him back of course.'

'I don't want him back. I just want her out of my hair.'

'Ah.' He stared at the floor. The shaft of light edged towards the coffee table. It made him impatient. 'Well, come on, give me the details.'

On the road to Walborough I had composed a description of B to give him, along with her address, her friends, and details of where she might be found. Now I couldn't even begin. I put a clumsy hand into the pocket of my jeans and pulled out the handbill for *Major Barbara* which I had taken from James's room. I had written her name on top and my phone number below. I tried to sound businesslike. 'She's in this play at the university. The first night's tomorrow.' I passed it to him.

'Ugh, Shaw – one of our more turgid exports.'

'I'll describe her. She's . . .'

'Don't. He pushed a palm towards my mouth, then looked down at the fender again. 'I never read the auctioneer's catalogue before a viewing. Other people's descriptions tend to cloud the instincts.' He held up the handbill. 'Time and place of sale is sufficient.' Without giving it a second glance, he folded the piece of paper and placed it in a dressing gown pocket. He might have been an assassin accepting a contract.

'More coffee?' he said.

It was a question expecting the answer no.

I shook my head. 'Ring me in four weeks to report progress,' I said.

'Or tell you I've failed – we'll see.'

'Think of the rug,' I said.

He picked up a newspaper and began reading.

I persisted. 'After the last night of the show there's a party . . .'

He waved me to the door. He had his own ideas.

In the hallway, I felt sweat trickle down my back. The tables and frames in the dark obstacle course leading to the back door were like people – my parents and Molly and Paul – remonstrating with me for my behaviour. Ruth was there too. 'One doesn't do this sort of thing,' she said with irrefutable authority. I was glad of the sunlight in the yard.

As I drove to Sheringham, unconcerned about being late for my duty day at the centre, the recriminating voices continued. I justified my actions to them aloud in the van. 'I've done nothing illegal,' I insisted. But this failed to impress them, and their accusations persisted through a dozen miles of country roads until, dropping between beeches towards the coast, on a bend I almost crashed into a coach coming up from the town. To recover I pulled into a layby at the foot of the hill and breathed deeply. Cars and caravans passed by. I tried to become absorbed by the normality of a Saturday morning by the sea. But the accusations and self-accusations refused to recede. Weakened, I gave way to them. Opposite the layby was a phonebox. I decided to phone Cosmo and cancel the deal. I climbed from my van and waited for more coast-bound cars to pass, so I could cross the road. But in a lull in the traffic, as I was about to walk over, I again heard B saying, 'It's only a game,' and 'Everybody happy then?' And I thought of James's face in the MG. His expression made the decision for me, silencing my accusers. I got into the van and drove on.

At the centre, Tara had already opened up.

'You look washed out,' she told me. She was wearing a grey 1930s two-piece of a sort which might have belonged to Aunt Hilda – another person who would have disapproved of me. 'Late night? Overslept?'

'Something of the sort,' I said.

'I'm glad you're getting out more. Good party?'

'Hardly a party.'

'The spontaneous ones are always the best. C'mon. Tell.'

To avoid interrogation I offered to look after the centre on my own for the day. She wouldn't hear of it, despite the fact that there were very few customers. To keep out of her way I began sweeping and tidying. These activities also precluded introspection, so that after an hour's work I could almost believe that my visit to Cosmo had never happened. The sight of my rare burst of housekeeping must have impressed Tara, since she suggested I go for an early lunch.

Forgoing my usual walk to the beach, I made for the secondhand bookshops in search of a copy of *Major Barbara*. At the first I had no luck, but at the next I was successful and bought an acting edition of the play. Excited at my purchase, under a darkening sky I walked back to the centre. By 2.00pm a north-easterly had got up, driving drizzle against the old chapel's windows and bringing in bored families, including dozens of members of a tandem bike rally. Brightening the building with their kagools and lycra shorts, they were interested only in old postcards and local memorabilia. Since this was Tara's speciality, she gave them her full attention, and I was freed from her inquisitiveness, while the incessant background chatter saved me from a drift into self-questioning.

Swings from guilt to the pleasure of at last having become proactive filled the weekend, during which my house and garden benefited from my need to be busy when alone. Early afternoon on Sunday, while I was giving the kitchen a rare clean, I pictured the last-minute preparations for *Major Barbara*. Soon I was there, backstage in the Wharfside Theatre, watching the arrival of stagehands and technicians in the converted warehouse. Anthony was rushing about checking the sets, while James was tagging along, trying to be helpful but thinking of fishing.

Before long, these pictures of a theatre I had never visited became almost as familiar as my own house. Around 4.00pm I sank into a chair and allowed the *Observer* crossword to give me some respite from thoughts of Norwich. Unravelling the clues made me think again of Adam, and sharing a crossword with him on our way to London. He had not yet been away two weeks – not halfway through his trip. I counted the days until his return.

With the newspaper spread on my lap, I dozed off. I woke in panic, worried I had missed the start of the play? No, it was an hour before curtain-up. I poured myself a glass of wine and pictured the leading lady gliding through the stage door. And for the first time I felt a step ahead of her. More powerful. At last, I had on my side an ally and the power of money. Previously, in all my dealings with her, I had been wretchedly alone and made aware of my financial insecurity. She had sensed this vulnerability and had attacked me where I was weakest. No longer. With these satisfying thoughts I opened my copy of the play and skimmed through Shaw's preface. That too was about the power of money, but it held no interest for me. This wasn't my play. I had come to see another drama, one of which I was playwright and director.

At 7.00pm I began to read Scene One aloud, trying hard to pace myself to what I judged to be acting speed. A previous owner of my edition had kindly underlined all Barbara's lines. I said them with great pleasure, thinking myself now on stage, now in the audience, looking around for Cosmo's red hair. At the end of each act I allowed myself gentle applause, while in the interval I stretched my legs and refilled my glass. At the final curtain I banged my book shut with a smile, tossed it across the room, and imagined that the roof-raising ovations at the Wharfside were not for the play they had seen, but the one I had written.

Just before 11.00pm when James was dropped off, it seemed superfluous to ask him how the evening had been. That night and for many nights afterwards I slept with the fragment at the end of my bed. It was protection against any mishap.

# 20

Monday started badly for me at Hillgate. Driving to school, I had warmed to the thought of another week's teaching. I was competent in my work, and my classes would prevent my mind drifting to Norwich. But these lofty hopes lasted no longer than ten minutes into my first lesson. While the Year Sixes were doing a simple translation, I slipped back into my imaginings. A boy in the front had a question. Impatient at staring towards me, his raised hand unnoticed, he called out, 'Miss, Miss.' Slowly, I was dragged away from outside the theatre back to my classroom. After that I forced myself to be vigilant against further lapses.

The morning had started worse for Alan Carter. During his first lesson, with Year Nine, he was kicked by Mark Jarritt, for no other reason, so Alan claimed, than a routine reprimand about paying attention. It was the talk of the school well before morning break, when I went to the staffroom to empty my pigeon hole of the almost hourly notes from Dr Lennox about Speech Day on Saturday week. Alan was in shock, slumped in an armchair, his hand shaking every time he lifted his cigarette to his mouth.

Duggy was revelling in the tragedy. 'That little shit should have been expelled the first term he was here. You want to go for compensation, Alan.'

'What did you tell the great doctor?' asked Renwick.

Alan stammered, 'I told him I wasn't prepared to have the animal in my class again.'

'Does that apply to all of us?' asked Brian.

Alan became agitated. 'It doesn't even apply to me. Lennox tried to fob me off with some nonsense that we can always expect high spirits in the run-up to Speech Day. Jarritt's gated for the rest of term, and that's the end of it.'

'Anything to stop the numbers falling,' said Renwick.

'Go to your union,' said Joan.

'And get myself top of the redundancy list when I'm in my unemployable fifties?'

They started arguing about teachers' unions. I was about to leave the room with Ruth when Renwick called out, 'You two might not like our company, but Jarritt doesn't care who he kicks.'

'Don't let them get to you,' said Ruth.

I tried not to, but knew that I would have to face Year Nine, lower set for the last lesson of the day. My fears proved groundless, since, from the moment they entered my room, the whole class was subdued. I guessed they were either exhausted by the morning's incident, or had been so stamped on during subsequent lessons, that there was no rebellion left in them. They succumbed without protest to my instruction quietly to read a chapter on Roman domestic life. Perhaps it was this rare unquestioning obedience which lulled me backstage to the Wharfside as it came alive two hours before the second performance.

A shout of 'Daydreaming, Miss?' disturbed me.

A general laugh followed.

Someone mumbled, 'Dozy cow.'

More laughter.

I struggled to extricate myself from my hiding place by the stage door.

A girl's voice said, 'Rough night, was it?'

I was back in class now, but my voice failed me.

'What's his name, Miss?'

'Or hers?'

Guffaws all round.

'Did he give you one?' said a boy.

'Shut it, Stan,' said Mark Jarritt.

'What's up with you, Jarritt?' he said.

'Do you want to get smashed?' snarled Jarritt.

No one replied to this. Mark Jarritt gave me the slightest of nods to say it was safe for me to continue the lesson. I mumbled, 'Back to work.' There were no more disruptions.

When the bell sounded, Mark lingered behind the others. He approached my desk. 'Sorry about the trouble, Miss.'

'You didn't join in.'

'No. Well, you know . . .'

I might have thought that he was making up for his violence in the maths room, but he gave me such a look of complicity – one criminal recognising another – I knew he had decided, by intuition or his own warped logic, that I was an ally in deviousness.

'If anyone gives you a hard time, Miss, let me know.' He left with a lip-curling nod, a welcome to his world of deceit.

Linda Baird must have heard the commotion in my class. On the path outside, she came up to me. 'Year Nine still a problem?' she asked.

'A little exuberance before Speech Day,' I said. 'I survived unscathed.'

'If there's anything I can do?'

I persuaded her to swap her Thursday duty evening next week for my Friday, so I would be free to have dinner with the Lennoxes.

During morning break the following day, when I visited my pigeon hole, an enormous wad of educational junk mail faced me. After my earlier feeling that Latin was the Cinderella of the educational world, I was now surprised that so unfashionable a subject could generate so many letters. As I consigned envelope after envelope addressed *The Head of Classics* to the bin, I looked at my colleagues sitting in silent exhaustion after eighty minutes of afternoon teaching. The exception was Duggy, who had used a spare period to take himself on a cross country run. In tracksuit and trainers, he was crouched on the edge of his chair, elbows on knees, purple head bent forward, pretending he was breathing deeply, not panting. He was probably trying to impress us with his athleticism, but it was more obvious that he was sweating out last night's alcohol. Renwick smiled at him. 'So you managed a sprint to the Gryphon before third period?' he said.

Duggy raised his wet, red cabbage of a head. 'Piss off,' he shouted. It could have been directed at everyone in the room.

Renwick regarded this response as a great success. His stifled laughter caused him to spill coffee over the pile of unmarked books on his lap. He brushed off the spillage, splashing his trousers. This sent Joan and Brian into hysterics. Renwick was furious that his barb had been blunted. Casting about for another victim, he turned on me.

'Ah, Latin, word from the jungle is that Jarritt has becomes teacher's pet. I hope you have a strong enough leash to keep him in check.'

'You can always borrow some good hempen ropes from Admiral Nelson here,' said Joan.

'And hang the little sod with them,' said Duggy.

'We didn't have chaps like him at Mel,' mimicked Renwick.

Duggy lurched forward, colliding with the coffee table. I thought he was about to throw himself at Renwick, but in this sudden exertion he had pulled a muscle. The pain held him back. He looked at me as if it were my fault. 'Siding with bastards like Jarritt won't get you anywhere.' In some agony he dragged himself to the door and slammed it behind him. Everyone but me laughed. I left the room in search of Ruth.

Wednesday proved to be one of my worst days at Hillgate. Since the start of the week my body clock had been haywire. The need for food and sleep became random, while all my energy was expended on appearing to be normal. This was the day of the final performance of *Major Barbara* and the last-night party. I guessed that, whatever charms Cosmo had or had not yet worked, this evening was critical in the scheme. During lessons I was an automaton; in breaks I avoided everybody, even Ruth, and took walks around the edge of the playing fields. In the afternoon my feeling of incarceration returned. I wanted to be an invisible presence moving about the Wharfside, not a member of staff confined in these grounds which often felt more like a badly run young offenders' prison than a school. At 4.15pm I found myself at the edge of the cricket field, staring over the wheat towards Hillgate church, visible only by the parapet of its tower, which seemed to float over a wood as if searching for its village. High above, swifts performed their acrobatics. Further on, invisible from view, the road, in a gentle incline – the hill in Hillgate – led to the marshes and the sea.

'Five minutes to lessons,' came the voice of a Year Ten girl beside me. I hadn't noticed her approach.

'Do you ever feel hemmed in here?' I asked her.

'You have to go to school somewhere, Miss. Hellgate's as good as anywhere.' She looked at her watch.

'I shall have to call you my personal assistant.'

'I want to be a PA when I leave school,' she said.

We walked together to the classroom block. I envied her straightforwardness. It made me feel guilty about my own enmeshed life. Again I wanted to phone Cosmo to cancel the deal. But that voice, 'It's only a game,' reverberated in my head and overcame any weakening.

After the end-of-lessons bell my van was the first vehicle to leave the car park. I raced back to Ulford, mentally preparing myself for the last night of the play. Between supper and curtain rise James and I played Monopoly. I then sat alone with my acting edition and again read until the interval. Here I opened a bottle of champagne Molly had brought back for me from France. I poured myself a glass, and gave James a thimbleful, by way of sharing my growing confidence in this evening's outcome. The final act of the play I spent in the bath, holding my acting edition in one hand and flicking soap bubbles with the other at each of B's entrances and exits. As she took her final bow I was happy to leave her with all the cheering and clapping.

'Enjoy it while you can,' I told her.

Emerging triumphant from the suds, I walked naked to my bedroom. Looking at myself in my long mirror, I thought of Molly's terracotta set of The Seasons. I told myself I was Summer, superseding B's Spring in the irrevocable progress of the year. From that moment, I enjoyed a week of calm reliance on destiny. I felt less and less the plotter and instigator; rather, I reassured myself, I had done no more than cooperate with the inevitable – Aestas, goddess of summer in obeisance to the Fates.

I spent many hours watching and replaying the scene of the party. Cosmo approaches her with congratulations and talk of Shaw. I hear him express his love of theatre and his descriptions of childhood visits to the Abbey Theatre Dublin. He mentions his plans for a few days in London to catch up with new plays, and has she ever been to Glyndebourne? Without a second thought she accepts a dinner invitation. There will follow a whirl of London hotels and theatres and shops and the sort of restaurants whose reviews I read in the weekend papers, but am never likely to visit.

Anthony arrives late for the party – he has had the set to strike. He sees B tête-à-tête with Cosmo, but is not in the least jealous – the Queen deserves these moments of triumph. Meanwhile B, without his knowing, has seen his arrival, and, looking towards her headgirlish attendant, makes that slight movement of head and eyes, only understood by a close friend, which signals that Anthony must be kept occupied for the evening. It is the first indication that a new consort has appeared, and the old one must now be gently handled and released, like her beloved brother Hector returning an out-of-condition salmon to the Esk. After all, Anthony was once a married man; he might slip into unacceptable behaviour.

The attendant loyally performs her duties. I have the occasional glimpse of her and Anthony as, later that night, they walk by the river between Foundry Bridge and Pull's Ferry. I watch them sit on a bench by the willow trees where, in the moonlight, they look at the reflections of the moored pleasure cruisers. In earnest conversation they stare at the water, but my picture of them is dimmed by the brighter lights of the party, while their voices are silenced by the band.

Cosmo and B are still there, still together. Each of the three of us, for very different reasons, celebrates a successful night.

* * *

So immediate was my return to equilibrium that, even for one used to precipitous mood swings, I was surprised at its suddenness. As ever when on the ascendant, I found it difficult to believe that my traumas at school earlier in the week had really taken place. In the classroom my teaching became a pleasure, while in breaks I found that at last, like Ruth, I was able to enter the staffroom undaunted. An easy rhythm returned to my life, and I envisaged next week's dinner with the Lennoxes as the seal on my contract of employment.

On Friday evening, as I wandered the school grounds, I was no longer the prison officer I had reverted to, but a teacher in regained control. Approaching the cricket field, I was not in the least surprised that Cosmo's Galaxy was not parked under the trees, nor that the distinctive head was not be seen on the cricket pitch, or among the players grouped in front of the pavilion. A cricket match, I thought, especially one at Hillgate Hall, would be the last place he would choose to work his charms.

The next day Anthony arrived alone to take out James. I made no remark about the fact, nor, on their return, did I question James about B's absence. Such probing might have invited bad luck – a lack of trust in a successful outcome. I had felt the same way when I had resisted questioning Dora about my Latin job.

On Sunday I took James, Ben and a football to the coast. We parked at the Cley beach café and headed for Blakeney Point, stopping midway to make driftwood goalposts and enjoy a kickabout on the windswept beach. At last we arrived at the Point, deserted apart from the seals asleep on the bank or lolloping to the sea. On our way back, we stopped by the dunes, where I sat and watched the boys exhaust themselves in more football, better fun now that the wind had dropped. When, perspiring, they had had enough, they paddled in the sea, then, having no swimming shorts, pulled off their clothes and skinny-dipped. Shouting from the water, they urged me to join them, assuring me it was warm. So, naked, I ran to the water and swam until the sky clouded over, when I clambered back to the dunes and watched them splash and shout and throw the ball around until, exhausted, they threw themselves on the sand to dry. There they sat, looking towards a far-off sailing boat – two small, white figures in an Anders Zorn beach scene, an ocean away from the wiles of B whom, I hoped, James would never see again.

Dressed, we trudged back to the car park, the boys dragging a piece of fishing net which they insisted on taking home and spreading on the lawn. Later, supper at Molly's was so much like earlier days that, even in a quiet moment away from the children, I was reluctant to disturb the atmosphere with weightier matters – I was glad not even to think about them. But when Paul lit a French cigarette, I thought of Cosmo, and as the smoke floated up in front of the dresser, for a moment I saw B's face appear, like an apparition in a medium's ectoplasm. In panic I blinked it away, scared someone else would see it. Then I realised my foolishness, and saw Bullace gazing down through the smoke in obvious disapproval.

On Monday my calm returned with a serenity I had never before experienced. I knew at once that B had disappeared from my life for good. Looking out through my bedroom window, I saw the fishing net, wet with dew on the grass, like flotsam from some freak tide. It made me scan the garden for other debris. In my head too, I felt there had been a curious ebb during the night: I was on a deserted beach, where the rollers had shrunk back to a strand of white wool on the horizon. She had gone. I was sure of it. And as I made my bed, I was tempted to remove the fragment of carpet. But since it was a piece of weaving, and weaving was the province of the Fates, I thought it best not to disturb it.

# PART IV

# 21

Five days before Speech Day we were still suffering from the Lennox paper plague. Earlier arrangements were cancelled, new ones made, information was repeated.

'It's the same every year,' Ruth said, 'and each Speech Day is just like the last.'

Perhaps knowing this, Duggy tipped all his memos unread into the bin, while the others allowed their pigeon holes to overflow. I alone had collected a complete set, and had devoutly read them all, in the hope of a chance to show off my knowledge over dinner on Friday.

It was with similar dedication, that, during my swapped duty evening on Thursday, I decided not to open my wine since, so close to Speech Day, I thought there might be governors on the prowl who would take exception to on-duty drinking. As it happened, I saw none on my wanderings around the grounds where, during the day, four marquees had been erected on the junior playing fields, the largest for speeches and prize-giving, three others for teas. Two of the ground staff, working late, were placing plastic vases of pelargoniums by the entrances. Peeping inside the main marquee, I saw a stage had been erected at one end, in the front of which were containers of petunias and trailing ivy. It was all too lavish for a small school – perhaps David Lennox was indulging his fantasy that he was head of somewhere more prestigious. But if Hillgate Hall which, I was certain, was soon to offer me a full-time contract, could afford to pander to his conceits, who was I to question it?

With no evening cricket that night, one of my walks took me across the cricket field. The boundary lines had been freshly painted, and a smell of creosote was drifting from the pavilion where a low fence had been newly treated, all in readiness for Saturday's match – the Headmaster's XI versus the School. Joan Tatham had tried to talk me into keeping the score, but I had pleaded such total ignorance of the game that she had looked elsewhere. On reflection, I considered my decision unwise, since in the last few days the salvo of memos had made it quite clear that this match was, at least in David Lennox's eyes, the high point of Speech Day. To show my support, I planned to stand in full visibility near the pavilion and clap with enthusiasm in the appropriate places.

I may briefly have thought of Cosmo as I walked to the edge of the cricket square, and turned towards the place under the oak trees where, almost five weeks ago, I had seen him waiting for me. But I was so confident he was diligently carrying out his part of the bargain, and I would have little more to do with him, apart from handing over my fragment of carpet, that I had relegated him and B to insignificant roles in the greater scheme of my life, over which I was at last in control. On the far side of the cricket field, I looked towards the direction of Ulford, and felt more certain than ever that my home and my future were secure. The bunch of duty keys in my hand affirmed it.

On Thursday evenings there were more children to oversee than on Fridays, when the weekly boarders had gone home, but now I had become an experienced, efficient teacher, the extra numbers posed no problem. Evening duty was a routine, and I carried it out almost without thinking. At 10.30pm I was in a hurry to leave, since the next day was a school day for James, and I needed to collect him from Molly's as soon as possible. But when James and I were home, I realised that, in my haste to leave Hillgate, I had left my bag and front door keys in the staffroom. Molly sometimes had spares, but not that day. A few weeks before, in a similar predicament, I might have pulled a ladder from the shed and entered a bedroom window. After my recent security measures this was no longer possible – all windows were closed. With no other choice, I drove back to Hillgate.

At the main entrance, I discovered that the caretaker had closed the iron gates. They weren't locked, and I could have opened them and driven in as usual. However, not wanting to cause a disturbance, I decided to lock James in the van, with the radio and his computer magazine for company, while I ran to the main building to retrieve my keys.

I sprinted down the grass verge at the edge of the drive, walked past the newly planted flowerbeds, and crept up to the front door, which was lit by the all-night light above it. I pushed the door open and entered, feeling like a burglar as I tiptoed down the corridor towards the staffroom. In the darkness, as I opened the door, the smell of stale cigarettes was stronger than in daytime. Not wishing to switch on the electric light, I waited and allowed a dull light from outside to bring the furnishings of the room into vision. I found my bag quickly, checked that the keys were inside and turned to leave the room. But at that moment, I saw through the window a figure moving in the direction of the front door. At first, I thought it was Brian, late back from the Gryphon, but I couldn't recall hearing his car. Nor did the silhouette I saw, although that of an adult, seem like his. As I stood by the door, considering who else it might be, a sound from the corridor froze me – someone had opened the front door. The footsteps approached the staffroom door. I held my breath. I heard them pass to the end of the corridor. Ear to the door, I continued to listen. My heart raced. I shivered. Two hours ago I had been here, a confident teacher on duty; now the footsteps of that silhouette had turned me into an anxious intruder. I waited a little longer, then, inch by inch, opened the door.

The corridor was empty, the building silent. Again I waited. I guessed it had been a senior boy returning after some late-night adventure. I relaxed a little. I had no reason to be afraid. I had a right to be here. As for miscreants – I wasn't on duty at this time of night; the behaviour of boarders was the responsibility of the residential staff. I needed to get back to James. Thanks to the fanlight over the front door, there was more light in the corridor than in the staffroom. Why should I be scared? I moved forward, but muffled sounds brought me to a halt. I looked up and listened: someone was walking along the passage on the floor immediately above me. I turned and looked at the staircase at the far end of the corridor. I had to investigate.

Silently, I removed my shoes, placed my bag beside them and barefooted approached the stairs. I felt the worn carpet under my feet. A cautious three steps told me that the old boards creaked less if I edged up against the wall of the stairwell. Slowly, I moved up until I reached the landing, where I waited in the shadows between the faint light which had helped me negotiate the staircase and the weak glow from a low watt lamp above me. Steeling myself, I inched up the second flight of the staircase. Six or seven steps from the top, I was able to look down the passageway along which the shadowy figure had walked. I knew that at this end there were only four rooms leading off it – two laundry rooms and the two one-bed dormitories. The doors of all four rooms were closed. Since this part of the passageway led nowhere, but ended with a permanently locked storage cupboard above the front door, I knew that the figure I had seen and heard was now in one of those rooms. Noiselessly, I moved to the top of the staircase. Here I paused and listened. There was silence. I moved along the passage, waiting and listening after each step. I heard nothing, but was drawn to the end dormitory by a dull light seeping from beneath the door. It was Mark Jarritt's room.

I put my ear to the door. No sound came from inside. I bent down to the keyhole. It had been stuffed with tissue paper. A thread-like strand was bent over the corner of the escutcheon plate. My fingernails were long enough to grip it. Millimeter by millimeter I prised out the complete wad. As I extracted it, a needle of light hit my face. I was petrified. I unbent my body. For what seemed a long time, the tissue paper remained crumpled in my hand. At last I pushed it into a pocket. Holding my breath, I lowered my eye to the keyhole. No lamp was switched on in the room. The source of the light was the lamp above the main entrance. It was shining through the window, lighting up the bed in front of me.

I was aware, first, of Mark Jarritt lying on his back naked, eyes closed, face contorted, head slumped on a pillow. Next, I saw, seated beside the bed, one hand on his abdomen, the other stroking him, Kate Lennox. Apart from her arms and hands, and the occasional tremor at the corners of his eyes and mouth, both of them were still, emotionless. I shall always regard it as fortunate that I never saw her full face. It was bad enough to see that profile and that one eye staring neither at him nor her hands, but at some distant point beyond the confines of the room. It was a look that terrified me.

With an effort I was certain they had heard, I lifted myself from the keyhole, stood motionless for a second, then, as quickly as I dared, escaped to the staircase. Not bothering to hug the wall, I dashed down. Near the bottom step I tripped. I almost fell, saving myself by grasping a baluster. I felt a sharp pain in my hand – a splinter. There was no time to examine it. I ran towards the main door, grabbing my bag and shoes from outside the staffroom. No longer caring about noise, I opened the door, left it ajar and ran out into the night.

For the first few yards fear propelled me, but I began to tremble. This slowed my pace, forced me into a walk until, involuntarily, I turned round, compelled to look up towards that first floor room. There, between half-drawn curtains, a face looked down at me, willing me not to move. It was the pain in my hand which finally broke its hold on me, allowing me to pull my head away from the window and direct my eyes towards the main gate. I ran down the gravel drive faster than I knew I was able. Stones cut into my bare feet.

At the van panic returned. I couldn't see James. But when I opened the door, I saw him stretched out across the front seats listening to the low-volume radio. I threw my shoes onto the floor of the van and hugged him, shielding him from the face at the other end of the drive.

I looked into his eyes. 'You're okay?'

'Of course I am.'

'No one has been here?'

'A car drove by, I think. Mum, what's the matter?'

'It's nothing.'

'You've hurt your hand.'

'Only a splinter.'

'Why did you take your shoes off?'

'I didn't want to disturb anyone. Let's get home.'

I did a U-turn in the wide opening in front of the gates, and drove off without looking back down the drive to the school, from where, I was certain, her eyes were still watching. Shivering, I switched on the van heating and asked James to turn up the volume of Radio 1. He increased it a little. I hoped the sound would drive out the picture in my head.

On the journey home, I was unable to think. Nothing was important except putting distance between us and Hillgate. But the picture lingered.

'Turn it louder,' I said.

He increased it to a deafening level. Now I felt safer. Every few seconds I looked to my left to see if James was still there, still safe. And once I looked over my shoulder to check that the rear of the van was empty. The worst part was stopping at road junctions. I was scared that someone would approach us from the shadows and try to get in. This was sometimes Kate Lennox, but once or twice John Copeford.

As soon as we were in the house, I double-checked that all the doors were locked. I made hot chocolate for James and myself, which we drank together in his room. It wasn't until he was asleep that I left him. Leaving all the upstairs lights on, I went down to the kitchen and there let the flood of questions flow into my head.

I must tell someone. I must phone immediately. But who? Molly? No, Ruth. But she was still away on her field trip and not due back until tomorrow. Had Kate Lennox recognised me? Did she even see me? Was I imagining that face at the window? No, I knew what I had seen. Yes, she had recognised me, and I was in danger. As I looked at the phone, the face at the window seemed to reappear in the dark against my kitchen window. I rushed upstairs, checked on James again, went to my bedroom and, fully clothed, climbed in. I tried to be rational. Since it was unthinkable to phone Dr Lennox who, I was certain, wouldn't believe me and would support all the denials his wife was sure to make – even provide her with an irrefutable alibi – I should contact the deputy head, Alan Carter. But here there was a problem. I didn't really know him, certainly had no confidence in him. Nor could I trust him. He had recently been kicked by Mark Jarritt; was there more to that outburst than I realised? And Alan Carter had shown himself too protective of his own job to want to cause any trouble for the Lennoxes. Who else could I talk to? No one came to mind. For all I knew, what I had witnessed was merely one corner of a web of abuse. I pictured the faces of the other staff, one by one, but now they appeared, not as cynical coffee-drinkers in break-times, some near-alcoholics, but as dark shapes like the silhouette I had seen glide past the window. Looking at each of them, I felt their eyes meet mine, and knew I could confide in none of them. I pulled the covers over myself, too frightened to think clearly.

I then remembered that I was due to be having dinner with the Lennoxes tomorrow. But now there could be no dinner. Before then I would have told someone. And as for Speech Day on Saturday, I couldn't imagine how that could now take place. I thought about the reaction of parents, children and governors when they learned about it. I imagined the investigation, the press, the publicity.

By the early hours, my head was racing with the legal implications of what I had seen, so that, when I eventually fell asleep, I was beset by fitful dreams in which I stood in a witness box while a barrister questioned me.

'So what you claim you saw was seen in the dark through a keyhole. No one else saw it, and, as the court has heard, the people you claim you saw totally deny it. Furthermore, as a mother of a small boy, your instinct did not make you enter the room and take action against what you would have us believe took place. Instead, Mrs Burns, you drove home. Am I correct?'

Somewhere beneath me in the court was Adam. I wasn't certain if he was on my side, nor, if he was, whether he really believed me. Kate Lennox was there, confident in her ability to be found innocent. She looked at me with loathing and disdain. I wasn't certain who was in the dock, she or I. When I looked up at the judge, I saw the drawn face of John Copeford, unrepentant, smiling as the barrister dissected my character.

'Now is it true that you have dealings with a certain Cosmo Butler?'

I nodded, then looked up. One of the faces in the public gallery was B's.

'Would you tell the court the nature of those dealings?'

## 22

Daylight was a consolation, but I was exhausted, even though I had overslept. As yesterday's fears again gripped me, I was aware, not of a need to talk to someone about the previous night, but of a wish I had never walked up that staircase.

It was a rush to throw a few things into an overnight bag for James – after school he was going away with Molly, Paul and Ben for a day's fishing on Graffham Water, followed by a ceramics event in Bedford. In my haste to drop him off at Molly's, so she could take him to school, all late-night resolve to tell her everything was pushed aside. At 8.15am that morning it felt wisest to wait, to go to Hillgate and attend assembly as usual, before seeking the right person to approach. I knew that boarding schools, to deal with matters of abuse, should have procedures, made known to governors, staff and parents, but if Hillgate had such a protocol, I had never been made aware of it. As I left home, I had no idea who could I safely speak to.

It was a cloudless, windless morning in which the calm of the country roads was disturbing, making me feel that the perfect weather was colluding in the concealment of a crime. So peaceful a morning was it, that I felt someone was offering me a chance to forget all I had seen. I dismissed the suggestion, but a mile from Hillgate, lowering the window and breathing in the summer stillness was like taking an opiate which promised to soothe away all harrowing memories. The drug might have worked, but the pain of the splinter, which had resisted my attempts to remove it, reduced its effect. The pressure to pretend that the events of last night had never happened increased as I approached the school. Beyond its iron gates, the school grounds with their weedless lawns, the edges precision-cut for Speech Day, the flashy geraniums – better suited to a municipal park – and the newly raked pea shingle in the car parks, insisted that my memories of the previous night were a phantasm. This time it was anger which resisted my compliance. Two maintenance men, one washing down the front door, the other sweeping the sills of the ground-floor windows, gave the impression of ordered efficiency, but to me they might have been two Secret Service clear-up men, removing all evidence of a covert operation the night before. Their work seemed cold-blooded and callous in the face of what had happened a few hours earlier behind a window above them.

As I parked, I watched children on their way to the library for assembly. Not wanting to enter the staffroom, I waited in my van until they had all gone in. The staff would now be walking from the staffroom to join them, moving down the passageway along which I had made my escape last night. A minute later, I saw David Lennox walk from his house towards the main door. I followed him at a distance. Last to enter the library, I took my place at the end of the row of staff, expecting to see all eyes bear down on me and read on my face the message publicising what I had seen last night. David Lennox greeted the school with his usual, 'Good morning, everybody,' and announced the Founder's Silence. I glanced at the Year Nines, and saw Mark Jarritt almost imperceptibly chewing gum and looking no different from usual, and no more or less bored than those standing near him. The ordinariness of it all distressed me.

That morning David Lennox replaced his customary sermonette with a diatribe about Speech Day, behaviour, manners towards visitors, punctuality and litter, during all of which I found it hard to believe that Speech Day would ever take place, at least not in its proposed form, presided over by this ranting misfit, with his smiling wife at his side. When he had run out of admonitions, he opened his lips as wide as possible without moving his teeth apart. It was either a grin or a threat to reinforce his point. He then strode out, his right hand reaching for his pipe pocket before he arrived at the library doors.

As Linda Baird hammered out one her of marching tunes, I saw in this woman, small in physique but strong in every other way, someone who might listen to me, believe me and know what should be done next. From none of the other staff did I receive such signals of reassurance. I resolved to speak to her after assembly. I would also speak to Ruth, not due back until later in the day; there had to be a contact number which I could obtain from the school office. I waited for Linda outside the library door.

'Ah, Phoebe.' A hand rested on my shoulder. Standing behind me in a powder-blue jacket and trousers, two buttons undone at the neck of her cream blouse, was Kate Lennox.

She smiled. 'Glad to have caught you. Still okay for tonight?'

She was so different from the creature seen through the keyhole that I replied with equal warmth. 'I'm looking forward to it.'

'Wonderful. Come as you are – we're never very formal. Now, there's Linda – I must have a word with her. See you later.'

As she left, I stared at her, for a moment doubting that this elegant figure, who might have stepped from the fashion pages of a county magazine, was the same woman I had seen last night. But looking at her chatting with Linda, I knew I had been outmanoeuvred. By what perverted intuition she had entered my skull and read my mind, I had no idea, but my instinct told me that this had indeed happened. Of course, I could still catch Linda on her way to the music room, but the sight of Kate Lennox talking to my would-be confidante threw me. I worried about what had been said between them. With no alternative, I turned to my classroom, defeated. I now feared Kate Lennox even more than before.

As I walked down the path, oblivious to the children around me, I felt her glance strike the back of my head. I knew she could sense my fear. And I could feel her smiling at this power over me. For the next hour I tried not to think of her, since I was certain she knew my thoughts more clearly than I knew them myself.

At break, I went straight to the office to ask for Ruth's contact number in Devon. But inside the half-open office door, Kate Lennox was standing, drinking coffee and chatting with Dora Prideaux. I walked past, thwarted again.

My next resort was the staffroom where, I thought, I could find the number of Hugh's office from a phone book or directory enquiries. However, the phone book had gone missing, Brian Devlin was monopolising the phone, and no one had a mobile I could borrow. I thought she, even at a distance, was controlling my life.

During the last lesson before lunch I made a decision. I let my class out five minutes early and walked, eyes fixed ahead, mind blank, to my van. Fifteen minutes later I pulled up outside Farrier's Arms Antiques, ran through the doorway and threw myself into the chair by the counter.

Frank appeared in the arch between shop and house. 'Tea?' he said. He raised his eyebrows. 'Or something stronger?'

He didn't wait for an answer, but left the room and reappeared with a bottle of whisky and two tumblers. He poured me a double which I gulped, spilling some on my dress.

'Ex-husband, is it? Or the posh blonde?'

'Neither. It's the school. It was last night. I saw the headmaster's wife with a boy . . .' I buried my head in my arms on the counter. I don't know how long I sobbed. I was glad he said nothing. When I looked up, he was holding a striped tea towel.

'Can't find a handkerchief,' he said.

I wiped its roughness on my face. Clinging on to it, I watched him refill my glass.

'It happened in a one-bed dormitory,' I said.

I gave him a description. When I had finished, he was silent. I watched him pull out a cigarette. He lit it.

'Have you told anyone?' he said.

'I don't know whom to approach.'

'How old is he?'

'Fourteen.'

'What are you going to do? It sounds like a police matter.'

'I don't know who to speak to.'

'Can't you speak to the assistant head? A senior teacher? Do you know any of the governors?'

I shook my head at each suggestion.

He picked up a bundle of lace bobbins from the counter and ran them through his fingers in thought.

'And last night – you weren't seen?'

'That's the worry. As I left the school, she looked out of the dormitory window – she must have recognised me.'

'So she could already be covering her back?'

I nodded.

'And I suppose the boy wouldn't admit anything?'

'Definitely not.'

'I wonder how much her husband knows.'

'Probably nothing. He lives in a dreamworld where he is head of some prestigious school. But if he does know something, or if he found out, I'm sure he'd protect her to save his own hide.'

'And give her some stick behind closed doors.'

'She wouldn't let him. I'm meant to be having dinner with them tonight. I can't go, of course.'

He dropped the bobbins on the counter. Some of their beads fell off and rolled to the floor. He left them there and finished his glass.

'Who runs this place – him or her?'

'Sometimes I think it's the school secretary.'

'Can you trust her?'

I tried to imagine myself approaching Dora Prideaux, to picture her face as she listened to me. 'I'm not sure.'

'Would she be involved in any network of abuse?'

'Most unlikely.'

'Would she believe you?'

I looked at Frank and imagined his face was hers. 'Yes, I think she would.'

'So you'd be safe with her?'

'I haven't considered it before now.'

'You weren't meant to.'

'What?'

'That woman in the dormitory has got to you, hasn't she?'

'I'm sure she knows every thought in my head.'

'That sort are cunning. Mind control is how they operate.'

'I feel she knows I'm here.'

Frank looked at me as, in fear, I clung to the tea towel with one hand and gripped my glass with the other. Watching his smoke rings go up to the ceiling, I counted the dusty jars on the shelf behind him. He again saw the tears in my eyes. After the next column of rings he left his mouth open.

'So . . . as a child,' he said, 'you've been . . . on the other side of the keyhole.'

I lowered my eyes and nodded. The tears streamed out.

'The bastards,' he whispered.

For several minutes the shop was silent, apart from the sound of my crying. When I looked up, he was reading the *Racing Post*.

He lit another cigarette. 'Phone the secretary from here. Fix a meeting outside the school.' He dragged his black bakelite phone through the ash on the counter towards me. I knew that by now she would be back from lunch. I dialled.

'Miss Prideaux? Phoebe Burns. Are you alone in the office?'

'I am. Why?'

'I must see you. Can I meet you somewhere outside school? It's urgent. I'm at a friend's now. I'll be in for afternoon lessons, but I can't speak to you on the premises.'

'Phoebe, are you all right?'

'Yes, but I must see you soon. But not at school.'

'Let me see. Speech Day preparations keep me here until early evening. After that I've a parish council meeting which I can't easily get out of . . .'

'This is very urgent.'

'Can you meet me at my home early tomorrow? Eight-thirty?' She gave me the address.

'I'll be there. Thank you.' I replaced the phone and sighed.

'You need some food,' Frank said.

He disappeared. When he returned, he was carrying a tray with two plates, bread, cheese and chutney. We ate in silence until he said, 'I think you'll have to go to that dinner tonight.'

'I can't.'

'If you don't, she'll suspect you're on to her. You could be in worse danger.'

'I'm too frightened.'

'That's in your favour. The more scared you look the better.'

'That won't be hard.'

I looked at him. He was framed by junk, dust, ash and crumbs. I trusted him. 'Okay,' I said. 'I'll go. They'll be other people there, but I'll still be terrified.'

'Good. At this stage she's got to feel she's ahead of you. Remember, she's banking on your fear. If you appear confident, she might think that you've already reported what you saw to a governor. Or worse, she might think you're about to blackmail her. Sometimes fear is your best friend.'

I pulled myself from my chair. Frank came round from the counter and opened the door. Another friend might have given me a hug. That wasn't his way. He just winked as I left. It told me he knew I was going to be safe. I was taking with me all his own experience in whatever life he had led before he fetched up at this crumbling former pub. I returned to Hillgate, feeling that the absurdity of relying on the advice of this world-weary armchair punter had more chance of seeing me through than anyone else's wisdom.

On my return to Hillgate, the outward normality was again disturbing, but the visit to Frank and the phone call to Dora had given me some strength, so that afternoon lessons drifted by in a welcome, if ominous, calm. But despite this strength, I was not up to going to the staffroom during the afternoon break, although I could have done with the tea to wash away the taste of Frank's whisky. But none of the children appeared to notice my breath; perhaps Duggy had made them used to it.

At the final bell, not wanting to see anyone, I remained in my classroom. It wasn't until shortly after 6.00pm that I ventured out, knowing that everyone would be in the dining room for the evening meal. Dinner at the Lennoxes was at 7.00pm. Needing this hour to nerve myself, I set out for a short walk around the cricket field.

Since there was no Pipistrelles' match tonight, after a single circuit, I walked towards the centre. But alone on the field, I felt vulnerable and under surveillance at every step. I moved towards the boundary, but here, close to the trees, I felt drawn by a hidden force towards the main school. In the car park, I regained some freedom and went to my van to listen to the radio. The voices of the evening news provided some safe company, but every few seconds I found my head turning in the direction of the headmaster's house where, I was certain, my every thought and movement was being monitored. Under this pressure, it was not enough to sit and listen. I looked around for reading matter. There was nothing, apart from the computer magazine, left behind by James last night. I thumbed through a few pages, trying to divert my mind among the readers' letters and adverts for expensive gadgetry. It was a different world, and to me incomprehensible. I turned some more pages. A photo fell out. I picked it up. It was a picture of B standing on a low cliff with the sea in the background – Southwold, I guessed. Her right arm was pointing down to the tops of the beach huts. Her left arm was nestled around James. The look on her face suggested she owned the whole town, James included. I turned it over. On the back she had written, *To Jamesey from your weekend Mum. X X X.*

Livid, I stared at it. At the kisses, written without removing pen from paper, like upturned fishing stools. At each letter *e*, written Greek-style, like the lipstick scribble in the pub, with their middle strokes pointing up, like barbs on hooks. I glared at the words *weekend Mum*, until *weekend* read like *weakened*, which was exactly what she had done to me. I crumpled the photo in my hand and stormed from my van to the staffroom phone, the woman behind the yew hedge powerless to control my movements.

Cosmo was in. 'Yeah,' he answered.

'When are you next seeing her?'

'What is this?'

'When do you see her next?'

'This isn't a convenient time.'

'I don't care.'

'All right, give me a moment.'

I heard him mumble. Was she with him? In bed perhaps? I hoped so. Then footsteps. I imagined him going to another room with the phone. I smoothed out the creased photo in front of me. Anthony must have taken it. That made it worse.

'What is it then?' he snapped.

'I want to know when you plan to see her next – after today?'

'Can't this wait?'

'No.'

'Look,' he said wearily, 'we've only just got back from two days in London. Verdi at Covent Garden, several doses of bloody Shakespeare, and *Starlight Express* in between. I'm carrying out my side of the deal. I'll phone in three weeks.'

'A few things have changed. Are you seeing her tomorrow night?'

'Of course.'

'Where?'

'A restaurant.'

'Which one?'

'Dunstan's.'

'What time?'

'Half-seven.'

'You won't turn up.'

'We should do this as planned – I've managed fine so far.'

'As I said, things have changed. Don't turn up. I'll be there instead.'

'This is not what we agreed.'

'Think of the money you'll save. The Opera House couldn't have been cheap.'

He made a grunting laugh. 'It was an investment.'

'Not too taxing, I trust.'

'One tries to enjoy one's work.'

I smiled at his coldness. 'I'll come over on Sunday with the fragment.'

'Enjoy the restaurant tomorrow.'

'Oh, I shall. By the way, how did she ditch my ex-husband?'

'Painlessly, I think.'

'How did she manage it?'

'Not entirely sure. One doesn't like questioning women about former partners. Sort of bad manners, isn't it?'

In the corridor, the first of the children were leaving the dining room. I rang off. Dunstan's was in central Norwich. It was expensive. I had been there only once – a birthday treat last year from Molly and Paul. As I recalled its layout – it was a converted church – I remembered my own dinner appointment. It mattered less now, and I wasn't afraid. I then remembered Frank's advice that Kate Lennox was banking on my fear. I struggled to recapture my terror, but found it impossible.

Linda Baird entered the staffroom. 'Still here?' she said.

'I'm not due there until seven.'

'There's some dust on your dress. Shall I . . .?' With her fortissimo fingers she began to brush it off.

I resented her interference, however kindly intended. 'I was told to come as I am.' I moved to the mirror and straightened my hair.

'You'll do,' she said. 'I expect they'll have the sherry open already.'

'No, twenty minutes to go. I'll wait.' I tried to relax in an armchair.

Linda sat near the window. For a minute we were silent. She looked out towards the car park. 'There you are,' she said, 'the boys are already walking over to the head's house.'

I stood and saw the three boys, not in blazers but in grey suits. There being no excuse to linger, I left the staffroom and hurried after them; it felt safer to enter the house in their company. But before we arrived at the gate in the yew hedge I was pre-empted. Kate Lennox, with dog on lead, appeared in front of us.

'Phoebe, come and join me for a pre-prandial stroll. Boys, walk straight in. Leave some sherry for us.'

They accelerated to the front door.

I turned on my heels and positioned myself next to the dog. To have it between her and myself felt like protection.

She smiled at me. 'We'll leave them to get on with their male talk – David loves that kind of thing. I've borrowed one of the kitchen ladies for the evening, so everything's under control. All set for tomorrow?'

'I finished my classroom displays some time ago.'

'Your predecessor hardly bothered. The most he'd do was to dig out some tatty posters of Latin phrases in everyday use – *tempus fugit*, *quid pro quo* – that sort of thing. I'm not sure about those reds in the flowerbeds, are you? Come away, Tabloid!'

The dog was sniffing at some salvias in a bed by the circular lawn.

'Better find him a tree,' she said, turning towards the cricket field, where a groundsman was marking out a wicket. 'A wonderfully English sight, don't you think?'

She bent down to let the dog off its lead. I looked at her svelte figure in the expensive-looking dress printed with an abstract green and grey design, and at her dark hair falling to her springer's coat as she unleashed it.

'David always gets very excited about the Speech Day cricket match,' she said. The dog bounded away in its freedom. She drew herself upright, seeming taller than ever. 'Yesterday he went through the annual ritual of making sure his old cricket whites still fitted. Do you play any sport?'

'My son James and I go swimming occasionally – that's all nowadays.'

'We hope to start building a swimming pool over the summer. You'll be able to bring James here. Staff and their families will, of course, have their own swimming times.'

Inwardly I recoiled when she mentioned James's name. I said, 'If I stay on.'

'Oh, we hope you will.'

She moved close to me, and I smelled her perfume, sweet but acrid, like damask roses and plastic. She hadn't worn it last night.

'Phoebe, you seem to fit in very well here. I'm sure that all the formalities of advertisements and interviews for a full-time job can be waived. Between ourselves, David's had several letters from Latinists about the September vacancy, but I'm sure I can work on him and one or two governors to secure your position. How does that feel?'

She was inches from my face. I wanted to run to the open space of the cricket field, but her look snared me to her side. She was smiling with her mouth, but her eyes were needles. Now I had no need to fake fear. 'That's very good of you,' I said.

'Well, you do seem to have a certain empathy with the school. Hillgate's a little eccentric in many ways ... that bloody dog.'

Tabloid was sniffing around the groundsman's paint pot, either about to drink from it or lift his leg on it. She ran after him. The snare loosened, but I felt half-hypnotised by her; collusion would be so easy. I followed her as slowly as I dared. The dog was leading her a dance around the cricket field. I felt it was on my side, keeping her away from me, drawing her fire.

When at last, with the groundsman's help, she caught the dog, she hit him on the back with such a vicious blow, that I was surprised the force of it didn't sting her hand. When she rejoined me, the springer was walking to heel.

As we walked back, she said, 'Tabloid has a weakness for all things cricket. Like his master, I suppose. He once stole the Pipisrelles' ball. Mind you, some of them are so old, they probably welcomed the break.'

I pretended to smile.

'Of course,' she said, 'you know one of them, don't you?'

I shuddered. Did she miss nothing which happened here? 'He's merely an acquaintance through the antiques trade.'

'Ah, your other persona. You must look at David's collection of snuff boxes.'

She paused at the garden gate. 'I really feel the hedge is getting too high. Slow-growing though it is, it needs taking down a little. David likes it this height. What do you think, Phoebe? You look as if you're a gardener.'

'You could compromise and just remove a couple of feet.'

'Good old compromise,' she said, again fixing me with the needle eyes. The dog was straining again. She pulled at its lead with some violence. The tug was for me.

She led me into a hallway lined with prints of leading public schools – Winchester, Eton, Charterhouse, St Paul's. 'They came with the house,' she said. 'I think the governors might question our aspirations if we replaced them. Very silly, I know, but one doesn't like to upset things.' The needles were on me again.

I looked to the floor, which was covered with a beige fitted carpet. It continued into the dining room where David Lennox, wearing a darker tie than in the morning, was well into the sherry with the boys. In the middle of a story, he didn't notice our entry.

'It was the tiniest cut on my thumb,' he said, holding up his right hand, 'yet every time I pulled back the oar, a blob of blood marked my white rowing vest.'

The boys tried to look interested, but betrayed themselves through their occasional glances to each other. There was a wall-to-wall tidiness about the room which made it more a hotel suite than a home. At the far end was a dining area. It overlooked a rose garden planted with hybrid teas in formal beds. A twin-pillar dining table was set for dinner. Apart from six mean, hard-looking modern armchairs, a small sideboard and more topographical prints, this end of the room was empty. I suspected that most of the house was equally sterile, although Kate Lennox, I guessed, would have a room of her own somewhere. Since they had no children, this might well be upstairs. Her husband's own retreat was his study over at the school.

'It was my first race on the Thames,' he said. 'By the time we reached

Chiswick I looked as if I'd been shot in the chest. The stains never came out of my rowing vest.'

Kate Lennox handed me a sherry and whispered, 'He's been dining off this story for years.'

David Lennox now noticed us. 'Tell me, Mrs Burns, did you row in your college's ladies' eight?' The last word was said with a grin which remained as I answered.

'I'm afraid I didn't,' I said. He didn't want to pursue it. Instead, he tried to amuse us with a story about a Classics teacher he once knew who had rowed in a replica of a Roman warship.

'And you won't believe this,' he said, 'but my friend had only just had an operation for piles.'

The boys laughed, more at him than with him.

I thought I heard the school minibus drive into the car park and stop, but peering through the window near me, my vision was blocked by the hedge. I assumed that this was the field trip returning. Ruth was now close at hand but inaccessible. The thought made me feel more trapped than ever. I would phone her as soon as I was home. I looked away from the window. Kate Lennox was staring at me, reading my thoughts. I glanced towards the other end of the room, where the woman borrowed from the kitchens appeared and placed plates of terrine on the table. With a nod to her husband Kate Lennox indicated it was time to eat.

David Lennox was seated at one end of the table, I was on his right. Kate Lennox, at the other end, was in easy eye contact with all of us. Her husband clearly wanted to monopolise the conversation.

'At Dean Notley,' he said, 'these occasions were always black tie dos.' He filled my wine glass from a silver-mounted claret jug, filled his own, then asked the boy on his left to pass it down the table.

To involve the others, I asked the boy opposite if his parents were attending Speech Day. His reply was drowned by more reminiscences.

'Mind you,' Dr Lennox said, 'at Dean Notley, the high master's dining room table was large enough for eighteen of us to dine together. My first dinner there . . .'

'Darling, do stop telling us about Dean Notley,' Kate said, 'or we'll begin to think we are there and not at Hillgate.'

I suspected she had made this sort of interruption many times before; it was part of their dinner table script.

He grinned at the boy on my right. 'Everything ready for Speech Day?' It was a rhetorical question. 'At my own school, the head boy had to make a speech himself, and in my father's day it had to be in Latin.' He looked at me. I thought he was going to ask me something about my subject, but he said, 'Very different here from Elveden College, I imagine.'

'Elveden was a much bigger school.' It seemed the kindest reply.

'I've plans to expand Hillgate. At the moment our size is so much against us, especially when it comes to teams. We're always hard-pressed to field a decent rugby fifteen, or even a cricket eleven. On the touchline, I always feel I have to cheer extra loudly to make up the balance.' He drank half his glass. It was a cue for his wife.

'And at one rugby match he got so carried away,' she said, 'that he shouted, "Come on Notley," instead of, "Come on Hillgate." '

The boys smiled politely, David Lennox too. It was another part of their act, as neat as the edges of the rosebeds. He noticed my glance through the window.

'A good show, aren't they? We head-hunted the gardener from Walborough Crematorium. My only complaint is that his colour scheme does tend towards the garish.'

'Probably a reaction to his former place of employment,' said Kate.

'It always worries me,' he said, 'when I see him sprinkle a top dressing on the roses. One does wonder where all those grey granules come from.'

'Not when we're eating, darling.'

The boys laughed. This was a polished routine, but it scared me to be caught between the cold eyes at one end of the table and the mad grin at the other. Respite came between courses. The kitchen assistant must have gone home, since it was Kate Lennox who removed our plates. For a minute she left the room. In her absence David Lennox told us of his plans to introduce an Air Force Section into the Cadet Force. I wanted to interrupt and tell him that it was unlikely that he would be here long enough to see it.

When Kate appeared with a casserole, he began to talk about proposals for a school gardening club.

'Perhaps Phoebe can help out with this next term,' she said.

'We shall have to see,' he said.

I met her smile which said that his 'we' related more to her than to him, that the decision was hers, and that she did not allow people to cross her. Well before the summer pudding I was shivering again.

Every few minutes David Lennox topped up our glasses, a ploy to disguise the fact that his was the only one which was empty. The boys were quick to work this to their advantage, and there developed a sly competition among them to keep up with their host, or even to be a sip or two ahead of him. I could imagine them arguing afterwards who the winner had been. Several times he refilled the claret jug from bottles on the sideboard, until Kate Lennox, who no doubt had seen it all before, removed the jug from the table.

Savouring the last glass, he said to me, 'Now, Mrs Burns, *By no means the least part of knowledge is to know good wine.* Isn't that from a Latin proverb?'

'I believe it is,' I lied.

His wife disappeared and returned with a very small decanter of port. She placed it in front of him with a gesture which said that this was the last of the evening's alcohol. He poured himself as much as he dared, then, having given the decanter a reluctant push to the boy on his left, gulped from his rationed glass, leaned back on his chair and, although perspiring, looked relaxed for the first time that evening. Perhaps the drink had finally performed its daily trick.

'One of the few occasions, tomorrow, for full academic dress,' he said. He turned to me. 'I trust you have a gown and hood?'

'I'm not sure I do,' I said. 'Perhaps I can borrow one.' Again, I felt certain she was in my head again, pleased to discover that I was degreeless, and smiling to have something to use against me if I ever even considered breaking my silence. I imagined a governor saying to me, 'You fraudulently became a member of staff, and now you want us to believe this other tissue of lies?' The room had now become hot and oppressive. My dress clung to me uncomfortably.

After coffee he sent the boys back to school. I wanted to go too, but he held me back. 'Brandy? Or a liqueur?' It was a blatant excuse for more alcohol, but he saw the frown from the other end of the table. 'However, with Speech Day tomorrow, we must keep our wits about us,' he said. 'I must show you my collection of snuff boxes. I have some in my study, but the best ones are here.'

He stood and walked unsteadily to the sideboard where he pulled out a drawer. I followed, pleased to leave the imprisonment of my seat. Kate Lennox, all composure as she had been throughout the evening, was close behind.

He showed me the boxes one by one: several silver examples mounted with agate, some wooden boxes whose shapes reflected the trades of their original owners – a coffin for an undertaker, a shoe for a bootmaker, a pistol for a gunsmith – and several beautifully decorated porcelain boxes. Trying to avoid comments which might prolong my stay, I made noises of appreciation, while all the time his wife's perfume hung in the air close to me. I thought we were at the end of the collection, but one last box remained. I was foolish enough to ask about it.

'That in fact is mine,' she said. 'David gave it to me on our tenth wedding anniversary.' She placed it in my palm.

It was a Staffordshire enamel box. There was a poem on the lid:

> *Remember me when this you see*
> *And do not turn away.*
> *I will be true, my love, to you*
> *Whate'er the world shall say.*

I forget what I said when I had read it, but as I gave the box back to her my hand was trembling. Shortly afterwards I was able to leave, not doubting that whatever the problems in their marriage, or whatever accusations might be brought against her, he would give her his unwavering support.

On the path outside, it was an effort not to run to my van. I knew she was watching my departure and reading my thoughts through the way I walked. This information would be added to the extensive dossier she had already built up on me, now a very comprehensive file following these last two hours of scrutiny. Again, I made an effort to blank my mind, to look ahead, not to turn back to the house. Driving away, I focused only on the gates at the end of the drive. Even beyond them I felt unsafe. The smell of her was on my dress. I could hear her whispering in my ear. Her words could not be drowned by the radio. With distance her hold slackened, but refused to fall away, her hand remaining on my shoulder where it had touched me twelve hours earlier. It was still there when I arrived home and thought about phoning Ruth. The most she allowed me was to go upstairs and pull out a dress suitable for Speech Day. Next, like a child late home, I quickly went to bed, even though it was not yet dark. Hiding under the covers, I tried to think of neutral things in which she would have no interest – the sort of gardening and household trivia one might turn to after a nightmare. But her face lingered. I fell asleep thinking of Frank looking at me across the dirty glass counter. She tried to replace his features with her own, but his unshaven face, creased clothes and the clutter of his shop were too strong for her ordered world, and he remained immovable.

## 23

I n the morning I woke slowly, aware only of fear. My mind dared my eyes to open. When they did, I lay in bed motionless, allowing the sounds in the garden to drown thoughts of the previous night. As full consciousness swept in, I remembered the dinner party and saw her face. But I knew at once that it was no longer close to me. She was not in this room, nor in this house. During the night, confident in my acquiescence, she had left. In this assurance I might have fallen asleep again, but I soon remembered that today was Speech Day, and I had an early-morning appointment. Since the act of remembering this risked her return, I lay in bed and waited until I was certain I was alone in the house. Only then did I feel I could get up with impunity.

It was now almost 8.00am. I was shocked that I had slept over nine hours. I dressed quickly, but not in my Speech Day clothes. They could wait – I was not required at the school until late morning. But I was annoyed at having overslept. I would have liked more time to prepare for this meeting. I was also hungry, but breakfast too would have to be delayed. My annoyance was increased by a thick mist which agonisingly prolonged the ten-mile drive to Dora's village. I felt that Kate Lennox had somehow conspired with the weather, until, a few miles from home, the mist lifted, and damp banks of mauve tufted vetch began to appear at the roadside. My mood calmed. I was now glad not to have been awake early, brooding for two hours on what to say to her – an exercise which would only have confused the facts in my mind.

Dora lived in Tylby, a village about the same size as Ulford but prettier, with its wide green and large pond. I imagined that her house would be one of the old cottages near the pub. However, her address in Front Lane proved to be at the far end of the village. It was one of a row of modern bungalows near the church – perhaps her reason for choosing it. Outside, the air was damp. I shivered as I walked down the path.

She opened the front door before I could ring the bell. Looking me up and down, she said, 'Coffee and toast for you, I think.'

She was in her Speech Day best – a Liberty print dress, thin stockings for once, new navy shoes, and a ruby ring I had never before seen her wear. She showed me into a sitting room whose walls were lined with bookcases and Victorian watercolours. While she was making my breakfast, they distracted me from thoughts of Kate Lennox. Among her books I noticed the *Mapp and Lucia* series. This encouraged me – Dora might be a kindred spirit. I liked her watercolours too. I hadn't progressed beyond some studies of the Italian lakes when she arrived with a tray.

'Lake Maggiore,' she said, and, while I ate and drank, I listened uneasily as she talked of her father's passion for Italy.

When I had finished my toast, she said, 'You sounded most distressed on the phone.'

As I told her every detail of Thursday night, I felt I was confessing to a crime. When I lowered my voice, she placed an elbow on the arm of her chair, resting her chin on her hand as she listened. I might have been a penitent confessing to a priest. I thought of Charlotte Brontë's Lucy Snowe, distressed, staggering into a Catholic church and kneeling in a confessional. And yet, like her, I had committed no crime. Our eyes scarcely met as I described what I had seen. Unaccountably, the guilt persisted. Her only reaction was one sharp, audible intake of breath. It made me shiver again. I paused. She broke the atmosphere by refilling my cup.

I faltered my way through an account of last night's supper. In tears I said, 'I'm certain she knows I saw her. And she'll deny it all. Jarritt too.' I clung to the arms of my chair.

Dora placed a hand on my shoulder. 'Phoebe, you were right in coming to me. I can see how distressing this has been for you.'

'I'm scared of Kate Lennox.'

'You don't need to be.'

'I feel she knows I'm here talking to you.'

'My dear, I'm sure she doesn't.'

'She prevented me from seeing you yesterday.'

'How could she have done?'

'She was in your office during break.'

From under her pewter-grey hair my confidante looked at me in silence, then, 'Are you absolutely certain of the identities of the people you saw on Thursday night?'

'Yes. And she'll be waiting for me again today.'

'Do you have any doubts whatsoever about what you witnessed?'

'None.'

Frowning, she sat down again. 'Now, tell me, I assume you have told no one else.'

I shook my head – Frank didn't count.

'Good. At this point it is most important that as few people know as possible. We must move cautiously. This would be a major crisis at any time, but today . . . I shall of course take this immediately to the Chairman of Governors. You will need to be at hand.'

'What will happen?'

'There is a procedure which the Chairman must follow. We'll take it step by step.'

'But you do believe me, don't you?'

'Phoebe, I'm sure you're telling me what you believe to be true. But I must counsel patience and discretion. This won't be easy.'

I looked at her. Did she believe me? I thought so, but wasn't totally convinced. Again feeling guilt, I shuddered at the prospect of having to repeat my story again, and to a stranger. She offered me more toast, but, hungry though I was, I refused. When I left, she walked with me to my van.

'Take care of yourself,' she said.

I returned to Ulford, wishing to God that I was with James and the others on Graffham Water. I imagined them sitting in silence in the boat. I saw James, his eyes on the fly, his left hand gathering in line, waiting for the elusive tug. My stomach churned at the prospect of my own day.

At home, I tried to rid my mind of a picture of Kate Lennox watching out for me in the car park later in the morning. Reason told me that the Speech Day programme and her guests would fully occupy her, leaving me free to hide myself among my colleagues or with parents and children. But at 10.40am, as I set off for the school, I was convinced that she would be standing at the iron gates, waiting for me.

I had been to Speech Days at the other schools where I had taught, but I was totally unprepared for the sight which hit me before I arrived at the car park. The grounds were ablaze with dazzling hats, summer dresses, bright ties and glittering shoes. Climbing from my van, I said, 'Good morning,' to a woman in a short, clinging, magenta dress as she slid out of a BMW. She appeared to have gold rings or chains on every inch of her tanned, bare flesh. Eyeing my own dress, grey and printed with understated sprigs – almost a governess fabric – she frowned at my van, managed half a nod and gave me a look which suggested she thought I was a caterer. As her husband, in a black blazer, clicked the BMW's central locking with a punching throw of his arm, the sun caught the stone in his ring, a diamond bigger than any on his wife's fingers. I fought through a crowd of similar couples and felt like a rogue swatch on a fashion house floor. Some of the mothers I must have met before, but since they had usually been in jeans or jodhpurs and in a 6.00pm hurry, not glammed-up for Speech Day, I struggled to recognise any of them. But they all knew each other, and were too busy talking about school fees or exotic holidays to notice me. They were certainly in no hurry to meet up with their children. Head down, I made for the staffroom, relieved not to have seen Kate Lennox.

I was hoping to find Ruth, but the room was empty apart from Joan, smoking and staring out of the window. It was the first time I had seen her in neither track suit nor khaki. Instead, she was wearing an unflattering dress of a design which included full-size sunflowers.

'Another bloody cow's carnival,' she said. She saw me looking at her feet, which were crammed into tiny gold sandals. 'Yes, and I've pulled out my fuck-me-quick slingbacks for the occasion.'

'Has Ruth arrived yet?'

'Not if she has any sense.'

'Perhaps she'll go straight to her classroom.'

She turned from the window. 'This classroom display nonsense is a waste of time. None of the parents gives a toss about it. All they want to do is to get to the playing fields and open their hampers.'

She continued to survey the car park. I stayed well away from the window, wishing Ruth would arrive. I wasn't sure what to tell her. I felt duty-bound not to say much, but I was desperate for her company.

The door opened. It was Renwick. He was wearing a tight-fitting pinstriped suit. He joined Joan at the window. 'I don't know what's more disturbing,' he said, 'seeing the parents *en masse*, or seeing some of one's former pupils ten years on.'

'When do we open our classrooms?' I said.

'Whenever you like,' said Renwick. 'Last year, I only had three parents through the door, and one of those only wanted to know the way to the kitchens, so he could get some ice for the G and Ts.'

Ruth and Duggy entered together. She was in pale yellow – one of the Ghost dresses of which she had so many – and carrying some roses which, I guessed, were for her classroom. I had planned some flowers for mine, but in the last two days such thoughts had evaporated.

Duggy was in a dark three-piece suit, blue shirt, and a white stiff collar which cut into his neck. He stood with the other two at the window. 'To think we rely on their wallets for our livelihood,' he said.

'So you'll be joining the state system in September?' said Renwick.

'No better there,' he said.

'Good field trip?' Joan asked Ruth.

'The sun shone, and we came back with the same number we left with.'

'Only half successful then,' said Duggy.

'We mustn't lose any more from the roll,' said Ruth.

I walked over to her and whispered, 'Can I have a quiet word – as soon as possible?'

She saw the desperation in my face. 'Come with me to my room. I must put these in water – they've got enough nicotine on them now to keep away any bug.'

To avoid the parents, Ruth led me out of the main building by the rear entrance. It was a route which worried me, since it was necessary to pass the dining hall and the school office, both places where we might meet Kate Lennox. But we arrived at the back door unseen and walked round to the safety of her classroom. The door to Ruth's room, however, was barred by a group of visitors intent on having their photo taken against the background of the old arboretum. I did a double take when I looked at the young woman with the camera. With her back to the classroom door, she was waving the group into position. It wasn't B, but with her fair hair, floaty gauze dress, braying voice and extravagant gestures, she might have been her twin. Standing to one side – Ruth patient with her roses, I shooting glances up and down the path – we waited while the group was arranged and rearranged for a dozen shots. The delay was unbearable. Somehow, Kate Lennox and B had joined forces and had contrived to send minions to obstruct me. My anger at this destroyed any resolve not to tell Ruth everything.

When the visitors had gone and we were safe in her room, I gave Ruth a full account. Telling her was easier than telling Dora Prideaux, since, as soon as I began, I had the absolute certainty that she believed every word. She listened without interruption, apart from a dash to the door, which she locked to ensure no disturbance.

Afterwards, with more sadness than surprise in her face, she took my hand. 'Phoebe, I'm so sorry for your having to go through all this. I'll do all I can to help you.'

'I wish I could have told you earlier. I've been so scared.'

'I can understand.'

'I'm not sure if I can get through today.'

'Don't worry. I won't let you out of my sight.'

'How am I going to handle it when I next see Kate Lennox? By now Dora's bound to have spoken to the Chairman of Governors. And he will have spoken to the Lennoxes.'

'You'll need representation as soon as possible. Do you belong to a union?'

'I never have done.'

'I'll get Hugh to help. We'll do the necessary today.'

In her face I saw her mind race. Her frown disturbed me. 'Ruth, what is it?'

'If she and Mark Jarritt both deny it . . .'

'My word against theirs?'

'Exactly.'

'What can I do?'

'We'll have to see how the day develops.'

'Should I speak to Mark Jarritt? He seems to like me.'

'You can't. That would harm the investigation.'

'Did no one have any suspicions about her before now?'

'No. About him and his drinking, yes. Not about her.'

Again I felt afraid. 'I should have spoken to someone sooner, shouldn't I?'

'I can see why you didn't, but . . .'

'It would have helped my case, wouldn't it?'

'This is where we need Hugh.'

I felt desperate. 'How can I face Speech Day? I feel like running away from this place.'

'That would play into their hands.'

'I should be in my classroom now. I'm not sure if I can face all those parents and visitors. And maybe her as well.'

'You probably won't see her.'

'How do you know?'

'She and David will be entertaining the General and his wife at the headmaster's house. They have lunch there too. I've only once known them to tour the classrooms.'

'I'm not up to standing and waiting to see if they do it again.'

'We'll work together. It's all fairly low key – an item on the programme, but one largely ignored. I'll leave this room open, we'll unlock your room, then together spend fifteen minutes in each.'

Happy to fall in with her plan, I followed her to my room. Over the next fifteen minutes we saw more than Renwick's three parents of the previous year, but their visits were quick and perfunctory; we spent most of our time staring out along the empty path outside. Only one visitor lingered for questions – a pupil's grandfather, who wondered if I wanted some shards of Roman pottery which had been dug up on his farm. I found enough patience to listen and accept the offer, but wanted to tell him that after today he might not feel so kindly disposed towards the school. Ruth stayed by my side. During our time in her classroom, I waited in a corner and prayed for as few visitors as possible. Kate Lennox had still not appeared.

At 12.30pm, when it was clear there would be no more visitors to the biology room, Ruth said, 'We can relax. She's sure to be at the house by now.'

'But won't any governors visit us?'

'You've already seen the Parent Governor, but I thought it best at the time not to tell you.'

'What about the Chairman and the others?'

'They occasionally wander in, but I imagine it's too late for them now. Anyhow ...'

She hesitated. I knew she was protecting me. 'They have other things to discuss,' I said.

She nodded.

There were no more visitors, and at 1.00pm we walked over to the dining hall for lunch. On returning to the main building, my anxiety returned.

Ruth tried to calm me. 'You're safe for the next hour. You might even find the food edible – the kitchen staff make more of an effort today.'

Lunch was set out on two tables, one for teachers, one for the remnant of children whose parents were not attending Speech Day. Among them was Mark Jarritt. I looked at his face, but failed to discern any sign that someone might have spoken to him about Thursday night.

Duggy was last into the dining hall. He was carrying a large tray of glasses and two open bottles of Chablis.

'With Lennox and the governors hard at it, and corks popping round the playing fields like a clay pigeon shoot, I'm buggered why we should be left out,' he said.

Our self-appointed host gave us glasses and filled them. I found myself with Ruth on one side, Brian on the other. He had made no effort to change his appearance for the day, apart from a sickly orange tie. Everyone at the table was for once in good spirits, appreciating the smoked salmon which appeared from the kitchen. I had no appetite, but was pleased to be anonymous in my colleagues' company, and to shelter under their rare affability.

Duggy continued to wait on us, serving us with salad and refilling our glasses; his restaurant days had not been entirely wasted. He was out to champion our cause against the headmaster and governors. 'It's an outrage,' he said between mouthfuls, 'Alan here, deputy head and not invited to lunch with the VIPs, but shoved in with us lot and the unwanted children.'

'Something of a relief,' said Alan.

'And the seating arrangements in the large marquee,' said Duggy. 'That's another disgrace. They should have built a stage big enough for all of us to be up there on either side of the head, not stuck in the front row like a load of prats.'

'Speak for yourself,' said Renwick.

At this point, the atmosphere degenerated into staffroom bickering.

'But we should be up there on the platform,' said Duggy.

'I suppose it depends on whether you like being looked at,' said Brian.

'On Speech Day we bloody well ought to be seen.'

I whispered to Ruth, 'I can't take much more of this.'

'You're doing fine,' she said.

I tried to ignore the contentiousness around me. I succeeded until, playing with the bowl of anaemic trifle in front of me, I felt a hand on my shoulder. I dropped my spoon, not daring to look round. But the voice above the hand was Dora Prideaux's.

'Phoebe, can you spare a minute after lunch? In my office.' Without waiting for an answer, she walked away.

'What did she want?' said Duggy.

'No idea,' I said.

'Not asking you to give a welcoming speech in Latin to the General?' said Renwick.

'I think one of the CCF officers should do that,' said Ruth.

Under cover of this answer I left the table.

Before going to the office I visited the loo. From its window I could see groups of parents and children making their way to the large marquee. The sight disturbed me. I was unable to imagine the governors, in the face of all these people on whom the school's future depended, being willing to entertain any suggestion of impropriety, let alone abuse, on the part of their headmaster's wife. And I also knew that more prestigious schools than this had successfully covered up far worse. These feelings were confirmed when I entered Dora's office. I had expected a governor, perhaps the Chairman, to be with her, but she was alone.

Her voice was slow, subdued: 'Phoebe, I have informed the Chairman of Governors of everything you told me this morning, and he has asked me to speak to you now. Later in the afternoon, he will be seeing you himself. He and I together spoke to Mark Jarritt this morning. I have to tell you that he totally denies that anything inappropriate has taken place between himself and a member of staff.' She hesitated, preparing herself to perform an uncomfortable duty. 'Now, I'm not saying that we must believe him – we all know his behavioural record – but he was quite adamant in his denial. And the Chairman . . .'

'I know what I saw.'

'I'm not disputing what you told me. But I have to pass on to you what the Chairman has asked me to say. He spoke with the headmaster this morning and said that a member of staff had witnessed, taking place between Mrs Lennox and a male pupil, the act you have described. His reaction was one of categorical denial. And when Mrs Lennox was informed, her reaction was the same. Apparently, he or she frequently looks in at the dormitories at night, but anything more than this was denied in the strongest possible terms. I have to say that Dr Lennox has already contacted his professional association to represent him and Mrs Lennox in any enquiry.'

'So no one believes me?'

'It's not that – it's a case of the Chairman's assessing whether there are sufficient grounds to contact the Local Authority or police. At the moment, he is not certain that there are.'

I became angry. 'Does this mean he does nothing?'

'No, it doesn't.'

'I shall be talking to my own solicitor before the end of the day,'

'Phoebe, please don't do anything precipitous. We are still at a very early stage in the procedure.'

'So what happens next? Do we wait for another round of abuse and hope that next time there will be more than one witness?'

'The Chairman would like to see you himself at four o'clock.'

'And meantime the day goes on with its speeches and strawberry teas.'

'No, the Chairman regards this as a matter of utmost gravity.'

'But he won't let it disturb Speech Day?'

'It's not like that.'

'But you believe me, don't you?'

'Phoebe, I said I believed you, and I've told the Chairman I believe you, but we must trust his judgement as to what action must be taken.'

'If any.'

'We must abide by whatever he decides.'

'Meanwhile, what will Kate Lennox, backed by her husband, do to me?'

'Your name has not been mentioned to the Lennoxes – only that a member of staff has reported the incident.'

'She'll know it was me, and already she'll have told him that it's me who's accusing her. And those two will stick together.'

'You must explain all this to the Chairman,' she said firmly. 'Now we have speeches to listen to, and I'm not relishing the next ninety minutes any more than you.' She showed me to the door. 'Your colleagues will be in the staffroom, robing.'

I recoiled at the word. It made me think of robing rooms in law courts.

The staffroom was full of the familiar after-lunch cigarette smoke, but different in that its occupants were in gowns and hoods. Ruth alone hadn't robed.

'There's a spare gown if you want one,' she said.

'I'll go as I am,' I said.

'I'm not one for this parade either. Any progress?'

I whispered, 'I've had as much as I can take. As we suspected, it's my word against hers. I've got to see the Chairman later. What's he like?'

'I've only met him once. A land agent, I think.'

Duggy noticed our lack of academic dress. 'You two letting the side down, are you?'

'We'll go in last if you like,' Ruth said.

We all processed in pairs to the marquee, Ruth and I at the rear.

'If nothing happens by the end of the day, I'll go to the police myself,' I told her.

'Please speak to Hugh first.'

'I have to do something.'

'If you go out on a limb, you'll be doing her work for her.'

'She just wants me to shut up.'

'She may have done so yesterday, but now she'll want to discredit you, perhaps make up some story that you've got it in for the school, because they won't give you a full-time job. If you go behind the governors' backs now, you'll strengthen her position.'

We were near the marquee. I could hear the sound of conversation from inside. I felt my case was hopeless. I turned to Ruth. 'What would you do if you were me? But then I suppose you wouldn't have looked through a keyhole in the first place – just walked in. That would have been simpler.'

We were by the vases of flowers at the entrance.

'Ready for the charade?' said Ruth.

I nodded. As we filed down the aisle, I tried not to look at the rows of parents and children on either side. When we took our seats below the platform, Ruth and I were the last to sit, and because there were more seats in the row than members of staff, I had empty chairs on my right. I felt vulnerable. There followed a torturous wait, made worse some minutes later when I heard the rows behind us beginning to stand, a sign that the headmaster's party was approaching. Ruth must have noticed my unease at being at the end of the row, since she swapped places with me as we got to our feet.

As the dignitaries appeared on the platform, I didn't dare look up, but fixed my eyes on the floral arrangements in front of me. It wasn't until David Lennox had said some words of welcome that I raised my head, but only far enough to notice the pale olive skirt of the woman in front of me. While the headmaster gave an account of the year's achievements, I stared at the petunias and ivy, but after a few minutes, raising my head and realising that the figure in the olive skirt was of the wrong proportions to be Kate Lennox, I risked lifting my eyes higher. I was relieved to see another woman. I assumed she was the General's wife, whose husband, in dark suit and regimental tie, was beside her.

Speeches were made and applauded. I didn't hear what was said, but concentrated on not looking further along the platform, distracting myself by counting and recounting the flowers in front of me. But during the General's speech, when he made some joke and the marquee filled with laughter, for a moment I relaxed and looked over towards the far end of the platform. First, I glimpsed a tall, grey-haired man with an authoritative face, whom I took to be the Chairman of Governors. His pale brown, windowpane suit was immaculately cut. I imagined that he conducted his professional life with cold efficiency. Whether he would give me a fair hearing I was uncertain. Then, next to him, I saw Kate Lennox looking down at me. Elegant in a cream dress, from under a wide-brimmed hat of the same colour, she fixed me with a stare of pure hate. For a second, I averted my eyes from her towards her husband. He was on her left, leaning back, proud and relaxed in a charcoal-grey suit. But she pulled back my eyes to her own and bore down on me with contempt. Slowly this turned to triumph. It told me that my accusation would be dismissed as unfounded, based on a grudge against the school. There would be a replacement for me before the end of term.

Fear held my eyes to the matting on the floor. The General droned on about lessons learned from the Falklands War, making me wince at the words 'right-mindedness' and 'justice'. His speech received prolonged applause.

At the end of proceedings, when a Year Seven girl presented the General's wife and Kate Lennox with bouquets, I found the ceremony so appalling that my face must have shown my anger. I looked at Ruth and could see that she felt the same way.

David Lennox now announced with great solemnity, 'The School Song.'

Duggy, in the centre of the front row, was first to his feet. From her piano, at the back of the marquee, Linda Baird banged out the first line. Everyone knew the words and most were shouting more than singing, but if Ruth knew them, she, like me, was silent. Duggy was the loudest. I thought it strange how a man who every day bemoaned the school was now singing its song with an enthusiasm far greater than was necessary to impress the platform. When the final chorus, with its mawkish *Floreat Hillgate,* had been bawled out, and the dignitaries had left the marquee, Ruth, like me, was eager to escape the crowd heading for the tea tents. We searched for some sanity and solitude elsewhere. For once, the safest refuge was the staffroom.

When she and I were alone, I looked at the clock. It was 3.30pm. 'Will you come with me when I see the Chairman?' I said.

'If it would help. Of course.'

'Not that I expect him to do anything. You saw them all up there. They'll close ranks to protect each other and the name of the school.'

'You can only repeat what you've already said. After that we must take advice.'

'He looked a cold fish, seated up there with the Lennoxes.'

'He still has a duty to listen to you.'

'And do nothing if he thinks fit.'

We waited in silence.

After some minutes Ruth's patience broke. 'Phoebe, there's no reason why she should imprison us like this. Stay here. I'm going to the kitchens to find us some tea.'

'Don't be long.'

I was left looking out of the window beyond the cars towards the cricket field. There was no one in sight, apart from a groundsman, in the far distance, carrying stumps to the wicket.

Ruth soon returned with a tea tray.

No sooner had she poured two cups than the door was kicked open and Duggy entered. 'Just been talking to a parent with his ear to the ground,' he said. 'He tells me that plans to change the curriculum are on the agenda of tonight's Governors' Meeting. What is bloody Lennox playing at? We know he doesn't go much for consultation, but this . . .'

'If you can find another cup . . .' said Ruth.

'I need something stronger than that,' he said. He stamped out and slammed the door behind him.

At 4.55pm we looked at each other. 'Ready?' said Ruth.

I nodded. It was like being called up from cell to courtroom to hear the verdict.

I knocked on the office door.

'Come in,' called a soft voice.

The Chairman was seated behind Dora's desk. He stood when we entered. He now seemed even taller than when I had seen him in the marquee. He was quite at home in an office setting. I could have been a tenant calling on the agent to discuss a problem with my lease.

'Ronald Maltby-Drew,' he said, smiling and shaking my hand. 'Mrs Burns, I assume.' He turned to Ruth. 'Mrs Stebbing, isn't it? I'm terribly sorry, but I'm afraid this is a personal matter between Mrs Burns and myself. I shall have to ask you to wait in the staffroom.' With firm politeness he moved to usher her to the door.

With matching civility, Ruth said, 'Mrs Burns has been advised not to be interviewed alone. In view of this, I really feel I must remain with her.

'I'm aware of the confidentiality of the meeting, and I shall absolutely respect that.'

'Very well,' he said, piqued and struggling not to show it, 'but you cannot take part in our conversation.' He turned to me. 'Mrs Burns, I was given to understand no one else knew of this allegation. May I point out that the procedure can only be hindered if you do not act with total discretion.' Forcing a smile, he pointed to two chairs and resumed his place at the desk, where he put on gold reading glasses, looked at some notes and frowned.

'Well, Mrs Burns, this is very difficult. I've heard in some detail what you claim you witnessed on Thursday evening.' He was struggling to speak gently, a style which came hard to him. 'As is my duty, I've spoken to both the individuals you claim you saw. I must say immediately that they both vigorously deny it. And the lady in question has been known to me for some years. That they were in the room is not in question. It was no more than a routine dormitory visit by a staff member. I suggest that you . . .'

'I know what I saw,' I said.

'I'm aware of what you think you saw.' He looked down at his notes, slowly removed his glasses and again frowned. 'Through a keyhole?'

'That's right,' I said.

'What puzzles me is that you, as a member of staff, with a responsibility for the welfare of children, and with, I believe, a young son of your own, did nothing about what you thought you had witnessed. Not the moment you thought you saw it. Nor later that night. Not even the next day. This to me is inexplicable.'

'I saw what I have reported,' I said.

'Somewhat late in the day. May I suggest that in the dim light of the corridor you may have been mistaken? You are free to reconsider your allegation. I am sure we can be understanding in this matter.'

The land agent was at his persuasive best. A small tenant was not going to interfere with the management of the estate.

'I was certainly not mistaken,' I said angrily.

He remained calm. His politeness was unnerving. 'Very well. As Chairman, I have to make a decision as to whether there is any reason to take your allegation further. On the evidence given to me, I do not believe I can.'

'Then I shall take it further myself,' I shouted. 'It's a travesty.'

'Please be calm, Mrs Burns.'

'How can I be, when the most awful abuse is being brushed aside?'

He stretched out an arm. 'Nothing is being brushed aside.'

I raised myself from my seat. 'You're covering up for a friend.' I pointed at him. 'And for the sake of the school's reputation.' I felt Ruth's arm restrain me.

The Chairman was now repressing his own anger. 'I've tried to be reasonable with you, Mrs Burns, and I will continue to respect you as a member of staff. May I suggest . . .'

'I don't want your respect,' I said. 'I want protection for that boy.'

'The boy in question is being well cared for here at Hillgate. After an unfortunate childhood he has settled in here, and this is in fact the one school where he has managed more than a year without expulsion.'

'But he is being abused.'

He paused, regaining composure. 'This is very painful, Mrs Burns. As I said, we respect you as a member of staff, but your allegation has insufficient foundation to demand further action. In the light of this – shall we call it an intractable misunderstanding? – it is difficult to see how you can continue working here. That said, we are grateful for your contribution – you stepped in when a Latin teacher was desperately needed – and I have every reason to believe that in the classroom you are a conscientious teacher. With this in mind, my fellow governors and I are happy to pay you as if you had worked for the complete term. In addition, we will pay you for the seven weeks of the summer holiday. I have also persuaded them that we should round this up so that, in total, you receive a quarter of your annual salary. I hope you will agree that this is the best way forward, and will avoid any unpleasantness.'

I was speechless. The land agent was offering to pay me if I agreed to quit and leave quietly.

'At the same time,' he continued with the same smooth gentility, 'Dr Lennox will happily supply a reference, if at any time you apply for a post at another school. I hope you think this is fair. We will, of course, require a signature from you on a form which I will have drawn up by the end of today, as a mutual safeguard against any further action which may be to our or your detriment.'

'You mean you're buying my silence,' I said. Angry, I turned to Ruth. 'I think this meeting's at an end.' I stood up.

'I suggest that over the weekend you reflect carefully on your options, Mrs Burns,' he said.

He slowly stood, a remnant of a smile lingering on his face. There was a chilling confidence about him. In his life he had dealt with weightier issues than this. He was in total control. He knew I would gain nothing by pursuing it. I imagined that he was on very good terms with the Local Authority and police.

Ruth and I left the room. Beyond the study door, we were both too angry to speak. At the same time, I felt my earlier fear resurfacing. Ruth led me to the staffroom. Shaking, I walked to the window. She stood beside me, resting a hand on my arm. In the distance a groundsman was sweeping the wicket. I knew I was defeated. For a moment, in that stillness, I even began to question what I had seen on Thursday evening. What had been my state of mind? It occurred to me that in any enquiry my medical history might be raised. It would be easy to prove that I was an unreliable witness.

There was a knock on the staffroom door. We both turned, expecting to see the Chairman again. The door opened. It was Mark Jarritt.

He looked at me. 'Can I speak to you, Miss?'

Without waiting for an answer, he turned away from the doorway. We followed him along the corridor to the games room. I entered. Ruth waited outside.

He stood at one end of a pool table. His fingers clenched the baize cushion.

'What is it?' I said.

'Sort of tricky this, Miss.'

'I'm listening.'

'You're not a teacher like the others.'

'No, I'm not.'

'And not like this load of tossers today, are you?'

'Definitely not.'

'Poncing around in their hats and Beamers. Don't know nothing, do they?'

'Not much, no.'

One of his fingernails dug into the baize, ripping it.

'Thing is, I don't like grassing anyone up. But I don't like being leaned on neither. And that's what she's doing.'

'She?'

'Mrs Lennox. We sort of . . . you know . . . she comes up to my room at night. She told me no one would ever find out. But now she says someone's sussed her. So she's leaning on me to shut up, like she don't trust me.'

'That's not good.'

'No, it's not. She's been crazing me for the last two days. She even gave me this wedge yesterday. Look.' He pulled from a pocket an envelope stuffed with twenty-pound notes. 'What does that make me?'

'You're not like that, Mark,' I said.

'After the first couple of times I didn't even enjoy it. And now she's chicken because she thinks she's been found out. And she's giving me a load of hassle.' He threw the envelope down on the pool table. 'She can stuff her money. I can get plenty of that without her.'

'What are you going to do?'

'I feel like grassing her up. I almost did when the old bag and that other git tried to get it out of me this morning.'

'Would it be grassing if she's leaning on you?'

'No.'

'What's the problem then?'

'I'd be in for it too, wouldn't I?'

'I think you'd find she'll get all the blame, especially if you showed them the money.'

'Yeah, maybe.' Thoughtful, he looked at the envelope, then picked it up and slid it into a back pocket. His hands gripped the baize again. 'Who should I tell?'

'Start with the old bag.' I wasn't going to risk sending him to the Chairman.

'Her?'

'Yes.'

His fingernails ripped some more baize. 'Okay. When should I see her?'

'Right now.'

'On bleeding Speech Day?'

'The best time.'

He smiled, then was silent for a while. 'It wouldn't be grassing, would it?'

'No. She's brought it all on herself.'

'That's what I thought.' He moved to the door. Turning, he said, 'You're one of us, aren't you, Miss?'

'Yes. I am.'

Ruth was waiting for me in the corridor. My face answered all her questions.

'He's going to Dora Prideaux immediately. Kate Lennox has been trying to buy his silence.'

'How?'

'He showed me an envelope full of notes.'

'You don't think it's a put-up job – that he'll now say you've been bribing him to dish the dirt on her?'

'No, I believe him. His world has its rules, and he thinks she's broken them.'

'Just to be safe, we ought to follow him to the tea tents.'

As we left the main building, we saw, over on the cricket field, some of the players having catching practice near the pavilion. Further on, we passed Dr Lennox and two men, limbering up as they walked, with swings of their arms and imaginary batting strokes. All three ignored us.

The party mood in the tea tent for governors and guests met us well before we entered. The formality of the marquee had disappeared, and the dozen tables seemed to be competing over their cakes and strawberries to carry on the loudest conversation. At the far end, the General and his wife were in almost hysterical laughter over a story Kate Lennox was telling them. Having her back to the entrance, she failed to notice our arrival. Nor did she see that by another table Mark Jarritt was bending down, whispering to Dora Prideaux. Ruth and I waited. We saw Dora's face blanch. She quickly mumbled some excuse to the guests at her table, rose from her place and walked towards us, Mark a step behind her. For a few seconds, this slight intrusion on the teatime jollity reduced the volume of chatter. A head or two turned to watch the school secretary and a boy weave though the tables towards the exit. Kate Lennox too, catching the momentary change of atmosphere, turned her head towards us. She saw Dora Prideaux's back, possibly Mark Jarritt's also, but the full force of her stare was reserved for Ruth and me. I saw Ruth pale, and felt myself do the same. As Dora passed us, she laid a hand on my wrist and clasped it in reassurance. Her touch also told me that she, as much as me, felt in need of support.

'Two spare seats here,' shouted a voice on our right.

We turned to see Renwick making some space among the guests at his table. Before we had a chance to refuse, he got up from his half-eaten chocolate cake and bullied us into chairs.

'Now, I was at Antietam, wasn't I?' he said. 'We'll spend two days there before heading over to Gettysburg. Then down south for some Confederate victories.' He glanced at us, then back to his guests. 'I just wish I could persuade one or two of my colleagues to join us.'

The others at the table were enthralled by his itinerary, but Ruth and I desperately searched for an excuse to leave. We needn't have worried.

Renwick, pausing after a gulp of tea, shot a glance at his watch and jumped up, scattering cake crumbs over us. 'Cricket match. Starting now.

Mustn't miss the headmaster's annual over of slow right-arm boundary fodder.'

We followed him out. He took a bowl of strawberries with him, offering some to us as we walked towards the cricket pavilion. As I refused, I saw Kate Lennox not far behind us. I signalled the fact to Ruth.

'I think we'll spectate away from the crowds,' she said.

'Suit yourselves,' said Renwick, marching on with his bowl.

From under the trees, well away from the pavilion, we saw that the match was about to start. The school team was batting first. David Lennox, captain of the Headmaster's XI, was at the bowler's end, setting his field with much shouting and waving of arms.

I said to Ruth, 'How on earth can the Chairman allow this mockery to continue?'

'I'm sure he'll need to confer with the other governors first.'

'When? Today? Or will he leave it till Monday?'

'There's a Governors' Meeting this evening, so it has to be today. My bet is he'll be talking to them right now.'

'Meantime the cricket goes on.'

Over at the pavilion, the spectators were clapping as the opening batsmen walked to the wicket. The game began, with every run, wicket or good piece of fielding given enthusiastic applause from a growing crowd. Ruth and I stood motionless on the boundary, occasionally stealing glances towards Kate Lennox who, hatless now, was seated with the Chairman's wife near the pavilion. After a few overs the two women stood and set out on a slow walk along the opposite boundary. Between balls, they paused and watched the cricket. A few minutes later, it was clear that they planned a compete circuit.

'We'll have to move,' I said to Ruth. 'I can't be here when she walks past.'

'No, wait,' she said. 'Over there.'

I turned towards the main building to see Dora and the Chairman walking purposefully in our direction. I expected them to stop when they reached us, but without a glance they walked past, heading for the pavilion. Here the Chairman had a word with a boy, who immediately ran onto the field to convey a message to David Lennox. While this was happening, I noticed Dora Prideaux walking round the boundary towards Kate Lennox.

The messenger arrived at David Lennox and spoke to him. Players and spectators heard him shout his reply, 'Not in the middle of an over!' With an angry wave he sent the boy back to the pavilion.

This goaded the Chairman into taking to the field. He received no reaction until he was a few yards from David Lennox. A brief exchange followed. At one point the Chairman took him by the arm, as if to escort him to the pavilion. He did this with such authority, he must have handled similar situations before – I could imagine him sending home early a badly behaved member of a shooting party. But David Lennox pulled himself free and refused to leave until he had delegated his captaincy to another player. Angry, instead of following the Chairman to the pavilion, he strode off towards the main school.

Kate Lennox's circuit had been halted by Dora's approach. She spoke only briefly to the two women before they followed Dora back to the pavilion. For the first twenty yards, from the way Kate Lennox and the Chairman's wife ambled, again pausing occasionally to watch the game, it looked as if they were being called back for some minor domestic problem. Ruth and I looked at each other in angry disbelief. But as they neared the pavilion, Kate Lennox's dignity left her. She ran ahead of her friend, snatched up her hat from a chair and walked towards us. Ruth and I stood our ground, expecting a confrontation. But she did no more than brush past us, head in the air, in the direction of her house.

Dora and the Chairman now came up to us. The Chairman gave me a reluctant handshake.

'Mrs Burns,' he said, 'I apologise for my earlier hesitancy in listening to the allegation.' He took a deep breath. Apologies didn't come naturally to him. 'As you know, the situation has now radically altered, and I can only thank you for your diligence, and indeed your tenacity, in this distasteful business.'

'We are all grateful to you, Phoebe,' said Dora. Her thanks were more sincere than his.

'We hope we can rely on your discretion,' said the Chairman. 'The next few days will be very hard for all of us. Sooner or later the press will get hold of it, but the less they know at the moment the better.'

'I assume the headmaster will be resigning,' said Ruth.

'I and my fellow governors will make a statement in due course. Meanwhile, I must ask you both not to speak about this to anyone, especially to other members of staff.' Another deep breath. 'I gather, Mrs Burns, that you would like to take up a full-time appointment with us. Since continuity is going to be very important for the school over the next few months, I'm sure we'll be able to offer you a contract.' A smile momentarily appeared on his face before giving way to the same calculating look with which, less than two hours earlier, he had tried to bribe me.

Dora rested a hand on my arm. 'I don't think you need to stay for the remainder of Speech Day,' she said.

When they had walked off in the direction of the school, Ruth gave me a hug. 'How about a small celebration?' she said.

'It doesn't feel like a victory.'

We watched Dora and the Chairman enter the doorway of the main school and disappear.

'If he thinks Duggy and Renwick won't know about this before tonight,' said Ruth, 'he's a bigger fool than I thought.'

Unaffected by the interruption, the cricket and spectating continued. The champagne corks were still popping, and the applause became ever more raucous.

'Shall we move elsewhere?' said Ruth.

'I think I'll take Dora's advice and leave.'

'Come and have supper with us this evening.'

I hesitated. 'Tonight's a little difficult.'

'Make it tomorrow then. James too of course. Tell him to bring a friend with him'

She saw me to my van. 'Phoebe, before you go, can you tell me something? How did Mark Jarritt bring himself to confide in you? He's not one to trust any teacher, let alone one new to the staff.'

'Can I tell you tomorrow evening?'

As I drove away, in my wing mirror I saw Duggy running up to her, bursting with scandal.

## 24

For some minutes I watched the rabble of pigeons at my feet. They pecked and jostled until, for no discernible reason, with the sound of a wave breaking on shingle, they rose as one into the air and made an anti-clockwise sweep over the market stalls below me, landing in untidy groups on the roof and ledges of the Guildhall. Their unity, I thought, was only in flight, not on the ground. Below them the early-evening city had all but emptied. Shops were shut and pubs and restaurants were preparing for the evening trade. At the coffee stall I had been the last customer of the day. Styrofoam mug in hand, I was seated on one of the low walls of the memorial garden, overlooking the multi-coloured roofs of the stalls – a child's picture of a market. Built in the Deco style of the City Hall behind me, the gardens must have been designed by an architect in sympathy with the city's snack-grabbers, footsore and weary. I had often sat here, shopping at my feet, staring over to Gentleman's Walk, a high-sounding name for a row of shops – Burtons, Next, Dixons and the others found in any large town. A few yards from me, a man in a brown coat unwound himself from the bench where he had been scribbling a frantic letter, then scurried away. Apart from the pigeons, descending again to invisible crumbs, I was alone. This was a place made for waiting – a place where I could allow Hillgate to recede.

I looked to my right where the Garnet Wolseley pub appeared to hang on to the corner of St Peter's church. I glanced towards the theatre; close by I had parked my van. These city buildings distanced the school, shrinking it to a rural remoteness, and encouraged me to think that I had never been there. Even so, I felt the occasional pang which suggested that somehow the Lennoxes would extricate themselves from their problems unscathed. So I sat and waited in the dusty sun until I had accepted that for them to remain at Hillgate was beyond question. Half an hour later, an old woman, pushing a shopping trolley full of lumpy plastic bags, appeared at the corner of the Guildhall. I watched her forage through a bin with the same degree of concentration I reserved for car boots and auctions. She pulled out some scraps of pizza, which I thought she was going to eat. Instead, she tore off tiny pieces which she threw on the ground. The pigeons soon joined her. I watched her feed them, my mind focused on the evening ahead.

Physically tired, but looking for another kind of energy, I pulled out from my bag the photo taken at Southwold. I read again the writing on the reverse: *To Jamesey from your weekend Mum. X X X.* I had no doubt that it was intended for my eyes. It had made James an unwitting messenger – a double injury. I wondered if she bothered to think about me now. I thought not. I had become an irrelevant part of her past, at most someone her ex-boyfriend, thanks to her, had outgrown – a mere adjunct to an old game. I gave the market stalls a wry smile and hoped that in the last two weeks she had forgotten about me.

As I watched the bag lady move to the next bin, it occurred to me how easily things might have been different. It was by a whisker of chance that I hadn't burst into B's house in Wyatt Square that night to enact what I had never dared, but had later dreamed. Again, in a different mood, I might not have remained silent in the Stanhope Arms. Both occasions, and others too in my garden, had been opportunities to bring matters to a head. But each time I had shrunk back, preferring avoidance to conflict until I chose this other way. Not that it felt like a choice. It was more the unavoidable course of action after all else had left me defeated. Perhaps the bag lady, as she followed the bin-to-bin path fate had given her, had similar thoughts about her own life. Any guilt I felt about my contract with Cosmo was dispelled by a quick glance at the photo on my lap. Returning it to my bag, I thought about the man behind the camera. Despite what Cosmo had told me, I imagined that Anthony would have been wounded by the split, but not badly and not for long. The coolness and pride he had learned from her would not have allowed any lingering anguish. And she would have used her powers to make the split seem no more than an altered friendship. He would have moved his things from her house to a room in a university hall of residence, without tears or resentment – that sort of behaviour might be expected from married couples, not from them. Sharing the same friends, they could remain friends themselves. She would have assured him of this. And he would have believed it. Any whiff of doubt on his part she would have blown away with some hint that this was a temporary break, good for them both. After all, he had tried marriage; this way was better. I had no wish to hurt Anthony. Two and a half years ago, in the face of his deceit, I had wanted to retaliate. Not now. It was her power over me, and, by association, over James, that I had wanted broken. Dealt with. This I had done. She was no longer with Anthony. She would no longer arrive at my house. She would no longer treat me with contempt. She would no longer make herself a mother to my son. She would no longer use her wealth as a weapon. For her, relationships were a game. She had said so in my hearing. I had now initiated my own game and was winning. There remained only the endgame.

My bag lady moved to Gentleman's Walk, then to the far side of the stalls and out of sight. High above me, the city clock, in a tone more suited to a Gothic belfry than a modern civic building, struck seven. Less patient now, I continued to wait until the minute hand had edged down beyond ten-past. Now I rose from the wall, and, looking ahead down Davey Street towards the castle, felt the first twinge of unease about what I was going to do. But I told myself the task would not take long, and if I found it distasteful, then it was far less objectionable than the role she had so often forced on me.

The first part of the plan was simple: a short walk would take me to Dunstan's. I judged that there would be little chance that she would be approaching it from my direction; in all probability she was already there. But my planning counted for nothing when, as soon as I stepped beyond the Market Place, the streets became part of a different city. The shapes of buildings seemed to change. In bewilderment, I noticed walls and windows I had never seen before. Familiar shopping precincts grew in size, where insignificant street signs and lamp posts became important landmarks. I was convinced that a pedestrian street I had walked down many times had recently been repaved with coloured slabs, and yet they looked well worn. The light was good, I wasn't ill, but I felt in danger of getting lost. An image came to me of Lucy Snowe, lost in a foreign town: *I grew embarrassed; I got immeshed in a network of turns unknown.*

With effort, I regained my sense of direction. I became more alert, suspicious, prepared for the outside chance that some contingency would necessitate her approaching the restaurant from this direction. Eyes behind me as much as in front, I moved from shop doorway to shop doorway, from corners to the tops of alleyways. At first, I saw no one, but when I saw walking towards me a group of youths on a lads' night out, I panicked. I thought they would try to obstruct me, or at least make some comment about this strange woman stalking the pavements. My heart pounded. I stepped to one side. But only one of them seemed to notice me, and he did no more than to give me a curious look as they laughed their way by. I halted by the entrance to an office to recover. I hated myself for coming to this. For a moment I was tempted to run back to my van, perhaps would have done, but a flow of adrenalin encouraged me to continue.

Nearer Dunstan's, I stopped in a small square to look at a group of students studying the menus on the door of a Chinese restaurant. I checked their faces. None was familiar. On the far side of the square was a pub. Outside, two men were seated at a table. I checked them too before moving on. The presence of these people made me feel less conspicuous. With fifty yards to go, I continued my approach with more confidence. But at the sight of the squat tower of Dunstan's I lost my nerve and hid behind a phone box, then inside it. There was no one in sight, but, despite this, I pretended to make a call, my back to the pavement, my face cradled in my hands. Voices in the street froze me. Frightened, I waited until I dared to turn my head. Looking between my fingers, I saw two girls pass. Neither was her. I replaced the phone, checked my watch, waited another minute.

She had to be there by now. I looked towards the flint walls of the church. I reminded myself of the interior: beyond the porch was an entrance lobby, separated from the main body of the restaurant by a glass screen; the tables were in the nave of the old church; there were two bars, one on a mezzanine floor under the tower, the other, where diners sat with their menus and aperitifs, was in the old chancel – I guessed this was where she would be. I left the phone box and walked to the porch. It was an unlikely entrance to a restaurant. Were it not for an unassuming sign in the tiny churchyard, a stranger might have walked past, unaware of the building's change of use.

Inside the lime-washed porch, I looked at the menu board and winced at the prices. Tensing myself, I stepped past the half-open oak door and walked into the lobby. It was darker here. Before I had time to take my bearings I was greeted by a waiter. As he spoke, I looked over his shoulder and through the glass screen, across vacant tables towards the chancel bar. It appeared empty – no waiting diners, no fair-haired young woman. I hesitated. I felt cheated.

He asked me again if I wanted a table.

I reasoned that she must be in the upper bar. To be certain, I checked the chancel again. Then I saw her – I still wasn't used to that shorter hair. She was seated in a black leather armchair by a wall. The dull red dress she was wearing merged with the colour of the floor bricks. She was looking at her watch. I stepped back, so that the waiter obscured the line of vision between her and me. He was impatient for an answer.

'I'll have a drink in the tower bar,' I told him.

He pointed me to a door beyond an imposing Elizabethan monument – a family kneeling in line: a gentleman in doublet, a nun-faced wife and a tail of daughters. I slipped past them and made my way up an enclosed modern staircase towards the bar. A few steps from the top I paused. From here I scanned the room ahead. It was all chrome and limed oak. Four men in dinner jackets were at a table. A barman was bringing them drinks. Beyond them I could see a large window fitted into the upper part of the tower arch. It overlooked the ground floor. From here I would be able to watch her. But there was a problem – most of this room was in full view of the chancel. I felt vulnerable – if she looked up, she might see me. I took a chance – she was looking for a man, not a woman – and I dashed up the last steps towards a stool at the end of the bar counter furthest from the window. Here I positioned myself, so that an oak post screened me from her view. However, by swaying forwards a little, she came into sight. My heart raced. I watched her fidget and look towards the lobby. I thought she looked up to the mezzanine bar. I swayed back behind the post.

The barman approached me. I ordered a red wine.

'On the bill?' he asked.

'No, I'll pay for it here.'

I peered out again. She was leaning forwards now, again looking towards the lobby. I placed an elbow on the bar and lowered my head. Like this, I was given extra cover behind the beer pumps. From here, I was sure I was invisible.

I looked at the drinkers at the table. They were talking boxing.

'It was a fix last time,' one of them said.

'With a glass jaw against him, it didn't need to be fixed.'

One of them looked at me. 'Want to join us, darling?'

I turned away and looked through the tracery of the west window and down into the street below. When I turned to pick up my glass, the four were back at their argument, ignoring me.

I leaned forward again. She was now holding a glass – something clear inside – mineral water, gin or vodka. She took quick, anxious sips. I looked at the clock behind the bar. It was 7.40pm. I drank deeply from my own glass. I looked over to the fresco on the far wall, an Italian landscape with pine trees and ruined temples. The men at the table burst into laughter at some joke. From the street below came the sound of car horns. The city was coming to life. I began to feel in control. I would give her another two minutes.

She was becoming more agitated, every few seconds craning her neck towards the lobby. I smiled, remembering each time she had climbed out of the MG with a new way to eviscerate me in my own garden. No more, I thought, no more. She pulled out her mobile and stabbed in a number – Cosmo's I was sure. It was good to see those white hands with their long fingers, so skilled in theatrical gestures, so adept at being dismissive, now half-clenched, frantic. Nervously, she looked up at the hammerbeam roof as she waited for an answer. There was none. She placed her phone on the table. She looked down towards the lobby. I saw her tortured face. She finished her drink and flicked a finger towards a waiter for another. Ever arrogant, I thought. I relished the chance of a longer wait. With great pleasure I finished my wine.

'Same again,' I said to the barman. 'And one for yourself.'

When her drink arrived, she stared into her glass, not bothering to drink. Without lifting it from the table, she swilled it around, her mind elsewhere, her anxiety palpable. Again she looked at her watch, again looked towards the lobby. Then, as I picked up my glass, she picked up hers. I paused before drinking. So did she. I drank. She followed. I enjoyed this control. I felt like James as he played a fish. She tried to sit back in her chair. She was unable. She leaned forward again, but was increasingly uncomfortable. It was time to reel her in.

I opened my bag and pulled off a sheet of paper from my notebook. I wrote on it: PHONE MESSAGE FROM COSMO BUTLER: DON'T WAIT. IT'S ALL OVER. FUN WHILE IT LASTED. I folded it, beckoned to the barman and whispered my instructions. With the £10 note I gave him, he was happy to be a discrete messenger. He walked down the steps to the lobby. As the door in the glass screen opened, I saw her face light up. A moment later, she sank back in her seat, despondent. I watched the barman approach her.

'Darling, it's only a game,' I whispered.

Without acknowledging the barman, she took the message, but fumbled as she unfolded it. It dropped to the floor.

'Nervous, are you?' I said.

She bent down and retrieved it. She read it. Her mouth opened. For several seconds, she held it in motionless disbelief. She slowly placed it on the table. She read it again. I watched her hands fall limp to the sides of her chair. Her face contorted. She fought to hold back tears. She failed.

'Not sulking?' I said.

I now saw the restaurant revert to a church, a country church in Kent, filled with wedding guests. I looked down on a sea of bright hats and fascinators, women in bright dresses, men in morning suits. The left-hand side was packed with her family and friends. I recognised the gang who had enjoyed tea in my garden. Anthony too. Orange blossom hung from the end of every poppy-head pew. Lavish pedestals of madonna lilies stood in front of the chancel step. The church was suffused with the scent of the pink and white roses on the window sills. The sun, flickering through the stained glass, caught their petals. Coloured shadows dappled the grey Norman pillars. An organ was softly playing. Every few moments, the best man, standing in the front, near the right-hand pedestal, glanced towards the back. He repeatedly looked at his watch. There was no bridegroom next to him. A clergyman in cassock, surplice and white stole, approached him and whispered in his ear. In the pew opposite, a woman in an emerald green hat, the bride's mother, turned her head towards them, then shot a glance to the other end of the church. Impatient, she left her seat and spoke to the best man, grasping his arm in desperation.

The bride had already entered the church. I could see her inside the west door. Her cream silk dress had a train as long as a princess's. She was holding a trailing bouquet of roses. Her hair, grown again, flowed over her shoulders. She was a pre-Raphaelite figure, and as distraught as one too. With her, in a grey morning suit, was her father, his face burdened with worry. A bridesmaid was making a hopeless attempt to reassure her.

'So you don't mind losing?' I said.

I saw guests turn anxious heads to one another, whisper, look at watches, turn round to her. They had waited too long. They were guessing what she already knew: today there would be no wedding.

I tried to laugh, but a new image surfaced – another church, another era. This one was almost empty, apart from the bride, the groom, a clergyman and a witness. Two other men walked up from the back, intent on halting the ceremony. They had proof that the groom was already married. Mr Rochester's insane wife had been locked away. Jane was too shocked to express any emotion. It was only later, when she was alone in her room, that the disaster struck her, and she *lay faint, longing to be dead.*

The image gave way to the present. The men at the table were looking at me. But at that moment, the four became two. I found myself staring at John Copeford and Kate Lennox. They were smiling at me, welcoming to their company a fellow manipulator of people, one as skilled as either of them. To drive away the unwanted visitors, I looked around the bar, focused on the fresco, and gulped the rest of my wine. The barman eyed me and frowned in puzzlement or revulsion, then, perhaps remembering his £10, turned away.

One of the dinner jackets called out, 'On your own love?'

I shook my head, feeling more alone than I had ever felt in my life.

B was still in her chair. She was red-eyed, forlorn. She looked as if she was unable to move. Other diners were arriving in the chancel bar, but she didn't see them. A vestige of malice made me pull out the photo again. But it meant nothing now, and the writing on the back no longer troubled me. I crumpled it in my hand, left it on the bar and ran to the stairs, knocking into a stool. Picking myself up, I heard some derisive comment behind me, then laughter. I didn't turn back.

I ran down the steps and across the lobby, colliding with a waiter and sending a pile of menus to the floor. I didn't stop to apologise. Outside, in my urge to keep running, I was almost hit by what seemed to be a driverless car. The Galaxy's tyres screamed into the kerb as it pulled up.

Cosmo exploded from the left-hand door, his face as fiery as his hair. 'Is she still there?'

I nodded.

'Deal's off. You can keep your fucking fragment.'

With a look which said he wanted to hit me, he dashed towards the porch. In his rush he tripped. He crashed to the pavement. A flailing arm couldn't break his fall. As he fell, his head struck the stone plinth of the porch entrance. He lay still. I thought he was unconscious until his head turned and his eyes met mine.

'You and your bloody deal,' he snarled.

I bent down to help him, but he knocked me aside. With great effort, he raised his upper body. He put a hand to his right temple. He looked at his palm. There was blood on it – on the pavement too. I approached him again and saw a gash on his head. I pulled a handkerchief from my bag and offered it to him. He ignored me. With another heave, he forced himself to his feet, clinging to the side of the porch. When he was almost upright, his knees gave way and he slipped down the wall. Using both my arms, I prevented another fall. This time he allowed me to hold him until, gaining more strength, he gripped my shoulder and hoisted himself up.

He looked at me with contempt. 'What did you say to her?'

'I didn't. I gave the barman a note.'

'What was on it?'

I told him.

'You bastard. Are you pleased now?'

I looked to the ground.

Tightening his grip on my shoulder, he managed two painful steps. I felt his full weight bear down on me. He stopped and panted for half a minute, during which his head was so close to mine that his angry breath was warm on my face. Finally revived, he shook me off and walked unaided to the door. There he waited, trying to compose himself. When he was ready to enter the restaurant, he turned back. Now his look was less hostile.

With some reluctance, he said, 'Tomorrow, I suppose, I might thank you.'

'Just get in there,' I said.

He gave me a sale-ground look. 'You won't mention this carpet business, will you?'

I shook my head.

He went in. I had no doubt that, before he arrived at the chancel, he would have found suitable explanations for being late and for the note. There was an odd justice in the way the two of them were so well suited, but the thought did nothing to ease my conscience. I wasn't certain who had won the endgame. I didn't care.

# 25

It was around 9.00pm when I passed the Ulford village sign. I was late arriving at Molly's, but wasn't yet ready to face her. I slowed just below the brow of the hill, pulled into my usual layby, and looked over the fields of barley towards Limepit House. Blanking my mind of Hillgate and B, I watched the black specks of house martins dart into their nests under the gable.

The day had left me with a heavy sadness. I was also exhausted. The emotional maelstrom of the past five weeks had given me inner strength, but at great cost. Too often I had been sustained, not by my physical resources, but by the energy of anger. Less angry now, I was more aware of my tiredness. I needed Molly's company, but found it almost unbearable to picture myself telling her, not only about today, but of so much in the recent past which I had withheld from her. I was on the point of braving myself for her kitchen, when I saw a shape move from the semi-wild end of my garden to the edge of the lawn.

It was a man. I watched him steal towards the far side of the house. He was little more than a silhouette. Was it . . .? No, surely not. I gasped. Yes. Him. My anger reignited. When he was out of sight – at the back door I guessed – I climbed from my van and walked to the ash trees at the side of the layby. There was no roadside ditch here, only a low bank. I climbed over it to reach the uncultivated strip at the edge of the field. From here, I sprinted the first fifty yards, knowing that the higher part of the field was more visible from the house than the lane end. As soon as I knew that I was in the safety area, I slowed, only stopping when I reached the hedge at the bottom. I knew every gap in this hedge – I had seen James and Ben run in and out of it often enough. I chose the most concealed hole, an opening more suited to a fox than a human. Having pushed my way through, I dashed across the lane to the bushes which marked the boundary of my garden. Again I selected a suitable gap and tunnelled through. A bramble pulled my hair. Eyes fixed on the back door, I ran across my herb garden towards the house.

On the doorstep, I recovered my breath. I struggled to be silent, aware of every heartbeat. The door was ajar. I listened. I heard nothing. I pushed it far enough open to allow myself in. I waited and listened again. No sound came from the rooms of the passageway. I took several steps forward and stopped. He was here, but in which room? Still I heard nothing. I pushed my head into the storeroom. He wasn't there. Kitchen next. This too was empty. I looked towards the hallway. I considered checking the remainder of the ground floor. I didn't need to. At the foot of the staircase was a pair of trainers. They weren't mine or James's – they were much larger. I looked up the narrow staircase. A sound came from a bedroom. Step by step, I went up. At the bend near the top, I avoided a stair which always creaked, stretching to the one above. On the landing, leaning on the wall by one of James's drawings of fish, I waited. A faint ruffling sound came from my bedroom. I breathed in deeply and walked to the open door.

The figure kneeling at my dressing table, hands in the top drawer, opened his mouth and froze. He was unable to release the clothes from his fingers. His round face turned white up to his crew cut hairline. His lips quivered. It was Steve, the brickie who had helped us restore the house. At that moment, what angered me most were his camouflage shirt and combat trousers – they suggested a planned intrusion. He looked away from me, but remained frozen.

'Close that drawer,' I shouted. He was twice my size, but the force of my voice withered him. It surprised me no less.

His hands dropped whatever garment he was holding and he pushed the drawer back. He remained on his knees.

'Stand up,' I said.

He brought himself up to a crouched position. I thought he might spring to the door, like a cornered animal, but the shock and fear were too much for him.

'You will go down to the kitchen,' I ordered. 'You will sit down. You will place my keys on the table. You will wait for me.'

He looked too terrified to move.

'Kitchen,' I shouted.

He shuffled out of the room. His footsteps on the stairs were erratic; he must have found coordination difficult. I heard the kitchen door open. A chair moved. Nevertheless, I glanced out through the window, looking over the garden and towards the lane, assuring myself that my school voice had been obeyed, and that he was not in full flight back to his home. Satisfied that he was not, I turned to the door, but in doing so caught sight of myself in the mirror. I looked at a dishevelled stranger. I brushed some leaves from my hair. There was a bloodstain on the shoulder of my dress where Cosmo had pulled himself up, and another on my hip. The hem was torn where I had pushed my way through the hedges. My ankles were covered in scratches from my run through the field, and my shoes were filthy. Shivering, I grabbed a cardigan and sat on the bed. The idiot downstairs deserved to wait.

When I entered the kitchen, I saw him slouched on a stick-back chair, his back to the door, his head making involuntary side-to-side movements. When I went to the opposite side of the table, he continued like this, his eyes staring blankly forward. His hands, palms down, rigid, could have been nailed to the table top. Two keys on a Coke keyring accused him from the far end. In the few minutes he had been waiting he seemed to have aged twenty years. He was grey and gaunt, like a prisoner of war after a brutal interrogation, barely strong enough to survive further questioning. This was as well. I had no intention of asking many.

Not certain whether he had noticed my presence, I grabbed the keys and banged down my fist to make him look up. His head ceased moving, but his eyes continued to stare ahead.

'You realise that this is a matter for the police.'

No response.

'You know you have broken the law?'

There was a faint nod of his head. He lowered his eyes.

'You have betrayed trust by getting keys cut when you were working here. You have intruded into my home and, for all I know, you have been stealing my property.'

He shook his head violently.

'And I know you have been here before – many times. And you've been in my son's room and interfered with our property. You have scared us. You know I should call the police.'

He opened his mouth. He tried to speak, but managed only a rasping from his throat. Then he was silent, his mouth left gaping. He raised his eyes. He looked pathetic.

'You've watched us, waited until we've been out. But for all that you've been caught.'

He dropped his eyes.

'Look at me.'

He looked up, closing his mouth.

'You have been incredibly stupid, haven't you?'

He nodded.

'Do you trespass in any other houses?'

He shook his head.

'You will not come near this house again. And you will have nothing to do with my son. Is that clear?'

He didn't answer.

'Is that clear?'

'Y . . . yeah.'

'I'm not going to the police. This time. But if you're mad enough to come near here again, I will. What would your family and your friends say if they knew?'

He looked at me, petrified. His mother worked mornings in the village shop. I saw her almost every day.

'Think how bloody stupid you've been. Now get out.'

Unpinning his hands, he wanted to run from the kitchen, but his back remained hunched, causing him to stumble. I watched him make for the back door. As he passed the stairs, I shouted, 'Shoes!' He grabbed his trainers, at last straightened his back and walked out. Beyond the back door, even though there was now drizzle, the trainers remained in his hand. He looked as if he wanted to run to the lane, but his body allowed him no more than an awkward jog.

From my bedroom window, watching him disappear, I struggled to believe that this was the same village boy who had been so invaluable when we were restoring the house. I wondered if I had been foolish in not contacting the police. I decided not. I certainly couldn't judge him to be as dangerous or perverted as the others who had haunted my life. In comparison to them he was pitiful. He may have harmed me by instilling fear and suspicion when I was vulnerable, but he had probably done more damage to himself by his secret visits and whatever warped gratification they gave him. The men who bought the top shelf magazines in the village shop, for whom his mother found brown paper bags in which to slide their purchases, measured much the same on any perversion scale. I shuddered. I wondered how close to him I had been when I sat hidden in the restaurant.

The trudge up the hill to my van was in semi-darkness. Now that the rain had stopped, the roadside breathed out a grassy-tar smell which recalled childhood walks. It was good company. I caught the village shop before it closed and bought two better bottles of wine than usual. When I had been served, the assistant asked me to wait while she went to the post office counter to fetch a parcel, which the postman had been unable to deliver in the morning.

When I arrived at Molly's, I carried in the wine and the unopened parcel. She was outside in her studio. Paul, Ben and James were in the back room, watching one of the *Ghostbuster* films.

James called out, 'You'll enjoy this, Mum. It's all about an old portrait in a museum. Your kind of film.'

'You can play it for me tomorrow,' I said, and returned to the kitchen.

Molly appeared, covered in studio dust. 'Long speeches?' she said, smiling as she pulled out a cork.

Shaking my head, I looked down at the table and noticed that the stamps on the parcel were American. Following my eyes, Molly noticed them too.

'I'll pour the wine while you open your parcel,' she said.

It was a gentle way to begin a painful account of the past few days. I unwrapped the parcel and found a small book on carpets, *The Study of Fragments*. Inside the front cover Adam had written: *Phoebe, remembering our trip to London.* I thought back to the last time I had seen him, here in this kitchen. I also thought of the poem. Today I was less angry with him.

Molly, watching me flick through the book, saw me pause, open-mouthed, as I looked at a colour plate of a fragment almost identical to my own but smaller. It had sold for $40,000.

'Is this a new line of dealing?' she asked.

'It could be,' I said.

Her raised eyebrows daunted me. But the accompanying smile eased my way for the unavoidable late night.

# POSTSCRIPT

To everyone's surprise, David Lennox took assembly as normal on Monday morning and did not resign until lunchtime. After that we saw no more of him. Nor did we discover where he went on leaving Hillgate, although Duggy heard various reports from different parts of the country. Kate Lennox somehow avoided legal proceedings, and was last heard of in a private psychiatric hospital. Mark Jarritt's parents removed him from the school. He became a day pupil at a school in London.

The Lennoxes abandoned Tabloid, or maybe he had abandoned them, since, a week after the headmaster's house had been vacated, he was seen wandering the school grounds. All attempts to capture him failed, but the kitchen staff left out scraps which disappeared at night. One lunchtime, when I was eating a sandwich in my van, he appeared, and I threw him a piece of ham. He must have loitered nearby, since, as I left the van, he jumped in and leapt to the back. He had decided his future. I took him home, where he was happy with the new name I gave him, Pilot – after Mr Rochester's dog.

I finished the term at Hillgate, but did not return in September. The following month I sold my carpet fragment for enough to pay off my mortgage, get the bank off my back and invest in some better stock for my business.

Ruth continued at the school for one more term and left at Christmas to take up a teaching post in Norwich. With falling numbers, Hillgate staggered on for two more terms before closing. After a legal battle between trustees and governors, it was sold and once again became a private residence.

After university Anthony got a job editing a woodland conservation magazine. He now lives in Bristol and is married to a fellow conservationist. B and Cosmo remained together and now live in Ireland.

Of my former colleagues, Duggy has created a Nelson Heritage Trail, Renwick has retired to Scotland, and Joan has opened a deli in Yarmouth. Linda, I believe, is still teaching, but in the state system. Of Alan and the others I have heard little, apart from the fact that Brian quit teaching. I occasionally go over to Tylby to see Dora, now in her nineties, but we tend to talk about pictures, not Hillgate, the portrait of whose founder now hangs on her staircase.

When the contents of the school were sold at auction, I was on holiday in Yorkshire with James. However, Ruth and Hugh attended, and at great expense bought the Regency sideboard from the library. Some months later, when an estate agent called in Frank to clear an attic the auctioneers had overlooked, he found a box of books which had originally been part of Lady Widwell's library. Among them were the battered but complete three volumes of the first edition of *Jane Eyre*. It remains, after twenty-four years, my most treasured possession. Frank also found a wine cooler in the same style as the sideboard. This now stands besides its companion in Ruth and Hugh's dining room. Those pieces of furniture stir bittersweet memories whenever Adam and I have dinner there.